Dear Reader,

It is so much fun to retur[n to] the fictional town I imag[ined]. [It's] literally like coming hom[e.]

I'm especially thrilled to see my latest Whitehorse book, *Dead Ringer*, offered with another of my earlier books set here, *Classified Christmas*.

If this is your first time in town, welcome to Whitehorse. It's a place where buffalo used to roam, where the prairie stretches all the way to the Little Rockies, where families have always had to stick together during rough times.

But it is also a place filled with mystery and awe, from the northern lights to the winter blizzards that close the roads, to the people determined to settle this wild country and the cowboys who tame it.

I hope you enjoy the McGraws in *Dead Ringer* as the family tries to find Oakley and Jesse Rose, the babies stolen from their cribs twenty-five years ago. Meanwhile, back at the ranch, Ledger McGraw is fighting to save the woman he loves from a man who is determined to destroy her.

In *Classified Christmas*, Cade Jackson is forced by a determined female reporter to face his past when Andi Blake comes to town to solve an old six-million-dollar heist.

Settle into my small Montana town and the wild country around it. But don't get too comfortable. Only the strong survive here. Good thing you can usually find a rugged, handsome cowboy when you need one.

I hope you enjoy your visit as there are now twenty-six books in the Whitehorse series—and more to come!

B.J. Daniels

B.J. Daniels is a *New York Times* and *USA TODAY* bestselling author. She wrote her first book after a career as an award-winning newspaper journalist and author of thirty-seven published short stories. She lives in Montana with her husband, Parker, and three springer spaniels. When not writing, she quilts, boats and plays tennis. Contact her at bjdaniels.com, on Facebook or on Twitter, @bjdanielsauthor.

Books by B.J. Daniels

Harlequin Intrigue

Whitehorse, Montana

Secret of Deadman's Coulee
The New Deputy in Town
The Mystery Man of Whitehorse
Classified Christmas
Matchmaking with a Mission
Second Chance Cowboy
Montana Royalty
Shotgun Bride

Whitehorse, Montana: The McGraw Kidnapping

Dark Horse
Dead Ringer

Visit the Author Profile page
at Harlequin.com for more titles.

B.J. DANIELS

NEW YORK TIMES BESTSELLING AUTHOR

DEAD RINGER & CLASSIFIED CHRISTMAS

HARLEQUIN® INTRIGUE®

ISBN-13: 978-0-373-83904-9

Dead Ringer & Classified Christmas

Copyright © 2017 by Harlequin Books S.A.

The publisher acknowledges the copyright holder of the individual works as follows:

Dead Ringer
Copyright © 2017 by Barbara Heinlein

Classified Christmas
Copyright © 2007 by Barbara Heinlein

Recycling programs
for this product may
not exist in your area.

Printed in U.S.A.

CONTENTS

This book is dedicated to JoAnn Hammond, who was one of the first in Whitewater to read one of my books. ☺ So glad we got to know each other—and share a love for quilting and reading.

DEAD RINGER

CHAPTER ONE

ABBY PIERCE OPENED her eyes and quickly closed them against the bright sunlight. She hurt all over. As she tried to sit up, a hand gently pushed on her shoulder to keep her flat on the bed.

"Don't sit up too fast," her husband said. "You're okay. You're in the hospital. You took a nasty fall."

Fall? Hospital? Her mouth felt dry as dust. She licked her lips. "Can you close the drapes?"

"Sure," Wade said and hurried over to the window.

She listened as he drew the drapes together and felt the room darken before she opened her eyes all the way.

The first thing she saw was her husband silhouetted against the curtains. He was a big imposing man with a boyish face and a blond crew cut. He was wearing his sheriff's deputy uniform, she noted as he moved back to the bed to take her hand.

She'd known Wade for years. She'd married him three years ago. That was why when she saw the sheepish look in his brown eyes, she knew at once that he was hiding something.

Abby frowned. "What was I doing that I fell?"

"You don't remember?" He cleared his throat, shifting on his feet. "You asked me to bring up some canning jars from the garage? I'm so sorry I didn't. If I had you wouldn't have been on that ladder…" He looked at her as if expecting… Expecting what?

"Canning jars?" she repeated and touched her bandaged temple. "I hit my head?"

He nodded, and taking her hand, he squeezed it a little too hard. "I'm so sorry, Abby." He sounded close to tears.

"It's not your fault," she said automatically, but couldn't help but wonder if there was more to the story. There often was with Wade and his family. She frowned, trying to understand why she would have wanted canning jars and saying as much.

"You said something about putting up peach jam."

"Really? I wonder where I planned to get peaches this time of year."

He said nothing, avoiding her gaze. All the other times she'd seen him like this it had been after he'd hurt her. It had started a year into their marriage and begun with angry accusations that led to him grabbing her, shaking her, pushing her and even slapping her.

Each time he'd stopped before it had gone too far. Each time he'd been horrified by what he'd done. He'd cried in her arms, begging her to forgive him, telling her that he couldn't live without her, saying he would kill himself if she ever left him. And then promising he'd never do it again.

She touched her bandaged head with her free hand. The movement brought a groan out of her as she realized her ribs were either bruised or maybe even broken. Looking down, she saw the bruises on her wrists and knew he was lying. Had he pushed her this time?

"Why can't I remember what happened?" she asked.

"You can't remember *anything*?" He sounded hopeful, fueling her worst fears that one of these days he would go too far and kill her. Wasn't that what her former boy-friend kept telling her? She pushed the thought of Ledger McGraw away as she often had to do. He didn't understand that she'd promised to love, honor and obey when she'd married Wade—even through the rough spots. And this she feared was one of them.

At the sound of someone entering the room, they both turned to see the doctor come in.

"How are we doing?" he asked as he moved to the foot of her bed to look at her chart. He glanced at Wade, then quickly looked away. Wade let go of her hand and moved to the window to part the drapes and peer out.

Abby closed her eyes at the shaft of sunlight he let in. "My head hurts," she told the doctor.

"I would imagine it does. When your husband brought you in, you were in and out of consciousness."

Wade had brought her in? He didn't call an ambulance?

"Also I can't seem to remember what happened," she added and, out of the corner of her eye, saw her husband glance back at her.

The doctor nodded. "Very common in your type of head injury."

"Will she get her memory back?" Wade asked from the window, sounding worried that she would.

"Possibly. Often not. I'm going to prescribe something for your headache. Your ribs are badly bruised and you have some other abrasions. I'd like to keep you overnight."

"Is that really necessary?" Wade asked, letting the drapes drop back into place.

"With a concussion, it's best," the doctor said without looking at him. "Don't worry. We'll take good care of her."

"We can talk about it," Wade said. "But I think she'd be more comfortable in her own home. Isn't that right, Abby?"

"On this, I think I know best," the doctor interrupted.

But she could see that Wade *was* worried. He apparently wanted to get her out of here and quickly. What was he worried about? That she would remember what happened?

If only she could. Unfortunately, the harder she tried, the more she couldn't. The past twenty-four hours were blank, leaving her with the terrifying feeling that her life depended on her remembering.

CHAPTER TWO

WHEN THE PHONE rang at the Sundown Stallion Station late that afternoon, Ledger McGraw took the call since both his brothers were gone from the ranch and his father was resting upstairs. They had been forced to get an unlisted number after all the media coverage. After twenty-five years, there'd finally been a break in the McGraw twins kidnapping case.

"I need to talk to Travers," Jim Waters said without preamble. "Tell him it is of utmost importance."

Ledger groaned inwardly since he knew his father had almost fired the family attorney recently. "He's resting." Travers McGraw, sixty, had suffered a heart attack a few months ago. He hadn't been well before that. At the time, they hadn't known what was making him so sick. His family had assumed it was the stress of losing his two youngest children to kidnappers twenty-five years before and his determination to find them. His father was convinced that they were still alive.

"Do you really think I would be calling if it wasn't urgent?" Waters demanded. The fiftysomething attorney had been like one of the family almost from the beginning—until a few months ago, when he and Travers had gotten into a disagreement.

"Jim, if this is about legal business—"

The attorney swore. "It's about the kidnapping. You

might recall that we originally used my number to screen the calls about the twins. Well, I am apparently still on the list. I was contacted." He paused, no doubt for effect. "I have reason to believe that Oakley has been found."

"Found?" Ledger asked, his heart in his throat. The twenty-fifth anniversary of the crime had come and gone, but after their father had hired a true-crime writer to investigate and write a book about it, new evidence had turned up.

That new evidence had led them all to believe that his father's gut instinct was right. The twins were alive— and probably adopted out to good families, though illegally. The McGraw twins had been just six months old when they were stolen from their cribs. The ransom money had never been spent and had only recently turned up—with the body of one of the kidnappers. That left whoever had helped him take the babies still at large.

Ledger was thankful that he'd been the one to answer the phone. His father didn't need this kind of aggravation. "All those calls are now being vetted by the sheriff's department. I suggest you have this person contact Sheriff McCall Crawford. If she thinks—"

"He has the stuffed toy horse," Waters interrupted. "I've seen it. It's Oakley's."

Ledger felt a shock wave move through him. The stuffed toy horse was a critical piece of information that hadn't originally been released to the public. Was it possible his little brother really had turned up? "Are you sure? There must have been thousands of those produced."

"Not with a certain ribbon tied around its neck." The information about the missing stuffed animal was recently released to the press—sans anything about the ribbon and other things about this specific toy. "Oakley's stuffed horse had a black saddle and a small tear where the stitching had been missed when it was made, right?"

He nodded to himself before saying, *"You say you've seen it?"* It was that small detail that no one would know unless they had Oakley's horse, which had been taken out of his crib along with him that night twenty-five years ago. "Have you met him?"

"I have. He sent me a photo of the stuffed horse. When I recognized it, I drove down to talk to him. Ledger, he swears he's had the stuffed horse since he was a baby."

Letting out a breath, he dropped into a nearby chair. A few months ago they'd learned that the babies might have been left with a member of the Whitehorse Sewing Circle, a group of older women quilters who placed unwanted babies with families desperate for a child. The quilting group had been operating illegally for decades.

Not that the twins had been unwanted. But the kidnapper had been led to believe that was the case. The hope had been that the babies had been well taken care of and that they were still alive, the theory being that they had no idea they'd been kidnapped. His father had made the decision to release more information about what had been taken along with the babies in the hopes that the twins would see it and come forward.

And now it had happened.

"What's his name?" Ledger asked as he gave himself a few minutes to take this all in and decide what to do. He didn't want to bother his father with this unless he was sure it wasn't a hoax.

"He goes by Vance Elliot. He's in Whitehorse. He wants to see your father."

"Abby doesn't remember anything," Wade said as he walked past his father straight into the kitchen to pull a can of beer out of the refrigerator.

He popped the top, took a long swig and turned to find his father standing in the kitchen doorway frowning at him.

"I'll pay you back," he said, thinking the look was because he was drinking his old man's beer.

"What do you mean she doesn't remember *anything*?"

"I was skeptical at first, too," he said, drawing out a chair and spinning it around so he could straddle it backward at the table. "But when I told her she fell off a ladder in the garage, she bought it. She couldn't remember why she would have been on a ladder in the garage. I told her she was going to get jars to put up some peach jam."

Huck Pierce wagged his head. "Where in the hell would she get peaches this time of year?"

"How should I know? It doesn't matter. She's not putting up any jam. Nor is she saying a word about anything."

"You are one lucky son of a gun, then," Huck said.

"Don't I know it? So everything is cool, right?"

"Seems so. But I want you to stay by your wife's side. Keep everything as normal as possible. Stick to your story. If she starts to remember…" He shrugged. "We'll deal with it if we have to."

Wade downed the rest of his beer, needing it even though he was technically on duty at the sheriff's department. He didn't want his father to see how relieved he was. Or how worried about what would happen if Abby remembered what had really happened to her.

"Great, so I get to hang out at the hospital until my shift starts. That place gives me the creeps."

"You're the one who screwed everything up. You knew what was at stake," his father said angrily.

"Exactly." Wade knew he couldn't win in an argument with his father, but that didn't stop him. "So what was I supposed to do when she confronted me? I tried to reason with her, but you know how she is. She was threatening to call the sheriff. Or go running to her old boyfriend Ledger McGraw. I didn't have a choice but to try to stop her."

"What you're saying is that you can't handle your wife. At least you don't have some snot-nosed mouthy kid like I did."

"Yeah, thanks," he said, crushing the beer can in his hand. "I've heard all about how hard it was raising me." He reached in the refrigerator for another beer, knowing he shouldn't, but needing the buzz badly.

Before he could pull one out, his father slammed the refrigerator door, almost crushing his hand. "Get some gum. You can't have beer on your breath when you go back to the hospital, let alone come to work later. Remember, you're the worried husband, you damned fool."

LEDGER HAD JUST hung up with the attorney when he got the call from his friend who worked at the hospital.

"I shouldn't be calling you, but thought you'd want to know," she said, keeping her voice down. "Abby was brought in."

"That son of a—"

"He swears she fell off a ladder."

"Sure she did. I'll be right there. Is Wade—"

"He just left to go work his shift at the sheriff's department. The doctor is keeping Abby overnight."

"Is she okay?"

"She's pretty beat up, but she's going to be fine."

He breathed a sigh of relief as he hung up. When it rained it poured, he thought as he saw his father coming down the stairs toward him. Travers McGraw was still weak from his heart attack, but it was the systematic poisoning that had really almost killed him. Fortunately, his would-be killer was now behind bars awaiting trial.

But realizing that his second wife was trying to kill him had taken a toll on his father. It was bad enough that his first wife, Ledger's mother, was in a mental hospital. After the twins were kidnapped, Marianne McGraw had a complete breakdown. For twenty-five years, it was believed that she and the ranch's horse trainer, Nate Corwin, had been behind the kidnapping. Only recently had Nate's name been cleared.

"I heard the phone," Travers said now. He'd recovered, but was still weak. He'd lost too much weight. It would be a while until he was his old self. If ever.

That was why Ledger wasn't sure how his father would take the news Waters had called with earlier—especially if it led to yet another disappointment. And yet Ledger couldn't keep the attorney's call from him. If there was even the slightest chance that this Vance Elliot was Oakley…

"You should sit down."

His father didn't argue as he moved to a chair and sat. He seemed to brace himself. "What's happened?"

"Jim Waters called."

Travers began to shake his head. "Now what?"

"He's still apparently the contact person for the family on some of the old publicity," Ledger said.

His father knew at once. "Oakley or Jesse Rose?"

"Oakley. Jim says the young man has the stuffed horse

that was taken along with Oakley from his crib the night of the kidnapping. He says he's seen the toy and that it is definitely Oakley's."

His father's eyes filled to overflowing. "Thank God. I knew they were alive. I've…felt it all these years."

"Dad, this Vance Elliot might not be Oakley. We have to keep that in mind."

"He has Oakley's stuffed horse."

"But we don't know how he got it or if it was with Oakley when he was given to the woman at the White-horse Sewing Circle," Ledger reminded him.

"When can I see him?" his father asked, getting to his feet.

"He's in town. Waters wants to bring him over this evening. I said it would be fine. I hope that was all right. If it goes well, I thought you might want him to stay for dinner. I can tell the cook." Their cook for as far back as Ledger could remember had recently been killed. They'd been through several cooks since then. He couldn't remember the name of the latest one right now and felt bad about it. "Let's just keep our fingers crossed that it really is Oakley."

His father smiled and stepped closer to him to place a hand on his shoulder. "I am so blessed to have such good sons. Speaking of sons, where are Cull and Boone?"

"Cull and Nikki are checking into some of the adoptions through the Whitehorse Sewing Circle." Nikki St. James was the crime writer who'd helped unlock some of the kidnapping mystery—and stolen Cull's heart.

"I doubt the twins' adoptions were recorded any-where, and with the Cavanaugh woman dying not long after the twins were kidnapped… You haven't heard any-thing yet?"

Ledger shook his head. "They said that clues to what happened to some of the babies were found stitched on their baby blankets. But the twins wouldn't have quilted blankets made for them because of the circumstances." Pearl Cavanaugh had been led to believe that the twins were in danger, so she would have made very private adoptions for Oakley and Jesse Rose.

"And Boone?"

"He went to check on that horse you were interested in, remember?"

Travers nodded, frowning. Loss of memory was part of the effects of arsenic poisoning. "Maybe I'll just rest until dinner."

Ledger watched his father go back up the stairs before he headed for his pickup and the hospital.

"You shouldn't be here," Abby said the moment she opened her eyes and saw Ledger standing at the end of her bed. Her heart had taken off like a wild stallion at just the sight of him. It always did. "Wade could come back at any time."

Ledger had been her first love. He'd left an ache in her that she'd hoped would fade, if not eventually go away. But if anything, the ache had grown stronger. He'd broken her heart. It was why she'd married Wade. But ever since then, he'd been coming around, confusing her and making being married to Wade even harder. He seemed to think he had to save her from her husband.

It didn't help that Ledger McGraw had breakfast on the mornings that she waitressed at the Whitehorse Café. She'd done nothing to encourage him, although Wade didn't believe that.

Fortunately, Wade had only come down to the restaurant one time threatening to kill Ledger. Ledger had called him on it, saying they should step outside and finish it like men.

"Or do you only hit defenseless women?" Ledger had demanded of him.

Wade lost his temper and charged him. Ledger had stepped aside, nailing Wade on the back of his neck as he lumbered past. Abby had screamed as Wade slammed headfirst into a table. He'd missed two weeks' work because of his neck and threatened to sue the Mc-Graws for his pain and suffering.

She knew his neck wasn't hurt that badly, but he'd milked it, telling everyone that Ledger had blindsided him.

Wade's jealousy had gotten worse after that. Even when she'd reminded him again and again, "But you're the one I married."

"Only because you couldn't have McGraw," he would snap.

Ledger's name was never spoken in their house—at least not by her. Wade blamed him for everything that was wrong with their marriage—especially the fact that she hadn't given him a son.

They'd tried to get pregnant when they'd first married. Since he'd joined the sheriff's department and changed, she'd gone back on the pill in secret, hating that she kept it from him. She told herself that when things changed back to what she thought of as normal, she would go off the pill again.

Now she couldn't even remember what normal was anymore.

Ledger took a step toward her. He looked both worried and furious. It scared her that he and Wade might get into another altercation because of her.

"I didn't come until I was sure Wade wasn't here," Ledger said as he came around the side of her bed. "When I heard, I had to see you. *You fell off a ladder?*"

She nodded even though it hurt her head to do so. "Clumsy." She avoided his gaze because she knew he wouldn't believe it any more than she did.

"What were you doing on a ladder?"

"Apparently I was getting down some canning jars to put up peach jam."

Ledger looked at her hard. "*Apparently?* You don't remember?"

"I seem to have lost the past twenty-four hours."

"Oh, Abby."

She could tell that he thought she was covering for Wade. It almost made her laugh since she'd covered for him enough times. This just wasn't one of them. She really couldn't remember *anything*.

Ledger started to reach for her hand, but must have thought better of it. She tucked her hand under the sheet so he wouldn't be tempted again. She couldn't have Wade walking in on that. It would be bad enough Ledger just being here.

"It was a stupid accident. I probably wasn't paying attention. I'm fine."

He made a face that said he didn't believe it as he reached out to brush the dark hair back from her forehead.

She flinched at his touch and he quickly pulled back his fingers. "Sorry," he said quickly. "Did I hurt you?"

Abby shook her head. His touch had always sparked

desire in her, but she wasn't about to admit that. "My head hurts, is all."

She looked toward the door, worried that Wade might stop by. When he'd left, she could tell that he hadn't liked leaving her. Even though he was supposed to be on duty as a sheriff's deputy, he could swing by if he was worried about her, especially since he was determined to take her home.

Ledger followed her gaze as if he knew what was making her so nervous. "I'll go," he said. "But if I find out that Wade had anything to do with this—"

"I fell off a ladder." She knew it was a lie, and from the look in Ledger's eyes, he did, too. But she had to at least try to convince him that Wade was innocent. This time. "That's all it was."

She met his gaze and felt her heart break as it always did. "Thank you for stopping by," she said even though there was so much more she wanted to say to him. But she was Wade's *wife*. As her mother always said, she'd made her bed and now she had to lie in it for better or worse.

Not that her mother didn't always remind her that Ledger hadn't wanted her.

"I'm here for you, Abby. If you ever need me…"

She felt tears burn her eyes. If only that had been true before she'd married Wade. "I can't." Her heart broke as she dragged her gaze away from his.

As if resigned, she watched out of the corner of her eye as he put on his Stetson, tipped it to her and walked out.

ATTORNEY JIM WATERS looked at the young man sitting in the passenger seat of his car as he drove toward the ranch later that evening. Vance Elliot. Here was Waters's ticket back into the McGraws' good graces.

He'd bet on the wrong horse, so to speak. Travers's second wife, Patricia McGraw, had been a good bet at the time. Pretty, sexy, almost twenty years younger than her husband. She'd convinced him Travers wasn't himself. That she needed a man she could count on. She'd let him believe that he might be living in that big house soon with her because Travers had some incurable ailment that only she and Travers knew about.

He'd bought into it hook, line and sinker. And why wouldn't he? Travers had been sick—anyone could see that. Also the man had seemed distracted, often forgetful and vague as if he was losing his mind. He'd been convinced that Travers wasn't long with this world and that Patricia would be taking over the ranch.

Little did he know that she was *poisoning* her husband.

As it turned out, Patricia was now behind bars awaiting trial. Since he had stupidly sided with her, things had gone downhill from there. He was hanging on to his job with Travers by the skin of his teeth.

But this was going to make it all right again, he told himself. He couldn't let a paycheck like McGraw get away. His retainer alone would keep him nicely for years to come. He just needed to get Travers's trust back. He saw a lot more legal work on the horizon for the Mc-Graws. If this young man was Oakley, he would be back in the McGraw fold.

His cell phone rang. Patricia McGraw again. Travers's young wife wouldn't quit calling even though he'd told her he wasn't going to help her, let alone defend her.

Nor did he need to hear any of her threats. Fortunately, no one believed anything she said. Since Travers

McGraw was idolized in this county, people saw her as the gold digger who'd married him—and then systematically tried to kill him. She got no sympathy. In fact, he doubted she could get even a fair trial.

"I'm innocent, you bastard," she'd screamed the last time he'd taken her call. "You did this. You framed me for this. Once I tell the sheriff—"

He'd laughed. "Like anyone will believe you."

"I'll take you down with me!"

He'd hung up and the next time his phone had rung it had been Vance Elliot.

Waters slowed to turn into the lane that led up to the main house. He shot the man next to him a glance. Vance looked more like a teenager than a twenty-five-year-old.

The man who might be Oakley stared at the house, a little openmouthed. Waters remembered the first time he'd driven out here and seen it. The house was impressive. So were the miles of white wooden fence, the expensive quarter horses in the pasture and the section after section of land that ran to the Little Rockies.

He couldn't imagine what it would be like to learn that he was part of this even at his age—let alone twenty-five. If Vance Elliot really was the long-ago kidnapped McGraw twin, then he was one lucky son of a gun.

"You all right?" he asked Vance as they drove toward the house.

The man nodded. Waters tried to read him. He had to be scared to face Travers McGraw, not to mention his three older sons. But he didn't look it. He looked determined.

Waters felt his stomach roil. This had better be real. If this wasn't Oakley McGraw he was bringing to Travers…

He didn't want to think about how badly this could go for him.

CHAPTER THREE

SHERIFF McCALL CRAWFORD happened to be standing at the window as Huck and Wade Pierce had come into work. Wade looked wrung out. She'd heard that his wife was in the hospital with a concussion after falling off a ladder.

McCall watched the two men. She'd inherited Huck when she'd become sheriff. Before that, she'd worked with him as a deputy. He'd made it clear that he thought a woman's place was in the home and not carrying a badge and gun. Huck hadn't been any more impressed when he'd been passed over and she'd become sheriff.

He was a good old boy, the kind who smiled in your face and stabbed you in the back the first chance he got. She didn't trust him, but she couldn't fire him without cause. So far, he'd done nothing to warrant it, but she kept her eye on him—and his son, Wade. The minute she caught him stepping over the line, he was gone. As for his son… She'd had hopes for him when he'd hired on, seeing something in him that could go a different way than his father. Lately, though…

Both looked up as if sensing her watching them from the window. She raised her coffee mug in a salute to them. Their expressions turned solemn as they entered the building.

Neither man was stupid. Both were hanging on by a

thread, and if the rumors about Wade mistreating his wife could ever be proved, he would be gone soon. But in a small community like this, it was hard to prove there was a problem unless the wife came forward. So far, Abby hadn't. But now she was in the hospital after allegedly falling off a ladder. Maybe this would be the straw that broke the camel's back.

McCall's cell phone rang. She stepped to her desk and picked up, seeing that it was her grandmother. It felt strange having a relationship with her after all those years of never even laying eyes on the woman.

"Good evening," she said into the phone.

"What are you still doing at work this late?" Pepper demanded.

"I was just about to leave," McCall said. The day had gotten away from her after she dropped her daughter off at day care and came in to deal with all the paperwork that tended to stack up on her desk. Most of the time, she and Luke could work out a schedule where one—if not both of them—was home with Tracey.

But several days a week, her daughter had to go to a day care near the sheriff's office in downtown White-horse. McCall had checked it out carefully and found no problems with the two women who ran it. Tracey seemed to love going because she was around other children. For a working mother, it was the best McCall could do.

"So is there any truth to it?" her grandmother demanded in her no-nonsense normal tone of voice. "Has one of the McGraw twins been found?"

The question took McCall by surprise. For twenty-five years there had been no news on the fraternal twins who'd been kidnapped. Then a few months ago a true-crime writer had shown up at the McGraw ranch and all hell had broken loose. While some pieces of the puzzle had been found, the twins hadn't been yet.

Now was it possible one of them had been located?

"I heard it's the boy, Oakley," her grandmother was saying. "Apparently your theory about who might have adopted out the children was correct. It was the Whitehorse Sewing Circle. That bunch of old hens. You should arrest them all." Most of the women involved in the illegal kidnappings were dead now. "On top of that, that crazy daughter of Arlene Evans almost escaped from the loony bin last night."

McCall hadn't heard about that, either. It amazed her that Pepper often knew what was going on in town before the sheriff did—even though the Winchester Ranch was miles south of Whitehorse.

"Thank you for all the information. Is that it? Or was the bank robbed?"

Pepper laughed. "You should hire me since I know more of what is going on than you do." It was an old refrain, one McCall almost enjoyed. Almost.

"Well, let me know when you find out something worth hearing about," Pepper said. "I'm having lunch with the rest of your family tomorrow. Maybe sometime you can come out." With that, her grandmother was gone, leaving McCall to smile before she dialed Travers McGraw's number.

VANCE ELLIOT WATCHED the landscape blur past and wiped his sweaty palms on his jeans.

"You all right?" the attorney asked from behind the wheel of the SUV. The fiftysomething man wore a dark suit, reminding Vance of an undertaker. No one wore a suit like that, not around these parts, anyway. So Jim

Waters must be some highfalutin lawyer who made a lot of money. But then, he worked for Travers McGraw, Vance thought as he saw the huge ranch ahead. Travers McGraw probably paid him well.

"I'm a little nervous," he admitted in answer to the lawyer's question. He was about to come face-to-face with Travers McGraw and his three sons. He'd heard enough about them to be anxious. Plus, the attorney had already warned him.

"They aren't going to believe you, but don't let that rattle you," Waters said. "They've had a lot of people pretend to be the missing twins, so naturally they're going to be suspicious. But having the stuffed horse will help. Then there is the DNA test. You're ready for that, right?"

Right. That alone scared the daylights out of him, but he simply nodded to the attorney's question.

He watched the ranch house come into view. He couldn't imagine growing up on a place like this. Couldn't imagine having that much land or that much money. Nor could he deny the appeal of being a McGraw with all the privileges that came with it.

He knew he was getting ahead of himself. There were a lot of hoops he had to jump through before they would accept that he was Oakley, the missing twin. But at least he could admire the house until then. It was huge with several wings that trailed off from the two-story center.

He'd heard stories about lavish parties where senators and even the governor had attended. That was before the twins were kidnapped, though, before the first Mrs. McGraw went to the loony bin and the second one went to jail.

But the house and grounds were still beautiful, and the horses… A half dozen raced through a nearby pasture as beautiful as any horseflesh he'd ever seen. Horses were in his blood, he thought with a silent laugh. And as Waters turned into the long lane leading to the house, he thought maybe horses were in his future.

"There is nothing to be afraid of," the attorney said. "Just tell them what you told me."

"I will." He swallowed the lump in his throat. Just stick to the story. The attorney had believed him. So Travers McGraw should, too, right? The stuffed horse had opened the door. The DNA test would cinch it.

As Waters brought the SUV to a stop in front of the house, Vance picked up the paper bag next to him and held it like a suit of armor to his chest.

"Try to relax," the attorney said. "You look like you're going to jump out of your skin."

He took a deep breath and thought of his run-ins with the law as a horse thief. He'd talked his way out of those. He could handle this.

Think about the payoff, he reminded himself. This place could be his one day.

"DAD, I DON'T want you getting upset," Boone McGraw said as they waited in Travers's office. "You know what the doctor said."

"I had a heart attack," his father said impatiently. "Given the state of my health and why it was so bad, I'm fine now. Even the doctor is amazed how quickly I've bounced back."

Ledger stood by the office fireplace, as anxious as the rest of his family. They all knew that their father had bounced back because even before this phone call, Travers McGraw was determined the twins were alive and that he would see them again.

And now, after releasing more information to the press, maybe one of the twins had come forward. Ledger couldn't help being skeptical. They'd been here before. Except this time, this one had Oakley's stuffed horse, which had been in his crib the night he was kidnapped. Would his father finally be able to find some peace?

Or, after twenty-five years, had too much time passed? Oakley would be a grown man, no longer that cute six-month-old baby who'd been stolen. He would have lived a good portion of his life as someone else, with other parents. He would have his own life and the McGraws would all be strangers to him.

Ledger feared this wasn't going to be the homecoming his father was hoping for as he heard a vehicle pull up out front. He looked from his father to his brother and then went to answer the door. Better him than Boone, who already looked as if he could chew nails. It was going to take a lot to convince Boone that whoever was headed for the door was the lost twin.

Unable to wait for a knock, Ledger opened the door. Attorney Jim Waters and the young man, who might or might not be his brother, were at the bottom of the porch steps. His gaze went right to the young man, who looked dressed in all new clothing from the button-down shirt to the jeans and Western boots. He was tall, broad shouldered and slim hipped like all the McGraw men.

At the sound of the front door opening, Vance Elliot looked up, his thick dark hair falling over his forehead. Ledger saw the blue eyes and felt a shiver.

This might really be his brother.

"Vance Elliot, this is Ledger McGraw," Waters said by introduction.

"Please, come in," he said, unable to take his eyes off the young man. "My father and brother are in his office."

LEDGER LED THE two men into his father's office and closed the door. The new cook, a woman by the name of Louise, he'd made a point of learning, was in the kitchen making dinner. Cull and Nikki should be back soon. Unless they decided to stay in Whitehorse and go out to dinner. He still couldn't believe how hard his brother had fallen for the true-crime writer.

"Please sit down," Travers said, getting to his feet to shake hands with Vance. He waited until everyone was sitting before he asked, "So you think you might be my son Oakley. Why don't you start by telling us something about you?"

Vance shifted in his chair. He held a large paper bag on his lap, the top turned under. Ledger assumed the stuffed toy horse was inside. He would have thought his father would want to see it right away.

"I don't know exactly where to begin. I was raised in Bear Creek, south of Billings, on a small farm. My parents told me when I was about five that I was adopted."

"Did you have other siblings?" Travers asked.

Vance shook his head. "Just me." He shrugged. "I had a fine childhood. We didn't have much but it was enough. I went to college in Billings for a while before getting a job on a ranch outside of Belfry. That's about it."

"And how did you become aware that you might be one of the missing McGraw twins?" his father asked.

"I heard about it on television. When they mentioned the small stuffed horse and showed a photo of what it might look like, I couldn't believe it. I'd had one just like it as far back as I could remember."

"Is that what's in the bag?" Boone asked.

Vance nodded and stood to place the bag on the desk in front of Travers. He took a step back, bumped into the chair and sat again.

The room had gone deathly quiet. Ledger could hear nothing but his own heart pounding as his father pulled the bag closer, unfolded the top and looked inside.

A small gasp escaped his father's lips as he pulled the toy stuffed horse from the bag. Ledger saw the worn blue ribbon around the horse's neck and swung his gaze to Vance. If he was telling the truth, then this man was Oakley, all grown up.

WATERS COULDN'T HELP the self-satisfied feeling he had when he saw Travers McGraw's expression. He'd felt the same way when he'd seen the toy stuffed horse. It was Oakley's; there was no doubt about that.

Of course, this wouldn't be a done deal until after the DNA tests were run, but he was in the homestretch.

"Would the two of you like to stay for dinner?" Travers asked, putting the toy back into the sack and rising to his feet. "I'd like to hear more about your childhood, Vance." It was clear he was fighting calling the young man by that name.

He'd also seen Travers's face when the two of them had walked into the office. The horse rancher had looked shocked by how much the young man resembled Travers's own sons.

Waters looked to Vance before he said, "We'd love to stay for dinner. If you're sure it isn't an inconvenience." He thought of the years he'd sat at the big dining room table and eaten under this roof. If this went the way he expected it to, he'd be a regular guest again.

"Wonderful," Travers said as he came around his desk. Putting an arm around Vance, he steered him toward the dining room at the back of the house. "Where are you staying?"

Vance cleared his voice. "I spent last night at a motel in town."

"You can stay here on the ranch if you'd like," Travers said. "I don't want to pressure you. Give it some thought. We can discuss it after dinner."

Waters smiled to himself. This couldn't have gone any better. Vance was in—at least until the DNA test. But if he passed that…

His cell phone vibrated in his pocket. He checked caller ID. Patricia, the soon-to-be former wife of Travers McGraw. He was sure his boss would ask him to handle the divorce. It would be his pleasure.

CHAPTER FOUR

ABBY WAS DRESSED and sitting in the wheelchair waiting when her husband came into her hospital room the next afternoon. She felt fine, except for a headache and no memory of what had happened to her. But hospital policy required her to be "driven" down to the exit by wheelchair after her doctor came in.

Wade stopped in the doorway. She gave him a smile to reassure him that she was all right. He'd been so worried. She'd never seen him like that before.

He tried to smile back, but his expression crumbled. He burst into tears, dropping to his knees in front of her wheelchair.

"Oh, babe, I'm so sorry."

"Wade, this wasn't your fault. You have to quit blaming yourself," Abby said, wishing it was true, as he squeezed her hand with what felt like desperation.

"I just don't know what I would do if I lost you," he was saying. "When I thought you were dead... Abby, I love you so much. Sometimes I do stupid things. I lose my temper or—"

"Well, fortunately, you didn't lose her," his father said from behind him in the doorway. Neither of them had heard Huck, so she didn't know how long he'd been standing there.

Her husband surreptitiously wiped at his tears but

didn't get up. Nor did he let go of the one hand he held of hers too tightly.

"In fact, son, she looks like she feels much better," Huck said as he entered the hospital room. "But you should have gotten those jars from the garage when she asked you to. I'm sure you won't make that mistake again."

Wade squeezed her hand even tighter. "No, I won't," he said, his voice sounding strained. "I swear."

"Then let's get this woman home. Can't let crime run rampant because of peach jam," Huck said with a laugh.

Wade got up slowly as if he had a terrible weight on his shoulders. Abby watched him use the wheelchair arms to support himself as he lumbered to his feet.

She'd blamed his job at the sheriff's office for the change in her husband, but as she felt the tension between Wade and his father, she wondered how much of the change in him was Huck's doing. Her father-in-law often talked about making his son a man. It was no secret that he thought Wade wasn't "tough" enough.

The doctor came in then to talk to her about her recovery. He still questioned whether she should be going home. She could tell that he was worried about her—and suspicious of her accident.

But Abby found herself paying more attention to what was going on out in the hallway. Huck had drawn Wade out into the hall. She couldn't hear what they were saying, but just from her husband's hunched shoulders, she knew that Huck was berating him. Talk about the kettle calling the skillet black, she thought.

"STOP YOUR DAMNED BLUBBERING," Huck said, taking Wade's arm and halfway dragging him down the corridor. "You didn't do anything wrong, remember? So quit apologizing."

"Easy for you to say," Wade said under his breath.

"You need to be more careful. If the doctor had overheard you…" His father shook his head as if Wade was more stupid than he'd even originally thought. "On top of that, the nurse said that Ledger McGraw stopped by to see your wife after you left," Huck said.

Wade swore and kicked at a chair in the hallway. It skittered across the floor, before Huck caught it and brought it to a stop with a look that told him to cool it. Wade wanted to put his fist through the wall. "He just won't stay away from my wife."

"So what are you going to do about it?" Huck asked, sounding as angry as Wade felt.

"I'm going to find the son of a bitch and kill him." He smacked the wall hard with his open palm. The pain helped a little.

"This is your problem—you go off half-cocked and just screw things up," his father said. "Listen to me. You want to get rid of him? I'll help you, but we won't be doing it when you're out of control. We'll plan it. As a matter of fact, I have a way we can be rid of Ledger McGraw and the rest of them, as well."

Wade stared at his father. "What are you saying?" He narrowed his eyes. "This is about the long-standing grudge you hold against Travers McGraw."

"What if it is? I don't just whine and cry. I take care of business."

He shook his head at his father. "I know you said you used to date Marianne before she married Travers, but—"

"But nothing." Huck wiped a hand over his face, anger making his eyes look hard as obsidian. "She was *mine* and then he had to go and marry her, and look how that turned out."

"You might be crazier than she is," Wade muttered under his breath, only to have his father cuff him in the back of the head as they headed back to Abby's room.

ABBY LISTENED TO the rain on the roof for a moment before she realized that she was alone. She rolled over to find the bed empty. More and more Wade was having trouble sleeping at night.

He'd said little after bringing her home from the hospital. Once at the house, he'd insisted she go to bed. He'd brought her a bowl of heated canned soup. She'd smelled beer on his breath, but had said nothing.

"I'll let you get some rest," he'd said after taking her soup tray away.

Sometime during the night she'd felt him crawl into bed next to her. She'd smelled his beery breath and rolled over only to wake later to find his side of the bed empty.

Now she found him sitting outside on the covered porch. He teetered on the edge of the chair, elbows on his knees, head down as if struggling with the weight of the world on his shoulders.

Abby approached him slowly, half-afraid that she might startle him. His volatile mood swings had her walking on eggshells around him. The floorboards creaked under her feet.

Wade rose and swung around, making her flinch. "What are you doing?" he demanded gruffly.

"I woke up and you weren't in bed. Is everything all right?"

"I just needed a little fresh air. You don't have to be sneaking up on me."

Abby desperately wanted to reach out to him, to comfort him, to plead with him to tell her what was making him so miserably unhappy. She blamed herself. They'd been good together once. Hadn't they?

But clearly he was in no mood for the third degree. Also she'd learned to keep her distance when he was drinking. But she knew he was hurting. Because of her fall? Or because of something else?

It was raining harder now. She hugged herself, the damp seeping through her thin nightgown. There'd been a time when he would have noticed just how thin the fabric was, how it clung to her rounded breasts and hips. Back then he would have pulled her to him, his breath warm against her neck. That husky sound in his voice as he told her how much he wanted her, needed her. How he couldn't live without her.

Wade didn't give her another look as he sat down again, turning his back to her. "You should go to bed."

She felt tears burn her eyes. Wade kept pushing her away, then losing his temper because he thought some other man might want her.

"I saw Ledger McGraw looking at you when you came out of the grocery store," Wade would say. "I'm going to kill that son of a—"

"You can't kill every man who looks at me," she would say.

"You like it when he looks at you."

She would say nothing, hoping to avoid a fight, but Wade would never let it go.

"He wants you. He isn't going to give up until he tears us apart. Not that he would ever marry you. He had that chance already, remember? Remember how he lied to you, cheated on you—"

There was nothing she could say to calm him down. She knew because she'd tried. "Wade, don't be ridiculous."

"Right, I'm ridiculous. I'm no McGraw, am I?"

"I married *you*."

"Only because you couldn't have Ledger."

She would try to hug him and he would shove her away, balling his hands into fists. "You never got over him. That's what's wrong with our marriage. You're still yearning for him. I can see it in your eyes."

He would shove her or grab her, wrenching her arm. It would always end with him hurting her and then being sorry. He would berate himself, loathing that he was now like his father. He would promise never to do it again, beg her forgiveness. Plead with her not to leave him.

And each time, she would forgive him, blaming herself for setting him off. Then they would make love and it would be good between them for a while.

At least, that was the way it used to be. Lately, it took nothing to set Wade off. And there was no pleading for forgiveness or any making up afterward.

"It isn't like anyone else wanted to marry you," her mother told her when she'd seen Abby wince from one of Wade's beatings. Her mother loved to rub salt in the wounds. "It's plain to see that you aren't making him happy. You'd better do whatever it takes or he's going to dump you for a woman who will. Then where are you going to be? Divorced. Left like a bus at the Greyhound bus station. No man will want you then."

Abby had bit her lip and said nothing. She'd made her bed and now she had to lie in it. That was her mother's mantra.

"And stay clear of that McGraw," her mother had

warned. "Men always want you when you're with someone else. But the minute they get you, they lose interest.
So don't be thinkin' the grass is greener with him. You
already know you can't trust him. Look how he broke
your heart. Just be glad Wade was willing to marry you
since you weren't exactly white-wedding-dress material,
now, were you?"

Now she stared at the back of her husband's head for
a moment, then padded barefoot back to bed. If only she
could remember how she'd gotten hurt. She had a feeling that would have answered all of her questions about
what was happening with her husband.

"ABBY'S STARTING TO REMEMBER," Wade told his father the
next day. He'd been relieved that he had to work. The last
thing he wanted to do was sit around with her. He felt
as if he was going to come unraveled at the seams as it
was. She knew she hadn't fallen off a ladder. He saw it
in her eyes and said as much to Huck.

"So what? It isn't like she's going to tell anyone," his
father said. "If she was going to do that, she would have
done it a long time ago."

"She's going to leave me."

Huck swore. "She would have done that a long time
ago, too. She's fine. It's you I'm worried about."

"*Everyone* knows." As he'd wheeled Abby out to his
patrol car parked at the emergency entrance, he'd seen
the way the nurses were looking at him. Everyone knew
now that he was his father's son—a bastard who mistreated his wife. He was thankful he and Abby hadn't
had a kid. What if he took his anger inside him out on
his *own* son?

"Snap out of it!" his father barked as they stood talking by their patrol cars. "You're in the clear."

Wade shook his head. "I'm afraid she's going to remember why we fought. If she remembers what she overheard you and me talking about…"

"I thought you said she didn't remember *anything*?"

He shrugged. "She says she doesn't, but the way she looks at me… She's going to start putting it together. I can see it in her eyes."

"Bull. If she remembered, she'd either go to the sheriff or she'd be in your face. What she needs to do is get back to work, keep her mind off…everything. In the meantime, you need to stay calm. You can't mess up again."

"I'll treat her real good," he said more to himself than his father. "I'll make up for everything."

"That alone will make her suspicious. Do what you normally do."

"Get drunk and stay out half the night?" Wade asked his father in disbelief. "And you think that will help how?"

"It won't make you seem so desperate. Stop saying you're sorry. It was her damned fool self who climbed up that ladder to get those canning jars."

Wade stared at him. He'd always known that his father bought into his own lies, but this was over the top. "She's not *stupid*. She knows damned well she didn't fall from a ladder." He felt a sob deep in his chest begging to get out. He wasn't sure how much longer he could hold it together. "You don't live with her. You have no idea what it's like. She knows she can do better than me. She's always known. If she ever finds out that we lied to her about Ledger McGraw and that girl at college—"

Huck swore a blue streak. "Stop feeling sorry for

yourself, you miserable little miscreant. It's our word against McGraw's. He swore nothing was going on, but if she didn't believe him then, she sure isn't going to now. She isn't going to find out unless you confess everything. She married *you*. Don't blow this. If she remembers what we were talking about when she overheard, then we'll deal with it. In the meantime, go get drunk, get laid, stop worrying."

ABBY COULDN'T SIT STILL. The doctor had told her to rest, but she felt too antsy. Not being able to remember nagged at her. She got up and turned on the television.

Standing, she flipped through the channels, but found nothing of interest and turned it off.

Out of the corner of her eye, she saw a book lying open on the floor next to her chair. As she bent to pick it up, she winced at the pain in her ribs. Dizzy, she had to grab hold of the chair arm for a moment.

She stared at the book, trying to remember. Had she been reading? It bugged Wade when she read instead of watched television with him. He took offense as if her reading made him feel dumb. It made no sense. No more sense than what had happened to her. Why would she have been reading if she was going to get canning jars down to make peach jam?

Marking her place, she put the book down and walked into the kitchen to open the refrigerator. Of course there were no peaches in there. Had she really thought there would be this time of year? Her ribs hurt worse as she breathed hard to fight back the nausea. She hadn't fallen off a ladder. Why did she keep trying to make Wade's story plausible?

She turned to look at her house, seeing her life in the

worn furniture, in the sad-looking cheap artwork on the walls, in the creak of the old floorboards under her feet.

Her gaze went to the floor as she caught a whiff of pine. Someone had cleaned the kitchen floor—but not with the cleaner she always used. Wade? Why would he clean unless...

Heart beating hard, she noticed that he'd missed a spot. She didn't need to lean any closer to know what it was. Dried blood. *Her* blood.

ABBY REALIZED SHE had nowhere to go. But she desperately needed to talk to someone. Even her mother.

She knew she shouldn't be driving, but her house wasn't that far from her mother's. Once behind the wheel she felt more in control. Seeing the blood, she'd quit lying to herself. She hadn't fallen off a ladder. Wade had hurt her. Again. Bad enough for her to end up in the hospital.

Only she had no idea why, which terrified her.

Too upset to just sit around waiting for Wade to get off his night shift, she'd finally decided she had to do something. If only she could remember what they'd fought about. A vague memory teased at her, just enough to make her even more anxious. It hadn't been one of their usual disagreements. It hadn't even been Wade drunk and belligerent. No, this time it had been serious.

As she turned down the road, she saw the beam of a flashlight moving from behind her mother's house toward the old root cellar. Abby frowned as her mother and the light disappeared from view.

Why would her mother be going down there this time of the night? She pulled up in front of the house and got out. As she neared the back of the house, she saw that her mother had strung an extension cord so she would have light down in the root cellar. It would be just like her mother to get it into her head to clean it out now, of all crazy possible times.

Abby had spent years trying to please her mother, but she felt she'd always fallen short. She almost changed her mind about trying to talk to her tonight. Her mother would be furious with her for not believing her husband—even though it was clear he was lying. Nan Lawrence was a hard woman to get close to. The closest they'd been was when her mother had pushed her to marry Wade after her breakup with Ledger Mc-Graw. Not that it had taken a whole lot of pushing since she had been so heartbroken.

She'd just reached the back of the house and was about to start down the path to the root cellar when she heard a vehicle. A set of headlights flashed out as the car stopped in the stand of cottonwoods nearby. Someone had just parked out there.

Her first thought was Wade. He'd stopped by the house to check on her, found her gone and figured she'd run to her mother.

Hanging back in the deep shadow of the house, she watched a figure come out of the woods. It was too dark without the moon tonight to see who it was, but it was definitely a man, given his size. Wade? He stopped for a moment at the opening to the root cellar before lifting the door and disappearing inside, leaving the door ajar.

Although she couldn't make out his face, she caught the gleam of a badge on a uniform. Abby almost turned back. She wasn't even sure she wanted to see her mother now that she was here. She definitely didn't want to see her mother and Wade. They would gang up on her like they often did, confuse her, make her feel guilty for not being a better wife. Make her believe that all of it was her fault.

And yet she was tired of running away from the truth. Wade had almost killed her. There couldn't be another time. Not unless she had a death wish.

She moved toward the open door of the root cellar. Wade had left it open. A shaft of light rose up out of the earth as she walked toward it. Her head ached and she told herself now wasn't the time to have it out with her husband.

But her feet kept moving, like a woman headed for the gallows.

The moon was still hidden well behind the cloud cover. She made her way across the yard until she reached the gaping hole of the root cellar.

The room belowground was larger than most root cellars. Having lived in Kansas as a child, her mother was terrified of tornadoes. No amount of talking had convinced her that tornadoes were rare, if not unheard of, in this part of Montana. She'd insisted that her husband build it large enough that if she had to spend much time down there, she wouldn't feel cramped. So he had. He'd have done anything for her. No wonder he'd died young after holding down at least two jobs all of his life.

Abby braced herself on the open door and took the first step, then another. The steps were solid. Also she could hear voices below her that would drown out any noise she made. They wouldn't hear her coming. She thought she might hear them arguing, but as she got closer, she realized there was only a low murmur rising up to meet her as if they were speaking in a conversational tone.

That alone should have warned her.

It wasn't until she reached the bottom step that she saw she'd been wrong about a lot of things. The man with her mother wasn't Wade. Nor was her mother down here cleaning.

Abby froze as she took in the sight. Black lights hung from makeshift frames along the earth ceiling. Under them green plants grew as far back into the root cellar as she could see.

Her mother and her visitor had frozen when they'd seen her. Deputy Sheriff Huck Pierce had a plastic bag filled with what looked like dried plants in his hand. Her mother had a wad of cash. Both quickly hid what was in their hands.

"What are you doing here?" her mother demanded. "You never stop by and tonight you decide to pay me a visit?"

Realization was like a bright white noise that buzzed in her aching brain. She stood stock-still. This, she realized, was why her mother had pushed her to marry Wade. It had nothing to do with him being her best choice. No, it was all about his father and the drug business her mother had been secretly running in her root cellar.

"Abby," Huck said casually. "I thought you'd be home in bed."

"I'm sure you did," she said and looked to her mother.

A mix of emotions crossed Nan's face before ending with resignation. "So now you know," she said.

Yes, now she knew why her mother had berated her for not being a better wife to Wade. Even when Abby had told her how Wade hurt her, she hadn't said, "Leave the bastard." No, she'd told Abby that it was her fault. That she needed to treat him better. That she needed to put up with it. Otherwise, she would be a divorcée, and look how that had turned out for her mother after Abby's father had died and she'd quickly remarried twice more and was now divorced again.

"I'll let you handle this," Huck said as he moved to leave. He tipped his hat as he edged past Abby as if she was a rattlesnake that couldn't be trusted not to strike.

But it wasn't Huck who she wanted to sink her venom into. It was her mother. All she'd wanted was her mother's love, she realized now. But the woman was incapable of real love. Why hadn't she seen that before?

"Don't be giving me that look," her mother snapped as she put away the empty jar that had held the dried marijuana the deputy had just bought. "I have to make a living. That's all this is. You have no idea what it's like being a single woman at my age. Anyway, it should be legal in this state. Will be one day and then I'll be out of business. But until then…"

She thought of all the things she wanted to say to her mother and was surprised when the only words that came out were "I'm divorcing Wade."

"You don't want to do that."

"*You* don't want me to do that, you mean. Or is it Huck who wants me to stay with his son?"

"Huck and I agree that the two of you need to work some things out. You two married just keeps things… simple."

"Simple for you since you're apparently in business with his father."

Her mother took a step toward her. "I won't hear any more about this. What are you doin' here, anyway? You should be home waiting for your husband. No wonder he has to take a hand to you."

Abby heard herself laugh, an odd sound down in the

root cellar. "It's not going to work, Mother. All I've ever wanted was you to like me if not love me. I tried to do what you asked of me, thinking that one day…" She shook her head. "Don't worry. I'm not going to turn in your little…operation or snitch on the deputy. Knowing Huck, he'd wiggle out of it and let you fry. But as for you and me?" She shook her head again and turned to leave.

"You're making a huge mistake. You leave Wade and things will only get worse for you. I'll tell you what. Quit your waitressing job and come into business with me. I'll cut you in and—"

"Save your breath," she said over her shoulder. "You and I are finished."

"I'm your *mother*. You listen to me," Nan yelled after her.

"I'm through listening to you." Abby topped the stairs and stumbled out. She took huge gulps of fresh air and fought tears. All this time she'd been trying to do the right thing according to her mother. It had all been to keep a drug dealer happy? Her mother had never cared what happened to her. It hadn't been about her marriage vows at all.

She staggered through the dark to her car, her ribs hurting as she took each ragged breath. She half expected Huck to be at the edge of the darkness, waiting to leap out at her. But apparently he'd left, believing that her mother could handle her. Look how well she'd done so far.

The moon peeked out from behind a cloud, startling her. Abby held her breath until she was behind the wheel of her car, the doors locked. She sat for a moment, gasping between sobs, the pain deeper than even her bruised ribs.

She started the car, desperately needing to leave here. Looking behind her, she saw her mother come out of the root cellar and stand, hands on her hips in the dim moonlight, scowling as she watched Abby drive away.

CHAPTER FIVE

"I DIDN'T EXPECT you to be back to work already," Ledger said, eyeing Abby a week later. "Are you feeling all right?"

"I'm fine," she said, handing him a menu and placing a glass of ice water in front of him. The familiarity of it after all this time had a nice resonance. She realized that if he ever quit coming in, she would miss him terribly.

That thought made her feel guilty. She knew what Wade would make of it.

Since the night she went to her mother's, Wade had been an adoring husband. Abby was sure his father must have said something to him about what she'd seen in the root cellar. Was that why he was being so attentive? Because he was afraid she would tell?

But tell what? She hadn't been able to remember anything from her lost twenty-four hours. She'd wondered if it hadn't had something to do with Wade's father's illegal business with her mother. Was that what she and Wade had argued about?

She didn't think so. All her instincts told her it was more serious than that. It nagged at her. She feared it was something worse, but couldn't imagine what that would be.

Seeing Ledger made her forget for a moment about that part of her life. He had always brightened her days.

She'd often regretted jumping into marriage with Wade, but had been determined to stick it out no matter what. She'd taken her marriage vows seriously—even without her mother's nagging.

"What would you like this morning?" she asked as Ledger picked up the menu. He had to have it memorized as often as he came in and the menu hadn't changed in fifty years except for the prices.

"Abby," he said, lowering his voice.

She fought the impulse to lean in closer. Close enough she could smell his distinct male scent, something that was branded on her memory. The soft sweetness of it was a painful reminder of when they'd been together. Ledger had been her first, something that Wade had never let her forget.

"I spoke to the nurse on your floor at the hospital. She told me that your injuries weren't consistent with a fall off a ladder."

"Ledger." The word came out a plea. He wasn't telling her anything she didn't already know. He couldn't keep doing this. It was killing her.

"I thought you should know. Wade lied to you."

Tears burned her eyes. She'd known Wade was lying to her the moment she'd seen his face. It wasn't the first time nor did she suspect it would be the last. But he was trying, something he hadn't done since becoming a deputy sheriff.

"He's going to kill you one of these days and then I'm going to prison for the rest of my life because I am going to tear him limb from limb." He said it so matter-of-factly that his words were like an arrow through her heart.

"Ledger. No."

"Why, Abby? Why have you stayed with him?" The

pain in Ledger's voice made tears blur her eyes. She hadn't just been putting *herself* through this.

She shook her head. All her reasons for staying no longer mattered. She took a step back, then another, bumping into a table before she got turned and rushed back to the kitchen.

"Get control of yourself," her elderly boss snapped as she rushed into the kitchen in tears.

"I can't do this anymore," Abby cried.

Ella took a step toward her. "If you're quitting, you aren't quitting in the middle of a shift."

"I'm not quitting." She lowered herself to a stool by the back door, her face in her hands. "I can't keep going back and forth, even in my mind."

Ella stepped to her and placed an arm around her shoulders. "Honey, this has been coming for a long time. You can't be that surprised."

"I'm a *married* woman."

Ella snorted. "And Wade is a married man. You think that means much to him? Now, wipe your face." She handed her a paper towel. "Honey, it's time to fish or cut bait. You're going to have to make a decision, and from where I'm sitting, it's pretty damned clear. You going to let Wade keep knocking you around? Or are you going to put a stop to it?"

She looked up, surprised, although she knew she shouldn't be. Of course her boss knew. "I've told him—"

"*Telling* him don't mean squat. Anything short of shooting him won't do any good if you don't leave him. I've held my tongue, but I can't anymore. Stop being a damned fool."

"But—"

"No buts. And stop listening to your mother. She

doesn't have the sense God gave a goose. I'm telling you straight. Dump that man and get on with your life before you don't have a life. Now, get back to work."

Abby went into the restroom and wiped her face. She'd cried enough over her situation. She looked as she came out to see that Ledger had left.

"I told him to get on out of here and to quit crowding you," Ella said. "You need to cut him loose if you don't have the sense to end your marriage. Now, do what women have always done—buck up and get back to work."

VANCE COULDN'T BELIEVE IT. He looked around the bedroom thinking he had to be dreaming. He'd downplayed how poor his adoptive family had been or how hard he'd had to work or how much debt he had from college.

As he walked to the window to look out, he felt a stab of jealousy for Cull, Ledger and Boone. They'd grown up here. They'd had all this and more.

But now you're one of them.

"Not yet." There was the DNA test. He'd managed to put it off as long as he could, knowing it was just a matter of time before he'd be forced to take it.

In the middle of dinner tonight Cull McGraw and his girlfriend had shown up. Both had looked at him like he was a bug under a microscope as if searching for his fatal flaw—just as they had the first night he'd met them. The girlfriend, Nikki St. James, the true-crime writer, had wanted to see the stuffed toy horse that night. He had watched her inspect it and seen that the horse had definitely been the ticket in.

But it would all come down to the DNA test.

"When is the DNA test scheduled?" Cull had asked his father tonight.

Travers had seemed taken aback by his son's abruptness.

"No reason to put it off any longer, right?" Ledger had interjected.

Vance had met Travers's gaze. "They're right. No reason not to schedule it," he'd said with more confidence than he felt. One more major hurdle and then he was home free, so to speak.

But he remembered that first night well. "So what have you been doing since college?" Nikki had asked.

"You can interview him for the book some other time," Travers had said with an embarrassed laugh.

"Sorry, questioning goes with the occupation," she'd said, but he had known he'd have to answer a lot more questions before this was over.

That was why he'd answered it that first night. "I've been working on some ranches in southern Montana. I'm apparently good with horses." That had pleased Travers—just as he knew it would. Vance had smiled to himself as he'd finished his meal.

Now over a week later and alone in his room, he tried to relax and enjoy how far he'd come. This was definitely an upgrade from how he'd been living, but, he reminded himself, it was temporary.

"How are you settling in?" asked a voice from the doorway.

He swung around to find the attorney smiling at him. "This place is beautiful."

Waters agreed as he stepped into the room and walked to the window to look out on the swimming pool, pool house and horse barns. Past them, the McGraw ranch stretched to the Little Rockies. "Dinner went well again tonight, don't you think?"

"I guess."

The attorney shot him a look. "Is there a problem?"

"No, but I think it's time I took the DNA test. Until I do…"

Waters nodded. "I don't see any rush, but it's up to you. Travers has accepted you. You seem to fit this place and this family."

He wasn't so sure about that. He might have won Travers over, but he wasn't so sure about the others.

"Now it is only a matter of tying up the loose ends," Waters said.

He wondered if the attorney was referring to the DNA test or the five-hundred-thousand-dollar reward. "I was wondering… The reward money? The friend who pointed out that I might be Oakley… I want him to have it."

The attorney studied him for a moment. "Minus my ten percent, you mean. I'm sure that can be arranged. Do you want me to speak to Travers?"

"No, not until after the DNA test." He swallowed back the bile that rose in his throat. "Once there is no question that I'm Oakley…"

LEDGER CORNERED HIS brother Cull.

"What do you want me to say?" Cull demanded after listening to what his brother told him.

"He lied about Abby falling off a ladder," Ledger repeated with more force.

"*Wade Pierce lied? Hell, stop the presses.* What should we do? I know—let's go over to his house and beat the crap out of him. Is that what you want me to say?"

"That would be a good start. Not that I need your help."

"Yep, you should go alone, that way I'll be able to get you out of jail on bail after you've gotten the hell kicked out of you by both Wade and his worthless father, who is also a deputy. Good plan."

"What am I supposed to do?" Ledger demanded.

"Do I have to remind you that Abby isn't your wife, not your responsibility, not even your business?"

"I'm just supposed to let him keep hurting her?"

Cull sighed. "She chose him. I know that's hard for you to accept but—"

"You don't know her. She sticks with whatever she promises to do. She promised to love him until death they do part."

"Then that's probably what's going to happen."

"I'll kill him."

"Oh, damn," Cull said and dropped his head into his hands for a moment. "Okay, what do you want me to do?"

Ledger looked at a loss for words. "We have to save her."

His brother nodded. "Okay, I reckon we could kidnap her."

"Kidnap who?" Boone had come into the room but stopped at his words and looked at him as if he'd lost his mind.

"Abby," Cull said. "We could wait outside the restaurant about the time she got off work and just grab her and—"

"And go to prison for kidnapping?" Boone demanded.

"Wait, this isn't such a bad idea," Ledger said. "Once we get her away from him, she will come to her senses and—" He stopped, seeing their disbelieving looks, and realized Cull had been kidding.

"Haven't you been trying to convince her to leave him?" Cull asked. "Has it done any good?"

"It's...complicated."

"Isn't it, though? I hate to tell you this, little brother," Cull said. "But as hard as it is, you need to step off."

Ledger flopped down in a chair. "I can't do that."

"What choice do you have?" Boone asked. "She doesn't want you."

"That's blunt enough, thanks, Boone," Cull said sarcastically. "Where are you going?" he asked as Ledger got to his feet and headed for the door.

"I'm going to find Wade," he said as he approached the door.

"He's going to end up in jail," he heard Boone say behind him. "Or worse if Huck and Wade tag team him. You ought to stop him."

"I suppose we could hog-tie him in the barn, but eventually we would have to let him go and then what?" Cull said.

Ledger let the door slam behind him as he headed for his pickup.

"Where have you been?" Abby asked when Wade finally showed up at home later that night.

He jumped, startled to find her waiting in the dark corner of the porch. "You scared the devil out of me."

Somehow she doubted that.

"I asked where you've been."

"You'd better change your tone and right now," he said, but it wasn't with the same meanness in his voice.

She really *had* scared him. The last thing he'd expected was to see her sitting in the dark waiting on him.

He reached in and turned on the porch light, blinked and then studied her as if trying to gauge what was going on.

"I'm still waiting," she said calmly.

"I was working," he said, starting to get belligerent. She could smell the beer on his breath from where she was sitting. But that wasn't the only scent she picked up on him. The cheap perfume turned her stomach.

She also noticed that he seemed to be swaying a little as if fairly drunk. Normally she wouldn't confront him. But tonight it was as if something had snapped in her. He'd been so good for weeks, but she'd known in her heart it wouldn't last.

"Don't bother to lie," she said, getting to her feet. "I know where you've been and what you've been doing." She started past him.

He grabbed her arm, spinning her around to face him. This was when she would normally hurriedly apologize, look at the floor, take whatever belittling he threw at her and then try to get away as quickly as possible.

Tonight she looked him in the eye with a fire she hadn't known she possessed. He seemed startled, his grip on her loosening a little.

Her gaze went to where his fingers clutched her arm. "Get your hands off me."

Amazingly, he let go. "You're getting some kind of mouth on you," he blustered. "You keep that up and I'll—"

"No, you won't," Abby said. She kept her voice calm but with an edge to it he'd never heard before because she'd never dared talk to him like this. "If you ever touch me again, you and I are done." She pushed past him, half expecting him to grab her from behind and backhand her.

But he didn't touch her. He let her go into the bedroom where she closed the door, the sound of the lock deafening in the house at this late hour.

Her heart was pounding like a war drum. She quickly moved away from the door, afraid he would charge it using his body like a battering ram and knock it down. The lock was fairly flimsy. It wouldn't take much.

But beyond the door she heard the shuffle of his heavy boots. He knocked over a lamp and cussed as it hit the floor. She heard him say, "I should bust down that door and teach that bitch what's what."

But with relief, she knew he wasn't going to do anything but pass out. She moved to the bed as she heard him collapse on the couch. Would he wake up in the middle of the night having sobered up just enough to be furious that she'd locked him out of his bedroom?

She climbed into bed, feeling the cold aluminum of the baseball bat she'd purchased in town. It lay next to her. She'd bought it on impulse today after work because as good as Wade had been, she'd known in her heart it wouldn't last.

Abby took hold of the bat. If he busted down the door and came in all raging fists and angry threats, he would get another surprise.

For a long time, she lay propped against the pillows, clutching the bat and waiting. Ella was right. She had to take control of her life. This was a start.

If she could save her marriage, she had to try. Ella was right about that. She was also right about Ledger. She needed to cut him loose.

CHAPTER SIX

LAST NIGHT LEDGER had driven around Whitehorse, looking for Wade's pickup. The deputy hadn't been at work. He also hadn't been at any of the local bars.

While he'd thought about driving out to Abby's house, he had enough sense not to. The more he drove through the sleepy little Western town, the more he realized something had to change. He'd been carrying this torch for Abby since high school. If he'd married her when he'd had the chance, none of this would be happening.

But they'd been too young and he'd promised his father that he'd finish college before they married. Unfortunately, Abby hadn't been able to wait. He'd heard that she was pregnant with Wade's baby, but that hadn't been true. Instead, he suspected the rushed marriage had been Abby's mother's doing. That woman just wanted to get her daughter married off—didn't matter to whom, apparently.

He'd finally driven toward home, telling himself he had to stop going by the café on the mornings Abby worked. He upset her too much. He had to back off. His brothers were right, as hard as that was to admit.

Feeling as if his heart was breaking all over again, he drove home. As he got out of his pickup, he saw that his brother Cull was sitting on the porch as if he'd been waiting for him.

"You don't have to get me out of jail," he said as he climbed the porch steps.

"Glad to hear it. Not that I was waiting up for you," Cull lied.

Ledger smiled at him as he took a step next to him. "I drove around looking for Wade for a while."

"Must not have found him."

"Nope, but I did do some thinking. You're right. Abby knows how I feel. It's in her court now."

Cull reached over and clasped his shoulder to give it a squeeze. "I know how hard this must be for you. But you've done all you can at this point."

He nodded. "I love her."

"I know." Cull was quiet for a moment. "So you think this Vance Elliot is our brother?"

Ledger shrugged. "He looks like us."

"He does that. Says he's good with horses." Cull chuckled. "I was thinking we'd put him on that new stallion."

Ledger actually smiled at that. "I'd pay money to see it."

Cull got to his feet. "It's late. Guess we'll know for sure when the DNA test results come back. I would imagine Dad will talk the lab into putting a rush on them. Or maybe not. I think he's enjoying the idea of Oakley being home. You going to be okay?"

"Don't have a lot of choice."

ABBY WOKE THE next morning, only her and the baseball bat in the bed. No Wade. He hadn't awakened in the night. Or if he had, he'd thought better about breaking down their bedroom door.

She realized that she felt better. Her ribs were still

sore. She still had a dull ache in her head, but even it was better.

Rising, she dressed, then she moved to the door and slowly unlocked it. She had no idea what to expect. The wear and tear of living in a relationship where she had to walk on eggshells had taken a toll on her. She felt jumpy, unsure, afraid as she slowly opened the bedroom door, the doorknob in one hand, the baseball bat in the other.

The couch was empty. She stood listening before taking another step. Was he waiting for her in the hallway off the bedroom, planning to jump her the moment she came out?

With the bat in both hands, she started down the hallway. She took a few steps and stopped to listen. The house creaked and groaned, but there was no sound of Wade.

She could see the indentation in the couch where Wade must have slept at least part of the night. One of the couch pillows was on the floor.

Cautiously she moved down the hallway toward the kitchen. The floor creaked under her step. She froze and listened again.

Just a few more feet and she would be able to see into the kitchen. He would have had time to think about what she'd said to him last night.

She prayed that he would know she meant it this time and that if he didn't change she would leave him. But she knew that her ultimatum might just as easily set him off and make things worse between them.

If what Ledger had told her was true about people at the hospital knowing she hadn't fallen off a ladder? Word would spread fast and everyone in the county would know the truth about her and Wade. Shame burned her cheeks. They'd know her terrible secret. All her lies had been for nothing. Because this time Wade had hit her hard enough that he'd had to take her to the hospital.

That story about her climbing the ladder in the garage for jars to make peach jam had been just that—a ridiculous story that he'd cooked up.

She shuddered as she realized that Wade hadn't come up with that on his own. His father's fingerprints were all over it. Wade would have panicked when he couldn't wake her up. He would have called Huck to ask him what to do.

Abby felt sick because all of it sounded so much more believable than the jam jar story. Yet she had wanted to believe it. Worse, she'd wanted Ledger to believe it.

What was wrong with her? She'd let her husband hurt her, telling herself that he was under a lot of pressure because he'd lost his job or because he wanted to make good at the sheriff's department or because he'd had a rough day at work. Like she'd never had one of those.

When he'd lost his temper and hit her, she'd told herself it was her fault. She'd promised to try harder to please him—just as her mother had said.

A wave of disgust washed over her as she moved to the doorway to the kitchen and stopped.

Wade was sitting at the table, elbows on the tabletop, his head resting in his hands. A floorboard must have creaked, because he suddenly lifted his head and turned it in her direction.

His eyes were red and shiny. Hungover? Or crying? She couldn't tell. Either, though, could change in a heartbeat and turn violent.

Those eyes focused on her, shifting from her face to the bat in her hands. His expression went from sorrowful to surprised, then deeply hurt. She realized he'd been crying. It was what he always did after he hurt her. She'd never doubted that he was sorry or that he didn't want to hurt her again. Until the next time.

"Abby?" His voice sounded lost.

She shifted the bat to one hand and let it rest against her leg.

"You don't need that," he said, still sounding shocked that she would either think that she needed a bat to protect herself or that she would consider hitting him with it.

She felt the irony of that soul-deep.

Yesterday she'd been determined to save her marriage. But looking at him sitting there, she knew that she no longer wanted to. The last few months had been so much worse than any she could have imagined. Him putting her in the hospital because of his temper… It was the last straw.

"I want you to pack your things and move out," she said, surprised how calm she sounded. Her heart was pounding in her chest.

"Abby, you can't mean—"

"I do, Wade. I can't live like this." He had started to get up, but her words stopped him. He settled back in the chair and put his head in his hands again.

"Don't do this, Abby. I'll change. I swear I will. In fact, things are going to get better."

The familiar words had no effect on her. She stared at her husband and wondered how long it had been over. She'd left him once. That night, running for her life, she'd made the mistake of going to her mother's.

"Don't you ever darken my door again. Your place is with your husband."

"You don't understand. He's going to kill me." She had pleaded with her mother.

"What did you do?"

She'd stared at her mother in disbelief. "I didn't do anything."

Her mother sneered. "You did somethin' to make him mad."

"He came home drunk, smelling of some other woman—"

"Grow up, Abby. He's a man. He has to let off a little steam. Be glad he took some of it out on that other woman before he got home. You want to be a good wife? Don't make him mad. Now, get out of here. He finds out you came here…"

She'd left, walking home in the dark and realizing she had no other place to go than back to Wade.

Now she felt a sadness deep in the pit of her stomach. She hadn't been strong enough to leave Wade then, but she was now. "It's over, Wade."

"You can't throw me out of my own house," he said belligerently. But he didn't make a move toward her.

She felt the weight of the bat. "If you don't leave, I'll call the sheriff. I don't think you want that."

He fisted his hands at his waist, glaring at her. Then knocking over the chair, he jumped up and stormed out. She listened to the sound of his pickup engine dying off in the distance before she went to the door, locked it and pushed the fallen chair under the knob.

But all her instincts told her he wouldn't be back. At least not until tonight.

WATERS SHOWED UP the next morning to see if Vance needed a ride to the lab for his DNA test.

"This really isn't necessary," Travers said when he opened the door to see his attorney standing there.

"I'm representing Vance through this," Waters said, surprising his old boss. "He asked me to on his behalf. I hope you don't mind."

"I guess I can understand how he might feel alone in this, though if this test comes back like I think it will, he'll now have family to take care of things. I hope, after all these years, that you won't be involved in any litigation with my son."

"I was the one who brought him to you," Waters reminded him. "I promised to look after his interests even though I've spent years looking after yours. But I'm sure once we confirm he's your son that he will have everything he needs."

Travers nodded.

"Since I am only on a retainer with you, I thought you'd appreciate me taking care of things on his behalf."

"You know I do." The horse rancher turned as Vance came down the stairs.

Just moments before, Waters was feeling good. Travers did appreciate what he was doing. He thought they might actually be able to patch things up. He was about to breathe a sigh of relief when he saw Vance's expression.

Worry wormed through him. The kid looked petrified. Maybe he hated needles. Waters could only hope that was all that was going on with Vance. Surely he wouldn't be so stupid as to think he could pass a DNA test if he knew he wasn't Oakley McGraw.

Then again, maybe Vance thought the toy stuffed horse would be enough.

He tried to relax. The kid had the horse. Unless he'd

picked it up at a garage sale, he was Oakley McGraw, right?

"I thought you and I would ride together to the lab," the attorney said to him. He promised to see Travers and his sons at the lab and quickly steered the would-be Oakley outside.

Once the two of them were in the car, he buckled up and looked over at the kid. "If there is some reason you think you might not pass this DNA test, then you need to tell me now."

ABBY WONDERED WHAT had made her think she could stay in this house. Everywhere she looked there were too many bad memories. Her first thought this morning was simply getting away from Wade. She didn't think her body could take another run-in.

But once she realized she didn't want to stay here, she knew she had to find a place of her own. Something small. Something she could afford by herself.

They'd been paying on this house for the past couple of years. If there was any equity in it, Wade could have it. She just wanted out.

That decided, she couldn't wait to pack up and leave. It wouldn't take much packing. She hadn't accumulated hardly anything she cared about over these few years of marriage.

When she looked around, she thought she could pack all of her possessions into the two suitcases out in the garage. She walked through the kitchen, opened the door from the house to the garage and froze.

A memory tugged at her the moment she saw the ladder lying on the garage floor. Was it possible she *had* fallen—just as Wade had said? She shook her head. No, the blood was in the kitchen. But there was something about the garage and the ladder.

Standing there, she tried hard to remember. Closing her eyes, she felt another nudge. Wade and his father. She frowned. They'd both been in the garage. She'd come to the door and heard them talking.

A shudder moved through her. Why had they been talking in the garage? Because they hadn't wanted her to hear. But she *had* heard. Had she let them know it?

Apparently not at once since she'd found her dried blood on the kitchen floor. Had she confronted Wade about what she'd heard and the argument had gone from the garage to the kitchen?

She squeezed her eyes closed tighter. They'd argued, but she'd already suspected that. But not in the garage. No, it had been in the kitchen. The two of them alone. But what had it been about?

Something important. Had Wade found out that she'd gone back on the pill and had been keeping it from him? She shook her head and tried to concentrate on what she'd seen and heard in the garage.

She could almost see Wade and Huck with their heads together, talking in grave tones in the garage. Almost hear... She opened her eyes with a groan, the memory just out of her grasp. But whatever it was, it was serious.

WATERS HAD FOUND a local lab to do the DNA test so they didn't have to travel out of town.

"Won't you need to get DNA from Mother?" Ledger asked. Once they'd seen that Jim Waters would be taking Vance to the lab, he and his brothers had insisted on driving their father.

"At this point, all they need is mine," Travers said

after lecturing them about babying him. "It should be conclusive enough. If needed, we can get your mother's."

As they walked in, Ledger wondered how long it would be before the news was all over town. He'd already heard the rumor going around that one of the twins had been found. Waters's doing? Or Vance's?

Vance had spent his first night in a motel in town. If Waters had checked him in, that could have been enough to get tongues wagging.

At the lab, his father walked up to the reception desk and was told that he could come on back. As he disappeared down a short hallway, Ledger looked around. The building was small. His brothers had taken seats in the waiting area, but he was too antsy, so he'd moved where he could see down the corridor.

There were a series of small rooms off the hall. His father had gone into one of those with the lab tech. He wondered where Vance was. At the sound of a familiar voice, he saw Deputy Sheriff Huck Pierce step out of one of the rooms with one of the lab techs, this one a redhead. She was laughing at something the deputy had said.

Ledger turned away, but not before he'd seen the lab tech move to open the door of one of the rooms. He got a glimpse of Vance sitting nervously on a gurney, waiting to have the test done. He didn't look like a man who believed he was Oakley McGraw.

"Good thing Dad is smart enough to demand a lab test," Ledger said when he joined his brothers. "I just saw Vance. He looks scared to death. What if he's lying?"

"Then we'll know soon enough," Boone said. "DNA doesn't lie."

"He had the toy stuffed horse." Cull shook his head. "What I want to know is what happens if he *is* Oakley."

CHAPTER SEVEN

LEDGER LET A few days go by before he stopped in the Whitehorse Café. He halted at the door to scan the room as he always did. Today, he would tell Abby why he hadn't been back. He would apologize for making things worse for her. He would step off.

But as always, there was that moment of expectation, that sense of hope, then concern when he looked around for her. If he didn't see Abby, there was always a painful disappointment that ruined his appetite. But he was too polite to turn around and leave on those days when she'd traded shifts. He would have a little something to eat even though the other waitress could tell there was only one reason he'd come in and it wasn't for the food.

"Abby took the day off," her friend Tammy said as she swung by on her way to a table with two plates full of biscuits and gravy. She didn't give him a chance to comment.

Abby never took a day off unless something was wrong. He waited until Tammy came back to ask, "Is she all right?"

Tammy slowed to a stop even though he could tell that she was really busy this morning. He saw her hesitate. He knew she didn't like telling something that Abby might not want him to know.

"It's okay," he said, not wanting to put her on the spot. "She needs loyal friends."

"She's looking for an apartment," Tammy said and gave him an encouraging smile.

"An apartment?"

"A studio," she said pointedly and then took off as she had another order come up.

A studio apartment. Did that mean what he hoped it did? That she'd finally left Wade? He tried to keep from getting too excited about the prospect, not knowing what it meant. There was always the chance she would change her mind. Or worse, that Wade would stop her.

He couldn't possibly eat a thing. He left and walked to his pickup, his step lighter than it had been in three years.

He'd just climbed into the ranch pickup when his cell rang. He thought for a moment that it would be Abby calling with the good news. He reminded himself that he wasn't part of the equation. He hadn't been since she married Wade. Just because she was getting an apartment—

Ledger quickly dug out his phone, still hoping. "Hello?" he said without checking to see who was calling.

"You need to get home," his brother Cull said without preamble. "Dad just got the DNA test results. He wants us all there."

"That quick?" Ledger asked in disbelief.

"They did just a preliminary one that should tell us if Vance Elliot has any of our blood running through his veins."

"I'm on my way." He disconnected and sat staring out over the steering wheel. It was the moment of truth.

He started the truck and drove as quickly as he could

toward the ranch, his thoughts straying radically from what was waiting for him at home to what Abby was doing right now.

He wanted to call her, but he resisted. He'd promised himself he would give her space. Ledger chuckled to himself, thinking about the times he'd wanted to pull some crazy romantic stunt like he'd seen in the movies. He'd ride into the café on his horse, scoop Abby up and ride off into the sunset with her. He'd save her from herself, from Wade, from her horrible mother.

Ahead the ranch came into view, the Little Rockies in the distance. He slowed the pickup to turn down the road past the bright white wooden fence that lined both sides of the road. A half dozen horses had taken off in the wind, their manes flying back as they ran.

The sight always made him smile. He loved this ranch, loved raising horses. He'd always thought that he would bring Abby here after he saved her.

Waters's car was parked in front of the house along with an older-model pickup he didn't recognize. Vance Elliot's?

Both trepidation and excitement filled him. For twenty-five years his father had searched for the twins. Was it possible the DNA test would prove that one of them had finally made his way home?

ABBY FELT STRONGER every day both physically and emotionally. She'd made a point of ignoring the pleading messages her mother left on her phone as well as the angry, threatening ones.

To her surprise, Wade had stayed away, as well. Each night she had expected him to get a snoot full of beer and come banging on her door. When she woke each morning to realize he hadn't, she felt like a woman in the eye of the hurricane. She didn't kid herself that it would be this easy to get her freedom from him.

Now she braced herself. The last couple of days had been nice not having to confront him. Unfortunately, she had to talk to him. She found Wade as he was getting off his shift. From the look in his eyes, his father had already told him everything, including that Abby now knew about the marijuana business.

"We should talk about all this at home," Wade said once he was close enough to whisper.

"I don't have that much to say and I don't want to be alone in the house with you." She saw the sharp ache of pain in Wade's eyes. The other times, she'd weakened. "I moved out of the house today. You can keep it or sell it, whatever you want. I don't want anything from you."

"You don't mean that. You're just angry and upset. Once you calm down—"

"No, Wade. I do mean it and I'm not going to change my mind. It's over between us."

A muscle jumped in his jaw. He got that familiar look in his eyes. If they hadn't been standing on the street in front of the sheriff's office, he would have lost his temper and they both knew what happened then.

"I saw a lawyer today and filed separation papers. There is a waiting period, but once it's over, if you sign the divorce papers, you won't have to pay for a lawyer of your own. Up to you, but dragging this out will only cost us both money."

He stared at her as if he couldn't believe the words out of her mouth. "You just hold up a minute. You didn't say nothin' about no divorce."

"I told you I was done."

"That ain't the same as a divorce," he said, taking off his Stetson to rake his fingers through his hair. "I just thought you needed some time to cool off."

"No, Wade. I can't be married to you anymore. Please don't put up a fight. It's over and I'm not going to change my mind."

He put his hat back on, looking like he was going to cry. "I'll change. You have to give me another chance."

"I've given you too many chances," she said, looking away from him.

His voice broke and, when she looked at him, fury was back in his gaze. "It's McGraw. Ledger McGraw."

"Believe what you want because you will anyway, but this is only about you and me." She started to walk back toward her car, hoping he wouldn't come after her.

But, of course, he did. "Abby, I know I've messed up…"

"Please stop," she said, continuing to walk. "I don't want to rehash this. You know exactly why I'm divorcing you. I won't tell anyone about how you physically abused me unless you fight the divorce."

She heard the breath come out of him in a whoosh. Clearly, he hadn't thought about that. Not that people didn't know already. Ledger had always known. But it was clear that Wade liked to think it was still their secret.

"It's my word against yours," he said, grabbing her arm and spinning her around to face him.

She jerked her arm free. "People saw the bruises on me, Wade. They'll testify in court. The doctor at the hospital is already suspicious after my…accident."

He looked furious but also scared. If it became public knowledge, he could lose his job. He grabbed her arm again.

"You're hurting me," she said, keeping her voice down. He released her arm and stepped back as if he didn't trust himself. "Just let me go. It's for the best. And, Wade? Don't let your father make you do something stupid."

"What does that mean?"

"My mother and your father have their own selfish reasons for wanting us together. I wouldn't take their advice." With that, she opened her car door and climbed in to roll down the window. "My lawyer will have the paperwork to you soon. Just sign it and let's part amicably, okay?"

She didn't give him a chance to answer as she turned the key in the ignition and drove away. He was still standing there looking after her when she pulled onto the street. They would never be *amicable*. She would be lucky if he gave her the divorce, let alone left her alone. No, she thought, fighting tears. She'd be lucky to get out of this alive.

LEDGER WATCHED THE celebration feeling strangely outside it. After twenty-five years, one of the twins was back. It was more than surreal. He glanced at his father. Travers looked so happy it made his heart ache with joy. But he was the only one, Ledger thought as he surveyed the family. They all looked as stunned as he felt.

He saw Nikki watching Vance. Or did they now start calling him Oakley? Nikki was sharp; that was what made her such an excellent true-crime writer. She saw things that other people missed. And she knew people. Look how much she'd uncovered in a very short time recently.

She was frowning as she studied Vance. Ledger

wasn't sure he could call him Oakley, even if the twenty-five-year-old would answer to it after all this time.

His father was suggesting another bottle of champagne as he put an arm around his long-lost son. Vance just looked uncomfortable in his new role.

Ledger moved closer to Nikki in time to hear her whisper to Cull, "Something's wrong."

His brother sighed. "He has the toy," Cull said quietly. "He has our blue eyes. He looks like us. But more to the point, he passed the preliminary DNA test with flying colors. So what are you saying?"

Nikki shook her head and looked to Ledger. "You feel it, don't you?"

He nodded. "It just feels…"

"Wrong," Boone said, joining them at the edge of the party.

Just then their father called them over so he could fill their champagne glasses.

"Whatever it is all of you think you know, keep it to yourself," Cull warned them. "Look at Dad. He's happy. So I'm happy. It will take some time, but let's make the best of this."

MEMORY IS A *funny thing*, Abby thought. One minute her mind nagged at her to remember what had happened that night in the garage and later in the kitchen. The next, she would get a flash. Just enough to make her stop what she was doing to try to hang on to it before it disappeared again.

She'd realized that she was missing one of her favorite earrings. Knowing that Wade should be working and away from the house, she'd driven out to look for the earring.

It was while down on her hands feeling around under the bed for the earring, when her fingers closed on it, that she had her strongest flash yet. She froze as the memory came to her like the trailer of a movie. She saw Wade and his father in the garage, their heads together in serious conversation. But this time, she heard what they were talking about.

At the sound of a vehicle pulling up in the yard, Abby jerked up, banging her head on the bed frame as she drew back, the earring biting into her fingers. Her head swam for a moment from the pain, from the memory, from the sound of a car door closing and heavy footfalls on the porch steps.

She rose and looked out the bedroom door toward the front of the house. At the sound of a key in the lock, she knew it had to be Wade. He would have seen her car parked out front.

Abby looked around as if for a way to escape. But the bedroom window was painted shut and she'd never be able to get down the hallway to the back door without being seen. If Wade saw her trying to get away from him, it would only make it worse.

Indecision froze her to the spot. She felt sick to her stomach from what she'd remembered. She wished she'd never remembered. Just as she wished she had forgotten about the earring. She should never have come back here.

But she realized that knowing what she now did, she would have to go to the sheriff. She had no choice. Wade wasn't a good husband. He had a miserable temper and he often struck out when he was hurt or mad or drunk, which was often. But she'd never thought he was a bad man. She'd often felt sorry for him, knowing how he was brought up by his father.

But after what she'd heard Wade and his father discussing in the garage… Once she went to the sheriff, she would never be safe. If Wade didn't get her, his father would. She would be just as good as dead. Her only other option would be to stop Wade before he and his father went any further—as if anything she could say would convince her husband to go against his father.

She'd forgotten all about her earring until she heard it hit the floor. She hadn't even realized it was still in her hand until she'd dropped it. Bending down, she felt around for it in the dim light of the bedroom. She'd just recovered it when she heard a floorboard creak behind her.

"Abby?"

She hadn't heard him come down the hallway. Now he was standing in the bedroom doorway.

He saw the look on her face and swore. "You remembered."

Now she really was trapped.

CHAPTER EIGHT

ABBY BACKED AWAY from her husband. She'd never seen such fear and fury in his eyes before.

"You are going to keep your mouth shut. Is that understood?" he demanded as he advanced on her, matching each of her steps with one of his own until he backed her into a corner.

"Wade, I'm begging you not to do this," she said, trying to keep the tremor out of her voice and failing.

"Begging?" He laughed. "I like the sound of that."

"I'm serious. I've gone along with a lot since we married, but this—"

"This is our ticket out of this hellhole. Come on, don't pretend that you wouldn't like a nice big house like the McGraws'." He snickered. "Just the mention of that name and your eyes sparkle, but it's not the house you crave, is it?"

"Please, don't start on that."

"Don't even want to hear Ledger McGraw's name on my lips, do you?"

She bumped hard against the wall. He had her trapped and he knew it. She'd put up with so much from him in the time they'd been married. At first he'd been so sweet, so understanding. He'd put her on a pedestal, but then he'd been fired at his feedlot job. His father had gotten him on as a sheriff's deputy and Wade had changed. He'd become more like the father he'd told her he despised.

He was close enough now that she could see the fire burning in his dark eyes. He desperately wanted to hit her.

Why had she tried to reason with him the night before he'd put her in the hospital? Why hadn't she gone straight to the sheriff when she'd found out what he and his father were up to?

Too late now. If only she could reach the gentle man who often cried in her arms after hurting her.

"Ledger McGraw," he repeated, his mouth twisting in an angry sneer. "I think my saying his name hurts you more than if I was to knock you into next week."

"Wade, this isn't about Ledger. This thing you're planning is cruel and illegal."

"Illegal?" He guffawed. "Honey, did you forget who you're married to? I'm a frigging deputy sheriff. There ain't nothing illegal when I'm carrying my badge and gun."

She feared he believed that. It would explain the change in him since becoming a deputy. She'd been a fool to provoke him by trying to change his mind. Even if she backed down, she had his ire up. He was going to hurt her.

And then what? Suddenly she wasn't sure how far he'd go to keep her from telling what she'd overheard him and his father planning.

"I NEED YOU to come right over," Wade said into the phone, his voice breaking.

His father swore. *"What did you do?"*

He glanced over the body lying on the floor. "It wasn't my fault but I might have hit her too hard."

His father swore again. "Don't do anything, you dumb ass. Just stay there. I'll be right over," he said before slamming down the phone.

Wade hung up and rubbed a hand over his face. Then pulled it away, shuddering as he saw it was covered in blood. He quickly wiped it on his pants.

"Stupid, stupid, stupid," he said, hitting his forehead with his palm. Why did he let it go so far? Why didn't he just walk away before it got so bad? Maybe he could have talked some sense into her. Why did he have to take it out on her?

"Because I'm my father's son," he said in disgust.

Walking over to Abby, he squatted down beside her. She didn't look that bad. His old man had taught him not to hit a woman in the face. Didn't want the neighbors talking or, worse, someone down at the sheriff's department being forced to call him on the carpet because everyone in town had seen his wife's black eye.

But he must have hit her in the face this time because her nose was bleeding and after her concussion...

His back door banged open. Angry footfalls marched down the hallway. He turned as his father came storming into the room.

"She still alive?" Huck asked.

"I don't know."

"You didn't check?" He let out an angry snort and, shoving Wade out of the way, squatted down to check her pulse. "You lucked out, you worthless little prick. She's still breathing. How long has she been out?"

Wade looked around as if the answer was in the room. "I don't know."

His father rose and glared at him. "What are you doing beating on her again?"

"You mean like you used to hit me and Mom?"

"Watch your mouth, smart boy," he said, stepping to him. Huck grabbed him by the front of his shirt and slammed him against the wall. "Why pick a fight with her today, of all days? Do I have to remind you that we have too much at stake for you to be calling attention to yourself with the authorities again because of some petty argument with your old lady? What were you thinking?"

"It wasn't petty," he gasped out. His father was choking him with the balled-up shirt at his throat. "She *knows*." He wiped a hand over his face, smelled her blood on him still and rubbed his palm against his jeans.

Huck let go of him and took a step back. "How?"

He shook his head. "I don't know. She must have just remembered. She'll tell."

Huck swore and turned to look at the woman on the floor. "We don't have any choice, then. We can't take her back to the hospital. I know someone who's an EMT. We can take her to him. He'll cover for you, and if she's smart, she'll keep her mouth shut and go along with it."

Wade bit at his cheek. He hated to tell his father but he didn't think Abby would be going along with anything anymore.

"It may take more than that," he said quietly.

Huck turned to look at him. "What are you saying?"

"I don't think she's going to keep this to herself. Not this time."

His father took a step toward him. Wade raised his arms to protect his head and waited for the force of Huck's punch to knock him to his knees.

Abby moaned.

Wade peeked from under his arms, surprised his father hadn't struck him.

"We'd better decide what to do with her," Huck said. "But first, you have any whiskey? I could use a drink."

ABBY DIDN'T KNOW how long she'd been lying on the floor bleeding. She groaned and tried to sit up. Her ribs protested violently and she had to lean back against the side of the bed. The room began to spin and she thought she might throw up. She closed her eyes, fighting the nausea. She could hear Wade and his father in the kitchen. From the clink of ice in the glasses, it sounded as if they were having a drink.

How was that possible with her lying in here on the floor, fading in and out of consciousness? Or had, this time, Wade thought he'd killed her?

They had lowered their voices, but she could make out most of what they were saying since this house was so poorly insulated. Her head ached. She had to concentrate hard to understand the words.

"...get rid of her body...have to do it tonight...can't just dump it anywhere."

Fear spiked through her. They couldn't be talking about getting rid of her. Getting rid of her for good. But even as she thought it, she knew it was true. Wade had gone too far this time. He thought he'd killed her.

She realized that he couldn't take her back to the hospital or questions would be asked. He might lose his job. He loved being a sheriff's deputy. He'd never give that up just because this time he'd hit his wife too hard.

Abby caught hold of the edge of the bed and pulled herself up. She realized she'd left a bloody handprint on the spread. For a moment, she stared at it, thinking the spread would have to be soaked to get that out.

A noise in the other room brought her back to the pain in her body, the ache in her head. She felt dizzy standing and wasn't sure how much longer she could stay upright.

Get out before it's too late, a voice screamed in her head.

She worked her way to the door and looked out. She could still hear Wade and his father in the kitchen. They were talking in very low tones now. She only heard the occasional clink of a glass or an ice cube.

They would be coming back for her soon.

She looked toward the back door. It seemed too far away to reach given how dizzy she felt, but she started for it, moving at a snail's pace as she used the wall for support.

She felt dazed, not even sure she was awake as she reached the door and tried the lock. Unlocked. It felt slick in her hand as she turned the knob and the door swung open.

A cool breeze hit her in the face, and from some survival instinct older than time, Abby knew she had to run for the trees now. If the men in the kitchen felt this breeze, they'd know she'd opened the back door. They would know that she was trying to get away.

She ran, the first step jarring her ribs and making her hurt all over. She ran bent over, her arms wrapped around her middle as if she could hold herself together. She didn't look back. She didn't dare. She had to believe she could reach the trees. She didn't think past that.

Abby stumbled on a tree root, lost her balance and went down hard. The fall knocked the air out of her and hurt her already aching ribs. She rolled over on her back and lay there, gasping like a fish out of water.

Over her head, stars glittered, making her think she was blacking out again. Her vision cleared as she caught her breath. She lay there listening, expecting Wade and Huck to find her and that her painful run for safety had only been a waste of time and effort.

Hearing nothing, she was suddenly aware of the weight of her cell phone in her pocket. She pulled it out, but for a moment, she couldn't think who to call.

Not her mother. Not her friends. She couldn't drag them into this. Wade had already warned her what he would do to them. As she held the phone, she felt a sob rise in her chest.

There was only one person she could call. She got up and stumbled deeper into the woods. She thought for a moment that she wouldn't be able to remember his number. But it was right there when she touched the keypad. She prayed he hadn't changed his cell number as she waited for it to ring.

The first ring filled her ear, making a sob escape. She held her breath as it rang a second time. "Please answer. Please."

She had no one else to turn to. She couldn't call the sheriff where Wade and Huck were both deputies. They would talk their way out of it even if she were believed.

It rang again. He wasn't going to answer. She gripped the phone tighter, feeling all hope slipping away.

She was just about to give up when Ledger answered on the fourth ring.

She began to cry so hard with such relief that she couldn't speak.

"Abby?"

She managed to get out two words. "Help me."

He didn't hesitate. "Just tell me where you are."

"SHE'S GONE!" WADE CRIED as he rushed back into the kitchen, where his father was finishing off the last drop of whiskey in the bottle. Fortifying himself for what had to be done.

"What do you mean, she's gone?" Huck demanded, slamming down his glass.

"She's not lying in there where we left her. There's blood on the spread and on the wall…"

"Come on, she can't have gotten far in her condition."

Wade returned to the bedroom, checked the bathroom and even looked under the bed.

"This way, you fool," his father snapped.

As Huck stepped out of the bedroom, he saw the handprints along the hallway. They led straight to the back door, which was standing open.

"What are we going to do?" Wade cried. He'd had just enough whiskey that he felt warm inside, but his head felt fuzzy. Everything about this felt surreal.

"She can't get far on foot," Huck said after checking to make sure she hadn't taken one of the cars. "We would have heard her start up the engine, if she had."

Wade headed for the stand of cottonwoods along the creek behind the house. It was a straight shot from the back door and seemed the obvious place to try to hide.

He hadn't gone far, though, when he found her shoe. It lay on its side next to the creek. He whistled for his father to join him as he looked deeper into the dark shadows of the trees.

I'm going to find her out here dead. That thought

immobilized him until he heard his father's heavy footfalls behind him.

"There's her shoe," Wade said, pointing at it.

"Pick it up. She must be close around here." Huck started to step past him.

"I don't think so," Wade said, holding him back with his free arm. He shone his flashlight on the tracks past the shoe. "They look fresh," he said of the tracks.

Huck bent down. "Someone picked her up and carried her." He glanced past the creek and the cottonwoods to the dirt road on the other side. "She have her phone with her?"

Wade swore under his breath. "You can damn well bet who she called. Ledger McGraw."

Huck rose right in front of his son. "You screwed this up royally. I could…" He reared back, but Wade blocked the punch.

"I'm not that boy you used to knock around," he said through clenched teeth. "You can call me a fool, you can say whatever you like, but if you lay another hand on me, I'm coming after you."

Huck scowled at him. "You think you can take me? You punk."

"Don't know but I'm going to try."

Huck laughed. "Tonight isn't the time to find out. If she goes to the sheriff—"

"She won't. She's gone to Ledger McGraw. If anyone comes looking for me, it will be him and I'll be ready."

CHAPTER NINE

LEDGER COULD THINK of only one thing. Take Abby to the hospital and then find Wade. He'd never been violent, but seeing what Wade had done to Abby had him to the point where he thought he could take the man's life. Wade had to be stopped and if it meant ending him…

"Where are you taking me?" Abby asked from the passenger seat of the pickup. He could tell that each word hurt her to speak. He would have brought the Suburban so she could lie down in the back but he hadn't known how badly she was hurt.

"To the hospital," he said.

"No!" She tried to sit up straight but cried out in pain and held her rib cage. "That's the first place he'll look for me."

"Abby, you need medical attention."

"Please."

He quickly relented. He couldn't let Wade near this woman, which meant no hospital. At least for now.

"I'll take you to the ranch and call our family doctor. But, Abby, if he says you have to go to the hospital—"

"Then I'll go." She lay back and closed her eyes. "I didn't want you involved."

"I've always been involved because I've always loved you."

She said nothing. He could tell that she was in a lot of

pain. It had him boiling inside. If he could have found Wade right now...

He slowed to turn into the ranch and called Dr. Johns. His service answered. Ledger quickly told the woman what had happened. "We need him to come out to the McGraw ranch." She put the call through. Doc asked a few questions about her condition.

Ledger answered best he could.

"I think you should take her to the hospital. I can meet you there."

"She doesn't want to go to the hospital because her husband can find her there. I'm taking her to the ranch."

"Then I'll meet you there."

Ledger pulled up in front of the house. He saw that she was looking at it, tears in her eyes.

"This is not the way I ever wanted to come back here," she said.

"I know. But right now the only thing that matters is that you're here and safe."

"Promise me you won't go after Wade." When he didn't answer right away, she cried, "Ledger, please. I can't bear the thought of losing you."

"I promise," he said, although they were the hardest words he'd ever had to say.

ABBY REMEMBERED LITTLE of the ride to the ranch or Ledger and his brothers helping her to a bed upstairs. The doctor had apparently told Ledger not to let her sleep because he stayed with her, asking her about everything but what had happened until the doctor got there.

It wasn't until the next morning, when the doctor told her she could sleep now, that Ledger asked, "Do you want me to call your mother?"

"No!" She'd looked so stricken that he hadn't pushed it as the doctor left.

"Is there anyone else I can call?"

She shook her head, tears filling her eyes. "He's already told me what he'll do to my friends if I involve them."

Ledger gritted his teeth, his anger a rolling boil inside him. What the man had done to Abby... But when he spoke, he sounded calm. "Okay, you just rest. Everything is going to be all right." As he started to turn from the bed, she grabbed his hand.

"You can't do anything to Wade. You can't let him know where I am. If you do anything... You promised."

He nodded as if he'd already figured that out for himself, but she could tell he wasn't happy about it. "Don't worry. He won't know where you are."

"Oh, he'll know," she said. "But he wouldn't dare come out here." Wade didn't operate that way. He would wait until she left here. He would wait until he could catch her alone.

And when that happened, she had no doubt that he would kill her. She'd done the unforgivable in his eyes. She'd gone to Ledger McGraw.

MCCALL TOOK ONE look at Abby and wanted to take a two-by-four to Wade Pierce. Locking him behind bars wasn't enough.

"How are you feeling?" the sheriff asked as she took the chair next to the woman's bed.

The changes going on at the house had surprised her. She'd heard that there had been quite a lot of renovation since Patricia was arrested and never coming back.

But McCall knew that wasn't all there was to it. With

one kidnapper identified and now dead, the money recovered and news that the twins had been adopted out to eager families through a member of the Whitehorse Sewing Circle, Travers seemed to have a new lease on life.

For twenty-five years, he'd kept the children's rooms and the entire wing of the house just as they were the night of the kidnapping. As if freed of some of the past pain, he was opening up the rooms and redecorating them.

The room where Abby was staying looked as if everything in it was brand-new. The walls had a fresh coat of a pale yellow. The curtains billowing in the faint breeze were light and airy. It was as if the room had been decorated just for her.

"I'm feeling better."

McCall could tell that it was going to be hard for her to open up and talk about what had been going on. Abby had tried to keep the secret, no doubt out of shame. McCall had run into this before. Often an abused woman never wanted anyone to know, blaming herself as her husband also did.

"Do you remember what happened?"

Abby shook her head and seemed to realize that McCall would think she was covering for Wade. "The doctor said having another concussion so close after the first one has caused even more memory loss."

"The first one? The fall from the ladder?"

Abby looked away. "That's what Wade told me."

"I spoke with your doctor. You need to know that he reported the incident as physical abuse. This time I think you realize that something has to change, right?"

Tears filled the young woman's eyes as she nodded. "I had left Wade, moved into an apartment in town and filed for a separation, the first step in the divorce proceedings. I remember going out to the house to get something." She frowned. "Wade must have come home early." She shook her head. "I'd told him earlier in the day that he would be getting divorce papers and to please sign them."

McCall nodded. "Abby, do you remember calling 9-1-1 and telling the operator it was urgent that you speak to me?"

She felt her eyes widen. Had she called 9-1-1 as a threat to Wade if he came near her? "I don't remember calling."

"The operator said you told her that you'd discovered something horrible that your husband and his father were doing."

She shook her head as she thought of her mother's marijuana operation. Surely she wouldn't have called the sheriff on her own mother. It was something Wade and his father were up to? She had a glimmer of a memory but it only made her head hurt worse. "I'm sorry. I don't remember calling and I can't imagine what I was calling about."

McCall nodded. "I think it's time you filed a complaint against Wade. Will you do that?" When Abby hesitated, the sheriff added, "And I wish you'd also take out a restraining order against him. True, it isn't worth the paper it's printed on if Wade ignores it and comes after you, but the order will tell him you mean business—especially if you call 9-1-1 the moment he breaks it." Both of them knew he would break it.

Abby closed her eyes for a moment. "I'll do it. The complaint and the restraining order." She opened her eyes and met McCall's worried gaze. "He'll lose his job, won't he?"

"Not right away, but once he breaks the restraining order, yes. When Wade first got on at the department he seemed to have so much potential. He was really excited about the job. I'd had hopes for him. This is his wake-up call. I hope he takes it. In the meantime, I just want to keep you alive."

Abby chewed at her lip. "Wade's just so angry right now about me leaving him."

"It's even more dangerous now. The operator heard Wade in the background before you disconnected. She heard him say something like, 'You'd get me sent to prison? Your own husband?' Whatever you tried to tell me about Wade and his father, it sounds serious. If they thought you might remember…"

THE SHERIFF DIDN'T need to tell Abby how much trouble she was in. Wade had almost killed her. She vaguely remembered hearing him and his father in the kitchen, their heads together. They'd been talking about what to do with her body.

She shivered at the thought, suddenly restless. The room where Ledger had brought her was beautiful, but she couldn't stay here forever. Then what?

Even with the restraining order McCall had her sign, she knew Wade would come after her. He'd told her that if she ever left him, he'd kill her and then himself. She'd never doubted that. But he'd also told her that if she ever went to Ledger, he'd kill him, as well.

Her heart pounded at the thought of what she'd done by calling him. But last night there'd been no one else. She knew Ledger would come and get her. She knew he would take care of her. If she had hoped to survive, she had to get away from Wade and his father last night. Otherwise…

Climbing out of the bed, she felt a little dizzy for a moment but needed to move. She felt anxious and afraid. Ledger had promised he wouldn't go after Wade. She had seen how hard it was for him to do that. She trusted that he would keep his promise.

But Wade coming after Ledger… Not that Wade would come out to the ranch. He wasn't that stupid. No, he'd wait until he could get Ledger alone.

She felt a memory pull at her. Something about the garage. It slipped past, refusing to let her grasp it long enough to make any sense of it. Wade and his father had been up to something that would send them both to prison if caught?

Abby felt sick to her stomach. What had the two gotten involved in? Something that apparently they would kill to keep quiet, she thought, remembering them whispering in the kitchen. The hair stood up on the back of her neck. If she hadn't gotten out of the house last night when she did, she'd be dead and buried out in the middle of the prairie.

MCCALL TOOK NO pleasure in calling Wade Pierce into her office. When she'd hired him, she'd hoped he would make a better deputy than his father. He had seemed to have that potential. But maybe his upbringing was harder to overcome than she'd hoped.

He tapped at the door and stuck his head in when she said, "Come in, Wade. Please have a seat." Not surprisingly, he looked nervous. He had to know what this was about.

"I wanted to give you a heads-up," she said once he was seated. "Your wife has filed a domestic abuse complaint against you—" She held up her hand, seeing that he was about to argue the point. "As well as a restraining order."

The man looked dumbstruck. He really hadn't expected she would do that. Then he looked furious.

"I want to make something perfectly clear. Right now I'm suspending you for two weeks without pay so you can think about your life and any changes you might want to make. However," she said quickly as again he was half out of his seat, mouth open and ready to argue. "However, if you break the restraining order or if there is another call from your wife, you will be dismissed."

"But it's a lie." He wasn't very convincing and she could see that he knew it.

"I don't take these kinds of charges at face value. I spoke with her doctor at the hospital. After that, I advised your wife to take these steps not just for her sake but for yours."

Wade shifted his gaze to look down at his boots. "So two weeks."

"This is serious, Wade. You can end up behind bars. If there is no trouble between now and then, I'm willing to give you another chance here. Anyone else I would have let go. Tell me that my faith in you isn't misplaced."

He looked up and swallowed, his Adam's apple bobbing up and down for a moment. "There won't be any trouble."

"Good. I'm glad to hear that. Wade, get some help." She slid a pamphlet across the desk to him.

"Anger management?" He let out a nervous laugh.

She saw his father in him then and knew she was

probably wasting her breath. "Often this problem is gen-erational. But it can be stopped."

"Generational," he repeated and frowned. He looked again at his boots. "Right."

"That's all."

He got up slowly, his hat in his hand. She could see that he was fighting all of this, going from embarrassment to anger and back. She feared anger would win.

"You know this will get all over town," he said quietly.

"Wade, everyone already knows what's been going on. Now's your chance to show them what kind of man you are."

He nodded slowly. "Two weeks." And he walked out, closing the door a little too hard behind him.

CHAPTER TEN

"I THOUGHT YOU said she'd never go to the sheriff," Huck Pierce demanded when Wade found him at his house and told him the news.

"She didn't. Apparently the sheriff went to her. It's that doctor at the hospital. The sheriff said he suspected physical abuse and reported it."

"So much for patient privacy," his father snapped.

"Isn't he required by law to report it? Maybe that's what happened."

"Or maybe your wife's boyfriend is behind all of this."

Wade ground his teeth. "As far as I know, she's still out there."

"Well, she can't stay there forever. I asked around. I found out where the apartment is that she rented."

"The sheriff was real clear. I can't go near her or I'll be fired."

"Well, there's no restraining order against me, but you're right. Now isn't the time to be worrying about this. We have bigger fish to fry." He winked at Wade. "Our plan went off without a hitch. Now it's just a matter of waiting for the money to roll in. Once you don't need this job anymore, you can get your wife back—if that's what you want."

"I'd rather die than see her with McGraw."

His father smiled. "That's what I thought. Believe me, she won't be for long."

LEDGER COULDN'T BELIEVE how different the house felt with Patricia and Kitten gone. But it was even better now, he thought, that Abby was free of Wade.

The biggest change in the mood at the McGraw ranch, though, was one of the twins being found. Vance had settled in upstairs in the wing where he'd once lived as a baby.

It had surprised Ledger when his father had announced that the wing would be remodeled. No longer would it be a shrine to the kidnapped children. Instead, it would be made into quarters for Vance—and eventually Jesse Rose, once she was found.

"You do realize that Jesse Rose might have a life she doesn't want to leave," Boone had pointed out. "She'll be twenty-five years old. She might not want to move back into the house where she was kidnapped."

It seemed odd to the three older brothers that Vance would move in. But he apparently had little going on in his own life and this had been his home.

"I'm aware of that," his father had said with a laugh. "But I want them to feel at home here on the ranch. I want them to have a place. Oakley might not end up staying, but he will at least know that he has a room here."

"Oakley?" Cull had asked. "Is he going to change his name?"

"We're discussing it. Of course, it would be an adjustment for him," Travers had said.

Ledger thought Vance would be up for whatever his father wanted. He seemed to have adjusted quite well to living on the ranch. Earlier, he'd seen him at breakfast putting away any and everything set before him. Later he was down at the pool swimming and napping in the sun.

"He said he had a way with horses," Boone pointed out. "When is he going to start working?"

Their father sent his son a disapproving look. "He's just getting used to being Oakley McGraw."

"Oh, I think he's gotten used to it quite well," Boone said, getting to his feet. "If you want me, I'll be in the horse barn. Working."

Cull rose, as well. "He has a point, Dad. Maybe you should discuss with Vance…Oakley what is expected of him." With that, he left.

Travers looked to Ledger. "Aren't you going to give me your two cents' worth, as well?"

"I think they pretty much covered it. I'm going into town to get a few things from Abby's apartment for her. You don't mind her staying on for a while, do you?"

"Of course not. Just be careful. Putting yourself in the middle of these kinds of things is very dangerous, especially with Wade Pierce."

Ledger nodded. "I'm not going to do anything stupid."

"But I don't think you can depend on Wade Pierce not to."

He smiled at his father. "I'll be careful."

As he started to leave, his father said, "I want to just enjoy having my son back for a while. But I don't want the rest of you resenting him. Am I wrong?"

Ledger turned at the door. "It's an adjustment for all of us. You just got him back. I don't think you need rush it."

His father smiled. "I could say the same about you and Abby."

He laughed. "Yes, you could, but you'd be wasting your breath. I'm going to marry that woman just as soon as she's free."

WATERS LISTENED TO Patricia McGraw's latest threat and realized he would have to go to the jail and have this out in person. It wasn't something he was looking forward to. He hadn't seen her since her arrest. He probably could have gone the rest of his life without seeing her. But she wasn't having any of that and somehow she'd hired herself a fairly good lawyer.

As Patricia was brought in, he picked up the phone. From the look in her eye, he was glad to have the thick, scarred Plexiglas between them. She sat down, glaring at him for a moment, before she picked up her own phone.

"You bastard," she said into the receiver.

"Nice to see you, too, Patricia. I'm a busy man, so if you have something to say, please do it."

She sneered. "I heard you're buttering up Travers so you don't lose your job. Good luck with that." He smiled and saw steam come out of her ears. "He's just stupid enough to keep you on. And what's this about Oakley being found?" she demanded.

He shrugged. "Seems that way."

She heard the suspicion in his answer and he could have kicked himself. "You think he's a fraud?"

"No. He looks like his mother, has the McGraw men's blue eyes and dark hair."

Patricia made a face. She never liked the mention of Travers's first wife. "But?"

"No buts. He passed the preliminary DNA test. Travers is convinced and Vance seems to have settled into your house just fine."

She let out a growl. "Vance?"

"Oakley. I think he'll be changing his name soon. So we have a happy ending."

"Maybe you do. Listen to me. I'm not going down alone, you hear me? I promised my lawyer that you will be helping finance my defense."

"You what?"

"You're in this up to your neck. Unless you pony up some money…" She smiled, no doubt seeing how uncomfortable he was with what she was saying.

"You can't drag me into this."

"Jim, darlin', I have dates and times. I have phone messages. I have phone calls. I have enough that my lawyer assures me you will go down as an accessory—if not the person who actually bought the poison and administered it. You were there almost every meal. Did you really think you could frame me for this?"

"I didn't frame you. This is all you."

"I don't think so, Jimmy." She hung up the phone and stood, smirking down at him as if she thought she had him by his private parts.

What killed him was that he feared she did.

ABBY COULDN'T HELP being nervous. Ledger hadn't returned from town. He'd taken one of the ranch hands with him to drive his pickup back after getting what she needed from her apartment and picking up her car at the sheriff's department.

"I want someone with you in case—"

He'd stopped her. "Wade is in a lot of trouble. He's not going to do anything that would get him thrown in jail."

She wasn't so sure about that. The sheriff had called to let her know that Wade had been warned—and that the restraining order would be served within the hour. On top of that, Wade had been suspended for two weeks without pay.

Abby couldn't even imagine how furious he was. It would only get worse when the restraining order was served—and he told his father.

"He's going to want to kill me—and you," she'd told Ledger before he left. "I shouldn't have involved you in this. I'm so sorry."

"Hey," he'd said, lifting her chin with his warm fingers until their gazes met. "I've been involved since the day I fell in love with you all those years ago. I couldn't let go. I know I should have but once I saw how he was treating you…"

"That's why you need to be careful. Give him time to cool down."

She had smiled at the man she'd loved for as far back as she could remember. So many times she'd regretted her hasty marriage to Wade. She knew now that Ledger would never have cheated on her. But back then she had her mother and Wade telling her different. She'd been afraid that the reason Ledger had put off marriage was because he didn't love her enough.

When she'd seen the photos of Ledger with some other woman at college…

She knew now that Ledger and the woman had just been friends. Her mother had wanted her with Wade for her own selfish reasons.

"I've made such a mess of things," she'd said, hating that she sounded near tears. She'd cried way too long over Wade and the mistake she'd made.

Ledger had cupped her cheek. "It's nothing that can't be rectified. I just want you to be sure of what you want to do now. I don't want to talk you into anything. Whatever you do, it has to be your decision. So maybe you should take this time to—"

"I've already filed papers to begin divorcing Wade. He knows it's over. I'd kicked him out of the house and I had packed up my things and moved them into the apartment in town. I guess I'd gone back to the house for something. I didn't expect him to be there…"

"That's all behind you, then." He'd leaned down and given her a gentle kiss. She'd wanted to pull him to her and kiss him the way she'd often dreamed—and felt guilty about. But it was too soon.

She'd jumped into a bad marriage. If she and Ledger had a future… Well, they could take it slow.

"As I was saying, I really think you should stay here for a while longer. I could go to your apartment and get you whatever you needed."

"My car is out at the house. I don't want you going out there."

"Why don't you call the sheriff and have someone bring your car into town for you," Ledger had suggested.

She'd agreed and made the call. McCall had said that was smart not to send Ledger out to get it, or worse, go herself.

"I'll have the keys here at the sheriff's office."

"Ledger will be picking it up," she'd told McCall.

"This afternoon would be good since Huck isn't working."

Yes, she didn't want Ledger running into Wade's father, either.

"Thank you for doing this," she'd said to Ledger as she'd hung up.

"Don't you realize by now that I would do anything for you?"

She'd smiled. "I do."

But he wasn't back yet and all she could think was that he'd run into Wade. Maybe even Wade and his father.

She got up, too nervous to stay in the room any longer.

OAKLEY MCGRAW. "OAKLEY MCGRAW." Down the hallway from Abby's room, Vance stood in front of the mirror and tried out the name. His new name. When Travers had asked him if he had considered changing his name to his birth name legally, he hadn't known what to say. Maybe because he never thought it would get this far.

"Oakley McGraw." He was Oakley McGraw. He wanted to pinch himself. Two weeks ago he was Vance Elliot, ranch hand. All of his belongings were in his beat-up, rusted-out pickup. He barely had a job let alone a nickel to his name.

Now he was Oakley McGraw, son of Travers McGraw, heir to all of this. Along with three brothers, he reminded himself. Three brothers who he could tell didn't like him. As if he cared. Their father adored him.

That was why he was going to tell him he wanted to have his name changed to Oakley McGraw legally. Then there would be no question, would there. He would be the missing son. Travers was even thinking about throwing a party to introduce him to his friends. His friends were powerful people in this town, in this state.

Vance couldn't believe his luck. He looked out his window at the swimming pool shimmering in the sun. Maybe he would go sit down there in the shade after he helped himself to a beer from the refrigerator in the kitchen. That he had the run of this place was unbelievable. He thought he could live like this without any trouble.

As he started down the hallway, a door opened at the other end and a young woman stepped out. The cook had mentioned that there was a friend of Ledger's staying in the house. Apparently the friend had her meals brought to her, though, since he hadn't seen her before. He'd thought she must be a "special" friend.

He let out a silent whistle when he saw her. Even from a distance, she was real pretty. She hadn't seen him yet, so it gave him time to study her. As she drew closer, her gaze on the floor at her feet as if distracted by her thoughts, he saw that she had a black eye and other bruises.

Also she was walking as if in some kind of pain. Clearly, something had happened to her. A car accident? A mugging? An assault? This explained why she'd been eating in her room—and Ledger eating with her.

He hadn't realized that he'd stopped just short of the stairs to stare at her. She must have sensed him, because her gaze came up quickly and he got his first good look at her. With a shock he realized that he recognized her. Wade Pierce's wife.

Worse, she recognized him. Her blue eyes widened in alarm. She stumbled a little, but caught herself. "I'm sorry. You startled me."

"Sorry." He waited, heart in his throat, expecting her to say more.

But she only stared at him, recognition in her eyes and yet… He realized that she was trying to place where she knew him from.

"Please, you go first," he said, motioning to the stairs.

She shook her head. "I wasn't going down. I was just stretching my legs." She took a step backward and another, before she turned and went back down the hall the way she'd come.

He watched her, knowing it was just a matter of time before she remembered where she'd seen him. All he could think was that when she did, she was going to take all of this away from him.

CHAPTER ELEVEN

WADE WAS SURPRISED to see Abby's car gone when he drove out to the house. Had she come out to get it? Or had that bastard Ledger McGraw retrieved it for her?

He pulled up in front of the house, threw the car into Park and sat just staring at where her car had been. He should go out to the McGraw ranch and drag Abby out by her hair. Frustration had him shaking all over. He couldn't do that any more than he could get her back. His dad was right. He'd have to bide his time if he wanted any satisfaction. Look what the woman had done to him. He wouldn't be able to hold his head up in this town ever again.

He turned off the engine and started to get out when he remembered the restraining order. He couldn't come any closer than fifty feet? Seriously, in a town the size of Whitehorse with only one grocery store, one post office, one damned theater?

Grabbing up the paperwork, he tore it into a hundred pieces and threw it in the air like confetti. He felt a little better.

His cell phone rang. For just an instant, he thought it might be Abby calling to say she'd changed her mind. All the other times they'd had problems she'd come back.

But it was only his father calling. He swore and picked up. "What?"

"I see your mood hasn't improved."

"Her car is gone. You think she came out and picked it up?"

"The sheriff sent two deputies out to bring it back to the office, where Ledger McGraw picked it up with one of his ranch hands."

Wade let out a string of curses. "I want to get out of this damned town."

"Oh, come on, don't you want a little retribution first? Have you forgotten? We have an ace in the hole, remember? We're in the catbird seat, son. Soon we will be calling the shots."

When his father had come to him with his plan, he'd thought the old man had lost his mind.

"You're going to get us both sent to prison. This can't possibly work."

His father had winked at him. "These years as a deputy, I've made a few…friends. Leave it to me. We can pull this off."

Wade had been skeptical at best. But to his amazement, the plan seemed to actually be working.

"So knock off the 'poor me' routine," Huck said. "Soon you will have the money to go anywhere you want. And we'll have gotten some retribution along the way."

"I HAVE GOOD NEWS," Travers said when he saw Vance.

He could use some good news. "How is that?"

"I'm calling a press conference tomorrow to introduce you to the world and announce that my son has been found."

This was not what he'd consider good news. Especially when Abby Pierce was upstairs, no doubt racking her brain to remember where she'd last seen him. "Do we have to?"

Travers put a hand on his shoulder. Vance tried not to flinch. He'd known all of this would feel...strange. A father he'd never known. A family he'd never met. A new name. He wondered if he was up to it. The money, the name that carried weight, the ranch and all the expensive horses, all that he could get used to. But the rest...

"Son, I want to introduce you to the world as a McGraw. I've waited twenty-five years. Can you indulge an old man?"

How could he not? "I understand, but I've never been good at getting up in front of people like that."

"It will be fine. You won't be required to say but a few words. Or none if you aren't comfortable."

Just stand there and smile into the cameras and let everyone speculate on me, he thought. "You're planning to tell the circumstances of how I was adopted."

Travers nodded. "I hope you don't mind. I think it might also help bring back our Jesse Rose."

Jesse Rose. His fraternal twin sister. He'd almost forgotten about her. Why not? Pretty soon they would be just one big happy family. Right, he thought.

"If I can help bring her home, of course I'll do it," Vance said, knowing he had no choice. He was Oakley McGraw. He needed to start acting like him.

For a moment, he forgot about Abby Pierce. "There is one thing, though," he said as Travers started to step away. "What do I wear for this...press conference?"

"I'm sorry. I should have thought of that. You'll want to pick up a few things. We can go into town—"

"Would you mind if I did this alone? I feel enough like a kid as it is."

"Of course you do. How foolish of me. Take one of the ranch pickups. There are keys on the board by the back door. I'll call the clothing store in town and tell them to put it on my account. Get whatever you need." He smiled. "Treat yourself, please. Head to toe. You're Oakley Mc-Graw. Nothing is out of your reach." He started to turn away. "There is one more thing. Your mother. You know she hasn't been well. But she is doing much better. In fact, she wants to see you."

All Vance could do was nod as he thought, *Holy crap! Just when I think it can't get any worse.*

LEDGER TOOK THE stairs two at a time, anxious to see Abby. He'd picked up what she'd asked for from her apartment. It wasn't much. He'd been shocked to see how little she owned.

He tapped at her bedroom door. No answer. He tapped again and tried the knob. She stood at the window, her back to him, hugging herself as if cold.

"Abby?"

Startled, she turned from the window, looking scared.

"I knocked. You didn't hear. What is it?" he asked as she quickly rushed to him and threw herself into his arms.

"I was so worried about you," she said into his chest. "I thought—"

"I'm sorry. I hurried as fast as I could." He stared at her. "You're as white as a ghost. Are you feeling worse?"

She lifted her head to look up at him. "I don't know." He could see the fear still in her eyes. "I think I might be losing my mind."

"Why? What happened? Wade hasn't come here, has he?" He held her at arm's length to look into her beautiful face. It was still bruised. Every time he saw it, he felt anger boil up inside him. It was all he could do not to go after Wade.

Abby shook her head. "I saw someone in the hallway." He frowned. "A man. He came out of a room down the hall. When I saw him—" She shuddered and he pulled her close again.

"Are you talking about Vance? Vance Elliot. He's staying here. Abby, I'm sorry. There's been so much going on. I thought you knew. My brother, the one who was kidnapped… He's been found."

Her eyes were wide with horror. "*He's* the missing twin? He can't be your brother." She sounded as scared as she looked.

He drew even farther back to look at her. "Why would you say that?"

She pulled away to pace the floor. "When I saw him, I recognized him. And he recognized me. I had this jolt of memory, nothing I could recall, really, just this frightened feeling."

Ledger didn't know what to say at first. "You say you recognized him? Could it be from the café in town?"

Abby shook her head. "It wasn't in that context. It was…a bad memory. I know that doesn't make any sense. It's just this…feeling more than a memory. But I know I've seen him before, and wherever it was, it wasn't…good."

"Okay," he said, wondering what to make of this. "And you say he recognized you? Did he call you by name?"

"No. He seemed as shocked to see me here as I was him. I made him nervous."

Ledger took this all in.

"I know I sound crazy," she said, stopping her pacing to step to him again. "I'm trying to remember where I saw him. So much of the past is a blank because of the concussions. I'm afraid I won't remember."

He held her, drawing her close and kissing the top of her head. "It's going to be all right. You're here." But so was Vance Elliot—soon to be Oakley McGraw, if his father had anything to do with it. He wondered how much he should worry. Wade had scrambled Abby's brain. Could he trust this feeling she had? Could he *not* trust it?

ABBY LEANED INTO Ledger's hard body. Breathing in his scent, she felt safe and loved in his warm, strong embrace. With his arms around her, she believed anything was possible. Even the two of them having a happy ending. She never wanted him to let her go.

But she couldn't shake off the bad feeling she'd had the moment she'd seen Vance Elliot in the hallway. Something was terribly wrong. If only she could remember where she'd seen him.

"Maybe I really am crazy."

"You're not crazy," he said, a smile in his voice. "You're going to be fine."

In his arms, she believed it. But when she was alone with her black hole of a memory… "I don't know." She stepped away to move to the window overlooking the ranch. She loved this view. It was so peaceful, unlike her mind right now. "Maybe my head is so jumbled up that I might never straighten it out again."

"The doctor said to give it time. You've been through so much," he said, stepping to her and clasping both shoulders in his big hands. His fingers tightened as if he was thinking of Wade. "Trying too hard to remember is only going to make your headache worse."

She nodded. "Thank you for not going after Wade."

His smile was tight. "You don't know what you're asking. You realize that, don't you?"

"Yes. I don't want you to lower yourself to his level."

Ledger let go of her. His laugh held no humor. "Oh, Abby, you don't realize how much pleasure it would give me to beat that man to within an inch of his life. I want to give him some of his own medicine." He smiled. "But for you, I won't go after him. All bets are off, though, if he shows up here."

She smiled and nodded through fresh tears. "Once this is over," she whispered as he took her in his arms. "Once this is over." But would it ever be over?

VANCE COULDN'T BELIEVE it as he sat behind the wheel of the ranch truck and looked at the fancy clothing-store bags and boxes piled high on the other side of the pickup.

"Treat yourself, please. Head to toe." That was what Travers—his father—had said. That meant Stetsons to boots. Any other time, he would have been over-the-moon excited. The truck smelled like good leather and expensive fabrics. It smelled better than anything he could remember.

As he looked down at his boots, he felt for the first time like Oakley McGraw. He'd never owned a good pair of boots before. Somehow it made him feel better about himself. At least temporarily.

He pulled out the burner cell phone, sick at heart that he had to make this call now, of all times. But he didn't know when he was going to be able to get back into Whitehorse alone.

It rang three times before a male voice answered with "You done good, boy."

"Yeah," he said, loving the feel of the fine leather on his feet as much as the new gray Stetson perched on his head. For a moment, he thought about hanging up, starting the engine and seeing how far he could get away before someone came after him.

He didn't want to give any of this up, let alone have it snatched from him. He liked being Oakley McGraw, but it would be hard to get rid of Vance Elliot after twenty-five years of him living in the man's body. As Vance, he'd made his share of mistakes that were bound to come out.

But he had a more immediate problem. "The thing is—"

"What's wrong?"

"Abby Pierce. I crossed paths with her in the house today. She recognized me, but I could tell she was having trouble remembering where she'd seen me. But I have to tell you, that look she got in her eyes... It won't take her long to put it together."

"Where are you?"

"In town. Travers treated me to some clothing. He's planning on a big press conference tomorrow to tell the world that I am his son. But if she remembers before that—"

"Meet me at the Sleeping Buffalo rocks. Fifteen minutes."

"I'M GOING TO see your mother," Travers said when Ledger came downstairs. "I was hoping you and your brothers would come, as well."

"Sure." He'd been once when he was younger. He

hated seeing his mother like that, and his father had said that he didn't want his sons going if it upset them. Cull was the only son who continued to visit her—not that she'd noticed.

"I heard she's doing better," Boone said as they started toward the front door for the drive to the mental hospital.

"She is," their father said, smiling. He looked so much happier now. His prayers had been answered. Now, if Jesse Rose would turn up... "She asked about each of you the last time I saw her."

"She's talking?" Ledger said.

"She is. Not a lot, but she's improved so much I have hope, and so do the doctors, that she could make a full recovery," Travers said.

On the drive to the hospital, they talked about the ranch, the horses and finally Vance.

"Is this press conference really necessary?" Boone asked. "Yesterday, I was out in the pasture and a drone flew over low with a video camera attached to it. Is it ever going to stop?"

"Not for a while," Travers said as Cull drove. "When Jesse Rose is found, we'll have to go through it all over again, but eventually we'll be old news."

"That day can't come soon enough," Ledger agreed.

"If it ever does," Cull said. "Whenever our name comes up, it's in connection with the kidnapping."

"And Nikki's book on it isn't going to help," Boone said.

Cull shook his head. "I disagree. We're in the public eye. People want the inside scoop. Well, they will get it in the book. After that there won't be anything to add."

"I hope you're right," Ledger said. "I want to marry Abby, but I don't want to bring her into all this."

"Patricia still has to go to trial," Boone said. "Who knows how long it could take to find Jesse Rose, if ever. I can't see this ending for years, so unless you want to make the mistake of putting off your marriage again—"

"Abby isn't even divorced from her current husband," Cull pointed out. "I think we should just be glad that Oakley has been found."

"Yes," their father said. "Let's count our blessings. After the press conference tomorrow, I have a good feeling about Jesse Rose being found, as well."

CHAPTER TWELVE

"WELL, WOULD YOU look at this dude," Deputy Huck Pierce said as Vance Elliot climbed out of the McGraw ranch pickup. "Oakley McGraw, all duded out. How ya likin' livin' in luxury?"

All the way out to the Sleeping Buffalo rocks, Vance had been thinking he should just take off. It wasn't like he'd left anything he wanted back at the ranch. And he knew Travers McGraw would never send the cops after him. Not his own son. He could just keep going.

The problem was that he would eventually run out of gas. He didn't have a dime to his name. But as Oakley McGraw, he could have it all. It meant staying, though, and taking his chances with Abby remembering where she'd seen him. It also meant dealing with Huck and his son, Wade, he thought with a groan as he glanced past the two deputies to the rocks.

"So what's this?" he asked, motioning to two brown boulders, a large one and a smaller one, under a roofed-over enclosure beside Highway 2. He was stalling for time and he knew it. As he stepped closer to the rocks, he saw that they appeared to be covered with tobacco and some loose cigarettes that had been broken and spread over the larger of the rocks.

"You ain't heard the story of the Sleeping Buffalo?" Huck asked. "These rocks are sacred. Indians—excuse me—Native Americans believe it has spiritual power. You see, the Native Americans were looking for buffalo, hadn't seen any and were worried. Then they saw what they believed was the leader of a herd perched high atop a windswept ridge overlooking Cree Crossing on the Milk River not far from here. It turned out just to be these rocks. But past it was a herd of buffalo. So they believe these rocks led them to the buffalo and that the rocks have some kind of special powers. That's why they leave tobacco on the rocks to honor the spirits."

"And you believe that?" Vance asked.

"You might, too, if you knew what happened back in the 1930s when the rocks were moved into town," Wade said. "Townsfolk swore that the rocks changed positions and bellowed in the night. So they hurried up and brought them back out here."

"No kidding?" Vance said, staring at the rocks. The larger one was way too huge for even a group of men in town to move by hand each night in order to scare people. He thought maybe there was something to the story since apparently a lot of the Native Americans believed in these rocks.

He wished he believed in something right now as he saw Huck fidgeting. He had something on his mind and Vance feared he wasn't going to like it.

"There's a hot springs up the road here, if you ever get out this way again," Wade was saying.

"Are we through shooting the breeze, because I want to know how things are going out at the ranch," Huck said impatiently.

Vance took a breath. He thought of his beautiful accommodations. He was now living in the lap of luxury— just as Huck had said—and he loved it. He'd never thought it would go this far. But now that he was so close to legally being Oakley McGraw, he didn't want it to end.

"There could be a problem," he said, turning away from the rocks. The sun beat down on him. Standing here, he could see the prairie stretched out in front of him for miles. This country was so open. He thought a man could get lost in it and thought he might have to before this was over.

"A *problem*?" Huck repeated, already looking angry.

He glanced at Wade. "It's your wife. I didn't realize that she was at the ranch because she's been holed up in a room down the hall. Well, I saw her today. And she saw me. I think she recognized me from that first night we met."

WATERS LOOKED AT the messages on his phone. Patricia. One of them caught his eye.

Travers came by to visit me.

He stared at the screen and swore. The last thing he wanted was for Travers to be talking to Patricia. Who knew what lies she'd tell him. She was determined to take Waters down with her. He didn't know how to stop her. Surely the sheriff and Travers knew that she was a liar.

But some things would have a ring of truth in them. He'd been so sure everything would be blamed on Patricia's conspirator, Blake Ryan. Blake had been the former ranch manager, an old family friend and one of Patricia's lovers. He would have done anything for Patty—and did.

Now, though, there seemed to be fallout around the case and Waters knew he was directly in the line of fire if Patricia kept shooting off her mouth. Plus, she said she had evidence in emails and texts.

He paced around his small apartment, telling himself that now would be the perfect time to leave the country. Except that what money he'd managed to put away over the years was in stocks and bonds and not that easy to liquidate. Also it was the worst possible time.

But if he could get his hands on some money…

"Calm down." He stopped pacing, tried to stop panicking. Vance Elliot was Oakley. He'd brought him to Travers. Everything was fine. Travers wouldn't take Patricia's word over his. If he could just hang in…

A thought struck him. If he could find Jesse Rose, Travers would be indebted to him forever. He thought about the strange call he'd gotten from that private investigator in Butte. Probably a dead end. But maybe he should mention it to Travers. Maybe make more out of it than it had been.

"WHAT THE HELL are you talking about?" Huck demanded. "I know Abby can't hardly remember her own name. That's right—not only do I have friends at the lab in town, but also I have friends at the doctor's office and in other places. She doesn't remember *anything*."

"Maybe," Vance said skeptically. "But if you had seen the way she looked at me."

Huck waved it off. "You're just being paranoid. Suck it up. So how are things going with Travers McGraw?"

"Like I told you, he's scheduled a press conference tomorrow to announce to the world that I am Oakley McGraw. After that, he wants me to change my name legally."

Huck burst out a huge laugh and pounded Vance on the back. "Nice work. I can see that you're enjoying the fruits of our labor. The accommodations up to your standards?"

"It's nice living out there."

Wade snorted. "I'll just bet. Abby eating it up?"

"She doesn't look good. I mean, she's still hurt pretty bad," Vance said. "She's kind of limping, holding her ribs, and there's bruises." He could see that this pleased both men. What had he gotten himself involved in? As if he hadn't known right from the get-go.

"So you stand up there tomorrow at the press conference," Huck said. "You tell the world how happy you are to be back in the bosom of your family and you start going by Oakley."

"What about the reward money? You said I'd get my share."

Huck's gaze narrowed. "You wouldn't be thinking about taking off once you got a little money in your pocket, would you?"

Vance looked away.

"Listen to me," the deputy said, closing the space between them. "This is for the long haul, not for a measly five hundred grand. You'll get your share but not until you are settled in and Daddy's put you in his will."

He blinked. "Why would you care about the will?"

"You let me worry about that," Huck said, patting him heavily on the shoulder. "I'll let you know when we're through doing business. In the meantime, stay clear of Abby. She's probably picking up on your nervousness. We're home free."

Vance could see now how this was going to go. At first it had been about the reward money. They were to split it and then part ways. But Huck was getting greedy. Which meant the deputies would bleed him dry for years if Vance let them.

LEDGER WAS STILL shaken from seeing his mother. He hadn't seen her since he was a boy. It had been shocking then. It was still shocking. Cull had gone to visit her at the mental institution over the years, but he and Boone had gone only once when she'd first been admitted.

He'd asked about her, though, when Cull had returned from a visit. "She's still catatonic. In other words, she doesn't know anyone, doesn't talk, doesn't respond to anyone around her," Cull had said. "She just sits in a rocking chair and...rocks."

Ledger had kept the rumors going around school about her over the years to himself. He didn't want his brothers or his father to know what the kids were saying about his mother.

"She's crazy scary. The nurses are all afraid of her."

"Her hair turned white overnight. She turned into a witch and puts spells on people."

"She sits and rocks and holds two old dirty dolls. She thinks they're the twins she kidnapped."

That was the hardest part, everyone believing his mother had helped kidnap her own children. Unfortunately, none of them still knew who inside the house had handed out the twins to the kidnapper on the ladder outside the window. The ladder had been found leaning against the house—one of the rungs broken halfway down. That had led the FBI and sheriff at the time to speculate that the kidnapper could have fallen with the twins and that the six-month-old babies had died.

Fortunately, they'd found out that that wasn't true.

Now Ledger stared at the white-haired woman in the rocking chair on the criminally insane wing of the mental hospital and wondered what *was* true. The woman in the rocker looked much older than fifty-seven—until he looked into her green eyes. There was intelligence there—and a whole lot of pain.

"Ledger," she said and held out her arms.

He stepped into them, kneeling down so she could hug him, and felt his heart break for all that she'd lost. Twenty-five years. Gone. Worse, only one of the twins had been found. If Vance really was the lost twin.

Ledger couldn't help thinking about what Abby had told him. Maybe it was just wires crossed in her brain. Or maybe not.

Worse, his mother was still a suspect in the kidnapping. But he didn't want to believe it. This woman who'd suffered so much… She couldn't have been responsible for helping the kidnapper take her own children.

"I want to see Oakley," his mother said as she looked at Travers. "Will you bring him to visit me soon?"

Travers promised he would. "He seems to have taken after you."

WADE WATCHED VANCE drive away. "We can't trust him."

Huck laughed. "You're smarter than you look. He's not going anywhere until he gets money."

"What if Travers gives him some?"

"He won't for a while. McGraw is no fool. He can see that Vance isn't comfortable in Oakley's clothes." Huck scratched his jaw, laughing at his own joke. "McGraw will spoon it out slowly to him so as not to scare him. Anyone can see that Vance has never had much. He won't want to overwhelm his son."

Wade had to hand it to his father. That night when he'd shown up with this crazy plan, Wade had been outside the garage putting new spark plugs in his old pickup. The moment he'd seen his father's face, he'd known something was up. He knew about the marijuana deal the old man had going on with Abby's mother, but he wanted nothing to do with it.

"Abby gets wind of this and she'll flip out," Wade had warned his father. "You're going to screw up my marriage."

"On the contrary, I'm helping you out. She'd never rat out her mother. This way we have leverage. One day, maybe you'll be as smart as me—probably not, but keep trying." He'd cuffed him and then changed the subject.

So that night when he'd seen the smug look on Huck's face, he'd thought, *Oh, hell, now what.*

"Somethin' I wanna show ya," his father had said. Wade had caught the smell of beer on the old man's breath even though he was still in uniform. Often he worried that Huck would get them both fired.

That was when he noticed the paper sack his father was carrying. Huck motioned for him to step into the garage. "Where's your wife?"

"In the kitchen making supper. Why?"

"Look at this." His father had opened the top of the large paper sack.

"What's that?" Wade asked after getting a glimpse of what appeared to be a stuffed toy horse.

"That is money, son." Huck had gone on to explain how he'd been one of the first law officers called out to the McGraw ranch the night of the kidnapping and how he'd found the stuffed animal lying on the ground and picked it up. "I was thinking eBay. People will pay a bunch of money for something from a crime scene."

Wade had interrupted to tell him what a dumb idea that was. "They'd have traced it back to you. They'd fire you, charge you with…tampering with evidence at a crime scene and who knows what else."

"Settle down," his father had said. "I put it away, all right, and forgot about it until I ran into this guy at the bar down in Billings. It was his blue eyes. Dark hair, too. I thought, hell, that kid could be the missing Mc-Graw twin." Huck had started laughing. "We got to talking and…" He'd motioned to his pickup parked behind Wade's. The passenger-side door had opened and out stepped Vance Elliot.

Wade had argued that it would never work. "They'll want a DNA test."

"Already got that covered. There's this cute little red-headed lab tech…" Huck had winked. "It gets better. Vance is adopted. No kidding. Tell me this couldn't be more perfect. And he's about the right age."

"But won't there be paperwork?" Wade had argued.

"Falsified to cover up the fact that his parents had knowingly adopted the son from what is now a famous kidnapping."

"But what if the real Oakley comes forward?"

"Who will believe him once our boy is in the big house on the ranch?" Huck had scoffed that things could go very wrong. "Five-hundred-thousand-dollar reward. Vance here gets a cut, but he will have the McGraw horse ranch."

"Along with his three brothers and his sister, if she turns up," Wade had pointed out.

"Stop looking for trouble," his father had said irritably. "This is going to work. Trust your old man."

That was when Wade had heard a sound from behind him. He'd turned in time to see the door to the kitchen close quietly.

CHAPTER THIRTEEN

WATERS COULDN'T HELP looking at his watch. Vance was late for dinner. He saw that Travers looked worried.

"Where is Vance?" Boone asked as Travers finally told the cook she could go ahead and serve the meal.

"He went into town to get a few things to wear," Travers said. "I wanted him to look nice for the press conference tomorrow."

"You're really going through with this," Boone said.

"Of course. He's my son. I want the world to know."

"Also it won't hurt to get the kind of publicity we need for Jesse Rose to see it and possibly come forward," Waters interjected.

Travers actually shot him a smile. "Exactly. I have faith that both of the twins will have been found by the end of the year."

Louise was serving the salads when Vance hurried in.

"Sorry I'm late. Getting clothing took longer than I thought."

Travers seemed to light up as the young man came into the dining room. Waters saw that his other sons noticed. Nothing like sibling rivalry. But he wondered how long it would be before the new rubbed off Vance and Travers wasn't quite so enamored with his long-lost now-found son.

"Did it go well?" Travers wanted to know.

"I took your advice and let the clerk help me," Vance

said, taking his usual seat next to his father. "I hope she didn't go overboard."

Travers laughed. "Not to worry. I just want you to have what you need."

Waters had been watching Vance and now saw him look around the table—and start. His gaze had fallen on Abby Pierce. She paled as the two met gazes across the expanse of the table.

"This is Abby," Ledger said as he, too, had noticed the exchange between his girlfriend and Vance. "Abby, I don't think you have officially met my...brother Vance. Or is it Oakley now?"

"Vance for now." The words seemed to get caught in his throat.

"But soon to be Oakley," Travers said, sounding pleased. "Unless you've changed your mind."

Vance looked again in his direction. "No, of course not. It will just take a little getting used to."

Waters noticed that Abby was still staring at the man as if trying to place him. He fought back the bad feeling that now knocked around in his chest. Things had been going so well. Except for Patricia. He and Travers had talked and now he would be handling some of the family affairs again. And he'd been invited to dinner almost every night since finding Vance.

He had his foot in the door. The last thing he wanted was for a problem to come up involving the soon-to-be Oakley. And yet, as he picked up his salad fork, he realized he'd been waiting for the other shoe to drop as if he was afraid to trust his good luck in Oakley turning up.

VANCE DIDN'T THINK he could eat a bite. He was still shaken from his meeting with the deputies. Huck scared him since he seemed to be carrying a grudge against the McGraws. His son, Wade, had mentioned something once about Huck having dated Travers's first wife, Marianne.

It must have been a long time ago since the woman had been locked up in a mental ward for the past twenty-five years.

"I think after dinner, Oakley and I are going to go out and visit his mother."

Vance didn't realize Travers meant him until he felt all eyes at the table on him. "Tonight?" His voice had risen too high.

"There's nothing to be concerned about," Travers said. "I'm sure you've heard stories, but Marianne is doing well now and she is very anxious to see you."

There was no way he was going to get out of seeing his mother. Not gracefully, anyway. So he smiled and nodded and took a bite of his salad. He could have been eating wood chips, for all he tasted.

With each bite, he could feel Abby's gaze on him, burning a hole in him headed straight for his soul. If he had one.

He hadn't taken Huck Pierce seriously the first time he'd met him in a bar down by Billings.

"I'm telling you, you're the spitting image of the McGraw boys," Huck had said, fueled by the half dozen beers he'd consumed. "I think you might be Oakley McGraw."

He hadn't known who Oakley McGraw was and said as much.

"It's the most famous kidnapping in the state of Montana. Where you been living, under a barrel?"

He hadn't taken offense because Huck had been paying for the drinks, so he'd listened as the man had filled him in. Two missing babies, a boy and a girl.

"They think they were adopted by well-meaning parents who kept it quiet," Huck had said.

Vance had felt a strange stir inside him. "*I* was adopted." He'd always been told that it was some teenager who couldn't raise him. But years later he'd heard that it was an aunt who'd dumped him off when he was a baby and his parents had finally had to adopt him.

His old man hadn't minded having a son around to help with the work on the dirt farm they had. Vance couldn't wait until he was eighteen to escape it. He'd taken off at sixteen and hadn't looked back. He'd heard, though, that both his parents had died in a gas leak at the house. The place had been mortgaged up to the rafters along with the land, so he hadn't gotten anything. He'd let the county bury them. They'd never liked him, anyway.

"Here's what I'm proposing," Huck had said that night at the bar. He'd spelled it out. Vance had said he'd have to think about it. "Doesn't look to me like you have much for prospects. Don't be a fool. This is too easy since I have something that was taken with the male twin the night of the kidnapping. Oh, don't give me that look. I didn't kidnap the kid. I was one of the first deputy sheriffs at the scene."

"You're a deputy sheriff?"

Huck had laughed. "You bet your sweet ass I am. You think about it. You call me tomorrow or forget it."

Vance hadn't been able to sleep that night. He'd looked up the kidnapping online. Huck had failed to mention that the McGraws raised horses. Vance had been making his living as a horse thief. He'd started to laugh until he saw something else Huck had failed to mention. The McGraws were rich.

He'd called the number the deputy sheriff had given him early the next morning. "This is crazy, but I'm in."

Huck had laughed. "You won't be sorry."

Now the meal ended too quickly. Travers got to his feet. "Let's go see your mother."

Vance rose. He shot a guarded look at Abby. She was putting the pieces together. He could see it in her eyes. How long before she figured it out and blew the whistle on the whole damned thing?

As he started to leave the dining room, he just wished she would do it now and save him the trip to the mental hospital to see his "mother."

"YOU OKAY?" LEDGER ASKED Abby as he led her back to her bedroom. She looked pale and he could tell she was still a little unsteady on her feet.

"I know you don't want to hear this, but I've definitely seen Vance before. There's something wrong."

"Wrong how?" he asked as they reached her room.

"You're sure he's Oakley?"

"He had the stuffed toy horse that belonged to Oakley. Also he passed the DNA test. It came back that he's Dad's son."

Abby sighed as she took a chair near the window. He took the other chair in the room. "I can't trust my memory or my instincts or…" She met his gaze. "But the feeling is *so* strong. I know him from somewhere and it's worrisome."

"It will come to you," he assured her even though he wasn't convinced. "Let your brain heal. I can tell you have a headache. Can I get you something?"

"No. When I take the pills the doctor prescribed I feel even more fuzzy. But I'm all right."

"You're telling me that you don't trust Vance," Ledger said.

"No."

"That's good enough for me. I'll keep an eye on him. In the meantime, I'm going to move into the bedroom next door. I don't like you being on this wing with him in case your…instincts are right." Ledger had been staying at his cabin on the ranch. She knew he'd been trying to give her space. As they both knew, she was still married to Wade.

She looked relieved, though, that he would be close at hand. It wasn't just that she didn't trust Vance. She was a little scared of him, as well.

"Thank you. I hope I'm wrong. Your father seems so happy to have him here. I hate to think what it will do to him if Vance isn't the person he believes him to be."

"That's just it. We know very little about him. Jim Waters did some checking and swears there is nothing to worry about. But I have my reservations, too. I do wonder how it will go with Mother."

THE SMELL HIT him first, then the noise of the mental hospital. Vance halted just inside the door, telling himself he couldn't do this.

"It's okay, son," Travers said. "Give it a minute. I'm sure this is hard for you, seeing your mother."

Vance wanted to laugh hysterically. The man had no idea. "There was this neighbor girl. She had to be… restrained. She ended up in a place like this. I visited her only once. I couldn't bear going there." He shuddered at the memory. Crazy Cathy—that was what the kids at school called her when they'd get a glimpse of her from the school bus. She would be tied up to the clothesline and she would run, her face stretched in a lopsided smile because she loved Vance—almost to death. She finally got sent away after she'd tried to kill him with a butcher knife one night after seeing him with another girl.

"I'm so sorry," Travers said. "This must be even more difficult for you. If you'd rather not right now…"

"No." He just wanted to get it over with. Trying to block out the sounds, the smells, the tension that sparked in the air like heat lightning, he walked down the hallway to be let into the violent wing. The sounds down here were worse—the crying, the screaming, the tormented shrieks that made goose bumps ripple across his skin.

A nurse opened the gate for them and led them down the hallway. Vance didn't look into the barred windows. He stared at the floor at his feet, telling himself he could do this, but feeling the weakness run like water through his veins.

His mother used to say that he wasn't strong. "We just need to toughen him up." Then she'd give him the worst chores she could find on the farm. The calluses he got were heart-deep and still rubbed him raw some days. He knew he wouldn't be here now if it wasn't for his childhood and that made him angry. His adoptive mother was right. He wasn't strong.

The nurse stopped at a door, used her key to open it and then told Travers she would be right outside the door if he needed her.

Heart in his throat, Vance followed him into the room and stopped dead.

The woman sitting in the rocking chair had lightning-white hair that hung around her shoulders like a shroud. But it was the face that froze his feet to the floor.

"Oakley?" the woman asked with a voice that cracked. She motioned for him to come closer.

It took every ounce of his courage to take that first step, let alone the second one, until he stood before her.

"Oakley?" she repeated, her green eyes narrowing.

He couldn't speak, could barely breathe. He swallowed, trying hard not to look into those eyes as if he might be looking into his own hell.

She reached for him before he could move. Her wrinkled hand caught his and held it like a vise as she dragged him closer. The green eyes widened in alarm and he felt a chill rocket through him.

Then the woman shoved him away and began to scream.

ABBY HADN'T BEEN able to sleep last night. Her mind had been alive with strange flashes that could be memory or could be her losing her sanity. Knowing that Ledger was in the next room hadn't helped. Several times she'd almost gotten up and gone to him.

But she'd known what would happen. She was still married. It didn't matter that it was a bad marriage. It didn't matter what Wade had done. She couldn't go to Ledger. Just the thought of him lying in his bed...

This morning she'd felt a little better.

"Stop trying so hard to remember," the doctor had said when he dropped by to check on her. "You will make yourself crazy. If your memory is going to come back, it will, and when you least expect it. Relax. Enjoy this beautiful place. In fact, I think you should get out of this room. Maybe sit by the pool."

Abby couldn't help herself. She could feel the memories just at the edge of her consciousness and she had the horrible feeling that it was imperative that she remember. And soon.

"I'll see that she takes it easy," Ledger had told the doctor after thanking him for driving out.

Abby had tried to relax as she and Ledger went out by the pool after breakfast. She'd been glad that breakfast was more casual, with everyone eating on their own in the large, warm kitchen. Boone and Cull had already gone to work in the barns and Travers was in his office, so she and Ledger had the kitchen to themselves since the cook had gone into town for more groceries.

She was glad that Ledger didn't mention marriage again. Right now, she couldn't think of the future. There was so much of the past missing in her memory. She had to deal with it first. Or maybe she was just afraid of rushing into another marriage for the wrong reasons. She knew Ledger wanted to save her from Wade. For so long, he'd been trying to get her to leave Wade. But was that enough to build a marriage on? Once she was divorced, would Ledger still want to marry her?

Her head hurt even thinking about it. She had too much to worry about, she realized.

Ledger seemed content to sit with her by the pool and talk about the horses and his family's plans for the ranch. She found herself smiling at him. He was a man with dreams. And she loved him so much it hurt.

"See that land on the mountainside over there?" He pointed toward a pine-studded hollow below a rock ridge. "That's mine. That's where I will build the house someday." His gaze shifted to hers and she saw so much promise in his eyes that she wanted to cry.

"It's beautiful."

"Like you," he said and reached over to take her hand.

She closed her eyes and told herself that everything was going to be all right. But deep inside she felt afraid. Wade and his father were up to something. Something she'd apparently overheard. They wouldn't trust that she might never remember. This wasn't over. Once she left here...

"Abby?" Ledger looked concerned.

She opened her eyes, realizing she'd been gripping his hand too hard. "I'm scared," she admitted. "I can't think about the future until I know what in my past has me so terrified."

Something moved past Ledger and she looked in that direction to see Vance. He saw her and quickly disappeared from view. The bad feeling washed over her, threatening to take her under.

Ledger followed her gaze. "You still think something is wrong, don't you?"

She nodded.

"My father said that the visit with our mother didn't go well. When she got a good look at him, she screamed. They had to sedate her. He's worried that this might have set her back. He can't bear that she might revert back into a catatonic state again."

Abby shivered at the news. "She must have sensed what I do about him."

"A BOOK?" WATERS COULDN'T believe what he was hearing as he stared through the scarred Plexiglas at Patricia. "You do realize that Nikki St. James is doing a book on the kidnapping."

"Nikki St. James wasn't there that night. I was," Patricia said into the phone at the jail. She gave him a smug look. "They're giving me enough money that it will pay for my decent lawyer. That's right. I'm going to get off, and when I do, they are going to start looking around for the person who really poisoned my husband."

He knew what she would be selling. The dirt on the McGraw family. The dirt on him, as well. "What is it you want?"

"*Now* you want to deal?" she asked, sweet enough to give him a toothache.

"Patty."

"Don't call me that."

"You don't want to hang out all your dirty laundry."

"Don't you mean your dirty laundry, Jimmy?"

"Think of Kitten."

"Oh, now you're going to show an interest in her?" Patricia snapped angrily.

She'd told him that Kitten was his, but he'd never been sure it was true given the way the woman lied. He had a feeling that she'd also told Blake Ryan, the former ranch manager, that Kitten was his. It would explain why Blake had done her bidding.

He lowered his voice. "You know why we had to keep this a secret."

"To protect your relationship with Travers. But look how that turned out. Unless you've managed to get back into his good graces." Her eyes lit. "Oh, you have! You… stinker you. You always land on your feet, don't you?" Her eyes narrowed. "Well, hang on for the ride of your life. I'm about to bring down your world and Travers's, too." With that, she slammed down the phone, rose and motioned to the guard that she was ready to go back to her cell.

VANCE COULDN'T HELP being rattled.

Travers had apologized at length for taking him to see his so-called mother. "I should never have taken you to see her so soon," he'd said on the ride home. "Marianne is just now recovering after all this time. This is all my fault. I'm so sorry."

"It's all right," he'd said. "Maybe I scared her." He hadn't scared her. He'd seen the look in the woman's eyes. She *knew*. Somehow she knew he wasn't her son.

"I think she was expecting to see you as a baby," Travers had said. "Or maybe it was just too much for her."

But Vance knew better and he feared Travers Mc-Graw was having his doubts. Just not enough doubts to stop all this craziness.

The press conference was a blur. He'd blinked into the flash of cameras, stepped up to the microphone to say how glad he was to have found his birth family and had then been ushered to the ranch Suburban as reporters shoved microphones at him and yelled questions.

He managed to escape after lunch, telling Travers he wanted to go for a ride and just digest everything that had been happening. He'd used the burner phone to call Huck, who'd been in a great mood.

"Saw you on the news! You looked real smart in those new clothes. Next step, legally becoming Oakley Mc-Graw."

"We need to meet and talk."

Huck's good mood had evaporated in a snap of the fingers.

"Okay," Huck said when the three of them met, this time out by Nelson Reservoir in a stand of trees. "So

Marianne freaked last night when Travers took you to see her. How did McGraw react?"

"He felt bad about taking me there, made excuses for Marianne, but I could tell he was shocked and taken aback. He has to be thinking she saw something he hadn't."

Huck waved a hand through the air. "It wasn't like she cried, 'This isn't my son!' Even if she had, she's...*sick*. So forget about it. You're still good as gold. McGraw wouldn't have gone through with the press conference if he had any doubts."

Vance raked a hand through his hair, his Stetson hanging from the fingers of his other hand. It was hot, but a breeze came off the water, and in the shade of the trees it wasn't too bad. But still he was sweating.

"I saw Abby looking at me again. Now she's got Ledger looking at me the same way."

Wade swore and kicked a rock into the water at the mention of Ledger's name.

"It's just a matter of time. I see her trying so hard to remember," Vance said, hating that he was whining. "She remembers just enough that she doesn't like me, doesn't trust me, and she's been bending Ledger's ear about me. How long before he goes to his father with this?"

"You just borrow trouble, don't you?" Huck demanded angrily. "She *hasn't* remembered. She isn't going to. What you need to do is dig in. Stop acting like a guest at the ranch. You need to go to work in the barns with your brothers."

Vance stared at him. How did he know...? "The cook? *Louise is spying on me?*"

Huck smiled. "I told you. I make friends easily. I know what is going on out there."

"I think Vance is right." Wade spoke up. "You know Abby. Once she gets her teeth into something…"

Huck swore.

"What are we going to do?" Wade cried. "Let me go get her. Once we have her back—"

"Don't be a fool."

But Vance could see that Huck was more worried than he let on.

"Okay, maybe it's time to take care of Abby." Huck turned to Vance. "Make it look like an accident."

"What?" He'd hoped he'd heard wrong, but one look at the deputy's face and he knew he hadn't. He took a step back. "I didn't sign on for murder."

Huck quickly closed the distance between them and got right into his face. "You signed on for whatever I tell you or you'll be meeting with your own accident. Is that understood?"

Vance's blood ran cold at the look in Huck's eyes. There was something bitter and heartless in that gaze. The deputy wasn't joking. Worse, he thought Huck was right about the places where he had "friends." He wouldn't look at the cook the same now that he knew Huck had her in his pocket.

"You are Oakley McGraw," Huck said, looking less dangerous even though Vance knew he wasn't. "You will have a great life if you don't weaken now, you understand? Abby *can't* remember who you are because that will raise suspicion and involve Wade and me. So take care of it."

"But that still leaves Marianne," he said, hoping to find a way out of this.

Huck laid a hand on his shoulder and squeezed just hard enough to make his point. "Marianne is mentally unstable. We aren't worried about her, okay? Don't make me worry about you. You're in this up to your neck. Just remember this. You double-cross me and you won't live long enough to see prison."

Go to the sheriff. Confess everything. But even as he thought it, he knew Huck was right. The deputy had friends everywhere. Look how he'd managed to get the lab tests to appear that Vance was a McGraw. He must have gotten someone to get him DNA from one of the real sons. Or maybe the lab already had something of the twins from the kidnapping.

It didn't matter how Huck had pulled this fraud off. He had. And now he'd painted Vance into a corner. When had it gone from simply pretending to be Oakley Mc-Graw to murder, though? Broke and now involved in fraud with a psychopath, he didn't see any way out of this but one. He had to kill Abby Pierce.

CHAPTER FOURTEEN

"You think he'll do it?" Wade asked after Vance had driven away.

"Nope," his father said. "He has it in him, but he's too gutless."

Wade shot his father a look. "But you made it sound as if you believed he would." He wasn't about to admit the sense of relief he'd felt. He still loved Abby. He figured he always would.

But that love came with such a sense of guilt over how he'd mistreated her it had turned into something hard as flint. In order to be rid of it, he had to be rid of Abby. Not that he wanted anyone else to have her.

"Son, if there is one thing I'm good at, it's reading people. Vance…well, he's damaged, no doubt about it. That's one reason why I knew he'd jump at the chance to be Oakley McGraw. But he's weak. I knew he'd never be able to go the distance."

"What the devil was the whole point of this, then?"

His father smiled. "Because we don't need it to. I've contacted Waters through a friend. He's taking care of getting us the reward money."

"But once they find out that Vance isn't Oakley—"

"That is never going to happen," Huck said with so much confidence that Wade wondered if the man had a screw loose. "By then anyone who could hurt us will be dead."

He stared at his father. "How—"

"You don't worry about that end of it. I have it all figured out. But first, we need to stop out by that rattle-snake nest in the Larb Hills." Huck grinned. "I brought along a couple of burlap bags. That wife of yours? You're not going to have to worry about her much longer. Neither is Vance."

WATERS COULD SEE his world exploding in front of his eyes. Patricia was the missile coming in hard and fast. He had to do damage control before she hit. But that meant telling Travers the truth. Well, at least enough of the truth to cover his behind. All he had going for him was the fact that Patricia didn't believe he would tell.

He found Travers in his office. "Do you have a minute?"

The older man looked up and waved him in. "Boone tells me that you've had another inquiry that sounds like it might be legitimate."

Waters had forgotten about the call from the private investigator in Butte. "Yes, there was something about the call. I mentioned it to Boone."

"Did you get any specifics?"

"Not exactly, but by the questions the PI asked, I think he might have information about Jesse Rose."

Travers leaned back into his chair and motioned Waters to sit. "This is great news. We should get on this right away. I'll talk to Boone about following up on it."

"The PI was called out of town. He said he'd be back in a week or so. I was planning to go myself."

"I'd rather have Boone go," Travers said.

Waters figured the lead would take Boone nowhere. But he had to look as if he was trying to help find Jesse Rose. "There was something else." He stopped. His role in this house was tenuous at best after he'd sided with Patricia. Now he wasn't sure how his confession would go down. Travers could fire him and that would be that. He hesitated.

"Yes?"

"I need to tell you something. I should have a long time ago, but Patricia begged me not to and I foolishly listened to her."

"If you're going to tell me that you're possibly her daughter's father, it isn't necessary. I've known all along."

Waters stared at him. "How—"

"I knew about the two of you before the kidnapping." Travers's gaze hardened. "I also knew about the two of you after I married Patty."

He didn't know what to say. *I'm sorry* didn't quite cut it. "I don't understand."

"Oh, I think you do. That old expression, keep your enemies close."

"You see me as your enemy?" That shocked him. He'd always thought that Travers trusted him, maybe even liked him. "If you knew, why didn't you say something?"

"I like to see how things play out. I was fine with you and Patty because I saw that she was using you the same way she was me. A leopard really can't change its spots."

He wasn't sure if Travers was referring to Patricia or to him. "She's doing a tell-all book to help pay for her lawyer's fees."

Travers nodded. "I heard."

"I can try to get an injunction to stop the book from ever being published if you—"

"Not necessary."

Waters couldn't help feeling confused. "But the bad press..."

Travers laughed. "Did you really think that would bother me? Jim, I believe you're the one who doesn't want to see Patty's book published. But I figure by then her trial will be over and the truth will have come out."

"The truth?" he asked.

Travers only smiled and said, "If that's all, please make sure Boone has all the information about this private investigator in Butte. I want him down there as soon as the man returns."

VANCE HAD NO idea how he was going to kill Abby and make it look like an accident. All the way back to the ranch, he cursed his luck. If he hadn't been in that bar in Billings, if he'd never met Huck Pierce, if he'd never gone along with this crazy idea for money...

Money was the root of all evil. If he had some right now, he'd be gone. He'd just disappear. Maybe go to South America. All he would need was a fake ID, and he'd heard that you could buy those if you knew the right people.

Except he didn't have money and he didn't know the right people. But Huck did. All this time, the cook had probably been watching him, reporting to the deputy that Vance was down at the pool or lying around the house.

Who knew how many other spies the man had at the ranch, he thought, reminded of the ranch hands he occasionally saw when he was down at the pool. It wasn't like Huck to show all of his hand, so Vance figured there were others watching him—not to mention Travers and his sons. He felt like someone was always watching him, looking for a crack in the story he'd built, waiting for him to unravel and admit he wasn't Oakley McGraw.

The house was unusually quiet when he entered. He looked around. Travers's office was empty. He thought he heard the clatter of pots and pans in the kitchen, but no voices. Happy not to be forced to make polite conversation with anyone, he took the stairs two at a time, wanting only to get to his room and hide out for a while.

He was almost to the top of the stairs when suddenly Abby appeared. Seeing her when she was so much on his mind, he reared back in surprise. Her eyes widened in alarm as he lost his balance.

Vance groped for the handrail, but it was slick and he wasn't close enough to get a grip on the highly varnished wood. He teetered and then felt himself start to fall backward. The irony of it didn't escape him as his arms windmilled wildly to no avail.

SHOCKED BY WHAT was happening, Abby rushed down a couple of steps to reach for the man. His hand closed on her wrist. He flailed, still off balance. But he held tight as she tried to keep her balance.

In those frantic moments, she realized he was so much heavier than her that she wasn't going to be able to keep him from falling. And with his hand clutching her wrist, he was going to take her with him.

She felt her heels lift off the step. Her free hand grabbed the railing, but Vance's pull was too strong. She felt herself falling toward him.

Abby let out a cry as Vance jerked her arm hard, then let go. She was thrown toward the center of the stairway as his body was pushed toward the railing. Her gaze tumbled down the long stairway to the marble floor below. She waited for her life to pass before her eyes as she felt herself falling through nothing but air.

Below her, the front door opened and Ledger stepped through. Their eyes met, his rounding in horror. He shot forward as if he thought he'd be able to catch her before she hit the bottom and the hard unforgiving marble.

She closed her eyes as a scream escaped her lips. She'd come so close to being with Ledger, but now fate had stepped in to keep them apart forever.

LEDGER'S CRY OF alarm mixed with Abby's scream as she began to fall. He rushed toward the stairs, his gaze locked on Abby. He'd only reached the bottom step when Vance's free arm shot out, the other looped over the handrail in a death grip. He grabbed Abby at the last minute.

For a moment, it looked as if Vance couldn't hold them both on the stairway. Ledger saw the pain in his face, the exertion as he looped his free arm around her waist and pulled.

He hadn't known he was holding his breath until he saw Abby find footing on the stairs. Vance let go of the railing and sat down hard on the steps. All the color had drained from his face, and even from where he stood, Ledger could see that the man was sweating profusely.

Abby had sat down, too. She was crying softly and holding her ribs after her close call. If Vance hadn't grabbed her when he did... But what were the two of them doing on the stairs together?

"Are you all right?" Ledger said when he reached Abby. He fell to his knees in front of her.

"Vance saved my life," she said between sobs.

His gaze went to the man.

"It wasn't like that," Vance said. "I was coming up the stairs not paying attention."

"I startled him. He started to fall backward," Abby filled in as they both seemed to be trying to catch their breaths.

"She grabbed me, but I was so off balance…" Vance finished with a look of such regret as he rubbed his shoulder. "I could have killed her."

"But you didn't," Ledger said. "You saved her. Is your shoulder hurt?"

"I think I might have pulled something," Vance said.

"I'll call the doctor to look at it." Ledger touched Abby's face, pushed back a fallen lock of her hair and wiped away a tear. "I'll have him take a look at both of you. I thought we agreed you'd stay off the stairs?" he said to her, smiling with such gratitude that she was all right. When he'd first seen her… If Vance hadn't grabbed for her at his own peril…

"Believe me, I'll take the elevator from now on," she said and let him enclose her in his arms. Past her, Ledger studied Vance.

"You're a hero," he said to his brother. "Thank you."

Vance shook his head. "I'm far from a hero."

VANCE'S HEROISM WAS the talk of the dinner table that evening. He'd pulled a muscle in his shoulder and had to ice it. Abby's ribs were even more sore from his saving her, but now when she looked at him, it was with gratitude as if her earlier suspicions were gone.

He tried to breathe, but his shoulder hurt like hell, and all this talk of how amazing he was hurt even worse.

He'd had a chance to let Abby tumble down the stairs and instead he'd saved her—after she'd tried to save him.

"Maybe you should both stay off those stairs," Travers joked. "Seriously, I've given all my other sons a piece of land for them to build on one day, if they can be talked into staying on the ranch."

The table had gone deathly silent.

A piece of land? Vance swallowed.

"We can look at a map of the ranch later if you'd like and you can pick out a section you might want," Travers was saying.

"That is very kind of you."

"Kind?" The man laughed. "Son, this is your birthright."

His birthright. He hung his head, muttering, "Thank you."

"Here's to your future," Travers said, lifting his wineglass. "May it be everything you've ever hoped for."

When he looked up to lift his glass, he saw the cook standing in the kitchen doorway looking right at him. His heart took off at a gallop. She would report all of this to Huck.

Vance took a sip of his wine and felt it instantly curdle in his stomach. His future was anything but bright.

CHAPTER FIFTEEN

ABBY STOOD AT the window looking out over the ranch. "I can't stay here," she said, more to herself than to Ledger as she shifted her gaze to him. She could see that he wanted to argue the point.

"You can't go back to your apartment. Not alone," he said.

She had a feeling that if she went back to her apartment—back to town—more of her memory would return. Travers was getting more attached to Vance. She'd heard Travers offer him a piece of land on the ranch. She knew that was a mistake. She just didn't know why.

"Wade doesn't know where my apartment is and there's the restraining order..."

Ledger cursed under his breath. "You aren't that naive. He's just waiting for you. And if you think a restraining order is going to stop him..."

"What about my job?"

"You don't have to work there anymore."

She shook her head. "Ledger, I enjoy my work. I miss the people. I miss feeling like there is a little normal in my life."

He sighed deeply, pain in his eyes. "What is it you're running from? Is it me?"

Abby quickly shook her head as she turned to him. "Never you. But I'm still married to Wade. I can't move on until I put that behind me."

He nodded. "You need time. I understand that."

"What will people think, my staying here with you?"

"Is that what you're worried about? What people will think?"

The moment she said it, she realized she sounded like her mother. The same mother who was growing pot in her root cellar, the same one who guilt-tripped her into staying in a bad marriage because it was to her benefit—not her daughter's.

Abby touched his cheek. "I want a fresh start."

"With me?" Ledger asked.

She smiled. "Oh, yes, with you. But I jumped into one marriage. I won't jump into another even with you."

He dragged her to him and kissed her. "I want you so badly."

"I feel the same way. It's been awful knowing you are just in the next room. I can't tell you how I have fought the need to come to you."

He let her go as if he felt the chemistry that arced between them as strongly as she did. "I'll wait as long as it takes." He grinned. "I've waited this long."

She had to smile.

"But you have to know Wade isn't finished with you. A man like him? His pride will be hurt. He'll take it out on you and this time he'll probably kill you."

"I know." She hated that she sounded close to tears. She'd cried so much over all this. "How do I get him out of my life?"

Ledger shook his head. "I don't know. But I wish you would stay here until the divorce is finalized. Maybe by then he will have realized it's really over. Maybe he will move on."

She nodded, but she knew neither of them believed

that. He reached for her again. The memory hit her so hard, she cried out, jerking back.

Ledger looked alarmed as if he thought he'd hurt her.

"I saw them!" The memory hung before her, crystal clear, before it flickered and died away as she tried to see more. *"I know where I've seen Vance. It was at the house. He was with Wade and Huck."*

LEDGER DIDN'T KNOW what to make of what Abby had told him. He found his brother Cull downstairs and pulled him aside.

"Since the first time Abby saw Vance, she felt she'd seen him before, and wherever it was, it wasn't good."

Cull lifted a brow. "In other words, she just had a feeling about him."

"Something like that, only just now she remembered where she'd seen him. He'd been at her house talking with Wade and Huck."

"What?" Cull rubbed a hand over his face. "Okay, if this is true—"

"Why are you questioning it?"

"Because Abby's had two concussions in a row. Her memory isn't the most reliable. After what happened earlier today on the stairs… Then add to that, the garage at the house is supposedly where she fell and got her first concussion…"

Ledger could see his point. "What if it's a true memory, though? What would Vance have been doing with Wade and Huck Pierce?"

Cull frowned. "Nothing good. We were led to believe that he didn't know anyone around here."

"Exactly. You think we should tell Dad?" Ledger asked.

"No," his brother said quickly. "It will just upset him.

And after everything that's happened, including Vance saving Abby yesterday on the stairs, I wouldn't suggest it. Anyway, if it's true and Vance denies it, it would be his word against Abby's."

Ledger nodded. "It could put her in danger if I'm right and the three of them are up to something other than the obvious."

"The obvious being that Vance isn't our brother," Cull finished for him. "Then how do you explain the DNA test?"

He felt a shiver race up his spine. "The day Vance was tested, Huck Pierce was in the lab. He was flirting with one of the techs."

"Interesting, but certainly not conclusive. We could do another test with another lab, I suppose," Cull said. "It would mean getting DNA from Vance. That shouldn't be too hard. We could have him tested against one of us."

Ledger smiled at his brother. He knew he could depend on Cull. Boone would have stormed upstairs and tried to throttle the truth out of Vance.

"This shouldn't be too hard," Cull said. "Let me handle it. In the meantime…"

"Right, just be cool."

WADE WATCHED HIS father storm up and down the floor, half expecting the floorboards to crack.

"He saved Abby! Saved her!" Huck roared. "Came out looking like a damned hero."

"Maybe that works to our benefit," Wade said when his father had calmed down a little.

Huck spun on him. *"What?"*

"When something happens to Abby, Vance will look innocent."

His father stopped pacing and stared at him. "You really aren't as stupid as you look."

"Thanks." Wade realized how sick he was of his father's belittling. He would be glad when they got the reward money. He was leaving town, putting all of this behind him for good. But then he thought of Abby. Did he really want her dead? No. Could he stop his father? It was too late for that, he feared.

Huck was muttering to himself as he paced again. "I think we need to step up the ending to all this."

Wade had no intention of being around to see whatever his father had planned. "When do we get the reward money?"

"My friend talked to the attorney. He offered to cut a check today, but my friend insisted it be cash, saying he wasn't alone in finding Oakley, that the others want to remain anonymous. Jim Waters doesn't care. He said he'd get the money. Won't be long now," Huck said, smiling broadly.

His mood could go from happy to furious in less than a heartbeat. Wade realized his own wasn't much better. The sheriff had the gall to suggest he go to something called anger management. He'd been insulted at the time, but maybe once he was gone from here, he'd check into it.

"So what happens now?" Wade asked, not sure he wanted to know.

WATERS LOOKED AT the stack of bills inside his briefcase. Five hundred thousand dollars. Travers had been adamant about going ahead and paying the reward.

"Are you sure you don't want to wait a little longer?" Waters had asked. "Maybe run another DNA test." He knew it was the wrong thing to say. Voicing his suspicions wasn't doing him any good.

But he was still shaken. Travers had known about him and Patricia all along. He'd known and not said anything. As he'd said, he'd wanted to see how it all played out.

The only thing the man hadn't known was that he was being systematically poisoned.

"Just pay the reward, Jim. Oakley is home. Boone will check out this lead on Jesse Rose. I feel good about it. So I suppose we should discuss your...retirement."

That had been plain enough. But at least he could continue billing the bastard until then. And he would, he thought as he slammed the briefcase. First he would get rid of this money. He felt as if Travers was throwing it away, but what did he care?

Vance wasn't Oakley. Waters would bet his stock portfolio on it. He had no proof, just a gut feeling. The same gut feeling that told him Patricia was going to take him down with her.

He looked at the briefcase again. His passport was up to date. All he had to do was book a flight to anywhere there was no extradition. He could live comfortably on what was in that case—even if he couldn't get his money out of his retirement.

Waters let out a laugh. He didn't even think Travers would turn him in to the sheriff. Instead, he'd pony up another five hundred grand to pay the reward and keep his mouth shut.

With a start, Waters realized this was exactly what the cagey old fool hoped he would do. This was kiss-off money. Travers expected him to run.

LEDGER FOUND HIS father in his office, but one look at him and he felt his heart break for him. "What's wrong?"

Travers looked up in surprise as if he hadn't heard

his son come in. For a moment, he seemed at a loss for words. "It's your mother. She's doing…worse. I blame myself. I should never have taken Oakley out to see her. Of course she expected a six-month-old baby—not a grown man. The doctor said she's trapped in that night twenty-five years ago."

"It isn't your fault. She asked to see him. You couldn't keep him from her."

His father laid his head into his hands, elbows on his desk. This was the most distraught he'd seen him. For so long, the man had lived on hope that his kidnapped children would be found. Ledger suspected it wasn't going quite like he'd hoped.

"I'm sorry," Travers said, lifting his head. "You wanted to talk about something?"

Now that he was here, Ledger almost changed his mind. "I want to marry Abby."

His father chuckled. "Son, that's not news."

"I know. I never got over her."

"I blame myself for that, as well. I should have let you marry her when you wanted to. I can't believe what she's been through."

Ledger nodded. "But your advice was good. Abby had a lot of pressure from her mother and Wade. Also she was lied to. I don't blame her for doubting me. I didn't handle things well."

"All water under the bridge."

"Yes. That's why I hope you don't mind her staying here a little longer."

"You know I don't. I just worry. She's still married to Wade."

"Yes, but not for long. She's filed for a separation. Unfortunately, she has to wait six months in Montana before she can file for the divorce. At least here at the ranch, she's safe. But I can't keep her locked up here for six months."

VANCE HELD THE phone away from his ear and looked toward the big house. He didn't think he could be seen from the shade of the trees where he stood. Nor did he think anyone was home. But Abby.

"Are you a complete idiot?" Huck demanded.

He didn't bother to answer.

"You could have finished it right there on the stairs."

"She saved my life. I would have fallen if she hadn't grabbed me."

The deputy let out a string of curses. "You sound like my addled son. Now you have a soft spot for the woman, too?"

"No." Actually, he was scared of her. He kept watching her, thinking she was going to remember. While she seemed less standoffish since their incident on the stairs, she still had that memory lodged somewhere in that head of hers. Once it came out...

He heard a vehicle coming up the road to the ranch. "I should go." He was hoping it was Travers back from town. His "father" had gone in to set up a bank account for him.

"I should have thought of it before," Travers had apologized. "A man needs a little spending money."

Vance wondered what his father thought was a little spending money. Hopefully enough so he could take off in one of the ranch trucks and never look back.

"Any word on the reward money?" he asked now into the phone.

"Not yet," Huck said.

A lie. Travers had told him that the reward was being paid today by special messenger. That had surprised him. He'd thought the lawyer, Waters, would be handling it and said as much to the man.

"Jim Waters is no longer in my employ," Travers had said.

That had surprised him even more. "I thought he was like family." At least, that was what Waters had told him once.

"Family," Travers had repeated. "It's odd what makes a family, don't you think? It isn't always blood. But even blood sometimes can't hold a family together. I think it's trust and love." The man had smiled. "One day my sons will all marry and our family will grow. I hope to see grandchildren before I die."

Vance had thought of Cull and Nikki. "I would think you'll be hearing wedding bells before you know it."

"Yes. I hope Jesse Rose is here to see it. This family won't be whole again until she's home. And her mother, too." Travers had brightened. "At least you're home."

"You still there?" Huck asked over the phone, sounding even more irritated.

"I'm here." Right here at home.

"Just do your job."

Vance disconnected and headed for the house. Once Travers handed him that checkbook... And yet as he walked up the back steps, he felt a pang. If only he truly was Oakley McGraw. Surprisingly it wasn't the ranch or the money or name that pulled at him. It was the idea of having a father like Travers McGraw.

CHAPTER SIXTEEN

"HERE, LET ME help you with that," Ledger said as he saw the cook struggling with a large box. He'd been busy making him and Abby a picnic lunch. He planned to surprise her with a ride around the ranch.

The fiftysomething matronly woman had just come into the back door with the box and seemed anxious to put it down. But when he tried to take it, the cook turned away from him. "I have it," she said, sounding as if out of breath. "But thank you." She set it down carefully.

He noticed that the top had been taped closed and wondered idly what was inside that so much tape had been used. Live lobsters?

She turned, looking nervous, and he realized he was making her so. "Did you need something?"

"No—sorry." He tried to remember her name. Louise? Elise? Eloise? He couldn't be sure. They'd had the same cook from as far back as he could remember. It was hard since they'd gone through a few before they'd gotten this one. Also he had the feeling that, like the others, she wouldn't be staying long. His family was a little too infamous and Patricia's arrest hadn't helped.

Ledger had forgotten why he'd come into the kitchen. His mind was on Abby, as usual. He'd realized that he couldn't keep her here like a prisoner. And yet he couldn't let her move back into town—not with Wade on the loose.

Now that she'd thought she remembered seeing Vance with Wade and Huck Pierce, he was all the more worried about her. He'd been so sure she was safe while in this house. But with Vance here, too...

Through the kitchen window, he saw Vance coming out of the trees at the back of the house. That was odd. He appeared to be pocketing a phone. Ledger realized he'd never seen Vance with a cell phone before. Who had he been calling that he hadn't wanted to make the call in the house?

"If you'll excuse me, I have work to do," the cook said.

"Yes, of course," Ledger told her distractedly and put the box she'd left on the counter out of his mind as he heard the elevator. Abby.

"VANCE!"

He'd practically run into Travers as he'd come in the back door of the house.

"This is for you."

He took the envelope and glanced inside. The paperwork from the bank—along with what looked like a savings account bankbook and a checkbook. He wanted to see how much was in his account. The waiting was going to kill him.

"You need to sign some forms in there and return them to the bank," Travers was saying. "But you should be all set."

"Thank you so much," Vance said sincerely.

"You're my son."

He felt the warm, large hand on his shoulder and swallowed.

"But we do need to talk about getting your name changed legally—if that's still what you want. Also I hope you've been thinking about what section of land on the ranch you would like. I've hired a new attorney. I'd like to get this taken care of right away."

Vance could only nod.

"There is one other thing, though."

He froze. Why did he always expect the worst?

"I want you to pick out a horse. A man should have his own horse." Travers chuckled. "There's a few out there. You do ride, right?"

"Yes. As a matter of fact, I'd been wanting to saddle up and take a ride. I wasn't sure if that was all right."

Travers looked sorry again. "Son, this is your ranch, too. I want you to enjoy it. I also hope that you might be interested in working it with your brothers."

He'd known that was coming. "Absolutely. I just need to learn the ropes."

The man looked delighted. "I'll tell Cull. He'll get you started. Tomorrow is soon enough. You're settling in here all right?"

"I am."

"I know it will take a while for it to feel like home."

Vance held the manila envelope with the bank papers in it to his chest. "Yes, this is all so new for me." He couldn't wait to leave the room, feeling as if he'd won the lottery. Except he didn't know how much he'd won. Or worse, how long it would last.

LEDGER MET THE elevator as it came down, anxious to see Abby. Her injuries were healing and he knew it wouldn't be long and he'd have to let her go. That scared him in a way that nothing on this earth did. She would never be safe as long as Wade Pierce was out there.

As the door opened and he saw her, his heart did a vault in his chest. He never saw her or heard her voice that it didn't send a thrill through him. He loved this woman. He'd never been able to let go because of it.

"Hey," he said, feeling like he'd been injected with helium.

She smiled broadly. She was almost her old self again. He could see it in her eyes. There was no reason for her to stay here—other than the fact that her husband was out there somewhere planning who knew what.

"I thought you might want to go for a ride. You've been cooped up too long. What do you say? Want to see my favorite parts of the ranch?"

"I'd love that, assuming you don't mean on a horse."

He laughed. "I'm not sure your ribs could take that. I've packed us a picnic."

"You think of everything," she said and squeezed his arm.

He wished he did think of everything. Otherwise, he would have better understood why Abby married Wade. If he'd known about the lies... As his father had said, "Water under the bridge." But still it was hard not to want to rewrite history and save them both a lot of pain.

As they started through the living room, he heard a vehicle pull up out front, engine revved. Through the window, he saw nothing but a cloud of dust. Someone was in a hurry. His father and Cull came out of the office, both having heard the vehicle.

The knock at the door sounded urgent. Or angry. Just like the thunder of the boot heels did on the porch.

"I'll get it," Ledger said and then turned to Abby.

"Wait here." He moved to the door, expecting it would be Wade.

Opening the door, he found a cowboy he'd never seen before standing there. He wore worn dirty jeans, a Western shirt with holes at the elbows and a belt with a rodeo buckle. The cowboy reached to take off his straw cowboy hat at the sound of the door opening.

Sans the hat, his dark hair caught the sunlight like a raven's wing. The young man brushed back a lock as he turned to look at him. Ledger found himself gazing into intense green eyes the same shade as his mother's. For a startled moment, Ledger thought he was seeing a male version of his mother.

"Can I help you?" he asked the man, his voice sounding calmer than he felt. There was something about this cowboy...

"No, but I can help you," the young man said, still standing in the doorway. "I heard there's someone here claiming to be Oakley McGraw."

That didn't surprise Ledger after the press conference had gone viral. What did surprise him was that this cowboy had not just gotten onto the ranch, he was standing at their front door.

"And what does that have to do with you?" he asked.

"The name's Tough Crandall. Before you ask, my father rodeoed and so did his father, thus the name."

"Well, Mr. Crandall, I'm not sure what that has to do with my brother Oakley—"

"I've been out of state. I just happened to see on the news that the McGraw kidnapping son had been found. I'm here to tell you that Vance Elliot is not your brother."

"How would you know that?" Ledger demanded.

"What's the problem?" his father said, moving from

where he and Cull had stopped just outside his office doorway.

"Mr. McGraw," Tough said to Travers, hat in his hand. "I heard you'd been sickly. I'm sorry to hear that. I didn't want to bother you, but I can't let you be tricked. The man staying with you pretending to be your son is a fraud."

"I think you'd better step inside," Ledger heard his father say. He could tell by Travers's shocked look that he'd seen the cowboy's green eyes and dark hair.

Once inside the office, his father asked Tough Crandall to sit down. The cowboy looked around at the expensive furniture and said, "I'd prefer to keep standing if you don't mind. I picked up a couple of horses over in Minot earlier today. I would have waited and come after I'd cleaned up, but I was afraid it couldn't keep. Anyway, this won't take long."

"Mr. Crandall…" Travers began.

"Please, call me Tough."

"All right, Tough. Why is it you think Vance isn't Oakley?"

Tough looked down at his straw hat for a moment before glancing up again. Ledger saw the effect those green eyes had on not just his father but his brothers, as well. Even Boone, who had quietly joined them, was staring at the man.

"Because, sir, I'm your biological son."

Travers cocked his head. "And what makes you think that?"

"My mother told me all about my adoption. I've known since I was five."

"Then why didn't you come forward before this?" Cull demanded.

Tough chewed at his cheek for a moment. "Beg your pardon, but I had no good reason to. I have parents who raised me just fine and I didn't want to bring that kind of trouble down on them. They are good people who believed they were doing the best for me. I agree with them."

"Are you saying you didn't want to be a McGraw?" Boone asked, sounding as if it wouldn't take much more to make him mad.

"No offense," Tough said quickly.

"Who did your mother say brought you to her when you were six months old?" Travers asked.

"Pearl Cavanaugh from the Whitehorse Sewing Circle. She, too, meant no harm. God rest her soul."

"Do you have any proof?" Boone asked.

"No, other than me standing here telling you what I know."

"But you'd be willing to take a DNA test?" Ledger asked.

"I didn't come here looking to be adopted into the family. I just thought you ought to know that Vance Elliot is an impostor."

"Vance passed the DNA test," Boone challenged.

Tough nodded as he seemed to study the lot of them. "Then you've got more vipers among you than even I thought." He took a step back. "I've done what I came to do. Believe me or not, doesn't matter to me. I just couldn't have this on my conscience without speaking up." He turned toward the door.

"Just a minute," Travers said. "My youngest son was taken from his crib with two items—"

"I saw that on the news," Tough said with a sigh. "I don't know anything about a stuffed toy horse. But I had a baby blanket with tiny horses on it. It was blue. The horses weren't quarter horses like you raise. They were Arabians. My mother gave me the blanket before she died. She told me to do with it what I wanted. I burned it."

A gasp came up from the room. "Why in the hell would you do that?" Boone demanded.

"Because I had no interest in doing what I'm doing right now," Tough snapped. "I won't be grilled. I won't be tested. I won't be looked at under a magnifying glass. I sure as hell don't want any press conference for the world to know. I *know* who I am, who my 'real' parents are, and I'm fine with that."

"But if you're Oakley—"

Tough cut Travers off. "Please, sir, don't make me sorry I came here. I couldn't let you be defrauded. But if you want to go on believing Vance Elliot is your son, that's fine with me. Please don't take offense, but I want no part of this family or what comes with it." He stuffed his straw hat onto his thick head of dark hair and lit out the door, leaving behind a stunned silence.

VANCE HAD WATCHED the whole thing from the doorway of the kitchen. After Abby had come down in the elevator, he'd gone into the kitchen and, finding it empty, had gotten himself a snack before opening the envelope.

Now he stepped back so no one saw him.

He heard a sound behind him and turned to see the cook. She had her phone in her hand. All the color had drained from her face.

She must have heard what was going on, as well. She was looking scared, no doubt because she'd been snitching to Huck about him. She was probably afraid she'd get drawn into all this.

"Please tell Mr. Travers that I'm not feeling well and have to go. I'm sorry about dinner." She headed for the door. He saw her glance at a large box sitting on the counter and she seemed to avoid it, increasing her speed as she went out the door. He noticed that some of the tape had been removed from the top of the box. There was a pair of kitchen shears next to it.

Whatever the cook had been getting out of the box, she seemed to have lost interest. Vance had the feeling that they wouldn't be seeing her again.

He wanted to run, too. He'd opened the envelope with his new bank account information but had seen right away that until he signed the necessary forms, he couldn't withdraw any of the ten grand Travers had put in his account. Ten grand. He'd had to count the numbers since he couldn't believe it. There was also a note in the envelope that read, "Thought you might want to buy yourself a vehicle. Let me know and I will see that the money is put into your account."

He'd groaned when he'd seen that. If he stayed, he got to buy himself a brand-new pickup. It was all too much. Worse, it was all a lie.

Had he really thought this was going to last? He couldn't stay. Even before that cowboy had shown up, he'd known that. But he also couldn't hide in the kitchen like the phony he was.

Vance walked into the living room, feeling the tension thick as fog. "The cook just told me to tell you that she isn't feeling well. She's sorry about dinner." He knew he couldn't ignore that tension. Or the way they all looked at him. "What's going on?"

"Some cowboy just stopped by claiming to be Oakley McGraw," Boone said. He was the most suspicious of the brothers. Vance couldn't tell who he thought was lying. Maybe both him and the cowboy.

"Well, he's too late, isn't he?" Cull went to the bar and poured himself a drink. The others joined him, all except Travers. "You passed the DNA test. You're Oakley, right?"

Vance swallowed, his throat too dry to speak. Anyway, what would he have said?

"That was disturbing," Travers said as he looked at his sons, his gaze finally taking in Vance.

He thought of how much he'd wanted this man to be his father. More than he'd wanted the money and the name. He felt an apology working its way up from deep in his chest.

His cell phone rang. He cursed silently. He'd stupidly forgotten to turn the darn thing off after his call to Huck. Pulling out the phone with trembling fingers, he looked at caller ID. *Huck*. It was marked Urgent.

He saw he'd missed an earlier text from Huck. It read: Unless you want to die, get out of the house. Now!

"I should take this." Quickly turning, he headed for the back door, wondering what this could be about.

CHAPTER SEVENTEEN

"DID ANY OF you know he had a cell phone?" Ledger asked the moment Vance was gone. Abby had sat down with the others. He joined her. She looked as shocked as he felt.

"Everyone in the civilized world has a cell phone," Boone snapped. "What is your point?"

"I just wonder who's calling him."

"You think he didn't have a life before he came here? Friends? People who care about him?" Travers asked as if he'd wondered the same thing.

They all looked after Vance for a moment before Cull spoke. "This Tough Crandall. He described the baby blanket perfectly. The type of horse on the blanket was never released."

"But he didn't have the toy stuffed horse," Ledger said.

"Vance did," their father said.

"For the sake of argument, let's say Tough Crandall is Oakley," Cull said reasonably. "How is it he had the blanket but not the stuffed horse?"

Boone brought his drink over to the couch and sat down. "The stuffed toy was taken the night of the kidnapping along with Oakley and his blanket, right?"

"Maybe the kidnapper dropped it when the ladder rung broke," Cull said.

"And the kidnapper's accomplice picked it up?" Boone said.

Ledger felt a chill. "Or whoever was the first person on the scene."

"Like maybe one of the deputy sheriffs?" Abby said.

Travers sighed. "All this is just speculation. Vance's DNA matched."

"Dad, there's something I need to tell you," Cull said and looked at Ledger. "I've taken DNA from Vance's room and some of mine. I've had another test done at a different lab."

"Why would you do that?" His father sounded angry.

"Because Abby remembered something," Ledger said, looking at her. She nodded and he continued, "She remembered seeing Wade and his father with Vance. It was at her house."

"What?" Travers shook his head. "When was this?"

"Before he showed up at our door claiming to be Oakley. That's not all," Ledger continued. "When we were at the lab getting Vance's DNA test done, I saw Deputy Sheriff Huck Pierce talking to one of the lab techs."

The room went deathly quiet again.

"Let's all take it down a notch here," Travers said, but Ledger saw that he looked worried. "You realize what you're accusing Vance of being involved in."

"Fraud," Boone said, putting down his drink and getting to his feet. "I think someone should go check on Vance."

Ledger reached for Abby's hand. "We're going on a picnic. Hope you get it all worked out before we get back."

They'd barely reached the pickup when the back of the house exploded.

VANCE HAD REACHED the trees past the pool house and was about to put in a call to Huck when the world behind him went up in flames.

He spun around in horror as he looked at the back of the house. The kitchen wing looked leveled while the rest of the house was quickly catching fire.

For a moment he couldn't move. Two ranch hands came running from the direction of the barns. Out of the smoke at the back of the house, he saw Boone. He'd been knocked to the ground but was now running back toward the burning house.

Vance's cell phone rang. Still in shock, he took the call.

"Did you get out in time?" Huck laughed.

"You did this?" he demanded.

"And just imagine what I will do if you cross me," the deputy said. "Now get rid of this phone. I'll find you when I need to talk to you again."

LEDGER GRABBED ABBY, not sure at first what had happened as glass showered over the porch as the front windows of the house were blown out.

The front door burst open. Cull and his father came stumbling out. "Call the fire department," Cull was yelling.

Ledger fumbled out his phone. Through the door he could see smoke billowing into the living room from what had been the kitchen.

He dialed 9-1-1 as he drew Abby farther away from the burning house.

"Are you all right?" he heard Cull ask his father. He noticed that the older man was holding his left shoulder.

"I'm fine. Go!" his father said as he stumbled toward one of the pickups parked out front.

Cull was running for their water truck parked next to one of the barns.

The 9-1-1 operator answered. Ledger quickly gave her the information, his mind reeling. What had happened?

"There was an explosion. The house is on fire."

"Is everyone all right?"

"I don't know," he said, suddenly terrified. Boone had started out the back door to go find Vance. The barns were far enough away that the ranch hands and the horses should be fine. But Boone...

"One of my brothers... I don't know where he is." And Vance. Ledger realized he'd never thought the man was his brother. "And another man."

"I'll send an ambulance, as well," the operator was saying. "The fire department is on its way."

HUCK HAD HEARD the call come over the radio and smiled. It just didn't get any better than this.

He drove partway out of town so he could see in the direction of the McGraw ranch. Black smoke billowed up into a cloudless blue sky.

With luck, Travers McGraw and at least some of his sons were dead, Abby along with them. If that damned cook had done her job, the box with the explosives in it would have been left under the front stairs, where it would have done the most damage.

Not that he'd told the woman what was in the box. He'd just told her to handle it with care and not say anything to anyone. It was a surprise.

Idly, he wondered if she'd been surprised.

You're a coldhearted bastard. He heard the last thing his ex-wife had said to him. "Yes, I am. Life made me that way."

And now he was getting back at everyone who'd wronged him. He had the five hundred thousand dollars from the reward coming. He'd give some of it to Wade and then he was gone. There was an island somewhere calling his name. Vance was now a McGraw. He'd be fine. And if he didn't like getting ripped off on the reward money, what could he do about it, Huck thought with a laugh.

For a moment, he watched the smoke rising higher in the sky as flames consumed more of the McGraw house. Things would have been so different if Marianne had married him and not McGraw. He would have done anything for her. Hell, he had that scholarship to the university. He was going to be an engineer, maybe build dams or skyscrapers; he hadn't decided.

But when she'd married McGraw, he'd lost his drive. Nothing mattered. He'd married Wade's mother on the rebound and his life had gone downhill from there.

An ambulance had been sent out to the ranch since they were unsure how many people had been injured. Huck waited patiently for the news, telling himself even if McGraw wasn't dead, his house would be gone. He would have been hit where it hurt the most. The house McGraw had built for Marianne? Gone. Just as Marianne was gone in every sense of the word.

He thought about the twins. They, too, were gone. In the months since more information had come to light about what had been taken from the house the night of the kidnapping, Vance was the only one to come forward.

McGraw had lost Oakley and Jesse Rose. He'd lost Marianne. And now he'd lost his house and hopefully his life.

"Got you," Huck whispered as he watched the cloud of smoke grow larger and larger against the skyline.

VANCE STEPPED BACK into the trees as Boone yelled at the ranch hands to let all the horses out. The two headed for the barns, while Boone raced back into the burning house.

A few minutes later, horses came running out, wild-eyed in terror and headed out across the pasture away from the burning house.

Vance was too shocked to do more than stare at the flames licking wildly at the large house and try to make sense out of what had happened. What would happen now? Who had been killed? Would they think he had done this?

Since this was Huck's doing, Vance was in it up to his eyeballs. No one would believe he hadn't had something to do with this, even if they couldn't prove it.

Was that the way Huck had planned it? Was he going to let him take the fall for this? Was that why he'd texted him to get out?

Had the deputy already gotten the five-hundred-thousand-dollar reward money?

There was also the possibility that Huck warned him about the explosion hoping he would be the only one to survive and all this would be his so Huck could blackmail him right into his old age.

But what to do now?

If he was a real son, he'd be helping with the horses or running to the house to see if he could help whoever was still inside.

But he wasn't and Tough Crandall's visit had raised enough doubt that this would soon be over. The sheriff would be investigating. More DNA testing would be done and when he failed…

Vance began to run in the direction of the house only to swerve at the last moment and race toward the front of the house and the pickups parked out there. If one of them had a key in it…

"HERE, TAKE MY father to my cabin up the road," Ledger said to Abby. "I have to help my brothers fight the fire until the rural fire department gets here." She started toward her car, but he handed her the keys to his pickup. "Take my truck. The road is rough. I'll have the EMTs come down there to look at his shoulder."

"I'm fine," Travers said. "We need to find your brother."

"Dad, I don't want to have to worry about you. Go with Abby. I'll do what I can here."

Abby could tell he didn't want his father watching the house he'd loved burn to the ground. She couldn't see how they could save it the way it had gone up in flames.

She was happy to help. Getting into the pickup, they started up the road when she had to pull over and let the fire trucks go by. She just prayed that Boone had gotten out.

Travers was looking back, tears in his eyes. "Still no word on Boone?" he asked. "Or…Vance?" She noticed he hadn't called him Oakley.

She shook her head. "I'm sure Ledger will call the minute he knows something."

Travers nodded and closed his eyes.

LEDGER WAS JUST about to go back inside to look for Boone when his brother came bursting out the front door in a cloud of smoke.

"Where is Dad?" Boone cried.

"He and Cull got out. Cull's gone to get the water truck. Abby and Dad are fine. I've sent them to my cabin. I didn't want Dad to see this. He's been through enough."

"What the hell happened?"

Ledger shook his head and called Abby to give her the news as his brother ran toward the second water truck. Cull was already watering down the closest barn. Clearly, he could see that it would be impossible to save the house without more resources.

At the sound of sirens, Ledger turned to see the fire trucks and ambulance in the distance.

VANCE CAME AROUND the side of the house as Ledger went to join his brothers to water down the barns. He rushed through the dark smoke toward the closest pickup. All he could think about was getting out of there. Let them think he died in the fire. It would be days before they realized his body wasn't in the ashes. Meanwhile, he would have put miles between him and this place.

No keys in the first pickup. Or the second. He swore. The smoke was starting to get to him. He spotted Abby's car and raced toward it. Behind him, the flames cracked and popped. Sparks flew into the air. The heat of the blaze felt as if it was frying his skin.

He could hear sirens and see the trucks coming up the road. He had to get out of there. If he stayed, he was looking at prison for a crime he didn't commit. He reached Abby's car, threw open the door and reached around the steering wheel, praying that the keys would be there.

They were!

His luck had changed. His mind was working again. If Huck had the reward money, he would get his share or blow the whistle on the deputy. Two could play at blackmail.

He dropped into the seat, reached for the key, turned it. The car engine caught and started. Vance glanced at the house, thinking what a waste and wondering who might still be inside.

He threw the car into Reverse, not letting his mind

go there. He braked and looked again at the house, his senses warning him not to run. He would look even guiltier if he did. Maybe he could turn state's evidence on Wade and Huck. Maybe he could get out of this with a little honor.

He put the car in Park and turned off the engine, thinking about Travers McGraw and wishing with all his heart that he really had been his son. How different his life could have been.

Did he really think there was hope for him, that he could change? He told himself he needed to help water down the barns. He needed to be a different man, the kind of man Travers McGraw thought he'd welcomed into his family.

He reached for his door handle when he heard a noise. At first, it didn't register. A buzzing sound that he could barely hear over the roar of the fire.

Vance looked down at the floorboard, shocked to see what was coiled there. Two rattlesnakes intertwined, both of their ugly heads raised and looking right at him.

He jerked the door handle in that instant before the first one struck. He threw himself out of the car as the second one caught him in the neck. Its fangs going so deep that the snake was still clinging to him as he fell screaming from the car. He tore the snake from his neck.

Over the roar of the blaze, he heard the sirens. Looking up, he saw the first fire trucks pull up. He ran toward them, screaming for someone to help him as venom raced like flames through his veins.

WADE STARED AT his father, then at the cloud of smoke in the distance. "What did you do?"

"Instead of merely whining, I took care of your wife

and her boyfriend," Huck snapped. "You should be thanking me. Hell, if it wasn't for me and Abby's mother, you would have never had Abby as long as you did."

"What are you talking about?" Wade demanded, his voice breaking.

"McGraw never had another girlfriend. He was in love with Abby and planning to marry her after college. And he would have if we hadn't tricked Abby into believing he was cheating on her. Why do you think she rushed into the marriage with you? You would never have stood a chance with her otherwise."

"You lousy son of a—" Filled with rage, he took a swing at his father. Huck easily stepped aside and hit him in the back of the neck. Wade staggered, turning to look back at his father. Lies, all lies. He felt as if his entire world had imploded.

He shook his head. He wanted to blame his father for all of it, but he couldn't. He'd gone along with this stupid plan. He could have walked away. He could have gotten help. He could have been a decent husband.

"Where do you think you're going?" his father demanded as Wade turned and walked toward his pickup.

He didn't bother to answer as he climbed behind the wheel. He had to find out if Abby was still alive. He had to see her. Restraining order be damned.

"Don't go out there," Huck yelled after him as he took off in a cloud of dust and gravel. He roared out of Whitehorse. Smoke billowed up into Montana's big sky.

LEDGER AND HIS BROTHERS, along with the hired hands, managed to get the horses to safety and save the barns. Now, covered with soot, he stared at the ashes of the house. The firefighters hadn't been able to save it.

Smoke still billowed up, a dark smudge on the skyline.

"At least no one was killed," Cull said as the brothers stood shoulder to shoulder in the front yard. "I talked to Dad. His shoulder is better, but Abby called the doctor, anyway."

"How long before we find out what caused it?" Boone asked.

"The fire chief said it should be a few days. Maybe a gas leak." Cull shook his head.

Ledger turned at the sound of a vehicle roaring up the road. "I'll be a son of a..." He stared in disbelief.

"Maybe you better let us handle this," Cull said, grabbing his arm as Ledger started toward the pickup that had just come to a dust-boiling stop in their yard.

He pulled his arm free. "Not a chance. I promised Abby I wouldn't go after him, but I told her all bets were off if he came out here." He stormed over to the pickup as Wade climbed out.

WADE DIDN'T NEED his father to tell him he was a damned fool for coming out here. But he had to know if Abby was all right. Now, though, as he saw the destroyed house, his heart lodged in his throat. If she was in that house when it exploded... His beautiful Abby.

He saw Ledger McGraw, the man he'd hated for years, stalking toward him. Abby had been in love with McGraw from the beginning. She would have married him if Wade's father and her mother hadn't lied to her. Wasn't that what had eaten him up inside for the past three years because he'd suspected it all along? He hadn't gotten Abby fair and square. She'd never wanted him. She'd always wanted McGraw. He'd never felt such pain. And all of it had been for nothing. Especially if Abby was dead.

"Wade? What the hell are you doing here?" Ledger demanded as he advanced on him. The cowboy was covered with soot from fighting the fire and he looked angry enough to kill.

"Is Abby…?"

Ledger kept coming. Wade didn't even bother to throw up an arm as the cowboy punched him. He staggered under the blow but didn't go down. His father had hit him a lot harder than that in his life.

"Just tell me she's alive."

Ledger hit him again, this time driving him back before tackling him to the ground. Wade took another blow before his survival instincts cut in and he started to fight back. This man had been his nemesis for years. He hated him. Hated that Abby loved this man more than him.

But still McGraw was winning this battle.

"That's enough," a male voice ordered as Ledger was pulled off him.

Wade looked from Ledger to his brother Cull. Behind him was the older brother Boone.

"I would have let him beat the hell out of him a little longer, if it had been me," Boone said. All three of them looked like they wanted to kick his ass. He couldn't really blame them.

He wiped the blood from his cut lip with the back of his hand as he sat up. "Abby?"

"She's alive," Ledger said, glaring down at him. "No thanks to you."

Wade covered his face with his hands and, unable to hold back the burst of emotion, began to sob in relief and regret.

CHAPTER EIGHTEEN

"YOU WANT THE good news first?" Cull asked. They had all gathered in Cull's cabin, the largest one on the ranch now that the house was gone.

"Huck and Wade have been arrested." He looked at Abby, who was sitting next to Ledger on the couch. "They've both been charged, along with a tech at the lab and our cook. Huck and Wade won't be seeing daylight for many years to come. Vance is going to live— and turned state's evidence against them. He'll get some time as well, but nothing like he should for his part of the charade."

Ledger saw his father nod solemnly. "I feel sorry for him. I saw something in him…" He shook his head. "I have more good news. While the house is a total loss, insurance will cover rebuilding. I actually think it's a good thing," he said, no doubt seeing that his sons were afraid he was taking it hard. "It's a new beginning. Let's face it, there was a lot of sadness associated with that house."

"It was haunted," Cull said. Ledger knew he was only partially kidding.

His father nodded. "I suppose it was. But my life has changed since I built that house for your mother and our future."

Boone had been looking at his phone. He glanced up suddenly, shock on his face. "Jim Waters has been arrested trying to leave the country with a briefcase full of money." His gaze shot to their father. "Do you know anything about that?"

Travers's smile was almost sad. "Human nature. Jim apparently couldn't overcome his. It's probably just as well since Patricia's trial is coming up. She has implicated him in my poisoning."

Boone swore. "That son of—"

"I have some good news," Ledger interjected. "Wade has agreed to sign the divorce papers when the six months is up. He isn't going to contest it. Also he'll be going to prison and locked up for some time to come."

Travers reached over to squeeze his son's shoulder. "I'm happy for you. I suppose you'll want to start building a house for the two of you on the ranch. Looks like there'll be a lot of construction going on. I like that. I like progress."

"Me, too," Ledger said and smiled over at Abby.

"Well," Cull said. "Nikki is going to be back this week. I hate to let my little brother beat me at anything…" He grinned. "I've asked Nikki to marry me. She's said yes!"

There was cheering. Travers suggested a toast.

"There's one more thing," Boone said. "Do you still want me to follow up on that last lead we had about Jesse Rose?"

"I do. But Vance taught me something," their father said. "I need to be more careful. If you don't mind checking it out…"

"Don't worry. If it's not legit, I'll know. Just don't get your hopes up."

"No," Travers said. "I'm going to drive down to the Crandall place. I need to talk to Tough."

"Dad—"

"Cull, I heard him just fine. He isn't interested in being a McGraw. I can live with that. But I believe he's my son. I can hope for some sort of relationship, can't I?"

LEDGER FOUND ABBY standing outside on the cabin porch, looking out at the ranch in the distance. For so long, smoke had curled up from the ruins of the house he almost thought he could still see. He would be glad when the debris was gone and the new house started.

Mostly, he wanted a fresh start with Abby. She'd been through so much. All he wanted to do was make her happy. He knew it couldn't be easy for her hearing about her soon-to-be ex-husband's arrest.

"Are you all right?" he asked as he joined her at the porch railing.

"I've made so many mistakes. If I had just followed my heart…" Abby began to cry.

Ledger pulled her into his arms. "Abby, we've all made mistakes. The moment I heard you married Wade, I should have come to you then. Maybe we could have sorted things out and you could have gotten an annulment since your marriage was based on a lie."

She nodded against his chest. "I should have trusted in our love."

"That's all behind us. I will never give you any reason to doubt it ever again."

"Your home, your beautiful…" She was crying harder. "It's all my fault."

He held her at arm's length. "Abby, it's just a building. No one was hurt. Dad is excited about rebuilding. You heard him. That house had too many ghosts." He wiped a tear from her cheek with his thumb. "I'm just sorry for everything you've had to go through. But that, too, is behind us."

She nodded and gave him a smile through her tears. "I don't know what I would have done without you."

"You'll never have to find out. I love you."

"I love you. My heart would break when you came into the café—and when you didn't."

He smiled at this woman he'd almost lost for good as he got down on one knee.

Abby's eyes widened as he squeezed her hand and asked, "Abby, will you marry me sometime in the future when you're a free woman?"

ABBY LOOKED DOWN at this man she'd loved for so long. He'd hung in, determined to be there for her even when she'd tried so hard to push him away. If it hadn't been for him, she knew she would be dead.

"Yes!" she said, her voice breaking. She'd never thought she'd see this day. "Oh, Ledger."

She dropped to her knees in front of him, falling into his arms.

He laughed and held her. "Don't you want to see the ring?"

She shook her head. "You can put a piece of string around my finger, for all I care. It doesn't matter. All I care about is being with you always."

"I guess I'll have to take this back," he said after pulling them both to their feet and opening the little black velvet box.

Abby gasped as she looked down at the pear-shaped diamond glittering up at her. "It's beautiful!"

"Just like you." He slipped it on her finger and then met her gaze. "I can wait as long as it takes."

"You've proven that," she said with a laugh.

"You can have any kind of wedding you want."

"I would love to marry you right now, right on this porch with your family as witnesses, if I could."

"I'll call the preacher the moment you're free—if that's what you want," he said, only half joking. "But I think we should do it up proud instead. I want you to have a wedding that you'll always remember." He looked into her eyes. "Meanwhile, I'll start building our house on the ranch. I need you to make it a home. You've seen my cabin."

She smiled. "But I'd still like to keep working at the café—at least until the baby comes."

"The baby?"

"The one you and I are going to make tonight," she said.

"Oh, *that* baby." He kissed her, knowing that things were finally as they should be. Ledger and Abby. Their marriage would be stronger because of the rough road that had gotten them here. And they would get married right here on the ranch.

But tonight they would be together again. He put his arm around her as they went inside and up the stairs to their room.

"Are you all right?" Ledger asked late that night when he found his father standing outside in the moonlight.

"I'm fine," Travers said, wrapping an arm around his son and pulling him over next to him for a moment. "I was just thinking about when your mother and I started this ranch. We had such dreams. I think that was the problem. We didn't want this much. It kind of snowballed as the ranch became so successful. We had no idea that our luck was about to change."

"You can't blame your good fortune on what happened," he said.

"Can't I? Your mother never wanted all of this."

He heard something in his father's voice that sent his pulse pounding. "The twins?"

His father had never looked so old as he did in the moonlight. "You boys were her pride and joy. She was happy with the way things were. I was the one who wanted to give her a girl." He shook his head. "It was all too much for her."

"I'm so sorry."

Travers smiled at him. "How are you, son? I feel as if I haven't paid enough attention to the children I didn't lose."

"We're all fine."

"Your brother Cull is in love. Boone, well, who knows if he will ever find anyone as contrary as he is." He smiled when he said it. "And you and Abby?"

"We're good. We got engaged tonight."

Sadness filled his father's eyes. "Years ago when you came to me—"

"You were right. I was too young to get married."

"But not too young to lose your heart."

"No," he agreed. "I gave it away. There was no getting it back." He smiled. "I've always loved Abby. Nothing changed even when she married Wade."

"Well, that is all behind you now."

"Yes. We all have a chance for a new beginning."

His father sighed. "Let's just hope Boone finds Jesse Rose. Even if it is to know that she's alive and happy. That will be enough."

EPILOGUE

THE SUN SHONE in a cloudless blue sky on Abby and Ledger's wedding day. Standing with her friends around her, Abby felt a shiver of excitement. This was how it was supposed to be, she thought, remembering her other wedding day.

It had been just the four of them, she and Wade, her mother and Huck. She'd worn a pink dress with navy flowers. It was one she'd had in her closet, one that Wade said he liked on her. Huck had gotten her a rose to hold as they drove to the judge's chambers to be married.

Afterward, she and Wade had gone back to the house he had bought. A honeymoon had been out of the question. "Honeymoons are for people with money to throw away since they have nothing to do with marriage," her mother had said.

Abby remembered crying herself to sleep that night after Wade had dropped off. He'd drunk too much champagne, some cheap bottles that Huck had opened on the way from the judge's chambers.

She pushed those memories away like a rainstorm moving on. The sun was out; her friends were all around her. She could feel their excitement.

"You are absolutely glowing," said Sarah, one of the young women she worked with at the café. "I always knew the two of you would get together. The way Ledger always looked at you when he came into the café, it was clear that he loved you."

"It's nice to have you back," another friend said. Abby hugged her. Wade had kept her from her friends, saying they would just put bad ideas into her head.

Ella stuck her head in the door. "You ready?" Her boss looked beautiful in a red velvet dress. It was the first time Abby had seen her in anything other than a white uniform. She'd asked Ella to give her away.

"I'm not even going to ask about your mother," Ella had said. "I'd love to give you away."

Now Abby looked down at the bouquet in her hands. She lifted the flowers and sniffed the tiny white roses. Was this really happening?

She looked up. From the huge terrace behind the new house Travers had built, she could see the Little Rockies in the distance. Horses ran across open foothills, their manes blowing behind them. The day couldn't have been more perfect.

She'd always thought of this ranch as paradise. The times she'd spent here before Ledger went away to college and she married Wade were something she'd hung on to for the past few years.

Now she looked out over the ranch realizing that in a few minutes she would be Mrs. Ledger McGraw. It felt like a fantasy, something she hadn't dared let herself believe was possible.

She thought of Ledger. He'd never lost faith. She felt tears burn her eyes.

"Can you ever forgive me?" she'd asked him that night after they'd made love.

"There is nothing to forgive, Abby. You didn't burn down the house."

"No, Wade and his father did because of me."

"Honey," he'd said, pulling her to him. "Huck Pierce has had it in for my father since they were boys. This has nothing to do with you."

"But I believed their lies. I didn't trust you and I should have."

"Oh, Abby, I knew you'd been lied to but there was nothing I could do. If I'd had my way, I would have ridden into the café and swept you up on my horse and rode out of town with you."

She'd smiled through her tears. "I dreamed of you doing that."

He'd laughed. "So did I. But I couldn't. Not until I knew you were ready to leave him. It was the hardest thing I'd ever done, waiting. But now there is nothing keeping us apart. The past is just that." He'd kissed her with such passion she'd let go of the guilt, the grief, the feeling that she could never be happy again.

With Ledger McGraw she could finally know passion, love, tenderness and happiness.

"I'm ready," she said to Ella. "I've never been more ready."

LEDGER LOOKED UP and saw Abby as the wedding march played. She stepped out in a shaft of sunlight. She wore a string of daisies in her long hair. The dress was a pale yellow that flowed as she moved. She had never looked more beautiful.

His heart soared, making him have trouble catching his breath. He'd dreamed of this day for so long. Now it was finally happening.

"You going to be all right?" his father asked, standing next to him with Cull and Boone.

"I am now," he said.

"Didn't you ever want to give up?" Cull had asked him last night after everyone else had gone to bed. "I think I would have given up."

"You wouldn't have if it had been Nikki. Once you fall in love...nothing can change that."

"I'm happy for you, Ledger," Cull had said and slapped him on the back. "Hope you're as happy as Nikki and I are being married."

"We will be."

As he watched his soon-to-be wife walk toward him, she smiled and their gazes met. He smiled back at her. The future couldn't have looked any brighter on this beautiful Montana summer day. Some things, he thought, were definitely worth waiting for.

* * * * *

CLASSIFIED CHRISTMAS

This one is for Jody Robinson,
for her encouragement and support and friendship.

CHAPTER ONE

THIS YEAR WAS DIFFERENT. Cade Jackson couldn't swear why exactly, just that he wasn't anticipating the anniversary of his wife's death with as much dread.

Maybe time *did* heal. Not that he didn't miss his wife. Or think of her. Especially with the anniversary of Grace's death only days away. He just didn't hurt as much when he thought of her. Nor after six years did he think of her as often.

There was something sad about that, he thought, as he watched the other ropers from the top rung of the corral. The thunder of hooves raised a cloud of dust that moved slowly across the enclosed arena.

Outside, snow continued to fall, promising a white Christmas. He breathed in the comforting scent of leather and horses, both as natural to him as the lay of the land beyond the arena walls.

Snow-covered open prairie ran to the deep cut of the Missouri River as it wound its way through Montana, the dark outline of the Little Rockies that broke the horizon.

He felt as if he'd come of out of a coma. Everything looked and smelled and felt new and different. He'd missed a lot of holidays with his family, lost in that dark place that his grief had taken him. But this year he felt as if he might make it through the holidays without having to hide out at his cabin or in his ice-fishing shack until Christmas was over.

Cade felt an odd prickling just under his skin and looked toward the window. Snow fell in huge flakes that floated down blanketing the earth with both cold and silence. He frowned at the sudden sense of apprehension he'd felt just moments before. What had that been about?

He shook it off. He wasn't going to let the old ghosts get to him. He was finally feeling as if he might make it.

ANDI BLAKE DISCOVERED a manila envelope on her desk when she got back to the newspaper from lunch. She'd spent her first morning at the *Milk River Examiner* cleaning off her predecessor's desk, only a little unnerved by the fact that he'd been murdered, thus the opening.

Glen Whitaker hadn't been neat. After boxing up all of his notes, she'd cleaned the desk, scrubbing away months if not years of grime.

She gave the envelope only a sideways glance as she slipped off her jacket and hung it over the back of her chair.

The envelope was addressed to her and had a Whitehorse postmark. Nothing unusual about that except for the fact that it was addressed to Andi *West*, the name she'd gone by as a television newscaster in Fort Worth, Texas.

She felt a shiver of trepidation. No one here knew her as Andi let alone Andi West. Her full name was Miranda West Blake. She had been named after her father, Weston Blake. He was the one who'd nicknamed her Andi.

To put Fort Worth and the past far behind her when she'd applied for this job, though, she'd used Miranda Blake and now wrote as M. W. Blake.

She'd thought by moving to Whitehorse, Montana, and using her real name that she would be able to escape from the terror that had run her out of Texas. Had it followed her?

Her heart pounded. All her old fears came back in a wave of nausea. Was it possible there was nowhere she could get away from it?

Fingers trembling, she picked up the envelope, turning it in her fingers. The contents felt light. And the package didn't sound like it was ticking. Something slid inside making her jump.

Her fear, though, gave way to anger. She was sick of being scared. She'd given up everything she loved because of some psycho. If he'd found her...

Taking out her letter opener, she sliced through one end of the envelope and carefully dumped the contents onto her desk.

She'd gotten enough of these at the television station that she knew what to expect.

A white cassette tape thudded to the desktop an instant before a piece of newspaper fluttered down beside it, surprising her.

She frowned and picked up the tape. It was file card size. There was nothing written on it. She glanced at the CD player on her desk and wondered where she might find a cassette player that played this size tape.

Not that she would play it. She'd learned it was better not to listen to the calls although she'd read most of the letters before handing them over to the police. Except the police hadn't been able to find her stalker let alone stop him or the threatening letters and calls.

Putting down the tape, she turned her attention to the other item from the envelope. As she unfolded the newsprint, she saw that it was a clipping of a local newspaper brief about a woman named Grace Jackson who'd died in a one-car rollover south of town.

She felt a wave of relief. Apparently someone thought the story warranted a follow-up. That's all this was.

True it was odd because the accident had happened six years ago Christmas Eve.

But at least it wasn't connected to Texas. Or her. She tried to relax.

Still the fact that it had been sent to Andi West bothered her. Who besides the newspaper publisher, Mark Sanders, knew her television name?

Just then Mark Sanders came in the door.

She held up the clipping and he took it from her as he walked by her desk, glanced at the story and handed the clipping back saying, "Yeah, that was real sad. They hadn't been married long." He started to walk off.

"Do you want me to do a follow-up?" she asked his retreating back.

He stopped to glance over his shoulder and frowned. "Can't see any reason. It's been what—"

"Six years," she said.

"Right. No reason to bring it back up," Sanders said.

"Someone sent it to me."

"Just file it. You're covering the Parade of Lights tonight, right? It's a pretty big deal in Whitehorse. You sure you don't mind shooting it, too?"

"No problem." She didn't bring up the name thing. It was possible, she realized, that Mark Sanders had told someone who she was thinking no one in Whitehorse, Montana, would care let alone cause her any trouble.

"I've got it covered," she assured him, imagining what her best friend back at the television station in Fort Worth would say if he knew she was covering parades for a small-town weekly newspaper, taking the photographs as well as writing the stories.

She hadn't talked to Bradley since she'd left Texas. Maybe she'd call him. She was sure he was probably worried about her since he'd tried to talk her out of coming up here. She missed him and hadn't wanted to call until things were going better. She didn't want to hear him say I-told-you-so. Even though he was right. She feared this move had been a huge mistake.

But she had some time to kill before the Parade of Lights and she really needed her friend.

"Hello?"

Just the sound of Bradley's voice brought tears to her eyes.

"Hello?" The apprehension she heard in his voice surprised and worried her.

"It's me," she said quickly. "Are you all right?"

"Hey." Instantly he sounded like his old self again. "I'm fine. I just thought it was someone else calling. I've been getting some obscene telephone calls. I might enjoy them if I was straight," he said with a laugh. "I am so glad you called. I have been worried to death about you. I was beginning to think you'd forgotten about me."

"No chance of that," she said, tucking her feet up under her. It was almost like old times talking with him over a delivery pizza and old movies.

"So how bad is it?" he asked.

"It's…interesting."

"I told you not to take that job. You must be bored to tears. You haven't been banished, you know. You can get on the next plane and be back in Texas in a matter of hours. I'll pick you up at the airport."

She laughed. It *was* tempting.

"So how horrible is it in the wild, Wild West?" he asked. "You can tell me."

"It's freezing cold for starters."

"I know. I confess I've been watching the weather. I knew you were going to freeze your cute little behind off." He laughed. "Seriously, how are you?"

"Homesick for you, for warm weather, for Mexican food." She smiled. "There isn't any in Whitehorse."

"Imagine that," he said with a smile in his voice.

"So how are things at the station?"

"It's been bloody hell. There was practically a revolt over your job even though everyone knew the position was only temporary."

Her boss had promised to hold her job for six months.

"So who got it? Anyone I know?"

Bradley let out a dramatic sigh and she knew.

"Rachel," she said. Rachel was as close a female friend as she'd had at the station. "I'm happy for her."

"Oh, please," Bradley said. "You can be honest. It's *me*, remember?"

Andi laughed. It felt good. "You're just jealous because she won't let you try on her shoes."

"I miss you."

"I miss you, too." She hated to ask, but she had to. "Has the station received any more threats addressed to me?"

That telltale beat of silence, then, "I made sure they were turned over to the police."

Hearing this surprised her. She'd thought the threats would stop once she wasn't on the air anymore.

"I'll bug the cops until they find this freak and lock him up so you can come home."

She smiled through her tears. "You're a good friend." She hung up, glad she'd called him. She felt better about her decision to come to Montana. If the television station was still getting threatening letters for her, she was much better off being as far away from Fort Worth as she could get.

As she started to file away the news article about the woman who'd died in the single-car accident, she stopped to read it through again, still curious why anyone would have sent it to her.

The deceased woman, Grace Jackson, had apparently been driving at a high rate of speed when she'd lost control of her car south of town. The car had rolled numerous times before landing in a ravine where it had caught fire.

As she had the first time she'd read it, Andi shuddered at the thought of the poor woman being trapped in the vehicle and burning to death. There were so few vehicles on the roads up here and miles between ranches let alone towns. Even if the car hadn't burned, the woman probably would have died before someone had come along.

According to the article, Grace Jackson had been married to a Cade Jackson. Wasn't the sheriff's name Jackson? Carter Jackson, as she recalled from reading back papers to familiarize herself with the town.

She wondered if Cade and Carter were related. Pretty good chance given their names. The sheriff's name had come up quite a lot in the news—including the murder of the reporter who'd had this desk, Glen Whitaker.

She looked again at the manila envelope the newspaper clipping and tape had come in, checking to make sure there wasn't a note that she'd missed. Nothing. The envelope had been mailed in Whitehorse so at least it was from someone local.

She filed the story, still a little anxious, though, that at least one person in town knew her other name.

As she pocketed the cassette tape, she wondered where she could find a tape player.

THE PARADE OF LIGHTS definitely was an event in Whitehorse, Montana. Andi stood on a curb with the rest of the county that had turned out, everyone bundled up for the cold, snowy December night, as one homemade float after another cruised by.

The air was filled with excitement, the stores along the main street open and lit brightly for the event. The smell of Christmas trees, hot cider and Native American fry bread wafted in the chilly air.

The streets were packed with not only townspeople, but also apparently ranchers and their families had come in from miles around for the event.

Andi shot a dozen photographs of the floats, surprised at how many there were given the temperature and how much work had gone into some of them.

She liked the small-town feel, which surprised her. It felt like an extended family as she heard people visiting and calling greetings from the floats.

Just as she was finishing up, she heard someone call out, "Cade!"

She looked up to see an attractive woman waving from one of the floats. Andi followed the woman's gaze to a man leaning against the building yards to her right. She could see only his profile, his face in shadow under the brim of his Western hat, but he was tall and all cowboy. He wore boots, jeans, a sheepskin coat and a Stetson, the brim pulled low, dark hair curling out from under the hat at his nape.

From the way he stood, back in the shadows, she got the impression he had hoped to go unnoticed.

Cade *Jackson*? The husband of the deceased woman from the newspaper clipping?

Andi lifted the camera and impulsively snapped his photograph. As she pulled the camera down, he disappeared into the crowd.

Cold and tired, she returned to the newspaper office just down the block, anxious to get her photographs into the computer. Warmer, she decided to go ahead and write up her story even though it was late.

She knew she was just avoiding the small apartment she'd rented on the other side of town. It wasn't far from the newspaper given that Whitehorse was only ten blocks square. She usually drove to work out of habit more than necessity, although she didn't relish walking through all the snow.

The apartment was small and impersonal to the point of being depressing. In time she would make it hers, but right now she preferred the newspaper office to home.

After she put in the photographs and wrote cutlines for each, she sat down at the computer to write an accompanying article.

Her mind wandered, though, and she found herself calling up the photograph of the cowboy she'd seen on the main street tonight, the one the woman had called Cade. How many Cades could there be in Whitehorse?

The publisher had said Cade Jackson and his wife, Grace, had only been married a short period of time before her death. That meant there should be a wedding announcement in the file, she thought, unable to shake her curiosity as to why someone had sent the cassette and clipping to her.

Five minutes later, she found the wedding announcement and photo. The two had married November 14—just weeks before her death.

Andi studied the photograph of the groom, comparing it to the one she'd taken of the cowboy she'd seen on the street tonight. Cade Jackson. The two were one and the same.

The cassette was still in her pocket. Now more than ever she was anxious to find a player and see what was on the tape.

Intent on the cowboy, Andi finally looked at the wedding photo of the bride, Grace Browning Jackson. Her mouth went dry, her heart a hammer in her ears.

She *knew* this woman.

Except her name hadn't been Grace Browning. Not even close.

CHAPTER TWO

ANDI BLAKE STARED at the photograph, telling herself she had to be mistaken. But she knew she wasn't.

It *was* Starr, she'd stake her life on it. Starr Calhoun wasn't someone she could have forgotten even if the first time Andi laid eyes on her wasn't indelibly branded on her memory. They'd both been only young girls. Andi remembered only too well the look they'd shared before all hell broke loose.

And it wasn't as if Andi hadn't seen Starr Calhoun since, she thought with a chill.

It made sense, Starr masquerading as this Grace Browning woman and marrying a local yokel. Starr Calhoun had been hiding out here, using marriage as a cover, waiting. Waiting for what, though?

Her brother Lubbock! He'd been arrested only an hour away from Whitehorse six years ago. She felt a chill as she realized she was meant to come here. As if it had always been her destiny. As if Starr Calhoun had called her from the grave.

She shivered and glanced toward the front window of the newspaper office along the main street, suddenly feeling more than a little paranoid.

A few shoppers straggled past. The Christmas lights still glowed in the park across the street by the train tracks. Next to the old depot, a half dozen passengers waited by their suitcases. Whitehorse's depot had closed years ago, but a passenger train still came through. Passengers had to call for tickets and wait outside until the train arrived.

Andi got up and closed the front blinds, double-checking the front door to make sure she'd locked it.

It didn't take her long to find a more recent photograph of Starr Calhoun on the FBI's most wanted list. She printed the photo, standing over the printer as it came out. The copy wasn't great. But then the original had been taken from a bank surveillance camera.

That had been six years ago August. Wearing masks and carrying sawed-off shotguns, a man and woman had robbed a series of banks across Texas amassing an estimated three million dollars over a two-week period.

During what turned out to be their last robbery, there had been an altercation and the mask Starr Calhoun had been wearing was pulled off by a teller exposing her face to the surveillance camera.

A warrant had been issued for Starr Calhoun, but she and her accomplice had gotten away and had never been heard from again. Nor had the money been recovered.

The accomplice was believed to be her brother Houston Calhoun, a known criminal who'd done time for bank robbery.

The Calhoun family shared more than their distinctive pale blue eyes and curly auburn hair. Nor was the robbery six years ago the first time Starr Calhoun had been caught on a bank surveillance video camera.

She was first filmed at the age of three when her infamous parents, Hodge and Eden Calhoun, hit a bank in Orange, Texas, with all six children in tow ranging in age from fifteen to three.

Hodge and Eden had eventually been caught, their children put into foster care and scattered to the wind.

Andi made a note to find out the latest on the rest of the Calhouns. At least she had a good idea where Starr had disappeared to, she thought, studying the wedding photograph.

She couldn't help the small thrill she felt. Her instincts had been right. As a reporter, she'd made a point of keeping track of the infamous Calhoun family. Whenever a news story from any part of the country mentioned one of the Calhouns, her computer flagged the story for her.

That's how she'd seen the article about Starr Calhoun being ID'd in the bank surveillance tape six years ago. Also the lesser story about her older brother Lubbock Calhoun being arrested not long after that.

She'd forgotten about where Lubbock had been arrested, though. It wasn't until she'd been looking for a job away from Fort Worth that her job search had popped up a newspaper reporter position in Whitehorse, Montana, on her computer and triggered the memory of Lubbock's arrest.

Too excited to wait until she saw him the next day, she had called her friend Bradley. Bradley Harris worked in fact-checking at the news station. The two had become good friends almost at once. He loved Tex-Mex food and old movies and was safe because he was gay and Andi didn't date men she worked with. Actually she didn't date at all—too busy with her career, she told herself.

"Why Montana? It sounds like a one-horse town," Bradley had joked when she'd told him about the job, leaving out the part about Lubbock being arrested near there. "Surely there is somewhere closer you could disappear to. Wait a minute." He knew her too well. "How close is this town to where Lubbock Calhoun was arrested?"

Bradley was one of the few people who knew about her interest—or obsession as he called it—in the Calhoun crime family. She'd thought he wouldn't make the connection.

Reluctantly she'd shown Bradley on a Montana map on her computer. Lubbock Calhoun had been arrested for an outstanding warrant in a convenience store in Glasgow, Montana, six years ago—an hour away from Whitehorse.

"I think it's a sign I should check into this job," she said and waited for Bradley to talk her out of it.

And Bradley had tried, pointing out that it had been six years, Lubbock was probably just passing through Montana, and "What could you possibly learn after all this time? Not to mention, you'll be stuck in One Horse."

"Whitehorse," she'd corrected, the job having taken on more appeal with the possible Lubbock Calhoun connection.

"I'm worried about you and this thing with the Calhouns," he'd said. She suspected he knew why they held such interest for her because he was the best researcher she'd ever known. But he never let on.

He'd finally given up trying to stop her, knowing how desperately she needed to get out of Fort Worth. And how she couldn't turn down even a remote chance to learn more about the Calhouns.

Coincidence? Starr coming to Montana, marrying a cowboy from Whitehorse and Lubbock being arrested just miles away? No way. Andi felt her excitement building. There was a story here, the kind of story that had propelled Andi's rise in broadcast news. That and her instincts when it came to investigative reporting.

And while she might have had to give up television news for a while, a story like this would definitely assist in her return when the time came.

Eagerly she planned how to proceed. She had to get the whole story and that meant hearing Cade Jackson's side of it, she thought as she looked up his address in the phone book.

As she took it down, she couldn't help but wonder. Did Cade Jackson know who he'd married? Or was he in for the surprise of his life?

CADE JACKSON WALKED home from the parade through the underpass beneath the tracks as the passenger train pulled in.

The night was cold and dark, the streets snow packed and icy. He breathed in the air. It felt moist, the clouds low, another snowstorm expected to come in by tomorrow morning.

A white Christmas. He could hear carols coming from one of the cars' radios as it passed. He quickened his step, anxious to get back to his apartment behind the bait shop. Going to the parade had been a mistake. Now he felt antsy. He thought about driving out to his cabin on Nelson Reservoir, but it was late and he was tired.

The parade had brought back memories of Grace and the night they'd come to the parade together, cuddled close as music played on a float with a Western band. She'd looked over at him, her eyes bright with excitement, her cheeks flushed from the cold. And he'd kissed her.

He could still remember the way she'd tasted. Sweet and just a little pepperminty from the candy cane she'd eaten. He recalled the way she felt in his arms and how happy he'd been. Newlyweds. They'd been newlyweds and he'd thought they had years together ahead of them.

That was the night they talked about having children, he realized as he finally reached the bait shop. He started around back to his apartment in the rear when he saw that someone had left a note on the shop's front door.

He stepped over to pluck it free before going around to the back. While he locked the bait shop door, like most everyone in Whitehorse, he left his apartment door open.

Stepping inside, he flipped on a light, glad to be distracted from his thoughts as he opened the note. Something fluttered to the floor, but he was busy looking at the note, surprised he didn't recognize the handwriting. He knew everyone in Whitehorse, having grown up in the area. He and his brother, Carter, had been raised down by Old Town Whitehorse to the south, but they'd both gone to high school here.

The town of Whitehorse had sprung up to the south closer to the Missouri River Breaks, but when the railroad had come through in the 1800s, the town had moved north, taking the name with it.

The note read: "Mr. Jackson, I need to talk to you, M. W. Blake." There was a local phone number at the bottom. And four little words that ruined his night. "It's about your wife."

The word "wife" jumped out at him. He glanced down at the floor and saw the business card at his feet. Bending, he stooped to pick it up. This he recognized. The logo was from the *Milk River Examiner*, the local weekly newspaper.

Under it was the name: M. W. Blake.

Under that was the word: *reporter*.

He crumpled both the note and the business card in his fist. He didn't have any idea who M. W. Blake was and he didn't care to know. The last thing he planned to do was talk to a reporter about Grace.

ON THE WAY home after leaving a note for Cade Jackson at his bait shop, Andi realized she couldn't wait until morning to find out what was on this cassette tape. She called the publisher and asked if anyone had a tape player that took regular-size cassette tapes.

His daughter just happened to have an old one she no longer used, he said. If she stopped by, she was welcome to borrow it. He also had a couple of tapes she could use if she needed to tape something.

Mark Sanders had bent over backward since she'd applied for the job. She'd told him she needed a change of pace. He, in turn, had needed a reporter after Glen Whitaker had been murdered. Not a lot of reporters wanted to come to Whitehorse, especially after they found out what it paid.

Sanders had been worried that Andi had too much experience and wouldn't be staying long.

"Whitehorse is nothing like Fort Worth," he'd said with a laugh. "Maybe you'd better come up here and have a look-see before you take my offer." He had already apologized for how little he could pay her.

She'd had to convince him that Whitehorse was exactly what she was looking for. She didn't tell him her real reason. Only her friend Bradley knew that.

Back at her apartment, Andi took the cassette tape from her pocket and popped it into one side of the player. Hitting Play, she turned up the volume and went into the kitchen to pour herself a glass of wine.

At first all she heard was static. She was beginning to think that the tape was blank as she took the wine bottle from the fridge.

But as she reached for a glass, she heard a woman's voice on the tape and froze.

Like a sleepwalker, she moved into the living room, the wine bottle in her hand as the tape continued.

She didn't recognize the voice—she'd never heard Starr Calhoun speak. Nor did the woman have much of a Texas accent. No, it was what the woman was saying that captured all of Andi's attention and convinced her that the voice was that of Starr Calhoun.

On the tape, the woman talked about robbing a series of banks. After a moment, a male voice could be heard on the tape. Her accomplice.

The tape went to static but Andi didn't move. Couldn't. She stood too shocked to do anything but stare at the tape player.

Who had sent this to her?

And why?

And where had it been the last six years?

She told herself not to look a gift horse in the mouth. Why not just revel in her good luck at having a story like this dropped into her lap?

But she knew that hadn't been the case. It was no coincidence someone had sent her this. Just as it was no coincidence she was here. Was it possible that someone had sent her the job notice, counting on her need to escape Fort Worth and her interest in the Calhouns? With Lubbock's arrest just miles from here the person who'd sent her the job notice knew she wouldn't be able to resist.

Just as she wouldn't be able to resist breaking this story once she had all the facts.

She stepped to the player, her fingers trembling as she rewound the tape and listened to it again before she went to the kitchen and poured herself a healthy glass of wine. She was shaking now, the realization of what she had in her possession starting to sink in along with the apprehension.

She needed to talk to her friend Bradley. He'd been her sounding board through the whole secret-admirer-turned-stalker trauma in Texas. She dialed his number, needing him to be home.

"So how's the weekly newspaper business," Bradley said after they'd exchanged pleasantries about the weather in Montana versus Texas and he'd told her the TV-station gossip.

She hesitated but only for a moment before she told him about the story she'd stumbled across. Bradley, being Bradley and a journalist at heart, was ecstatic.

"What an incredible story," he cried. "So you were right about there being something to Lubbock Calhoun's arrest up there. Well, that's why you're the hotshot news celebrity and I'm the lowly researcher," he joked. "And to have this story dropped in your lap..." He suddenly turned serious. "Oh, sweetie, I almost forgot. I saw on the news that Lubbock Calhoun was released from prison three weeks ago and has already broken his parole."

Her heart leaped to her throat. Lubbock was on the loose?

"You don't think he's the one who sent you the information, do you?" Bradley asked.

"Why would he?" she asked, although she already knew.

"Isn't it obvious? He figures a hotshot reporter like you will find the money," Bradley said.

She bristled at the hotshot reporter comment. "I work for a weekly newspaper."

"Now you do. Stop being so modest. You are a great reporter. Lubbock must have seen you on TV during one of your stories that made national news," Bradley said. "Sweetie, I don't like this. I think you should hightail it back to Texas. If Lubbock Calhoun's feeding you this information, then it's too dangerous. The man is a hardened *criminal*."

"You know I can't come back to Texas."

"But can you stay there? What if I'm right and he's hoping you find the money for him?"

"It would make quite the story," she said, only half joking.

"Sweetie, but what if you don't find the money?"

"For all I know Starr faked her death and has already spent all the money," Andi said and took a drink of her wine, unnerved by the news about Lubbock. "Don't forget Houston. He could have already blown the money. No one has seen him since he and Starr pulled off that last robbery six years ago."

"If Houston *was* her accomplice," Bradley pointed out. "We know it wasn't Lubbock. He didn't resemble the man in the bank surveillance photos. Plus he was arrested on an old warrant so he wasn't even a suspect in the robberies apparently."

Andi had been thinking about the millions of stolen dollars. "You can bet one of the Calhouns has already spent that robbery money."

"If that were the case, wouldn't Lubbock Calhoun know that—if he's the one who sent you the information?" Bradley asked.

He made a good point.

"Maybe he doesn't know what happened to the money—or Starr or Houston. Maybe he's winging it just like me," she said.

"Maybe. Or maybe Starr hid the money, planning to take off with her new identity, but hadn't planned on losing control of her car and dying."

"That's another possibility," she admitted. "That's the problem. There are too many possibilities."

"Oh, wait," Bradley said, "but if Starr had hidden the money, surely her husband would have found it by now. Unless he *did* find it!"

"Is there some way to find out if any of the stolen money ever turned up?" she asked.

"The robberies were during the day, right? Banks have what they call 'bait' money. It's traceable. So if any of it has surfaced… I'll see what I can find out and get back to you," he said, sounding as excited as she felt about the story.

She gave him her new cell phone number and they both promised to keep in touch.

After she hung up, she shot a glance at her front window as a car drove slowly by. Lubbock wasn't just out of prison, he'd already broken parole.

Quickly she stepped to the window and closed the curtains, telling herself that the smartest thing she could do was to take everything she knew to the local sheriff, Carter Jackson, Cade Jackson's brother.

But then the story would break prematurely. A story that belonged to her. And not the whole story. Not to mention that she might never find out who was sending her the information or what they wanted.

She checked to make sure her door was locked before she rewound the tape and listened to it again, her mind racing. She took one of the blank tapes Mark Sanders had given her and put it in the second cassette deck and made a copy of the original.

Wouldn't anyone who wanted the story to come out have gone to the sheriff? Or the FBI? Or if not that, a major television station?

Whoever had given her the newspaper clipping and the tape wasn't after a story—or justice. No, they wanted something else. Bradley had to be right. They wanted the money.

She took the tape out of the player and stared down at it. The big question was what was *she* going to do with this?

CHAPTER THREE

THE JACKSON BAIT SHOP was on the edge of town. The sign was weathered, the building small. As Andi got out of her car the next morning, she wondered how Cade Jackson made a living in such a remote place selling bait.

Or was he living off the three million dollars Starr had stolen?

Andi had gone into the newspaper early, gathering everything she could find on Cade Jackson. There hadn't been much. A local cowboy, he'd grown up on a ranch south of here near what was called Old Town Whitehorse.

Since then he'd won some horse-roping events and caught a few big fish that had made the newspaper.

His only claim to fame just might turn out to be marrying Starr Calhoun, she thought as she saw that the closed sign was still up in the bait shop window. There were no store hours posted. Did anyone even fish this time of year?

She knocked at the door and waited on the small landing out front, hugging herself, trying to keep warm. She guessed he was already up since the *Great Falls Tribune* newspaper box next to the door was empty. It had snowed again last night, coating the entire town with a couple of inches. The snow glittered so bright it was blinding. But it was the breeze that cut through her, chilling her to the bone. She'd had no idea it would be this cold up here.

As a gust of wind whirled snow around her, she instinctively reached for the doorknob. To her surprise, it turned easily in her hand, the door falling open.

She was hit with a blast of warm air. She leaned into it, stepping into the room and closing the door behind her as she tried to shake off her earlier chill.

Apparently Cade Jackson sold more than bait. The room was divided into four long aisles by three high shelves filled with lures and jigs, rods and reels, paddles and oars, nets and an array of boat parts and sporting equipment.

Cade Jackson was nowhere in sight but she thought she heard water running somewhere in the back.

She moved through the shop toward the sound. It was warm in here and she was in no hurry to go back outside into the cold.

But she reminded herself: for all she knew this man had known about the robbery, might even have gotten rid of his wife to keep all the money for himself.

But if he had the three million dollars or even some of it, he didn't appear to be enjoying it much, she thought as she saw his living quarters.

The shop opened onto a small apartment. The lack of stuff made her wonder if anyone could live this simply. Certainly not Starr Calhoun.

For a moment Andi considered what she was doing. This felt all wrong. Not to mention she couldn't guess what Cade Jackson's reaction was going to be to not only her being here, but also what she had to show him.

What if she was wrong?

She wasn't and she knew it.

But she still felt apprehensive. She had no idea what this man was like. The fact that Starr Calhoun had married him was a clue, though. Andi was wondering if she'd made a mistake coming here alone.

She was no fool, though. In her large shoulder bag, along with a copy of the cassette she'd made and the boom box, she had a can of pepper spray and her cell phone.

"Mr. Jackson?" she called from the doorway into the apartment. No answer.

She called his name again. The sound of running water stopped. "Hello!" she called out. "Hello?" She stopped to look at a bulletin board filled with photographs of fish being held by men, women and children. Some of the fish were as huge as the grins on the many faces.

When she looked up, she was startled to find the apartment doorway filled with a dark silhouette. She got the impression Cade Jackson had been standing in the doorway for some time studying her.

To make things even more awkward, his dark hair was wet and droplets of water beaded on his lashes as well as on the dark curls of his chest hair that formed a V to disappear into the towel wrapped around his slim hips.

"I'm sorry, the door was open," she said quickly.

He smiled either at the fact that he had her flustered or because of her accent. "The shop isn't open yet, but then again you don't look like a fisherman," he said eyeing her. "Nor do you sound local."

"No, I'm neither," she said, getting her composure back. He was even more handsome up close and personal.

He cocked a dark brow at her.

"I'm Miranda Blake. I left my business card and a note on your door last night? But I can wait while you dress."

He'd looked friendly before. He didn't now. "M. W. Blake, the new reporter over at the *Examiner*?" He was shaking his head and moving toward her, clearly planning to show her out. "I don't talk to reporters."

"You'll want to talk to *me*," she said standing her ground as she put her hand on her shoulder bag, easing the top open so she could get to her pepper spray.

He stopped in front of her and she caught a whiff of his soap. Yum. He stood a good head taller. She had to tilt her face up to look into his eyes. Eyes so dark they appeared black. Right now they were filled with impatience and irritation.

"I'm afraid you're mistaken about that, Tex."

"I have some information about your wife," she said, determined not to let him intimidate her but it was difficult. The look in his eyes alone would frighten someone much larger than herself. She clutched the pepper spray can in her purse.

He was as big a man as she'd first thought, a few inches over six feet and broad at the shoulders. Solid looking, she thought. Not like a man who worked out. More like a man who worked. That surprised her given that selling bait and tackle couldn't be all that strenuous.

He settled those dark eyes on her. Everything about him was dark. She tried to imagine someone like Starr Calhoun with this man. Starr with her wild, curly auburn hair and those pale blue eyes, as fair as this man was dark.

"You're new here," Cade Jackson said as if roping in his irritation. "You don't know me. So I'm going to cut you some slack. I don't want another story about my wife's death. It's Christmas and I don't need any more reminders that she's gone, all right?"

"I think you'd better look at this," she said, slipping her hand from the pepper spray can to the copy of the photo taken from the bank's surveillance camera. It had gone out to all news media six years ago, but she doubted it had made it as far as Whitehorse, Montana.

Cade didn't take the photo she held out. He stood with his hands on his hips, dripping on the wood floor of the bait shop, the white towel barely wrapped around his hips showing way too much skin.

"Please. Just take a look and then I promise to leave," she said.

With obvious reluctance he took the copy of the photograph. She watched his expressive dark eyes. Recognition then confusion flashed in them. "What the hell is this?"

"It's your wife. Only her name wasn't Grace Browning. It was Starr Calhoun. That photo was taken by a surveillance camera in the bank she robbed six years ago—not long before she showed up here in Whitehorse."

"Get out," he said. "I don't know what your game is, Tex, but I'm not playing."

"Neither am I," she said as he reached for her arm. "Starr Calhoun was one of the infamous bank-robbing Calhouns from Texas," she said, dodging his grasp, her hand again clutching the can of pepper spray in her purse. "The three million dollars she and her male accomplice stole was never recovered."

"If you don't get out of here right now, you're going to be sorry," he said through gritted teeth. "What the hell do you keep reaching in that purse for?" He grabbed her arm.

As he jerked her hand out of the shoulder bag, her finger hit the trigger on the pepper spray.

ON THE LAPTOP propped up in her kitchen, Arlene Evans studied the latest applicant on her Meet-A-Mate site with pride as she whipped up a batch of pancakes.

Since she'd started her rural online dating service she'd had a few good-looking men sign up but none who could match Jud Corbett, a former stuntman and actor, who liked long walks in the rain, horseback riding, dancing in the moonlight and was interested in finding a nice cowgirl to ride off into the sunset with.

Arlene had proved she was a great matchmaker when she'd gotten the Whitehorse deputy sheriff together with that Cavanaugh girl.

But that was nothing compared to who she had picked out for the handsome Jud Corbett.

Her very own daughter Charlotte. True, Charlotte wasn't a cowgirl, so to speak, but she could ride a horse. And Jud Corbett was just what her daughter needed right now.

Charlotte had seemed a little down lately. But a man like Jud Corbett could bring her out of it quick!

The two would make beautiful children together, Arlene thought with longing as she broke a couple of eggs into the batter and stirred as she admired Jud Corbett's good looks. If she were twenty years younger...

"Are the pancakes about ready?" her son, Bo, demanded. At twenty-one, Bo had gotten his looks and personality from his father, damn Floyd Evans to hell.

Floyd had up and left them a few months ago. The divorce papers were somewhere on the overflowing coffee table. The bastard had left her with their three children to finish raising.

Not that the three weren't pretty much raised since the oldest, Violet, was in her thirties, unmarried and no longer under the roof, but that was another story. Bo was of legal age, although that didn't seem to mean anything other than he drank beer in front of her now. Charlotte had just celebrated her eighteenth birthday, eating most of the cake all by herself before going out with her friends and getting high.

The phone rang before Arlene could come up with a proper retort for her son. It rang another time but neither of her offspring seemed to hear it.

"Let me get that, why don't you?" Arlene said doubting they got her sarcasm, either, since neither seemed to hear anything over the blaring television.

"Mrs. Evans?" a woman said on the other end of the line.

Arlene didn't correct her. "I'm not buying anything," she snapped and started to hang up the phone.

"I'm calling about your daughter Violet."

Arlene put the receiver back to her ear. "Yes?" she asked suspiciously. Calls about Violet were never good.

"My name is Myrna Lynch, I'm the media coordinator here at the state hospital. Your daughter Violet would like you all to come up for Family Day."

"*Family* Day?" Arlene Evans echoed into the phone. "You can't be talking about my daughter. Violet is completely out of it and the last time I came up there to see her you guys wouldn't even let me in."

Arlene was still mad about that. As if she enjoyed driving clear up to the state mental hospital to be turned away.

"No one told you?" asked the woman whose name Arlene couldn't remember. "Your daughter Violet has made remarkable progress. She's no longer in a catatonic state."

"What are you saying? She's not nuts anymore?" How was that possible? "Did she tell you what she did to end up there?"

"Mental illness is a medical disorder that is treatable, Mrs. Evans. Your daughter is getting care that will let her be a responsible member of society again," the woman said, clearly upset at Arlene's use of the word *nuts*. "In order to do that, she needs to work through any issues she has with her family. So can I tell the doctor you and your family will be here Saturday?"

"Wait a minute. Issues? She tried to kill me!" Arlene bellowed.

"Your daughter doesn't recall any of that, Mrs. Evans."

Arlene just bet she didn't.

"Violet needs the support of her family. I'm sure you want to do what is best for her."

Arlene bristled at the woman's tone. "I've always supported Violet. You have no idea what I have done for that girl and what did I get for it? Why she—"

"Mrs. Evans, if you can't attend Family Day Saturday, then—"

"I'll be there," she said with a sigh.

"Violet has asked that her brother and sister also attend," the woman said.

Arlene glanced over at her daughter Charlotte curled up on the couch chewing on the end of her long blond hair. Bo was slouched in the recliner, a jumbo bag of corn chips open on his lap and an open can of beer at his elbow, in his own catatonic state as he stared at some reality show on the television where a woman was shrieking at one of the other contestants.

"Turn down the damned TV," Arlene yelled, covering the mouthpiece. "Can't you see I'm on the phone?"

Neither of her grown children responded.

"I have to bring Charlotte and Bo?" Arlene asked the woman, turning her back to the two. "I'm not sure it's a good idea for them to be around Violet."

"It's important for *Violet's* healing process."

"Well, whatever is important for Violet," Arlene snapped. "Never mind the rest of us. She really is better?"

"I think you will be surprised when you see her. We'll plan on your family Saturday."

Arlene hung up, wondering how Violet could surprise her more than she had. Her old-maid daughter had plotted to kill her and even gotten her brother and sister involved.

Arlene could never forgive Violet for that. She'd been so sure her daughter would never get out of the mental hospital and now this. *Family* Day.

Surely those fools at that hospital weren't really considering letting Violet out?

As she spooned the pancake batter into the smoking skillet, the scent of oil and sizzling pancake batter filled the kitchen and adjoining living room.

Behind her, Charlotte made an odd sound, then sprung up from the couch to run down the hall, her hand over her mouth. It was the fastest Arlene had seen the girl move in years. A moment later she heard Charlotte retching in the bathroom.

"What on earth is wrong with her?" Arlene demanded of her son.

He glanced away from the TV to scowl at his mother. "What do you think? She's pregnant. Haven't you noticed how big she's been getting? Where have you been?" He looked past her and swore. "Damn it, Mother, you're burning the pancakes!"

CADE JACKSON SWORE as he wrenched the can of pepper spray from Andi.

Unfortunately the spray nozzle had been pointed in the wrong direction—her direction. Fortunately only a little had shot out. Enough that her eyes instantly watered and she began to cough uncontrollably.

He grabbed her, cursing with each step as he tried to drag her to the back of his apartment. She fought him, although it was clearly a losing battle, unaware of what he was trying to do until he shoved her out the back door and into the fresh air.

She took huge gulps, tears running down her face as she coughed and tried to get the fresh air into her lungs.

He stood for a moment shaking his head, his arms crossed over his bare chest, his dark eyes boring into her.

"I think you're going to live," he said, giving her can of pepper spray a heave. It landed in the deep snow out by the trees along the Milk River and disappeared. "Now, get the hell off my porch."

He stepped back inside, not even looking chilled though still only wearing a towel, and slammed the door behind him. She heard the lock turn.

ON THE OTHER side of the door, Cade Jackson took a ragged breath and looked down at the grainy photograph still clutched in his hand.

It wasn't Grace. True it looked enough like her to be her twin. Enough like her to rattle the hell out of him.

The woman in the photograph, Starr Calhoun, had

robbed a bunch of banks and gotten away with three million dollars?

He wanted to laugh. Not for a minute would anyone believe that this Starr Calhoun was Grace except some wet-behind-the-ears reporter. It was beyond crazy.

He realized he was shaking. From anger. From shock. From the scare she'd given him. Earlier, for just a fleeting panicked instant, he'd thought the woman in the photo was Grace.

It was clear why the reporter had thought so as well as he took one last look at the photo. Even the poor quality print revealed a little of Grace in this woman and it shook him to his core. It was the eyes. She had Grace's eyes.

The reporter had made an honest mistake, he told himself as he balled up the photo of Starr Calhoun and tossed it in the trash can. The rumpled-up photograph landed on the note and business card the reporter had left the night before. M. W. Blake. He still wanted to break her pretty little neck for giving him such a scare. And that stunt with the pepper spray...

He shook his head as he returned to his apartment at the back of shop to get dressed. Someday he would look back on this and laugh. Let Tex wait by the phone. He wouldn't be calling her.

Still he felt shaken by the encounter. Anyone would have been rattled, though, he told himself, after being caught coming out of his shower first thing in the morning by someone like Ms. Blake. He'd foolishly left the shop's front door open after getting his newspaper this morning. Maybe he'd better start locking his apartment, as well.

When he'd first seen her standing there, he'd been a little surprised but he sure hadn't expected what was coming. Not from someone who looked like her, small, demure, sweet looking and sounding with that Texas accent of hers. And a determination that rivaled his own.

Too bad he couldn't shake off the worry that pressed on his chest like a two-ton truck. The woman wasn't foolish enough to run the story, was she?

As he started to leave, he went back into the shop to retrieve the photo, note and business card from the trash. Smoothing the photo, he felt his original jolt of surprise. He quickly folded the paper and stuck all three items in his coat pocket as he headed for the door again.

Cade would just show the photo to Carter, have him find out who this Starr Calhoun was and put an end to this foolishness before the reporter made a fool of herself and tarnished Grace's memory. That, after all, was the benefit of having a brother who was sheriff.

Cade glanced at his watch, knowing where to find his brother this time of the morning. At the same place he was seven days a week, the Hi-Line Café.

Leaving his closed sign in the window, Cade headed for the café just a few blocks to the west. It was one of those beautiful December days, cold and crisp, the sky a crystalline blue, the clouds mere wisps high above him and the new snow brilliant and blinding.

It was supposed to snow again by evening, he'd heard on the radio this morning before his shower. The shower brought back the image of M. W. Blake standing in his bait shop. He remembered now that his first impression had been one of male interest—before he'd found out who she was and what she wanted.

He recalled being a little taken aback by the sharp pang of desire he'd felt. But given how long it had been, he supposed he shouldn't have been surprised. The feeling had been more than lust, though. He'd actually been interested.

Even before she'd opened her mouth, it had been clear she wasn't local. She was wearing some fancy black boots with a gray pin-striped three-piece suit and a lightweight leather coat, her long dark hair pulled up to give him a good view of her long, graceful neck.

When she'd turned, he'd been thrown off guard by how young she was. It was the freckles she'd failed to completely hide with makeup and those wide green eyes. Wisps of dark hair curled on each side of the high cheekbones. She was a stunner. The soft Southern drawl was just icing on the cake.

He swore under his breath. She wasn't even half as appealing when it turned out she was a damned reporter, though. And it had only gotten worse when he realized she was a reporter who didn't have her facts straight. What could he expect of someone who was obviously too young to be anything but a rookie?

As he passed the big bare-limbed cottonwoods along the Milk River etching dark against the bright day, he thought of the fall day he'd met Grace and felt a sharp jab of longing.

The woman in the photo hadn't been Grace, but even the resemblance to her made him hurt all over again. He cursed the damned reporter all the way to the café.

Sheriff Carter Jackson was sitting at the counter. Cade dropped onto the stool next to him and motioned to the waitress that he would have the same thing he always did. Coffee.

"Good mornin'," he said to his brother as the waitress slid a cup in front of him.

"Is it?" the sheriff said.

The waitress brought Cade extra sugar packets. He tore open a half dozen and poured them into his cup.

"If you don't like coffee, why drink it?" Carter asked irritably.

"Who says I don't like coffee?" He poured in most of the small pitcher of milk the waitress brought and glanced at his brother, wondering what had put Carter in such a foul mood. He suspected he knew. Eve Bailey.

Carter had been trying to get Eve back for months now. They'd dated in high school but Carter had married someone else. Now divorced, he wasn't finding Eve Bailey very forgiving. Not that Cade could blame her, although it was clear his brother had always loved her.

"You're up early," Carter said, eyeing him. "What's goin' on with you?"

Cade had planned to show his brother the photo of Starr Calhoun and tell him about the ridiculous claim made by the new reporter in town. But something stopped him.

"Nothin'," Cade said. "Just thought I'd join you for a cup of coffee this morning."

His brother turned now to stare at him. "You sure you're all right?"

"Don't I look all right?" Cade shot back.

"You look a little peaked."

Cade concentrated on his coffee, telling himself he was a fool not to show his brother the Wanted poster and put an end to this. So what was holding him back?

"You're usually out in your ice-fishing house by now," Carter said, sounding suspicious. That also went with having a sheriff for a brother.

"I haven't got my house out yet," he said, although that had been his plan just this morning. Before his early visit from Tex. Normally as soon as Nelson Reservoir froze over he would be on the ice.

"I heard Harvey Alderson speared a nice northern pike the other day," Carter said.

Cade nodded. "The photo's already on the wall at the shop." Harvey had come straight there to have his photograph taken. It was a Whitehorse tradition.

"Maybe you're starting to realize there is more to life than fishing," his brother said, sounding as if he thought that was progress.

On any other day Cade might have argued the point. "So how is Eve?"

"She's impossible as ever," Carter groused. "And I don't want to talk about her."

Cade laughed as he watched his brother wolf down his breakfast and between bites, go on and on about Eve. Some things didn't change and today Cade was damned glad of it.

ANDI FINISHED HER story on the Parade of Lights and laid out the page for the next day's edition, trying to keep busy.

She'd expected Cade to call. He hadn't.

Wouldn't a man who'd been given evidence that his wife was a known criminal call? Unless he'd already known and was sitting over in his bait shop planning how to keep her from telling another living soul.

She slammed the drawer on the filing cabinet and cursed mildly under her breath. It was time to use her ace in the hole: the cassette tape.

It was dangerous, but once he heard the voice on the tape, he would confirm that the voice was Starr Calhoun's and she would have the proof she needed. She hoped that faced with even more evidence and his own innocence in all this, he would break down and tell her everything about his relationship with Starr.

Unless of course he wasn't innocent.

Andi couldn't help the rush of excitement she felt at just the thought of playing the copy of the tape she'd made for him. Maybe she should have told him about the tape when she'd shown him the photo.

No, she thought, given how angry he'd been she doubted he would have listened to the tape. He had needed time to calm down, to let it sink in, to realize he couldn't hide from the truth.

Right. But how was she going to get him to listen to the tape if he refused to talk to her again? The man was obviously more stubborn than she had anticipated. She'd been convinced, guilty or innocent, he wouldn't be able to rest until he heard her out. So much for that thought.

She sighed as she sat down and checked her schedule. She didn't have another story to cover for several days. The newspaper would hit the stands in the morning and she would have a whole week before the next edition. She couldn't believe how laid-back weekly newspaper work was compared to broadcast news in a metropolitan city.

But it would work out well for her. She'd need time to mine this story. Time to convince Cade Jackson to talk to her.

That was the problem. To get the story she wanted, she needed Cade's side of it. She needed to know how he and Starr had met, how she'd deceived him into marrying her.

Andi felt a twinge of guilt. Cade hadn't just been furious this morning. He'd seemed stunned. Even though he denied the photo was of his wife, she'd seen his shock. He'd recognized Starr.

What would his reaction be when he heard his wife's voice on the tape, callously planning the bank robberies with her accomplice? Unless, of course, Cade *was* her accomplice.

No, the man caught on the bank surveillance cameras had pale blue eyes. Cade Jackson had dark, expressive eyes. Nor was he built like Starr's accomplice.

If Cade Jackson was involved, then it was from the sidelines. Which didn't mean he hadn't known who his wife really was—or that he didn't know what had happened to the robbery money.

A thought struck her like a bolt out of the blue. How badly *had* Starr deceived him? Hadn't the article in the newspaper about her death said that the car had rolled numerous times before catching fire? Her body had apparently burned beyond recognition.

What if Starr had faked her death just as Andi had first suspected? What if she was somewhere living off that three mil with her accomplice? Then who had been killed in the car wreck?

Mind racing, Andi realized the pieces still didn't fit. Lubbock was out of prison and missing. But whoever had sent her the job information about Whitehorse knew she had information about Lubbock's arrest in Montana. That meant the person knew about her interest in the Calhoun family. Might even know about her connection to the Calhouns.

She groaned, realizing how that was possible. A few years back, she'd driven over to the prison where Amarillo Calhoun had been sentenced. The eldest of the Calhoun children, Amarillo had followed in his parents' footsteps, his life of crime going from bank robbing to murder.

She'd seen him sitting in the glassed-in cubicle. Their eyes had met. He must have recognized her because he told the guard he didn't want to speak with her—backing out on their interview. Her face had been all over the TV news. She'd just broken a big news story. That was right before she'd gotten her newscaster job in Fort Worth.

So it was possible Lubbock knew who she was and why she would jump at digging into this story.

If her friend Bradley was right, then Lubbock was after the missing money. Or Starr *and* the money, if she'd faked her death. Or there was Houston Calhoun, who'd disappeared the same time as Starr.

Clearly if Lubbock had left her the tape and newspaper clipping, he wasn't interested in the truth coming out. And he wasn't the only one, Andi thought. Cade Jackson wouldn't want a story about his wife being Starr Calhoun, the bank robber, hitting the news, either, she thought, remembering the look on his face when he'd recognized the woman on the Wanted poster. If he'd loved his wife as much as he appeared to, what would the truth do to him?

She pushed the thought away. She'd never backed down from a story and wasn't going to now. The best stories rose out of someone's pain. This was one of those stories.

A niggling concern wormed its way into her thoughts, though. Whoever was sending her the information was playing her like a marionette until he got what he wanted. Then what?

Her phone rang, making her jump.

"Hello?"

Silence.

"Hello?" she said again, feeling suddenly spooked. Lubbock?

Then to her relief, Cade said, "It's me." He didn't sound happy about it, though.

She waited, suspecting he was sorry he'd called and might even hang up.

"I need to see you," he said gruffly.

"All right. Do you want me to—"

"I'm right outside."

CHAPTER FOUR

CADE WATCHED MIRANDA BLAKE come out of the newspaper office. She had to be freezing. The temperature was still hovering around zero. Another snowstorm was expected before evening. And here she was dressed like she was still in Texas.

Didn't she notice that no one dressed up in Montana let alone in Whitehorse? And she had to be kidding in those high-heeled boots that certainly were never intended for walking on ice and snow.

He reached across to open the passenger-side door, shaking his head. What the hell was he thinking? He should have just told her what he had to say on the phone. At least he'd left the pickup running. He'd make this quick.

There was a regal air about her that set his teeth on edge as she climbed in and smoothed her suit skirt. She'd brought along an old-fashioned black boom box. What the hell was that about? He turned up the heat, furious with himself for doing this. Why hadn't he left well enough alone?

Because he knew M. W. Blake sure as hell wasn't going to.

"I just wanted to tell you that you're wrong," he said, looking out at the snowy day through the windshield. He'd just have his say, then get on his way. "That woman in the photo isn't Grace. Admittedly it resembles her. It sure sent me for a loop." He cleared his throat. "But if you'd known her, you'd know that she wasn't some bank robber and you would have realized your mistake."

She didn't say anything and he was finally forced to look over at her.

"It was an honest mistake, I'm sure," he said. "I just didn't want you doing a story and having to retract it. Nor am I looking for an apology."

She laughed softly. "Well, that's good because I wasn't going to give you one. You're the one who's mistaken."

He jerked off his Stetson and raked a hand through his hair. This woman was impossible. "I'm telling you that photo isn't of Grace."

"No, it's of Starr Calhoun, the woman you married," she said in that sweet Southern drawl of hers.

He slapped his hat back on his head and gave the pickup a little gas as he gripped the wheel to keep from strangling the damned woman. "I don't know why I bothered to come by and try to talk sense into you, Tex."

The inside of the pickup cab was warm and smelled of the soap he'd used that morning in the shower. Andi recognized the pleasant scent. "My name is Miranda and you came by to see me because you recognized her and whether you want to admit it or not, you want to know the truth about the woman you knew as Grace Browning."

"Like hell, Tex," he snapped.

As intimidating as he was, she turned to face him. "You can't keep me from doing the story."

"Maybe I can't keep you from making a fool of yourself, but I can sure as hell keep you from involving me in it." He shifted the pickup into gear and gave her a pointed look. "You and I don't have any more to say to each other."

"You're wrong about that. You *are* involved," she said calmly as he reached across and opened her door. A blast of freezing air rushed in.

"Maybe, but you'll have to do your story without my help," he snapped.

"Then I guess you'll have to hear the truth with the rest of the town when it comes out in my article." She started to get out. "Oh, by the way, you should know I'm not the only one who knows about your wife's true identity. Someone sent me a newspaper clipping about her death along with a cassette tape of Starr Calhoun and her male accomplice planning the bank robberies. Want to make a bet it's your wife's voice on the tape?"

He swore and looked away for a moment before he said, "When were you going to tell me about the tape?" He sounded scared and she felt again that prickle of guilt that she was about to destroy this man's life.

"When I thought you could handle it."

He cut his eyes to her, his expression one of anger and fear. He let out a humorless laugh. "And you think I can handle it *now*?"

CADE TOLD HIMSELF that the tape would prove this woman was wrong and that would be the end of it. Not that he didn't realize she was banking on the tape proving just the opposite.

"Fine, let's hear the tape," he said, and reached across her to slam her door.

"I think the sound quality would be better without your pickup truck's engine running in the background, don't you? Also the player's batteries are low. I need to plug it in."

He didn't really want to take her back to his apartment behind the bait shop, but he had little choice. He much preferred doing this on his own turf. And the newspaper office was out. Anyone could come walking in. He sure as hell didn't want an audience.

Pulling out, he flipped a U-turn in the middle of the main street and headed back toward the bait shop.

One of the benefits of living in Whitehorse was the lack of traffic. But today he would have loved a traffic jam. Anything to postpone this.

It wasn't that he feared the voice would be Grace's. All this talk of Grace had brought back the pain. He just wanted to hide as he'd done the last six holidays. He didn't need to see more photographs of women who reminded him of Grace. Or hear some woman's voice that might sound even a little like his dead wife's.

But clearly Miranda Blake wasn't going to give him any peace. Not until he proved her wrong. He glanced over at her, worried about her apparent calm. Did she know something he didn't?

"PREGNANT?" ARLENE EVANS cried as she threw the spatula at her son.

"Why are you yelling at me? Charlotte's the one who got knocked up, not me," he said and picked up the remote to turn up the sound on the TV.

Arlene grabbed the skillet, tossing the burned pancakes in the trash and turning off the burner before she wiped off her hands and stormed down the hallway.

She wished she were Catholic because she had the

strongest urge to cross herself. First Violet and that disgrace and now Charlotte? She couldn't bear it.

Tapping lightly at the bathroom door, she said, "Charlotte, precious, can I come in?"

"No!" Then more retching and the *whoosh* of the toilet as it flushed.

"Open this damned door now or I will break it down," Arlene yelled.

The door opened slowly and Charlotte's bloated face appeared.

Arlene had seen her daughter getting heavier by the day and had just assumed it was all the sweets the girl put away. Violet had always had a weight problem and Arlene hadn't known how to deal with it. She'd told herself that Charlotte, who'd always been slim, would outgrow it.

"What do you want?" Charlotte asked irritably.

Arlene pushed open the bathroom door and stepped in, closing it behind her. She spoke carefully, determined not to lose her temper. "Aren't you feeling well?"

Her daughter gave her a withering look.

"Your brother seems to think you're pregnant but how is that possible?"

Another withering look. Arlene fought the urge to smack the look off her youngest daughter's face.

"You're pregnant?" Her voice broke. One daughter in the nuthouse and one pregnant out of wedlock. She'd never be able to hold her head up in this county again.

Charlotte didn't answer, just looked down at her stomach as she smoothed her large sweatshirt over her protruding stomach.

Arlene was stunned. "Good heavens, how far along are you?"

Her daughter shrugged. "Four months, I think."

Arlene stumbled over to the toilet, dropped the lid and sat. "*Four* months? Four *months* and you don't say a word? What were you thinking?"

Charlotte was still looking down at her stomach as if admiring it.

"Who is the father? Tell me who he is and the two of you can run down to Vegas. No one has to know you didn't get married four months ago."

"I'm not getting married."

Arlene stared at her daughter. Lately Charlotte had been reminding her more and more of Violet, an unpleasant similarity at best. "Of course you're getting married."

Charlotte raised her gaze. "Not likely since he's already married," she said with a chuckle.

Arlene thought she'd have a stroke and imagined the paramedics hauling her out of the bathroom on a stretcher. As if her life wasn't already humiliating enough.

She willed herself not to have a stroke. "Who is he?" She would castrate him. Then kill him.

Charlotte shook her head. "I'm not telling you. I'm never telling you." She gave Arlene a challenging look. "And there is nothing you can do to make me tell."

THE CLOSED SIGN was still in the front window of Jackson Bait Shop and no customers out front waiting, Cade noticed with relief as he pulled around to the back and got out.

The reporter followed him, bringing along that huge shoulder bag of hers and the boom box. He opened the rear door and stepped aside, clenching his jaw as he let her pass. Now that he was here, he just wanted this over with—and as quickly as possible.

"I don't have a lot of time," he said.

She smiled at that no doubt noticing that there hadn't been a crowd of fishermen beating down his door this morning. But she walked right to his kitchen table and set down the boom box.

He wondered if she had retrieved the can of pepper spray from the snowbank out back or bought more as he watched her plug in the boom box and then produce a tape from her pocket. She dropped the cassette tape into the player and lifted a brow in his direction.

He sighed and stepped over to the table to pull out a chair. Swinging it around, he straddled it and sat down, resting his arms on the back as he gave her an impatient nod. "Let's get this over with."

She hit Play.

At first all he heard was static. The sound was like scraping a fingernail down a blackboard and he flinched, his nerves on edge. He tried to find calm, to breathe. This would be over soon. And yet his heart thudded in his chest with an apprehension that scared him as much as the impossible thought he could have been wrong about Grace.

The static and whir of the tape stopped abruptly with the sound of a female voice.

His heart stopped as well, as he heard a voice from the grave. He tried to catch his breath, his pulse a bass drum in his ears and his limbs numb with a bone-aching chill that rattled through him.

The woman across from him hadn't missed his reaction. Hell, she'd been expecting it. His blood ran colder than the Milk River outside his door and he thought for a moment that he might black out.

There was no doubt about it. The voice on the tape

was Grace's. Staggered, he hadn't even heard what she was saying. But slowly, the words began to register.

And just when he thought it couldn't get any worse, he heard another voice, this one male, as the two planned what banks they would rob and in what order.

There was no denying it. The woman he'd married six years ago and lost wasn't who he thought she was.

He stood, knocking over the chair as he lunged at the table to shut off the tape player.

"There's more that you might want to hear," the reporter said.

"Not now." His voice felt as rough as it sounded. "Please go. I need to be alone."

She started to collect the big black tape player.

"Leave it. I'll make sure you get it back."

Her gaze locked with his. "I made a copy of the tape."

"I was sure you had."

She seemed to hesitate, but then rose slowly, all the time watching him as if worried he might come unglued on her.

"I'm fine," he said a little sharper than he'd meant to.

She nodded but didn't look convinced. He figured he probably looked as horrible as he felt.

"Call me when you're ready to talk."

He walked over to the door, opened it and stood waiting, not looking at her. He was afraid of what he'd do if she didn't leave soon.

"Take my truck," he said, removing the keys from his pocket and holding them out to her.

"It's not far, I'll walk."

"Suit yourself."

She stepped out and he slammed the door, leaning against it as he fought to breathe. Grace. Her memory blurred in his mind and he knew even if he pretended this had never happened, Grace Browning was lost to him. More lost than she'd been even in death.

He lurched forward, slamming into the bathroom to be sick.

THERE WAS NOTHING Arlene Evans enjoyed more than a mission. Finding the father of Charlotte's baby was now at the top of her list.

"Take a shower, you smell," she told her daughter as she left the bathroom and walked down the hall.

The television was so loud it made the old windows in the farmhouse rattle. Arlene walked calmly over to where her son slouched in the chair. She picked up the remote and pressed Off.

"What the hell?" Bo demanded, sitting up.

She shoved him back down, snatching the bag of chips off his lap and carefully folding the top down before she put the bag aside. "Who is the father of that baby?"

"You're asking *me*? Why don't you ask her?"

Arlene wet her lips. She liked to think of herself as one of those patient mothers.

"I'm asking you, Bo. Now, please tell me. Who has she been with?" Arlene tried again calmly.

"Who hasn't she been with?" he said with a laugh.

Arlene hadn't meant to smack him. If she had, she would have cuffed him harder.

He recoiled, looking hurt and angry, even though she'd barely touched him.

"She said the man is *married*."

"So?"

"I would think that would narrow the field some,"

Arlene snapped. "Now, think. You're going to help me with this."

Bo groaned and reached for the chips.

Arlene held them out of his reach. "I'm going to make you some pancakes and when I'm done, I expect some names."

ANDI WALKED BACK to her office, the frigid winter air like a slap in the face. The snowstorm moved in before she'd traveled a block. She welcomed it. She was still shaken by Cade's reaction to the voice on the tape—even though she'd known it had to be the woman he'd known as Grace Browning.

The look on his face, the shocked horror, the devastation. If Andi had wondered how he felt about his wife, she didn't anymore. His stricken face had been filled with pain and anguish. Sticking a knife in his heart might have been less painful.

She shivered from the cold, glad she had only a few blocks to go. The fact that she'd been right—Grace Browning *had* been Starr Calhoun—gave her little satisfaction. She glanced back toward the bait shop, hoping Cade was all right, wishing he wasn't alone, a little afraid of what he might do.

Not that she had any choice but to leave. She'd known better than to argue with him. He'd already thrown her out once today.

Afraid he's going to off himself before you get the rest of the story?

She bristled, hating that he'd been hurt. But he'd needed to hear the truth. It wasn't as if this all wouldn't come out even if she didn't do the story.

Not that this wasn't going to be an amazing story and

it wouldn't do even more amazing things for her career. She would get national recognition.

But that really wasn't the point. She wasn't doing this story for her career. This one was personal and she'd see it through till the end—no matter how difficult this was for Cade.

Clearly he hadn't moved on with his life since his wife had died. Once this was over, maybe he finally could.

When Andi looked at it that way, she was doing him a favor.

Nice spin, her irritating conscience noted sarcastically.

"I haven't gotten where I am today by backing down from a story," she snapped, her words lost in a gust of wind and snow.

Yeah, just look where you are.

She told herself that she refused to feel guilty for doing her job and walked a little faster, the earlier chill no longer refreshing.

By the time she reached the newspaper office her teeth were chattering. The air shimmered with snowflakes that whirled around her as if she was inside a snow globe.

She opened the door and hurriedly ducked inside. Immediately she saw that she had the office to herself. Without sitting down at her desk, she pulled out her cell phone and dialed Bradley's number.

"I've been on pins and needles waiting to hear from you," he said without preamble. "Did he hear the tape? What was his reaction?"

"He was devastated," she said, surprised how close she was to tears. "Until he heard her voice, I don't think he believed she was Starr Calhoun."

"So he really didn't know?"

"No. I just feel so badly for him."

"Let me guess. He's ruggedly handsome."

She shook her head, smiling a little. "He's good-looking, if that's what you're asking, but that has nothing to do with—"

"You feeling sorry for him. Right?"

"He loved her. From what I can gather, he hasn't even dated since she died. Everyone in town who I've mentioned his name to has told me he became a recluse after he lost her."

"So you have a great story," Bradley said.

"Yeah, I guess."

"Excuse me, that isn't you getting emotionally involved, is it? Miss Hard-Core News Reporter."

"He's a victim of the Calhouns. I can relate."

"Yes, I guess you can. I guess when the story breaks it will be a form of justice for you both then."

She smiled ruefully. She'd always suspected he knew her connection to the Calhouns. His comment confirmed it. "You always know what to say." She spotted Shirley heading back to the office. "I have to go. I'll call you." She snapped off her phone and walked to her desk.

It wasn't until she was taking off her coat that she saw the envelope on her desk. Manila, with her name and address neatly typed on the front. Nothing else. Just like the last one.

CHAPTER FIVE

WITH CHARLOTTE STILL refusing to divulge the name of the baby's father and Bo, it turned out, knowing little or nothing about his sister's "friends," Arlene was forced to do her own investigating.

Four months ago her daughter had worked at the Whitehorse nursing home. Arlene realized that she'd been remiss in not visiting one of Old Town Whitehorse's leading citizens. The Cavanaughs were as close to royalty as it came in Old Town, and Pearl Cavanaugh was the queen. A few months ago she'd had a stroke and had gone into the home for a while.

Pearl's husband, Titus, still ran Old Town and Whitehorse and half the county if the truth was known. He did everything from preach at the community church to organize every Old Town event. Arlene had heard that he spent hours at his wife's bedside.

Not prone to jealousy, Arlene still couldn't curb her irritation. How had Pearl gotten a man like that when Arlene had gotten *Floyd*? Life wasn't fair, that was for sure, she thought as she pushed open the door to the nursing home carrying the Christmas cactus she'd bought for Pearl.

Arlene asked directions to Pearl's room. She passed Bertie Cavanaugh who scowled at her as she slunk down the hall. The woman always looked guilty.

As she passed Nina Mae Cross's room, Arlene stopped to say hello to McKenna and Faith Bailey who were visiting their grandmother—not that Nina Mae had a clue who they were. Alzheimer's, Arlene had heard.

"I sent you an email," Arlene told McKenna. "I'm still looking for the perfect man for you."

The cactus was getting heavy so she hurried on down to Pearl's, anxious now to get this over with.

She'd checked out the staff on her way and was disappointed to find that most of the people who worked here were female. The new doctor in town was practically a baby himself—and single. And the one male orderly was anything but her daughter's type.

To Arlene's surprise, Pearl was sitting in a wheelchair by the window. When had she gotten well enough for a wheelchair? She turned as Arlene entered the room.

"Pearl," Arlene said loudly. "How are you?"

"Her hearing is fine," said a male voice behind her.

Arlene turned to find Bridger Duvall standing in the doorway. He moved to Pearl's side. "She can understand you but she's having a little trouble talking, aren't you, Pearl?" He took the elderly woman's hand in both of his and gently stroked the pale skin.

Pearl smiled, a lopsided smile but nonetheless a smile, shocking Arlene.

"I didn't realize you knew Pearl," she said. After all, Bridger Duvall was a mystery. No one really knew who he was or why he'd come here. He'd opened a restaurant in town with Laci Cavanaugh, Pearl's granddaughter.

That, Arlene realized, must explain this odd friendship.

"I brought you a cactus," Arlene said to Pearl, enunciating each word carefully.

"How thoughtful," Bridger said, taking it from Arlene to place the plant over by the window.

"She's certainly doing well." The last Arlene had heard Pearl was paralyzed and unresponsive. Now she looked alert. But then Pearl Cavanaugh had always been a sharp old broad.

"I just stopped by to say hello," Bridger said, returning to Pearl's side. "Laci and I are cooking for parties all month. Not that we're complaining. Business has been good."

Pearl smiled up at him and said something Arlene couldn't understand.

"I'll give Laci your love. She's busy baking Christmas cookies. She'll be bringing some down to the staff. You know how she is."

What could have been a chuckle arose from Pearl.

As Bridger started to leave, Arlene said, "I'll walk out with you." She waved over her shoulder at Pearl. "Glad to see you're doing so well."

Once out in the hall, Arlene said to him, "You spend a lot of time here? You might know my daughter, Charlotte."

He nodded.

"I was wondering if you've seen her with anyone, you know, a man, romantically, you understand?"

From the look on his face, he understood perfectly. "I'm sorry, but I wouldn't know anything about that. Now, if you'll excuse me."

As Arlene watched him hurry away, she looked back at Pearl. The old gal had a sympathetic look on her face. There was nothing Arlene Evans hated worse than pity, she thought, as she hurried down the hall and out into the cold December day.

ANDI STARED AT the envelope on her desk for a long moment. Then she put her coat on the back of her chair and, rubbing her freezing hands together, sat down. Like her coat and boots, her gloves were a thin leather that had been perfect for winters in Fort Worth.

Gingerly she picked up the envelope, turning it in her fingers. No return address, of course. No clue as to who might have sent it.

Shirley, the newspaper receptionist/bookkeeper, had stopped outside to talk to a passerby.

The newspaper had little staff, just Shirley and several columnists who stopped by on occasion. The only time the office was busy was when the publisher and his oldest daughter put the paper together the night before it came out.

Shirley was a grandmother who only worked part-time. Most of that time she was next door at the coffee shop. Apparently everyone in town knew where to find her if they needed anything.

With a sigh, Andi took out her letter opener and sliced the envelope open. Inside was another newspaper clipping. Andi unfolded it, flattening it, then turned the clipping over, frowning.

On one side was an article about Kid Curry's last holdup in the Whitehorse area. On the other side was an ad for tractors. What could this possibly have to do with Starr Calhoun or Grace Browning?

Shirley entered with a latte and fry bread from the shop next door. "Oh, if I'd known you were here I would have brought you something." She was tiny with white hair and small brown eyes.

"Thank you, but I'm fine," Andi said.

Shirley saw the article lying on the desk and smiled.

"You like our colorful history?" she asked. "Kid Curry and his brothers hung out up here for a while. Had a place to the south."

"Really?" Andi couldn't imagine what that had to do with Starr Calhoun and the missing bank robbery money.

Shirley quickly warmed to her subject. "This area was home to many an outlaw. It was the last lawless part of the state. You might be surprised how wild this town used to be. Why, one of the outlaws' six-guns is on display at the museum. Can't think of his name right now and my fry bread is getting cold, but you should check it out."

"I'll do that," Andi promised.

As Shirley hurried to her desk in the back, Andi dug out the first envelope she'd received. She compared the type on both. Identical. Sent no doubt by the same person. Both postmarked Whitehorse.

But what was the connection to Kid Curry? Other than they were all outlaws?

A thought struck her and she wondered why she hadn't considered it before. Was it possible Houston was still in Whitehorse? He could have done what Starr did, found someone, gotten married under an alias and was still living here.

Although if Houston was behind this, she had to wonder why he'd waited six years. Lubbock had been in prison until just recently so the timing made more sense.

She told herself that she didn't care who was pulling her strings. All she cared about was the story. But even as she thought it, she knew that eventually she'd find out who was behind the information being fed to her. And what that person wanted from her.

Folding up the newspaper clipping she shoved it back

into the envelope and put it with the other one in her drawer.

"Shirley?" Andi called as she reached for her coat. "If anyone wants me, I'll be at the museum learning about Whitehorse's infamous past."

CADE COULDN'T MOVE, couldn't breathe. He dropped into a chair at the table and covered his face with his hands, telling himself this wasn't happening. Not after six years of grieving. Not after he was finally coming to grips with losing Grace.

Too stunned to hear or feel anything, the hammering at the front door of the shop didn't register for a while. Not that he would have opened the door even if he had heard it before the knocking abruptly stopped.

He stared at the tape player but didn't touch the play button. Not after hearing it three more times. Each time he thought the voice wouldn't be Grace's. Each time, he prayed it wouldn't.

Each time it was.

He heard the crunch of snow outside, then the rattle of the knob as someone tried the back door only to find it locked, something nearly unheard of in Whitehorse.

"Cade?"

At the concern he heard in his brother's voice, Cade rose and went to unlock the door.

One glance at Carter's expression and he knew he must look like hell.

"What's wrong? It isn't Dad, is it?"

Cade shook his head. "Everyone's fine."

His brother came in, closing the door behind him. "Everyone's not fine. You were acting weird at breakfast. And now you look like your best friend died. What's going on?" He glanced toward the large black tape player on the table, the worry in his expression deepening.

"I need a favor," Cade said, knowing his brother. Carter would keep after him until he gave him at least a plausible explanation.

"Are you in some kind of trouble?"

He shook his head. "A *couple* of favors actually. There's a new reporter in town from Texas. Her name's Miranda Blake. She goes by M. W. Blake."

"This is about a *woman*?" Carter asked incredulously. He laughed, looking relieved.

"I hate to ask but could you see what you can find out about her?"

Carter was smiling. "You had me scared. You looked so horrible, I thought…" He quit smiling and shook his head. "I thought for sure someone had died."

"There is something else," Cade said. "It's about Grace."

His brother instantly looked worried. "Grace?" He seemed to be holding his breath.

Carter had once asked him what it was about Grace that Cade couldn't forget. "Everything," he'd said. *"Everything."*

"I want to close that chapter on my life," Cade said now, meaning it more than he thought possible.

His brother's relief was palpable. After the first couple of years when Cade couldn't seem to get over Grace's death, Carter had become concerned.

"I'm worried about you," he'd said. "I'm afraid you're never going to get over this."

Cade had smiled ruefully. "I don't think I am."

"In order to move on," Cade said now. "I need to find out if Grace's parents are still alive."

"I thought she said they were dead?" Carter asked in obvious surprise.

"That's what she told me, but I learned something recently that makes me wonder," he said. "Could you see what you can find out? I don't want to contact them, I just want to find out if what Grace told me was true."

"Grace have a middle name?" Carter asked, pulling out his notebook and pen. Cade had known his brother would do anything to get him to move on with his life.

"Eden," Cade said.

His brother looked up. "Eden? Like in Adam and Eve?"

Cade shrugged. "I guess so. Her birthday was July 4, 1974."

"Birthplace?"

"Los Angeles, California."

Carter looked up and frowned. "No kidding? I always thought she was born in the South. I wonder where she picked up the accent?"

"Accent?"

"You never noticed her accent?" Carter laughed. "It only came out when she was upset. Like that time you got thrown from the horse. When we were at the hospital waiting for the doctor to tell us how bad it was, I could really hear her Southern accent." He frowned. "Wait a minute. This new reporter..." He glanced at his notes. "She's from Texas?" He swore. "She's got a Southern accent, too?" He looked at Cade with suspicion.

"She's nothing like Grace," Cade said quickly. "And anyway, Grace didn't have a Southern accent."

Carter raised a brow. "You never noticed it?"

"No." He realized that wasn't quite true. A few times he had picked up an accent, but she'd said her father was in the military and they'd spent some time in Alabama when she was young. He'd noticed after that how she seemed to do everything she could to hide it.

Carter put away his notebook and pen and placed a hand on Cade's shoulder. "Don't worry, bro. I'll find out what I can. You didn't say what you heard that made you think Grace's parents were still alive."

Cade shook his head, hating that he was lying to his brother. But he wasn't ready to talk about this. Maybe he was still holding on to the hope that there had been a Grace Browning. Another woman besides Starr Calhoun who looked and sounded just like his wife.

"I saw a couple on CNN," Cade said. "Their name was Browning. They lived in Los Angeles and were about the right ages. I swear they looked enough like Grace that they could have been her parents. It just seemed like too much of a coincidence. I know it's crazy."

He saw that his brother agreed. "Heck, why not check it out? I'll let you know what I find," Carter said as he headed for the door. He stopped and glanced back at Cade. "Does it matter if her parents are still alive or not? I mean, are you sure you want to dig up the past?"

"To me Grace was perfect, you know? But the truth is I sensed that she wasn't telling me something about her past. I guess if I found out that she'd lied about her parents being dead it would make it easier to let go for good," Cade said, knowing his brother would buy this explanation.

Carter nodded. "Speaking of favors… I have one to ask of you."

Cade braced himself. He hoped this wasn't about Christmas. He wouldn't be having any happy holidays this year.

"The families are getting together Christmas Eve at Northern Lights restaurant," Carter said. The families being the Jacksons and the Baileys.

"Yeah, about that…" Cade said quickly. "I'm probably not going to make that."

Carter looked upset. "Not good enough. Not this year. You have to come."

"Maybe I could drop by—"

"Cade, you've missed Christmas now for six years. You can't this year. It's important. The truth is I need you there."

Cade stared at his brother. "You're going to ask Eve to marry you."

Carter gave an embarrassed laugh. "Am I that transparent? Yeah, I am and I need as much of the family there as I can get. Less chance she'll say no."

"She won't say no. She loves you."

"I mean it, Cade, I need you there. You can bring the reporter if that's what you want."

Cade swore silently. "Naw, that's all right. I'll be there."

"Thanks, I really need the moral support." Carter didn't ask why Cade hadn't wanted to come originally. He'd probably just assumed that it was because of Grace. He had no idea just how true that was.

"So you've bought the ring I assume?" Cade asked.

"Dad gave me Mother's," he said a little sheepishly.

Of course Dad would have given it to Carter, their mother's favorite. "Cool," Cade said. "That's great."

"Dad didn't think you'd mind." Carter stepped to him, surprised Cade by pulling him into a hug. "I've missed you, bro. It's good that you'll be there this Christmas."

Cade felt bad that he'd been a recluse for the past six

years. He'd burrowed in with his pain, just wanting to be alone to grieve.

He'd been so much better this year. Until that damned reporter had shown up.

Carter drew back looking a little embarrassed. "Okay. I'll see what I can do about finding Grace's parents." He smiled. "And I'll also check on the new reporter for you. I've heard she's a stunner."

"She is that," Cade agreed. She sure as hell stunned him.

CHAPTER SIX

THE WHITEHORSE MUSEUM was housed in a small building on the edge of town. A couple of elderly ladies were behind the desk as Andi entered.

They greeted her warmly.

"Are you doing a story on our museum?" the shorter of the two asked. "She's the new reporter at the *Examiner*," the woman informed her coworker who nodded.

Andi couldn't help being amused. So few newcomers moved to Whitehorse that apparently she stood out even before she opened her mouth. The way news traveled in this town, she wondered why they even bothered with a newspaper.

On the way to the museum, she'd driven by the bait shop and seen a sheriff's department patrol car parked out front. That worried her. She had no idea what Cade would do.

Had he called his brother and told him about Starr Calhoun? she wondered, as she paid her admission price and wandered through exhibits that chronicled everything from the story of the hundreds of thousands of buffalo that had roamed this prairie to the coming of the railroad and the birth of present day Whitehorse.

She found the outlaw exhibit at the back. Apparently Shirley was right. This part of Montana had remained lawless late into the 1800s. Along with Kid Curry,

Whitehorse had seen Butch Cassidy, the Sundance Kid and other less known outlaws. It had been a place of murder and mayhem. Curry had been the leader of the notorious Wild Bunch, was alleged to have killed ten men, although it was said he'd grown up reading the Bible.

According to the museum exhibit, there'd been Western holdup artists, bank robbers, road agents, killers and railroad thieves.

While interesting, Andi was wondering what something that had happened so long ago had to do with Starr Calhoun when she spotted a name that leaped out at her. It was in the part of the exhibit detailing an outlaw named Long Henry Thompson.

Long Henry was credited with having belonged to the Henry Starr gang out of Texas that robbed everything they could, along with stealing livestock on the Texan-Mexican border. Long Henry, wanted in Texas for these crimes, had allegedly hired on to bring cattle to Montana along with some others from the Starr gang.

Andi had heard of Henry Starr. He was descended from the Starr criminal dynasty that began with Tom "Giant" Starr and his son Sam.

Hadn't she read somewhere that Hodge and Eden Calhoun had named their daughter Starr after the famous Henry Starr criminal family that had operated in Texas during the 1800s?

And now it seemed at least one of the Starr gang had ended up in Whitehorse, Montana, back when this part of the country was known for its outlaw hideouts.

Was this the Calhoun connection to Montana? Was this why Starr had come here—just as some of her namesake had more than a hundred years before? The Texas outlaws had changed their names, she realized, and re-invented themselves.

Just as Starr had done.

Was that why she'd been given the Kid Curry clipping? Was whoever had sent her the clippings just seeing whether or not she would follow up each lead?

That would mean, though, that she was being watched. She glanced toward the large plate-glass windows, but all she could see was the falling snow.

She turned back to the exhibit, studying the black-and-white photographs of robbers—not unlike the one she had of Starr, she thought as she heard the tap of boot heels behind her and turned to see Cade Jackson.

He glanced at the outlaw exhibit and she caught his surprised—and worried—expression. "We need to talk."

CADE WALKED OUT to his pickup. This woman had knocked him for a loop. And now to find her standing in front of the outlaw exhibit… Idle curiosity? Or something more?

He feared he knew exactly what that more might be. But how had she found out?

Because she was hell-bent on finding out everything there was to know about Grace. And, in turn, him.

If he'd doubted before that the woman meant business, he no longer did. His whole life was about to be opened up and every detail exposed to the media. And he didn't need Miranda Blake to tell him that a story like this would go nationwide.

He was losing his past like a shoreline being washed away by waves. He could feel a little more of it drop out from under him, swept out by the storm.

And Tex was that storm. She'd blown in and now she was causing havoc in his life. Worse, with Grace's.

"How did you know I was here?" she asked, stopping short of his truck as snow fell around her.

"I called the newspaper. Shirley said you were at the museum. Get in."

She crossed her arms over her chest and glared at him, unmoving. "What did you want to talk to me about?" Her dark hair sparkled with ice crystals as snow fell around her.

"You want to talk about this out in the middle of a snowstorm? Go right ahead, Tex. I'll be in the truck." He didn't wait for an answer.

"As I told you before, my name is Miranda. Or Andi. *Not* Tex. Remember?" she snapped as she got in and he started the engine.

Miranda sounded too old. Andi was a little too friendly and he was feeling anything but friendly.

"I saw your expression in there," she said. "What was it about the outlaw exhibit that ties in with Starr?"

He shook his head, not in answer, but in awe. The woman was like a bloodhound on his scent and she was tracking his life with an instinct that scared him.

"Don't even bother to tell me that you don't know what I'm talking about," she said, sounding angry. "You *know* something about all this. You couldn't have lived with Starr and not suspected *something*. Why do you keep fighting me?"

He looked over at her. "Because it's my life you want to destroy for a damned news story and fifteen minutes of fame."

She looked chastened. "I'm sorry. I know how hard this must be on you. But this isn't going away just because you want it to."

"*You're* not going away, you mean," he said, trying to curb the anger he felt the instant he was in her presence.

"Even if I left tomorrow, do you really think whoever fed me the information about Starr is going away, as well?"

He didn't know what to think. Or feel. Other than numb. Just not numb enough.

"There's something you should know. Lubbock Calhoun, Starr's brother, was recently released from prison. Apparently he's broken his parole. No one knows where he is."

Cade shot her a look. "You think he's the one who sent you the tape?"

"Well, if it's him, then he's already in town," she said. "The envelope was postmarked Whitehorse."

Cade swore. Just when he thought things couldn't get any worse. What a fool he'd been to think that this might all blow over. "What does he want?"

"Probably the money. Until the three million is found..." She looked up as he backed out onto the highway and turned north. "Where are we going?" She sounded worried.

"I thought we'd take a ride."

"I put the original cassette tape with a copy of all my notes in a secure place," she said, looking away. "In case I should disappear."

He laughed. "I wasn't planning to kill you, Tex."

She glanced over at him. "I guess neither of us have anything to worry about then."

He wished that were true as he drove north out of town on the wide two-lane. A few locals were trying to get the highway across what was known as the Hi-Line

made into a four-lane. They had some crazy idea that it
would bring more people to this isolated part of the state.

He wasn't opposed to the idea, he just knew it would
never fly—not when he could go for miles and never see
another car on the highway.

"Tell me about Starr Calhoun," he said after Whitehorse disappeared in his rearview mirror.

The question seemed to take her by surprise. "Like
what?"

"Everything you know about her."

"Okay." She took a breath and let it out slowly. "She
is one of six children born to Hodge and Eden Calhoun."

Eden? Grace had picked her real mother's name for
a middle name. He felt sick. There was no doubt about
who Grace had been.

"Her parents took all the kids with them when they
robbed banks until they were captured and the children
were put into foster homes."

Grace had been in a foster home? He couldn't help but
feel for her, just as he couldn't help but think of her as
Grace even if she really had been Starr Calhoun. "What
happened to the kids?"

She shrugged. "They grew up. Some of them made
the news as they followed in their parents' footsteps."

"And the parents?"

"Hodge and Eden died in prison a few years apart.
Hodge was killed by another inmate. Eden killed herself."

He practically drove off the highway. He remembered
how sad Grace had looked when she'd told him that both
her parents were deceased. Killed in a plane crash, as he
recalled. A lie. On top of the biggest lie of all.

"All of the kids dropped off the radar until one after

another all but one turned up on police reports," she was saying. "Amarillo, the oldest, died in prison of hepatitis C. Dallas is doing time in California. Houston has been missing since the robberies six years ago. Worth seems to be the only one who went straight. He was the youngest of the boys so he was probably adopted and his name changed. Lubbock…well, who knows where he is?"

Cade couldn't believe what he was hearing about Starr and her family.

"For all we know, Houston could be living in Whitehorse," she was saying. "Did Starr ever mention her family, her brothers?"

"She told me she was an only child." Another lie. "You know an awful lot about the Calhouns," he said.

She looked out her side window even though there was nothing to see but snow. "I'm a reporter. I do a lot of research."

There was more to it, he thought. He couldn't wait to see what his brother found out about Andi Blake. "That's all you know about Starr?"

"I know she robbed a bunch of banks and disappeared," Andi said bristling. "And now I know where she disappeared to   at least for a while."

"What does that mean?"

"Are you sure she's dead?"

"What?" he snapped. "I buried her. You think she walked away from that car accident?"

"Someone died in that car, but how can you be sure it was your wife?"

"She was wearing the wedding band I bought her." He wished he'd left Tex at the museum.

"Was an autopsy done? Was any DNA taken?"

"You think she faked her death?" he asked incredulously.

"She had three million good reasons to fake her death."

"She had at least one damned good reason not to," he snapped and shook his head, wondering how this could be any more painful. If it hadn't been the middle of winter he might have just dumped Tex off beside the road. Let her find her own way home.

"Grace didn't fake her death," he said, trying to keep his voice down. "I know because…" He took a breath and let it out. "Because she'd gone shopping in Billings for my Christmas present. She called on her way home to tell me she had a surprise for me and couldn't wait to tell me. An early present." He glared over at Andi. "She'd been to a doctor. She was pregnant with our baby."

He took satisfaction in the shock he witnessed on Andi Blake's face before he turned back to his driving and fought to swallow back the gutting pain of the memory. "The woman who died in that car on the way back to Whitehorse was two months pregnant with my child. And yes, I know that for a fact. I got a copy of the results from the doctor after she died."

Andi stared at his granitelike profile for a moment before turning to gaze out at the snow-covered landscape. It suddenly felt colder, definitely more isolated.

Starr had been pregnant. The story just kept getting better and better. All she had to do was keep badgering Cade, keep getting the bits and pieces he was trying so hard to keep from her.

She knew she was treading on thin ice. She'd hurt this man, angered him and feared what he might do if she pushed him too hard. She was 99 percent sure he hadn't known who Grace was. But he had to have suspected something wasn't right.

"I'm sorry," she said. Starr hadn't just married Cade Jackson, but she'd also gotten pregnant with his child? That didn't sound anything like the woman Andi had read about in the police reports. Nor the one planning the robberies on the cassette tape.

Starr Calhoun hadn't been talked into robbing banks. She'd been the ringleader. Even if she was pregnant, it didn't mean she'd died in that car six years ago. There was no way of knowing if Starr Calhoun was dead without doing an exhumation.

But Andi wasn't about to voice that. Especially right now, she thought, looking out at the desolate landscape. She couldn't even be sure where they were let alone where they were headed.

Ahead all she could see was snow. It filled the sky, drifted in the barrow pits, clung to the fence posts on each side of the road and covered the rolling hills for miles.

And it was still falling. Earlier on the radio she'd heard something about a winter storm warning alert— whatever that was.

The women at the museum had told them as they were leaving earlier to bundle up because there was a storm coming. Another foot of snow was expected and temperatures were going to drop. She couldn't imagine it getting any colder.

She saw Cade look in his rearview mirror as they topped a hill. Glancing back she saw nothing but empty highway. As she turned around she felt a little sick. The lack of contrast gave her the feeling that the earth was flat white and that if Cade kept driving, he would drive right off the edge of it.

Cade slowed the pickup and turned off the highway. She caught a glimpse of a sign that read Sleeping Buffalo.

"What was that?" she asked as they passed a manger-like structure that housed two large rocks. She hoped he was taking her somewhere public. Being alone with him was wearing on her nerves. She didn't like how upset he was.

"It's Sleeping Buffalo," he said. "During the Ice Age, glaciers carved this country leaving behind a field of large boulders the Native Americans thought looked like buffalo. The buffalo had been scarce. When the Natives saw the two rocks, they thought they were buffalo and rode toward them. Just as they reached the rocks, though, they saw a huge herd of buffalo beyond them. The two buffalo-appearing rocks were then considered sacred, having led the hunters to the buffalo. The rocks are kept so the Native Americans can pay their respects by leaving tobacco on them."

She took that in as they passed a cluster of buildings that according to the sign was Sleeping Buffalo Resort. She recalled something about a shoot-out there a few months ago. If she had any doubt she was in the Wild West, all she had to do was read the old newspaper stories.

Over the next rise, she saw an expanse of ice dotted with a half dozen small fishing huts. "People really don't fish when it's this cold, do they?"

"If cold stopped 'em, nobody in Montana would fish," he said. "And I'd be out of business."

They drove in silence as the snow-packed road narrowed and a few houses gave way to nothing but rolling, snowy hills. Out here there was no hint of the fast-approaching holiday. Just as there was no Christmas tree or any decorations at her apartment. Or at Cade's. No reminder that Christmas was just days away.

"So what's your life story, Tex?" Cade asked. "Let's hear it. Seems only fair since you're so interested in mine."

She ignored the "Tex." "I don't have a story."

He let out a humorless laugh. "We all have a story. Isn't that how your profession works? You prey on our life stories for the amusement and edification of your readers? But *your* life is private?"

She didn't answer, more concerned about where he was taking her.

"Wasn't there some man you left in Texas?" he asked, glancing over at her. He must have seen the answer in her face although he misread it. "That's what I thought. And you give me a hard time for trying to run away from this?"

"You're mistaken."

"Right," he said with a laugh as he slowed to turn on an even narrower road, the deep snow scraping on the undercarriage of the pickup as he busted through drifts, snow flying.

Andi held on for dear life, afraid now of not only where he was taking her, but also what he planned to do when he got there.

"A woman who dresses like you working for a weekly newspaper in Whitehorse, Montana, and you're telling me you're not running away from something?" He had to fight to keep the pickup in the narrow tracks. "Save your breath."

Had he found out about her broadcast news job in Fort

Worth through his brother the sheriff? "This isn't about *me*. But if you must know, I worked for a television station but I wanted a change of pace."

"A change of pace?" He shook his head. "Come on, Tex, you're into this up to your eyeballs. You're the one who got the newspaper clipping and cassette tape. Not me. Don't tell me you haven't wondered: Why *you*? I sure have."

She'd wondered all right. "I'm a reporter. Whoever sent me the information knew I would follow it up."

"Lubbock Calhoun, straight from prison, would know that about you?" he asked.

"Or Houston. For all you know he married someone right here in Whitehorse just like his sister did. He could be your neighbor."

Cade shook his head. "I know all my neighbors and have for many years. Any other theories?"

"I don't know who is sending me the information. I'm sure they have their reasons. If it's Lubbock, then he must have seen me on the news."

"You made the news?"

"I was a TV broadcast newswoman."

"Oh, you *read* the news," he said.

"I did more than *read* the news. I—" She stopped abruptly as she saw the trap he'd laid for her.

"Yes?" he asked smiling over at her. "What? You want your life to remain private? You just tell the news. Forget that it's my life and Grace's memory that you're trying to destroy."

"There was no Grace," she snapped.

"Like hell there wasn't," he shot back. "She was Grace when I fell in love with her, when I married her, when I buried her."

Andi heard the horrible pain in his voice and was hit with a wave of guilt that angered her. She didn't start this. The Calhouns did. She was just doing her job. She was sick of him trying to blame her because his wife was a liar and a criminal.

"You might never have known the truth if I had just ignored it," she snarled.

"Yeah, and wouldn't that have been terrible?" he said sarcastically as he glared over at her for a moment.

"You can't just stick your head in the sand and pretend none of this happened. Whoever is sending me the information about Starr, you think that person is going to keep quiet?"

Cade realized where he was headed and swore under his breath. He hadn't really planned to come out here. Hell, he hadn't planned to go anywhere with this woman. There was no place he could find peace right now, but he especially didn't want her near the home he'd shared with Grace.

So why had he come here?

He glanced over at her, wondering how she fit into all this. It was no act of fate that she'd ended up in Whitehorse—or that she was the one someone had chosen to tell their secrets to. No coincidence at all.

And Andi Blake had to know it.

CHAPTER SEVEN

"WHERE ARE WE?" Andi asked, squinting into the storm.

Cade had taken the back way into the cabin, circling around the north end of Nelson Reservoir, figuring he'd give her a taste of rural Montana in the winter. He took perverse satisfaction in the way she'd been forced to hang on. ·

As the cabin came into view and the frozen reservoir beyond it, he thought about the first time he'd laid eyes on Grace Browning.

He'd been driving northwest on Highway 2, headed toward Saco when he'd seen her crouched beside her car just off the highway with a flat tire on the left rear.

He'd stopped, seeing that she appeared to be a woman alone, and got out to walk back to her.

She hadn't looked up, just flicked a glance at his boots before she said, "Thanks, but I've got it."

He'd smiled to himself. She was a little thing but she was tackling that flat tire as if she was a truck driver. He'd thought about telling her not to be ridiculous, to move aside and let him change it.

But he'd stood back instead and watched her, seeing how not only capable she was, but also how determined. If he'd learned anything about women it was to give them their space when they had that particular look in their eyes.

But he wasn't about to leave her alone on this empty stretch of highway. So he stood back and watched with a mixture of amusement and awe.

Now, though, he wondered if she hadn't wanted him to help her because she had something to hide. Like a trunkful of stolen cash and a bounty on her head.

Clearly she'd been hiding everything, he thought bitterly.

But a part of him argued that if she had the robbery money, why had she married him? Why had she stayed in Whitehorse, Montana? Why had she gotten pregnant with his child?

The memory was like a stake to his heart. His foot came off the gas, the pickup's front tires sliding off into the deep snow. He fought to wrestle the truck back into the tracks.

"Are you all right?" Andi asked beside him.

"Fine," he snapped. He'd thought he'd been grieving the last six years. It was nothing compared to now. At least he'd had his memories of Grace. And now even those were tainted because didn't common sense tell him that Grace had just been hiding out here, the marriage to him having just been a cover until she divvied up the money with her accomplice and split, just as Andi suspected?

But if Starr had had the money from the bank robberies in her trunk that day, what had she done with it? She'd have had to hide it somewhere, otherwise he would have known about it. Three million dollars wouldn't have fit in her purse. Or one of her shoe boxes.

And why the hell hadn't she just kept going?

She'd finished changing the tire, then looked up for the first time at him.

He'd been startled by the same thing that had given away her identification when Tex had seen her photograph in the newspaper clipping. Her eyes.

They were pale blue and bottomless.

"You're still here," she'd said, sounding amused. "Haven't you ever seen a woman change a tire before?"

"Not with that kind of determination," he'd admitted.

She'd laughed.

He'd often wondered if he'd fallen in love with her the moment he'd looked into her eyes—or if it had been when she'd laughed. Either way, it had been like a jolt of electricity straight to his heart.

The day had been hot and he'd said the first thing he'd thought to say.

"Buy you a beer at the bar up the road."

She'd smiled at him, those eyes twinkling. "A beer?" She'd nodded thoughtfully. "I could use a beer."

"Cade Jackson," he'd said and held out his hand.

"Grace Browning." Was that the moment her alias and her cover had been born? There had been no hesitation when she'd said the name, no clue that this woman was anything but who she said she was.

Or had he been so enamored that he just hadn't noticed?

A part of him hadn't expected her to follow him to the bar, let alone come in and have a beer with him.

But she had.

"You're from here," she'd said.

It really hadn't been a question, but he'd answered, anyway. "Born and raised south of here on a ranch."

She'd eyed him for a moment. "So you really are a cowboy."

He'd laughed. "If you mean do I ride a horse, yes. My

father sold the ranch, but I bought a smaller one to the north. I raise horses more as a sideline. The rest of the time I run a bait shop here in town."

He remembered her smile, the amusement that played in her eyes.

"Horses and a bait shop." She shook her head. "Diversification, huh. Well, Cade Jackson, that's quite a combination. You make any money at it?"

He remembered being a little defensive. "I have all I need."

Her expression had changed, her features softening. "I envy you. Most people never have enough."

"Most people want too much," he'd said.

He smiled at that now as he realized that the woman he'd said that to had more than three million dollars.

So why hadn't she kept on going down that highway? Why had she hung around to have another beer and dinner? Hung around long enough that he fell more deeply in love with her? Hung around long enough to get pregnant with his child?

"Starr could have kept on going," he said as he parked in front of the cabin. "Why didn't she?"

"You tell me," Andi said as he saw her look down the plowed road that led to the cabin, her eyes narrowing. "Do you think you can scare me into not doing the story?" she demanded, clearly irate.

Was that what he thought? Or was he just angry at the messenger? He reminded himself that she hadn't just brought him the bad news. She planned to *publicize* it. Once her story broke, the media would have a field day and he'd be right in the heart of the storm.

He knew then why he'd brought her here. He wanted her to know the woman he had. He wanted to convince

Andi that Grace Browning had existed. And while a part of him knew he was wasting his time, he knew he had to try. Not so much for Andi as for himself.

"Grace could have chosen a life on the run with the money. She didn't. How do you explain that, Tex?" he asked as he cut the engine and turned his attention on her.

"I can't. So are you telling me that there weren't things she said or did that made you wonder if there wasn't more to her staying here? Things that made you worry she wasn't telling the truth?"

"Stop looking at me like I'm an idiot. I knew my wife. I'm not a fool."

And he'd known something was wrong. He'd seen her fighting a battle with herself. He just hadn't known what it was. Or how to help her. He'd hoped whatever had been haunting her would blow over. When she'd called from Billings about the baby, she'd sounded completely happy.

And he'd known then that she'd won whatever battle had been going on inside her. A battle he'd just assumed had something to do with another man.

Maybe he was a fool after all.

"Isn't it possible that Grace wanted to put her past behind her and start over?" he asked, hating the emotion he heard in his voice. "Isn't it possible that she was tired of that life, that she wanted something more, that she'd found it with me? That maybe Grace was exactly who I believed her to be?"

He knew what he was saying. That he and his love had changed Starr Calhoun into Grace Browning Jackson, a woman he would have died for.

Something caught his eye in the rearview mirror. The wind whipped the snow past and for just a moment he saw the glare off the windshield of a car on the road by the reservoir.

Earlier he'd had the strangest feeling that they were being followed. Crazy. This was Whitehorse. All this talk of outlaws was making him paranoid.

He lost sight of the vehicle in the falling snow and felt a wave of relief. But as he looked at Andi, he saw both skepticism—and pity—and felt his temper boil. Not only had she turned his life upside down, but she was also making him doubt everything—including the safety of the community he'd lived in his entire life.

"Maybe you just saw the woman she wanted you to see," Andi said.

"Were you this cynical before or does it come with being a reporter?" he demanded with no small amount of disdain.

"Now who's being contemptuous? I'm proud of my profession."

He lifted a brow.

"People have the right to know the truth." She snapped. "If there weren't individuals willing to go out on a limb to get the truth, what would that leave?"

"Peace?" he asked with a laugh.

She scoffed. "Some people just can't take the truth obviously."

Obviously. "Truth is relative. Your truth apparently isn't mine because you're wrong about my wife." He could feel her gaze on him like a weight. "Maybe she was Starr Calhoun."

"Maybe?"

"You want to know about Grace Browning? Take this down, girl reporter. Grace was as different from

Starr Calhoun as night and day." With that he opened his pickup door and climbed out.

ANDI HEARD HOW desperately he wanted to believe that Starr had changed before she died. That she'd become Grace Browning, the woman he'd fallen in love with. That Starr had wanted to put that other life behind her.

Who knew what Starr had been thinking when she hit Whitehorse? But Andi could see that Cade needed to believe that the woman had stayed because she'd fallen in love with him instead of merely using him and this place as a hideout like the outlaw she was.

As she watched Cade stride away from the pickup through the snow, she wondered. Had he grieved six years because he'd loved his wife that much? Or had his pain been one of disillusionment and denial?

"You knew her best," Andi said diplomatically as she caught up with him.

"I *did* know her," he said, stopping to turn to face her.

That was why she needed his part of the story. Not that she believed for a minute that Starr Calhoun had changed. How could someone go from being the cold-hearted, calculating criminal on the audio tape to becoming an upstanding citizen and a wife to this man in a matter of months?

But if true, it would make a great story.

Not that anyone would believe the transformation except Cade. Look at the woman's genes. Had anyone in the family stayed out of prison? Maybe Worth. Unfortunately that was hard to verify since he could be breaking the law at this moment just under another name.

Starr and a change of heart? No way. Not even for this good-looking cowboy, Andi thought.

As she followed him toward the small cabin, she wondered how Starr could have stayed as long as she did here. A woman used to big cities and everything stolen money could buy would have gone crazy here, wouldn't she have?

All Andi could figure is that Starr had been waiting for something. The money? Or for her brother Houston to meet up with her? Then where did Lubbock come in?

She doubted Starr would trust Houston to bring the money. Rightly so apparently since Houston hadn't shown up. Or had he?

Andi's suspicious nature couldn't help but come back to Starr's death. Just as she worried about the person who had wanted her to know that Grace Jackson was really Starr Calhoun.

She was still going with the theory that Starr had staged her death and taken off with the money and that someone possibly in Starr's own family might be looking for her and using Andi to do it.

Cade had stopped at the edge of the porch and was looking back at her. He didn't seem like anybody's fool, she thought. So how had Starr tricked him into not only buying her act, but also falling madly in love with her and now defending her even when he knew who she really had been?

Andi saw him frown as he looked past her back up the road from the way they'd come.

"Is something wrong?" she asked, turning to follow his gaze. Through the falling snow she caught the glint of the dull gray light off a vehicle just before it disappeared over a hill.

"I think we might have been followed," he said distractedly but she could tell he was worried. She recalled how he'd been watching his rearview mirror earlier. Or maybe he was just trying to scare her.

"I didn't see anyone." She was still irritated that he'd taken some back road through the deep snow no doubt just to frighten her. But she felt a stab of apprehension as she realized they could have been followed.

The cabin couldn't have been in a more deserted place. She shivered as she stared through the falling snow at the reservoir and saw an ice-fishing shack not far off shore. She realized it must be Cade's since there was no sign of anyone else around.

What an isolated place, she thought as she clutched her shoulder bag to her side, slipping her hand in to make sure she had her new can of pepper spray.

CADE WAITED TO SEE if the vehicle he'd spotted earlier drove by again. Could just be someone lost since no one used this road this time of year. From this side of the reservoir, there was no way to drive out onto the ice.

Other than ice fishing, there wasn't any other reason to come down this road since it ended at the bottom of a rocky outcropping.

If not someone lost, then they had been followed. Which would mean Andi Blake might actually know what she was talking about. In which case, there just might be cause for concern.

"You realize you're being used," he said. She didn't answer. "Aren't you worried as hell what this person wants and what he'll do when he doesn't get it?"

"What do you suggest I do?"

He ignored the sarcasm in her tone. "Go back to Texas. Forget you ever saw that clipping or heard that tape."

She raised a brow. "And what will you do? Can you just forget it? I didn't think so."

"I'll turn it over to my brother because frankly, I don't give a damn what happened to the money." His gaze fell on her. "But you're in it for the story to the bitter end, aren't you? Whoever is feeding you the information knows that. They know you won't back down."

"And they're right."

He shook his head.

"Do you really think they are just going to let me stop now?" she asked.

"You're in *danger.*"

"Not as long as I keep digging until I find what that person wants."

"You think you're going to find the money." He let out a laugh. "That's the topping on your story, isn't it?"

What had he been thinking bringing her to the cabin he and Grace had shared. It felt like a betrayal. The thought made him want to laugh. Grace had *betrayed* him.

He scowled over at Andi. What did any of us know about each other really? All his instincts told him that Andi Blake had her own secrets—but not for long. At this very moment, his brother was working on finding out everything there was to know about her.

And Cade was anxious to know. He knew he was looking for some kind of leverage. So far Andi Blake had been holding all the cards.

"What are we doing here?" she asked impatiently.

What were they doing here? He'd thought maybe here, in the home that he and Grace had shared, would be proof that Grace Browning had existed. But the only proof was what he felt in his heart and even he was starting to question whether it had been real.

As Andi had pointed out, the three million dollars was still missing. Apparently someone was looking for it. And Andi Blake wasn't the only one who knew about Grace being Starr.

Something had happened in Texas to catapult her to Montana. He'd bet the ranch on it. He had a bad feeling whatever it was would end up being connected to Starr and the Calhoun family.

He thought about turning around and going back to town. But he'd come this far…

"Come on," he said. "You want to know about Grace…" He headed toward the arena, not ready to take Andi inside the cabin, if ever.

"Where are the horses?" she asked once inside. He'd taken his time showing her around, stalling.

"I board them during the winter," he said. The truth was he had boarded them in town ever since Grace died, avoiding the cabin and thoughts of the future they had planned here.

It was cold in the arena. He could see his breath and Andi wasn't dressed for winter in Montana. The fool woman was still wearing that lightweight leather coat and high-heeled boots. She was shivering, her teeth practically chattering. She had her arms wrapped tightly around herself and looked as if she was close to hypothermia.

He swore silently. Whatever animosity he felt toward her for coming into his life and blowing it all to hell, he hadn't meant to let her freeze.

"You look cold," he said.

"I'm fine."

Her teeth were chattering now.

"Right," he said. "Come on." There would be no getting out of it. He'd have to take her into the cabin and get her warmed up before they headed back to town.

For just an instant it crossed his mind how alike Grace and Andi had been when it came to stubborn determination.

He quickly pushed that thought away with distaste. Andi was nothing like Grace. At least the Grace he'd thought he'd married.

"WHAT IS THAT?" Andi asked, trying to keep her mind off the freezing cold as they walked toward the cabin. The snow was deep and the ice under it slick. She couldn't feel her fingers in her leather gloves. Nor her toes in her boots.

"What?" He stopped to look back at her.

She pointed in the distance to what appeared to be the skeleton of a house someone had started and abandoned. The wood was weathered gray against a backdrop of rocky bluffs.

"I was building a bigger place for us when Grace was killed," he said, following her gaze.

"You plan to finish it?"

"No."

"So you're just going to leave it like that? I would think it would only act as a constant reminder of what you'd lost."

He turned to glare at her. "I don't know what I'm going to do with it, all right? What's it to you anyway?"

"Nothing. I was just curious," she said.

"Maybe one of these days I'll raze it. Happy?" With that he turned and strode off toward the cabin.

She stared at his strong back, the determined set of his shoulders and shook her head. Would she ever understand this man?

Reminding herself that she didn't need to understand him, she tucked the information away, already weaving it along with this place into her story as she trailed after Cade, colder than she'd ever been in her life.

A gust of wind whirled snow into her face as she neared the house. She felt her boot heel slip on the ice and would have gone down if Cade hadn't grabbed her.

He shook his head in apparent amused disgust as he took her leather gloved hand and led her up the steps to the cabin.

She drew her hand back once they were on the porch, angry with herself and with him. She was out of her realm—just as he would be in Fort Worth. So she hadn't walked on anything but sidewalk most of her life. So she was cold and not as sure-footed on the ice as he was. She didn't need his condescending attitude.

As he unlocked the front door of the cabin, she realized she could no longer feel her feet. And she couldn't stop shaking.

Cade ushered her inside where the interior of the cabin was only a little warmer than the arena.

Andi stood just inside the door looking around. She hadn't been sure what to expect. The outside of the cabin was rustic, appearing to have been built back in the 1930s. It was log-framed with chinking between the logs and a weathered rail porch, all grayed with age.

So it was a surprise to see that the inside of the cabin was quite homey. She instantly recognized a woman's touch—this cabin was so different from the apartment where Cade stayed in town behind the bait shop.

Cade must have noticed her startled expression. "It was all Grace's doing."

The decor was warm and inviting with comfortable furniture and welcoming colors. Also the place was more spacious than she would have guessed from the outside.

There was a rock fireplace against one wall with bookshelves on both sides to the ceiling. She walked over to glance at the books. They all looked as if they'd been read, and more than once. The variety of topics surprised her given that a cowboy and a bank robber had lived here. She looked up to find Cade's dark gaze on her.

"Most of the books are mine." He sounded defensive. "Or didn't you think I could read?"

She ignored that as she moved around, trying to warm up her hands and feet. What had she been thinking moving to Montana in the middle of winter? It was literally freezing up here.

She pulled several books from the shelves, then put them back.

"I'll make us some coffee," he said, then seemed to hesitate. "Maybe I'd better make a fire."

She glanced around as he got a blaze going in the fireplace. All of the walls had interesting black-and-white photographs of what she assumed was the area. They had such a Western feel to them that Andi was reminded of old movies she'd watched as a child with her father. He loved Roy Rogers and Gene Autry films.

"Grace took those," Cade said behind her.

It surprised her that Starr was such a good photographer. "I had no idea Starr was this talented."

Cade met her gaze. "There's a lot you didn't know about my wife."

Apparently so. But a lot he didn't know, either.

"She was going to have a show in Great Falls in the spring. She was shy about her work, but I talked her into it." He stopped as if he realized another reason Starr might not have wanted to go public with her work.

"Wrap up in that quilt on the couch. You need to warm your fingers and toes slowly otherwise they'll hurt," he said as he turned and went into the kitchen.

Her fingers and toes already ached from the cold. She couldn't imagine them hurting any worse as she went to stand by the blaze he'd gotten going in the fireplace.

Within moments, she felt a painful tingling in her fingers. Her toes were starting to tingle, as well. She could hear him banging around in the kitchen. She sat down on the couch, her eyes tearing with the pain.

Why had he brought her here? She pulled her shoulder bag with the pepper spray in it closer—just in case she might need it, then wrapped the quilt around her, wondering if Starr had made it as she stared into the flames.

Cade came out of the kitchen and handed her a mug of steaming instant coffee.

Her hands and feet hurt, just as he said they would. She grimaced as she wrapped her fingers around the hot mug.

"Here," he said. "We need to get those wet boots off." Before she could protest he knelt in front of her and taking one of her boots in both hands began to unzip them. "If you're going to live here, you've got to dress for the weather."

"I'm fine," she lied and attempted to pull her foot back.

He gave her an impatient look, pulled off her boot, then reached for the other one. He removed the second boot, put both boots to warm near the fire and began to gently rub her feet.

"They're hurtin', aren't they?" he said, nodding before she could answer. "They'll be better in a minute."

She'd have to take his word for it. She sipped her coffee, trying to ignore the feel of his strong but gentle fingers rubbing her feet.

The cabin felt much smaller. Cade Jackson seemed to fill the entire space with his very male presence. She knew how much this was hurting him, being here in his cabin he'd shared with his wife. Clearly he didn't spend much time here since her death. Andi could tell that he'd been reluctant to bring her here. So why had he? As hard as he tried not to show it, she could see that this was killing him.

"Better?" he asked after a few minutes.

She nodded. "Thank you." The moment he stood again, she tucked her feet under her. Not that she didn't appreciate his kindness. As she sipped her coffee she watched him. He stood next to the fireplace, the flames playing on his strong features.

Had Starr fallen so deeply in love with this man that she really had wanted to change? As Andi studied him, she thought it actually possible. There was something so comforting about this man, a strength, and yet an aliveness that drew even her.

"What now?" Cade asked quietly.

She shook her head, not understanding since only moments before her thoughts had been on anything but Starr and the news article she would write.

"I've shown you my life with Grace," he said. "You can do your story. What else do you want from me?"

There was one thing she needed before she broke the story, but she knew it would be over Cade Jackson's dead body.

However, none of this felt as if it was in her hands anymore—if it ever had been. She was being led by whoever was providing her with the information. That person knew her, knew that this was personal for her, knew she wouldn't quit until she got to the truth.

"It isn't about what I want," she said, believing that to be true. "Whoever is supplying me with the information, wants something."

He nodded solemnly. "The money." He said it with such distaste she didn't doubt he'd never seen it let alone spent it.

"That would be my guess," she said.

"We already know that." Cade rubbed a hand over his face in frustration. "But I don't know where the money is. If Starr had it, I was never aware of it."

She nodded. "I believe that. The question is, does Starr still have it?"

"You're not back to your theory that Starr walked away from that wreck, are you?"

Her gaze locked with his. "What if she isn't dead? What if you didn't bury your wife? Then she is alive somewhere with your child. We need to know if that body you buried is actually Starr's. You're the only one who can have her body exhumed."

Cade froze, his mug partway to his mouth, his eyes suddenly hard as stones.

Andi rushed on, "If her DNA matches that of one of her brothers in prison—"

He threw the mug with enough force that it shattered when it hit the wall. Coffee made a dark stain across the woodwork and floor.

Without a word, he stormed out of the cabin.

CHAPTER EIGHT

"You can go visit my cousin in Minnesota until the baby is born and then come back," Arlene said.

Charlotte looked up at her from the couch where she was eating cold leftover pancakes dripping with syrup. "I'm not going anywhere. It's not like everyone doesn't already know I'm pregnant."

"What about the father?" Arlene asked, wiping up crumbs from the plastic on the couch beside her daughter.

"What about him?" Charlotte asked, licking her fingers.

"Have you told him the baby's his?"

Charlotte turned her attention to the last pancake on the plate. She dredged it through a lake of syrup but didn't lift it to her mouth. "He doesn't believe me that it's his."

"And you're *protecting* this man?" Arlene demanded. "What is wrong with you?"

"Nothing. It's my baby. I *want* it."

Arlene raised a brow. "Want it? What do you intend to *do* with it?"

"Raise it," Charlotte snapped.

"You? Raise a baby?"

"I figure I can do a hell of a lot better than you have," her daughter said, shoving away her plate. The pancake spilled to the floor in a pool of syrup as Charlotte stormed off to her bedroom, slamming the door solidly behind her.

Arlene stared down at the pancake and syrup soaking into the rug for a moment, then dropped to her knees to hurriedly clean up the mess. She'd always kept a clean house, prided herself in her neatness. Floyd had hated the way she fussed around the house.

"Sit down, for cripe's sake, Arlene," he'd bark. "You're driving me crazy with your cleaning."

Nervous energy. She'd always had more than her share.

She scrubbed at the rug, frantic to get the syrup up before it stained the rug, wondering why she'd tried so hard. She'd wanted to be a good wife and mother. Her own mother had been cold and uncaring. Arlene had never been able to do anything right according to her.

She quit scrubbing at the rug. The dishrag felt sticky in her hands. Her eyes burned hot. She couldn't remember the last time she'd cried and was surprised when scalding tears began to run down her face.

Her body shook with chest-rattling sobs. Through blinding tears, she saw herself on the floor crying as a child, her mother standing over her.

Her mother had always said Arlene wouldn't amount to anything. Even when Arlene had kept her house and her kids spotless, her mother had found fault until the day she died.

But that day, on the floor, her mother standing over her with the leather strap, Arlene had prayed that she could prove her mother wrong as she cried for the father she'd never known to save her.

He hadn't and her mother's prophecy had now come

true. Arlene Evans was a disgrace, a failed wife, a failed mother. How could she allow another generation to be born into this mess?

ANDI STARED AFTER Cade as a gust of cold air blew in with the slamming of the door.

She'd known he wasn't going to take the idea of the exhumation well. Not that she blamed him. She found she was shaking and wondered if it was from his reaction—or her own. She'd just asked a man to dig up his dead wife, a woman he had clearly loved almost more than life itself.

She felt sick. Had she no compassion anymore? Not for the Calhouns. And even less for Starr who had obviously broken Cade Jackson's heart—and Andi feared would completely destroy it by the time this was finished.

She hated being a part of it. But she was and had been for more years than she wanted to admit.

Not that she thought the person who sent her the clippings and tape would let her stop now, anyway. How far was he willing to go to get what he wanted? And what exactly did he want besides the money?

She rose from her chair in front of the fire to retrieve her boots. They felt warm as she slipped her feet into them. As she did, she noticed a row of books—all about the outlaws of the Old West.

Andi pulled down one with a well-used paperback cover and thumbed through it, stopping on the title page. It was signed: "Grace, I know how much you like these stories. Love, Cade."

She heard a sound outside the cabin and put the book back. Now she understood Cade's expression when he'd found her in the outlaw section at the museum. He'd known about Grace's interest in the outlaws of the Old West.

So what did that have to do with anything?

And where was Cade? she wondered as she took her mug to the kitchen. She rinsed it out and set it on the counter, admiring what Starr had done with the house.

Why had Starr bothered fixing up this place if she was planning to take off? Or had the decorating just been something to do until she could take the money and leave?

Andi cleaned up the broken mug and spilled coffee. Past the kitchen was an open door. Through it she could see the bedroom. The colors alone drew her toward the room. An antique high bed with an iron frame sat in the middle of the room. The iron bed had been painted white, stark next to the color-crazy quilt on the bed.

But it was the photograph over the bed that drew her. She moved closer. The shot was of Cade. Starr had captured the man so perfectly, both his strength and his stubbornness as well as a vulnerability that pulled at Andi's heart. This was the man Starr had fallen in love with. The man who had changed her into Grace Browning.

"Are you ready?"

Andi jumped at the sound of Cade's voice directly behind her. She'd been so taken with the photograph and what it said about Cade—and Starr—that she hadn't heard him come back. "It's a wonderful photo of you."

He said nothing as he waited for her to leave the room before he firmly closed the door behind them.

"I should get you back to town," he said, taking her coat from where he'd hung it earlier to dry.

She wanted to tell him she was sorry. Sorry for sug-

gesting the exhumation. Sorry that she was the one who'd
brought this to him. But what she was really sorry for
was that she hadn't believed him that Starr had become
the woman, Grace Browning, who he'd loved.

She understood his pain more acutely. It was another
reason she said nothing as he drove her back to Whitehorse in a fierce silence that brooked no arguments or
discussions.

CADE MENTALLY KICKED himself all the way back to town.
What in the hell had he been thinking? All Tex cared
about was her damned news story. Seeing the home
Grace had made for him had only given the reporter
something more to write about.

But now she wanted him to exhume Grace's body?

It had been all he could do not to dump her in a snowbank on the way back to town.

Fortunately she'd had the good sense not to say a word
all the way back, otherwise he couldn't be responsible
for what he would have done.

He dropped her off without a word at the newspaper office and drove toward the bait shop, still kicking
himself.

As he drove home, Christmas music played from
somewhere down the street. Everywhere he looked there
were twinkling Christmas lights.

Grace had been so excited about their first Christmas together. She'd decorated the cabin and made sugar
cookies and eggnog.

It had started snowing the week before Christmas that
year. Grace had been like a little kid, catching snowflakes in her mouth, making snow angels out in the yard.
She'd said she'd never seen that much snow before. He

promised they would make a snowman when she got back from her shopping trip to Billings.

He had wanted to go with her, but she'd been insistent that she had to go alone.

"It's a surprise and you're not going to ruin it," she'd said. "The roads are plowed and sanded. I'll be careful." She'd kissed him, holding his face between her warm palms, those blue eyes of hers filling with tears.

"You make me happier than I ever dreamed possible," she'd said.

He shoved the memory away, no longer sure what had been a lie, and looked in his rearview mirror.

His mood didn't improve at the sight of his brother's patrol car behind him. With a curse, Cade pulled into the bait shop, his brother pulling in behind him.

"Where you been?" the sheriff asked after motioning for Cade to get into the patrol car.

Cade cringed under his brother's intent gaze as he slid into the passenger seat. "Out to the cabin. Fishing." Why was he lying? Why didn't he just tell Carter he'd been with the reporter? "Why? What's going on?"

Carter had his bad news look on.

"Just tell me." Cade hadn't meant to sound so abrupt. "Is it about Grace. Or Andi?"

"Andi?"

"Miranda Blake," Cade snapped, knowing he'd given himself away. He already knew about Grace. What he didn't want, he realized with surprise, was bad news about Tex.

Cade wanted the news, short and sweet. He didn't want sympathy. Nor did he want to have to explain himself.

"I can't find any record of Grace Eden Browning,"

his brother said. Carter looked more than a little uncomfortable. "No record of any kind. All I can figure is that she must have been born under another name. Do you happen to have her social security number?"

Cade shook his head. This wasn't news but hearing it from the sheriff definitely made it all the more real. "I'll see if I can find it. I'm sure there's an explanation."

"Yeah." Carter didn't sound convinced. "You don't seem surprised by this."

Cade knew it was just a matter of time before he was going to have to tell his brother the truth. But not yet. "What did you come up with on Miranda Blake?"

Carter seemed a little taken aback that Cade appeared more interested in Ms. Blake than this news about his former wife, but opened his notebook and said, "As for Miranda Blake..."

Cade listened, not surprised that Andi had been a top news anchorwoman in Fort Worth, working her way up as an investigative reporter and making quite a name for herself.

But her reason for leaving Fort Worth did surprise him.

"She took the job up here to get away from a stalker. Apparently one of her viewers had a crush on her," Carter said. "At first he sent her flowers, candy, love letters all anonymously. But when she asked him on the air to please stop, he felt rejected and started threatening her."

"Didn't she contact the police?" Cade asked.

The sheriff nodded. "But it's hard to catch these kinds of secret admirers. The threats escalated and she left the station. Not even her former boss knew where she'd gone."

"You didn't tell him where she was," Cade said, unable to hide his fear for Andi.

His brother looked even more surprised. "He knew I was with the Phillips County Sheriff's Department in Montana, but I doubt he was her secret admirer."

Still, Cade couldn't help being concerned.

"Her boss said they are holding her job for her for six months," his brother was saying. "That's why I would hate to see you get involved with this woman since you know she won't be staying for probably even that long."

Cade wanted to laugh out loud, but he had to go on letting his brother think his interest in Andi was romantic for a while longer.

"Don't worry," he told Carter. "I've already figured that out. I just thought it would be smart to know what I was dealing with."

His brother eyed him. "Dealing with?"

Cade shrugged and looked away, realizing he'd been too truthful. "Well, it has been a while since I've...dated."

"Yeah," Carter agreed quickly. "You'll want to take it slow." But he sounded pleased that Cade might even be thinking of dating again.

He felt a little guilty for leading his brother on like that. But in time, he would have to confide in Carter on a professional basis.

Cade didn't want to spoil the holidays. This could wait until after then. Until after his brother popped the question to Eve Bailey. Cade just hoped to hell she accepted Carter's proposal. There was enough heartbreak as it was.

"I'm glad you're doing better. I really am," his brother said. "I've been worried about you."

Cade knew he'd put his family through a lot. "I'm sorry I haven't been around much for you."

"Hey, I'm not complaining," Carter said. "I know

you've been through hell." He smiled. "Just don't forget Christmas Eve. Unless I lose my nerve."

"You won't," Cade assured him. "You and Eve are made for each other."

"You care about this Andi Blake," Carter said.

He nodded. He could have argued the point, but didn't.

"Just be careful, okay?" his brother said. "I don't want to see you get hurt."

Carter had no idea just how he'd been hurt by the woman. "Don't worry. I know what I'm doing."

Carter didn't look as if he believed him.

"I have another favor," Cade said, quickly changing the subject. "I was hoping you could find out about a woman named Starr Calhoun for me."

His brother's expression didn't change. "Starr Calhoun?"

"She was originally from Texas."

"Texas? Like Miranda Blake," Carter said.

"Yeah. Thanks for doing this." Cade reached for the door and opened it.

Carter reached past him and closed it. "When are you going to be honest with me and tell me what's really going on?"

Cade felt the full weight of his brother's gaze. He squirmed. "Soon. Just trust me a little longer?"

Carter met his gaze and held it. "I'll trust you. But I have to know. Are you involved in anything illegal?"

"No." Not unless you considered withholding evidence illegal.

A WINTER STORM warning alert had been put out for Whitehorse and all counties east of the Rockies. With the blowing and drifting snow, the road south of Whitehorse was closed to all but emergency traffic.

Andi did what she had to at the newspaper, then headed back to her apartment. In this part of the county during winter, it got dark shortly after 4:30 p.m.

Once home, she got out of her cold car since the drive hadn't been far enough for the engine to even warm up a little. Snow fell silently around her. She didn't want to go up to her apartment, but she had nowhere else to go.

And while she was too upset to sit still, she didn't feel like unpacking any boxes. She wasn't even sure why she'd brought so much stuff. She wouldn't be staying. Especially the way she was feeling right now.

She was cold and tired and sick at heart as she climbed the stairs to her second-story apartment. Her thoughts kept coming back to Cade Jackson. He was a victim in all this. And the woman who'd involved him was allegedly dead and buried. Andi could understand how Cade didn't want to exhume the body of the woman he'd loved.

But how could he still love a woman who had deceived him the way Starr had? And wouldn't he need to know if she'd pulled a disappearing act, possibly with his baby?

The moment she flipped the light switch and nothing happened Andi knew someone was there in the dark waiting for her just as the man had been in Texas.

He came out of the blackness. She felt the air around her move an instant before he was on her. She caught his scent, a mix of body odor and cheap aftershave.

He slammed her back into the wall, knocking the air out of her, his fingers closing around her throat.

She tried to call out, but she had no breath and the pressure on her throat choked off any sound. She scratched at his face, only to get a handful of thick mask.

He let go of her throat with one hand and slapped her

hand away, wrestling her arms behind her as he pinned her body to the wall, his fingers digging into her throat.

She'd been wrong. It wasn't her attacker from Texas. This man was larger, stronger. She couldn't breathe.

"Listen, bitch. Hurry up and find the money like you're supposed to. Run and I'll track you down and kill you. Don't even think about telling your friend's cop brother."

At the sound of pounding footsteps on the stairs to her apartment, he loosened his hold, then slammed her hard against the wall before letting her go. "I'll be in touch."

She saw stars. She gasped for breath, her throat on fire. Her legs gave out. As she slid down the wall to the floor someone burst into the apartment. She caught the glint of a star—and a weapon.

"Help." The word came out in a whisper. But even as she said it, she knew that her attacker was gone. She could feel the cold breeze blowing across the floor and knew the back door was open.

"Stay with her," the man with the badge ordered as he turned on a flashlight and swept the beam across her small apartment. She looked away, blinded by the sudden light.

"Are you all right?" The voice surprised her. Just as Cade did as he knelt down next to her.

She looked up into his face and began to shake. He gently pulled her toward him.

"It's okay," he said as he rubbed her back.

His kindness brought the tears. She hated this feeling of weakness, and worse letting him see her like this. She'd always had to be strong. For her mother. For herself because there was no one else.

"You're okay," he said, as if he knew how hard it was for her to be vulnerable in front of him.

She leaned into his strength, no longer able to fight back her emotions as she remembered the man's threat—and the sensation of knowing she was going to die if she didn't get air.

The lights flickered on. She pulled herself together and Cade handed her a tissue from the end table nearby.

"How is she?" the sheriff asked standing over them.

Cade got to his feet, gently pulling her up and easing her over to the couch. "Give her a minute."

"I'm all right." Her voice came out in a whisper. She was far from all right.

The sheriff took out his notebook. "I'm going to need to ask you some questions. I'm Sheriff Carter Jackson, Cade's brother."

She nodded and told him about reaching for the light. When it hadn't gone on, she'd known someone was in her apartment.

"How did you make the call?"

She shook her head. "I didn't." She'd wondered how they'd gotten to her so quickly. She saw the sheriff exchange a look with his brother.

"I was with my brother when he got the call about the break-in," Cade said as if seeing her confusion.

"Someone must have seen him break in." It hurt to talk. She swallowed, her eyes tearing from the pain.

The sheriff looked up from his notebook. "Is your apartment number 555-0044?" he asked.

She nodded numbly, knowing what was coming.

"According to the dispatcher, the call came from that number. From inside your apartment."

She felt her eyes widen in alarm. "I don't understand."

"Neither do I," the sheriff said as he walked into her kitchen and picked up the phone near the back door and hit Redial.

She watched his face, knew the emergency operator had answered.

"This is Sheriff Jackson. I was just testing the line." He hung up and looked at Andi. "The last call made was to the 911 operator. If you didn't make the call from here, then who did?"

CHAPTER NINE

"WHAT THE HELL was that about in there?" Cade demanded the moment he and his brother were outside again. "Did you see her throat? She was *attacked.* You're acting as if she staged the whole thing."

Carter said nothing as he opened the door of his patrol car. "You want a ride home?"

"No, I want you to tell me what the hell is going on."

"I don't know," his brother said calmly. "I just know that the 911 call originated inside that apartment. Either she made the call, or her attacker did."

"That's crazy. Did the dispatcher say whether it was a man or a woman on the phone?"

"The voice was muffled."

Cade swore. "You should be out looking for her attacker."

Carter was studying him. "This has something to do with why you wanted me to check on her, doesn't it?"

"Forget it," Cade said, holding up his hands in surrender as he backed away from the patrol car. "There's no talking to you."

"Try telling me what's going on with you and that woman in there. She's trouble. Can't you see that?"

Carter called after him as he headed down the street. "Come on, I'll give you a ride."

Cade didn't answer as he kept walking toward home

and his truck. He didn't know what to think, but he wasn't leaving her alone tonight.

ANDI BOLTED THE door behind the sheriff and Cade. She was still shaken but the sheriff had checked the apartment and assured her there was no one in it. He'd found a window that had been ajar and shut it for her.

The sheriff had offered to take her to the emergency room to have her throat checked, but she'd declined. It was feeling better and she didn't want to be seen with the sheriff after the threat her attacker had made.

Lubbock Calhoun. That's who it had to have been. Hadn't she suspected once she'd learned he was out of prison and on the loose that he was the one sending her the information?

She shuddered at the memory of his hands on her throat. Why did he think *she* could find the money? This was crazy, but no crazier than her coming to Montana because of the Calhouns. This was where her obsession had gotten her—in worse trouble than she could imagine. Bradley was right. She should never have come up here.

She had to get out of Montana. But even as she thought it, she reminded herself that she'd already run from trouble in Texas. She'd thought she was safe here in Whitehorse, Montana. But Lubbock had found her.

She remembered what he'd said and began to shake. *Hurry up and find the money like you're supposed to.* Like you're supposed to?

Was it possible someone had tricked her into coming here? Feeding on her obsession with the Calhoun family?

Her heart began to beat harder. The stalker in Texas. "Oh, no." She put her hand over her mouth, tears burning her eyes. She'd been set up from the beginning. First the stalker to scare her out of Texas, then the job ad that had been sent to her.

Whoever had done it had known that she'd been running scared and had wanted to get away from Texas. She would never have come to Montana if Lubbock hadn't been arrested just miles from here.

She shook her head. She'd been set up. By Lubbock? It was too preposterous that a man like Lubbock Calhoun had planned this, manipulating her through each step to the point where he would physically threaten her into finding the money? As if she could.

She tried to imagine the man who'd almost strangled her to death having the patience to lay the groundwork to get her here and couldn't. It would have had to have been someone in Texas. Someone who knew her. Someone…

Fear curdled her stomach as she dug out her cell phone.

Bradley answered on the first ring. "I'm so glad you called. I have news."

She said nothing, all her fears growing inside her. Bradley knew her better than anyone. He was the one person who knew about her obsession with the Calhouns and how she would jump at a chance at retribution. But he'd also fanned the fires of her terror when her secret admirer had become a stalker. He'd encouraged her to leave Texas, for her own safety. If Bradley had hired someone to stalk her…

"Are you all right? You sound funny," he asked as if hearing the change in her.

"News?" she said, her voice breaking. How could she be thinking these things about her friend? Her closest friend?

"Great news," Bradley said with a flourish. "There's been an arrest. The police found your stalker."

"What?" It was the last thing she'd expected. She dropped into a chair.

"And wait until you hear who it is." He did a drumroll. So like Bradley to play the moment to the hilt. "Rachel, your nemesis. That's right, sweetie. The police found evidence in her locker—and in her boyfriend's car. She got her boyfriend to do the dirty deed."

"Rachel?" Andi was still in shock. "Why would she—"

"Isn't it obvious? She wanted your job—and it worked like a charm, didn't it? She continued sending the threats hoping you wouldn't return and the newscaster job would become permanent."

Andi didn't know what to say. Her whole theory that there had been an elaborate plot to get her to Montana came unraveled. Just moments before she'd been suspecting Bradley... She began to cry.

"Sweetie, I thought you'd be *happy* to hear this."

"I am," she managed to say. "I'm just so relieved." So relieved that her stupid suspicions were unfounded and feeling guilty for even having them. "Rachel confessed?"

"Right, sweetie. She's denying everything and so is her boyfriend but the police found enough evidence between the two of them so it's a slam dunk and truthfully, no one at the station is surprised in the least. So now you can come back to Texas. Your old job is waiting for you—and you have one fantastic story to break."

She didn't know how to tell him. "There's news up here, as well."

"You sound funny. Are you all right?"

She told him about the attack.

"That's it," he said. "You're getting out of there."

"If I thought there was someplace I could run and get away from him, I would."

"You're that convinced it was Lubbock Calhoun?"

"Yes." Her throat was sore and painful again. "I shouldn't talk anymore."

"Then just listen," Bradley said. "I have some more news although I was hoping you'd forget about the Calhouns and just come home. But the robbery money? It's never turned up. At least none of the 'bait' money. I'm betting one of them hid it and for one reason or another couldn't get back to it. Which could explain why Lubbock, if that's who it is, put you on Starr's trail."

What he said made sense. "Bradley, I feel as if I've been set up. I knew someone was pulling my strings once I got here, but I think it goes deeper than that." She told him what Lubbock—if that's who it had been—had said to her.

"I didn't want to say anything, but I think you're dead-on," Bradley said. "It seemed pretty obvious why. They have to know who you are, your connection to their family, and given the amount of exposure you've gotten in Texas..."

"But why would they think I could find the money? That's just crazy."

"Are you serious? Look, I've given this some thought. What else do I have to do at work all day?" he joked. "Number one, Lubbock sure as the devil couldn't get close to Cade Jackson, but you can. Two, you're trained to get information. Look at the stories you broke, including that famous murder case that you practically solved single-handedly."

She groaned, realizing that there were viewers out there who thought they knew her.

"The good news is that it must mean that there is information to be found," he was saying. "Whoever is after the money, Lubbock or Houston or even Starr possibly if you're right and she faked her death, knows who you are. They're using you, kiddo. Maybe even one of them got to Rachel for all we know."

She felt sick. "How am I going to find the money?"

"The same way you go after news stories," Bradley said. "If anyone can do this, it's you."

"You haven't seen this country. It's vast and right now it's covered in snow. A lot of it looks the same. It would be so easy to get lost in."

"Exactly," he said, sounding excited. "You've just hit the nail on the head. The Calhouns would have had the same problems when they hid that money."

Even as exhausted and scared as she was, she saw where he was going with this. "You think they would have made a map back to the money."

Bradley laughed. "Isn't that what you would have done? So now all you have to do is find the map. Don't thank me yet," he joked.

"It seems like a lot of trouble to go to," she said. "Why didn't Starr just split the money with Houston and skip the country?"

"Don't forget Lubbock. He would have wanted a taste and I have a feeling him being arrested on that old warrant near Whitehorse was no coincidence. I'm betting the cops got an anonymous tip."

"Starr?"

"That would take care of one brother for six years," Bradley said. "Now all she had to do was contend with

Houston. So she hid the money where she's the only one who knows how to find it. Gives her leverage."

Especially if Cade was right and she wanted to start her life over. But then why not give up all the money?

"I'm not so sure about the map, sorry," she said. "Wouldn't Cade have found it by now if there'd been one?"

"It wouldn't have been something obvious," Bradley said. "It would have to be disguised as something else."

Andi laughed. It felt good to talk to him even if it did hurt her throat a little. "You're really getting into this, aren't you?"

"I can't help it. I'm down here where it's safe and I can live vicariously through you," he said. "Aren't you scared?"

"Terrified. I'm afraid the Calhouns think I'm a lot smarter than I actually am."

"I'd argue that. But you can quit, go to the cops, get out of there. Just tell me what time I should pick you up at the airport."

"You know I'm no quitter and quite frankly I'm afraid to go to the cops. The ones in Fort Worth certainly didn't do much to find my stalker when I was down there." She didn't mention that the sheriff up here was more suspicious of her than her attacker because of a phone call she couldn't explain.

If she told Sheriff Jackson what she was really thinking about this whole mess, she knew he'd be as disbelieving as she was.

"You are so much braver than I would be," Bradley said.

"Goes without saying," she joked, so glad her fears about him were baseless. Talking to Bradley, it was easy to forget the trouble she was in. At least for a while. "I do miss you."

"Good. So keep in touch, okay? Call me every day. I need to know that you're all right. And be careful of this Cade Jackson character. I think he knows more than he's telling you. I'd hate to see you get taken in by a pretty face."

She thought of Cade, remembering his expression when he'd seen her looking at the outlaw exhibit. There was no doubt that he knew more than he was telling her.

"You're probably right," she said noncommittally as she thought of the way he'd rubbed her feet, the way he'd thrown the mug of coffee and stomped out at even the suggestion of digging up his wife's grave and how he'd held her earlier after the attack.

"I do love a treasure hunt. Except for the fact that it's a killer sending you the clues."

She groaned. "I thought gay men are supposed to be so sensitive?"

He laughed. "Sleep tight. And by all means, be careful."

After she hung up, she wished for a moment that she'd taken the sheriff's advice. "You might consider staying at a motel tonight if you don't feel safe here," he'd said before he left.

She'd seen his suspicion. He didn't believe that she hadn't made the call. She couldn't blame him. It made no sense to her, either. Why would Lubbock make the call? Unless someone else had been in her apartment.

With the blinds closed and the doors locked, she had to check the apartment again for herself. She didn't expect her attacker to return. He wanted the money. His threat had been strong enough that he didn't need to come back tonight to make sure she got the message.

She knew she should have told the sheriff everything. But then she would have to tell him the rest of it and she didn't doubt that Lubbock's threat was more of a promise. A man like Lubbock Calhoun could and would carry out that promise.

Look what had happened in Texas with her stalker. The police hadn't been able to protect her. Nor had they caught the people behind it until after she left—and as Bradley said, it was so obvious who had the most to gain with her gone. If the police hadn't been able to catch Rachel until now, then Andi had even less faith that the local sheriff could stop someone like Lubbock Calhoun.

At least the stalker had been caught. She still felt guilty about her suspicions about Bradley. Thank goodness she hadn't voiced them.

She turned on the television, found an old Western, Bradley's favorite, and curled up to watch it, knowing she would never be able to sleep.

She was still shocked about Rachel even though she'd known how ambitious and competitive the woman had always been.

A little after midnight, though, Andi's apartment windows began to rattle from the wind. Snow pelted the glass that had already frosted over. She scraped at the frost on the inside of the glass, trying to see out. But she couldn't even see across the street because of the falling and drifting snow.

She realized she couldn't tell if Lubbock Calhoun or anyone else was out there watching her apartment. But as a gust of wind whirled snow down the street, she saw a familiar pickup parked directly below her window. Cade?

Andi told herself it couldn't be, but secretly she hoped it was him keeping a vigil over her.

She finally fell asleep in the wee hours of the morning, after she'd talked herself out of going down and seeing if Cade was in that pickup. What would she do if he was? Invite him up?

CADE SPENT THE night in his pickup parked outside Andi's apartment. He was angry at his brother but after he'd cooled down, he had to admit he had a lot of questions himself.

If this was the stalker from Texas, then why hadn't Andi mentioned it to his brother? Instead she'd acted like she didn't know who had attacked her.

He'd seen how scared she'd been. Wasn't it time to tell Carter everything? And yet, he hadn't spoken up, either, he reminded himself.

His sleeping bag was good to fifty below zero and he was damned glad of it. Snow swirled around the truck, burying it by morning.

Her light was on late into the night. He could see the flicker of her television screen. He took comfort in the fact that she couldn't sleep, either.

Several times he thought about going up to her apartment. He had a lot he wanted to talk to her about, including the attack and what she was keeping from him. His biggest fear was that the attack had something to do with Grace. And that damned money.

But he talked himself out of going upstairs. At this late hour and feeling the way he was toward her, going up to her apartment wasn't a good idea.

At one point, his brother had cruised by in his patrol

car. Cade had slid down in his seat, but he was sure his brother had seen him—and thought him a fool.

THE NEXT MORNING Andi heard on the radio that because of the chill factor with the wind the temperature was twenty-four degrees below zero. She'd never been anywhere that cold and when she looked out the icy window she was startled to see that the snow had blown into huge sculpted drifts.

Cade's pickup was gone, she noted with a disappointment she had no business feeling. Her own car was buried in the snow, a huge drift completely hiding the rear of the car.

What was she doing here? All her life she'd felt more than able to handle anything that came her way. But she was completely out of her league. Not just that a hardened criminal was threatening her life. She wasn't prepared for this kind of weather.

This morning, her throat bruised and raw, she didn't feel strong enough to do this. She hated what she was doing to Cade Jackson. She was completely inept in this wild and dangerous country. And common sense told her she was so far in over her head that it was doubtful she'd get out of this alive.

Feeling the chill of the apartment, she turned up the heat and went to shower, angry with herself for bailing out of Texas. She'd jumped out of the frying pan and into the fire. If she hadn't run, none of this would be happening. But even as she thought it, she knew it wasn't true.

Come hell or high water, someone had been determined to get her here—and now she knew why. And she wasn't about to leave without the story.

When she came out of the shower after drying her hair

and dressing for work, she put on her warmest coat, hat, boots and gloves—which she knew would be sorely inadequate for this weather. Unfortunately she would have to wade through the drift to get to the hardware store to buy a snow shovel.

But when she opened the door she was shocked to see that a walkway had been carved through the drifted snow to her car.

The snow was piled deep on each side and as she neared the street and her car she saw snow flying through the air.

Closer she saw that someone with a shovel was on the other side of her car making that cloud of snow as they dug out her car. Some Good Samaritan. She only caught a glimpse of a stocking-capped head coming out of the cloud with each shovelful, but she was more than grateful for the help.

She'd reached the end of her car and had to yell to be heard over the howling wind and the scrape of the shovel.

The man stopped shoveling to turn around to look at her.

Cade Jackson. And he didn't look happy.

She couldn't have been more surprised. "What are you doing?"

"What does it look like?" he snapped and went back to shoveling.

"I could have done that myself," she hollered at him, wondering why he was angry with her. Because he'd had to sleep in his pickup last night in the cold? Whose idea had that been? Not hers.

"You have a snow shovel?" he asked as he stopped to lean on his. "I didn't think so." He held out his hand.

"Give me your keys. I doubt your car will start since you forgot to plug it in last night, but I'll try it for you."

Plug in her car? Was he joking?

He seemed to see her confusion.

"When it's this cold you have to get a head-bolt heater and plug your car in every night. Welcome to Montana."

She dropped her keys into his outstretched palm. "Thank you," she said meekly.

He grunted something she couldn't hear and handed her the snow shovel as he went to her car and tried to start the engine. The engine growled a few times.

"Come on," Cade said, getting back out of the car and slamming the door. "I'll give you a ride to work." Without waiting, he turned and started toward his pickup parked down the block, leaving her holding the snow shovel. "Keep the shovel, you're going to need it," he said over his shoulder.

Chilled to the bone, she wasn't about to argue as she stood the shovel against the wall of snow next to her apartment and hurried after Cade.

He'd left his pickup running. The inside of the truck was warm when she climbed in. She wanted to kiss him she was so glad to be inside somewhere warm. Just that few minutes outside had chilled her to the bone.

He glanced over at her as he put the truck in gear. "How ya like Montana now, Tex?"

"Just fine," she managed to say through her chattering teeth. "It's beautiful."

He smiled at that. "It's a lot prettier if you're properly dressed. Stop by the department store. They'll get you outfitted. Unless of course you're having second thoughts about staying after what happened."

He'd stopped in front of the *Milk River Examiner* office. He glanced over at her. "Anything you want to tell me?"

"Thank you for the ride and the snow shovel," she said as she opened her door. She had to hang on to the handle to keep the door from blowing away. The cold took her breath away. "I'm not going anywhere."

"You might change your mind about that sooner than you think," he said and revved the engine.

She was already halfway out of the pickup or she would have demanded to know what that was about. As she hurried into the office and Cade Jackson sped away, she saw Sheriff Carter Jackson waiting for her inside.

CADE WENT BACK to the bait shop to find Harvey Alderson waiting in his pickup.

"'Bout time," Harvey said irritably and glanced at his watch.

"Kind of cold for ice fishing, isn't it, Harvey?" Cade said, opening the shop.

"It's warm in the icehouse," Harvey said and began going through the fish decoys before he began to inspect one of the spears.

It was clear to Cade that Harvey was just killing time and had no intention of buying anything let alone going spearfishing out on the reservoir even though the ice was plenty thick.

The moment Harvey left without buying anything, Cade put up the closed sign. He'd been mulling over everything his brother had told him, especially the part about Andi Blake.

Could he believe that a stalker had run her out of Texas and that she just happened to end up in Whitehorse, Montana?

He wondered if he was just a fool when it came to women. He'd believed Grace Browning was the woman she appeared to be. Look how wrong he'd been.

And now he'd bought into Andi Blake's story when clearly it was no coincidence the woman was here.

His head hurt from trying to sort it all out. Part of him wanted to go over to the newspaper office and get the truth out of her. But his good sense told him he needed to calm down, to figure a few things out before he talked to her again.

What he needed more than ever was to do the one thing that had kept him sane the last six years—fish. He'd always thought better out fishing.

"Ms. Blake," Sheriff Carter Jackson said, his hat in his hand. "I need to have a few words with you."

Andi glanced toward the back of the newspaper office. Empty. "Please have a seat," she said and turned back to lock the front door. "This won't take long, will it?"

He shook his head.

She felt his eyes on her as she walked over to her desk and sat down behind it. He pulled up a chair next to it.

"I would imagine you know why I'm here," the sheriff said.

She waited. It was a technique she'd learned quickly as a reporter. Let them do the talking.

"I know about the problems you had in Fort Worth," he said. "Why didn't you mention that you'd had a stalker after you in Texas yesterday when you were attacked?"

"I had no reason to connect the two," she said carefully.

He frowned. "Two different men are after you?"

"Actually I just learned last night that my stalker in Texas has been caught so there is no way it was the same man. It turned out to be the boyfriend of a coworker who apparently wanted my job."

"That's good news about the stalker being caught," the sheriff said. "May I see your throat?"

It was so badly bruised that she'd worn a turtleneck, not wanting to have to tell anyone about the attack. She pulled down the top of her turtleneck.

He whistled and shook his head. "That's some bruising you got there. It must hurt to talk. I'll try to make this quick. Did he say anything, make any kind of threat, demand your money?"

"You got there so quickly and scared him off, he really didn't have time to tell me what he had planned for me."

"Yeah," Carter said and scratched his jaw. "That phone call still bothers me."

"Me, as well." She made a point of looking at her watch.

"Am I keeping you from something?" he asked.

"I have an interview. If there isn't anything else…"

He studied her for a moment. His eyes weren't as dark as his brother's and while he was probably the better looking of the two men, he didn't have the raw maleness that Cade had.

He slowly rose from the chair across from her desk. "What are your plans now?"

"My plans?"

He seemed to hesitate. "Now that it's safe for you to return to Texas."

She shook her head. "I have no plans to leave Whitehorse. At least not yet."

"You do know you can come to me if you need help."
He said the words quietly. His gaze met hers.

"Thank you. I appreciate that."

Andi watched him drive away before she put on her
coat again and left the office, locking the door behind
her. The wind whipped at her Texas-climate clothing and
she knew it was time she took Cade's advice.

CHAPTER TEN

JUST AS CADE was loading a few fishing supplies into his pickup, his brother pulled up in the patrol car.

Cade swore under his breath as Carter got out and walked toward him. A few more minutes and Carter would have missed him.

"I need to talk to you," Carter said in his cop voice.

Cade nodded and reached for his keys to open his apartment door. "What's up?" he asked, surprised how the snow had drifted around his back porch just in the time he was getting packed to go.

"When did you start locking your door?" Carter asked.

Cade didn't answer as he unlocked the door and stepped inside to flip on the light. It was one of those dark snowy days when the only good place to be was sitting in a fishing shack on the ice.

Opening the refrigerator, he took out two beers. He shot a look at Carter. "Isn't it your day off?" Carter grunted in response and Cade handed his brother a bottle. Carter took it reluctantly but didn't open it as Cade screwed off the top of his and took a drink. He knew he was going to need it.

"What the hell, Cade?" Carter said, shaking his head at him.

Cade tilted his beer toward a chair in the small living

room, dropping into one. He couldn't remember ever seeing his brother this angry and was betting Carter had run Starr Calhoun's name through the system as he'd requested. Once Carter saw a picture of Starr…

"I feel like running you in," Carter said.

Cade took a drink of his beer, watching his brother over the bottle.

With a curse, his brother twisted off the cap on his beer and sat down, tossing the cap onto the end table.

"First you say you want to know about Grace's parents," Carter said, biting off each word. "Which we both know was bull. You wanted to know if Grace Eden Browning existed, but I suspect you wouldn't have asked me to find out if you hadn't already known that no one by that name did."

Cade said nothing as his brother rushed on.

"Then you ask me to check out Miranda Blake, leading me to believe your interest in her was romantic." He hesitated but seeing that Cade wasn't going to comment continued. "Then you want to know about Starr Calhoun. When I ran the names I also requested photos. Why the hell didn't you tell me?"

Cade shook his head. "I was still trying to assimilate it myself."

"Grace was Starr Calhoun."

"So it appears," Cade said. "I couldn't come to you with this until I figured out some things for myself."

"The Lone Ranger," Carter said under his breath. "You've always been like this. Can't stand to ask for help. You're just like the old man."

Cade couldn't argue that.

"So what have you figured out?" Carter asked sarcastically.

Cade shook his head.

Carter glared at him for a long moment, then took a pull on his beer. He swallowed and put the bottle down on the table beside him. He pulled a thick file from inside his jacket and tossed it on the small coffee table between them.

"Starr Calhoun and her family of criminals."

Cade looked down at the file, but didn't pick it up.

"Why do I have the feeling that nothing in there is going to come as a surprise to you?" his brother asked.

Cade said nothing, waiting for Carter to run out of steam. He knew his brother. Carter needed to get everything off his chest, then they could talk.

Carter took another drink of his beer. "How long have you known that Grace was Starr Calhoun?" he asked more calmly.

"Not long." He'd been two steps behind on all of this from the time he'd seen Grace on the highway that summer day more than six years ago.

He wasn't equipped to handle any of it given the way he'd felt about her. Worse, his brother was right about him. He wasn't good at asking for help. But right now he wanted nothing more than to turn this all over to him. Carter was the sheriff. He would know what to do when Cade didn't. Mostly it would take it out of his hands.

"I've been behind the eight ball on this from the moment I met Grace… Starr," he corrected.

"Then you had no clue she wasn't who she said she was?"

"I knew something in her past was bothering her. I thought she was still in love with some man." He chuckled at his own foolishness.

Carter shook his head and took another drink of his beer as Cade told him about Miranda Blake showing up at his door with the photograph of Starr Calhoun. "I still have trouble believing it, let alone accepting it."

"I assume you know about the bank robberies."

Cade nodded. "And before you ask, I don't know anything about the money."

"Three million dollars," Carter said. "Never found. On top of that, one of Starr's brothers was released from prison about three weeks ago. He's broken his parole and no one knows where he is. He's considered dangerous. Name's Lubbock Calhoun."

His brother must have seen his expression. "So you know about that, too." Carter swore. "Then you know the connection between the Calhouns and Miranda Blake."

Cade frowned. Connection?

"Other than the fact that they were both from Texas, it turns out that Ms. Blake's father was killed in a bank robbery. He was gunned down by Amarillo Calhoun, the eldest son of the Calhouns. It's all in the file, including the fact Miranda Blake was there that day at the bank." He nodded at Cade's no doubt shocked expression. "It gets better. Both she and Starr Calhoun were there. They were both about five at the time."

Cade couldn't have spoken even if he'd wanted to. Andi and Starr. Hadn't he known there was more to the story?

"What does Miranda Blake want out of this?" Carter asked.

"The story," Cade said slowly, still stunned by the import of what his brother had told him.

"You don't think she might be looking for a little revenge?" Carter asked.

"For her father's death? I would imagine there's some of that, too."

"You don't really believe it's a coincidence that both Starr and Miranda ended up here, do you?" Carter asked.

Cade smiled ruefully. "Someone wanted her to uncover this story. They've been giving her information anonymously."

"And that doesn't worry you?" Carter snapped.

"Yeah, it worries me. Especially after what you just told me."

"Especially after whoever was at her apartment last night," Carter said. "Three million dollars. Men have killed for a lot less. And so have women."

"Andi isn't after the money," Cade said.

His brother raised a brow. "And you know that how?"

Cade glanced at the file on the coffee table, no longer sure of anything.

"There's something else in that file," Carter said. "It's about Houston Calhoun, the brother Starr allegedly robbed the banks with."

"I know he's been missing—"

"Not anymore," the sheriff said. "That body we found in the abandoned Cherry House down in Old Town a while back? Well, I finally got an ID on it. It was Houston Calhoun."

Cade took the news like a blow.

"We were able to identify the remains through DNA. He'd had his DNA taken the last time he did prison time."

Cade swore, knowing what was coming next.

"You still have that .45 Colt Dad gave you?" Carter asked.

"I haven't seen it for a while," Cade said, surprised how calm he sounded when his whole life was about to blow sky-high. "Why?"

"Because Houston Calhoun had a .45 slug embedded in his skull. That's right, big brother. Houston was murdered and you better hope to hell you can find that gun and it doesn't match the slug taken out of the back of your former wife's brother's skull."

"Stop looking at me like I'm a suspect," he said, more angry with himself than his brother. He'd gotten himself involved in this when he'd fallen for Starr Calhoun. Not just fallen for her, but married her and fathered their child. A woman he'd never really known.

"Did you ever meet her brother?" Carter asked, sounding more like the sheriff than his brother.

"No. I didn't even know she had a brother. She told me she was an only child."

"He would have been a threat to your life with her," Carter said. "Based on the way the body decomposed, the anthropologist at the crime lab says Houston Calhoun died before winter set in approximately six years ago."

Cade swore. "I didn't know who Starr was or that Houston Calhoun even existed. And I sure as hell didn't kill him."

"Someone did. Knowing what we do now, he probably came to get his share of the money."

Cade watched another chunk of his life with Grace wash away. Soon there wouldn't be anything left but the lies. He had to face the fact that she might have killed her brother—and possibly with Cade's own gun.

He told himself if she'd done it, she did it because Houston was threatening to expose her. She would have wanted to stay and have Cade's baby, to put that old life behind her, to protect him from her past.

"If Grace killed him, she'd only been defending herself." Cade just didn't want to believe it had been about the money.

"No way to ever prove that now," Carter said. "You should be more concerned about keeping yourself out of prison."

"Damn, Carter, I'm your brother. You really think I shot that man and hid his body in the old Cherry House?"

"No. But you have to admit given all the facts, including that the body was hidden in an old house that you and I used to play in when we were kids, makes you look damned suspicious."

Cade knew what his brother was saying. How had the killer known that the house was abandoned, boarded-up and marked with no-trespassing signs? Or that the house was considered haunted by most everyone in Old Town Whitehorse?

"You ever mention the place to Grace? Maybe even show it to her on your way out to see our old ranch?" Carter asked, then read his expression and swore. "Damn, Cade, this is one hell of a mess."

Andi had been right. He was up to his neck in this whether he liked it or not with little way out unless he could prove he didn't know Grace was Starr Calhoun.

And there was little chance of that.

AT THE MERCANTILE STORE, Andi told the clerk that she needed some Montana winter clothing.

The clerk laughed. "Did you have something in mind?"

"Whatever it takes for me to be warm."

Forty minutes later, Andi left the store carrying her business suit, leather coat and stylish boots in a large bag. She wore flannel-lined canvas pants, a cotton turtleneck, a wool sweater, a sheepskin-lined coat, heavy snowpacks on her feet and a thick knitted wool hat, leather mittens with wool liners and a knitted scarf.

She felt like a sumo wrestler, but she *was* finally warm. She smiled as she called the local automotive shop to see about getting a head-bolt heater for her car and whatever it would take to get it running.

Once she had her car, she went looking for Cade. She had to tell him the truth about last night. He was in this almost as deep as she was. He had to be careful.

At his bait and tackle shop, she found a note on his door: Gone Fishing!

Great. At the convenience store, she filled up with gas and asked where everyone fished.

"This time of year?" the clerk said. "The reservoir. Drive north. You can't miss it."

The clerk was right. About fifteen minutes out of town, Andi spotted the white, smooth surface of the reservoir wedged between the low hills, and realized this was where Cade had brought her, only she didn't recall how to get to his cabin.

She parked on the edge of the ice, debating what to do. She could see four-wheelers and pickups parked out on the ice beside a dozen or more fishing shacks spread along the reservoir, but she wasn't about to drive her car out there because she could also see places where the ice looked thin or had a break in it. One of those shacks was Cade's.

At the sound of a four-wheeler coming across the ice, she got out of her car and waved down the man driving.

"You can drive out on the ice, it's plenty solid," the fishermen said over the thump of the four-wheeler's engine.

Andi stared out at the frozen expanse. She could see places where the ice had buckled. There wasn't a chance she was going to drive out there. It had been frightening enough just driving out from town on the snow-packed highway even with the new tires the automotive shop had put on for her when they'd added the head-bolt heater for the engine to keep it warm.

As if seeing her hesitation, the fisherman added, "Or I could give you a ride." He motioned to the seat behind him on the four-wheeler.

At least a four-wheeler would be lighter than a car, and the man obviously knew where to go to avoid any thin ice. At least she hoped so.

"Thank you. I will take you up on your kind offer," she said.

"Best get your warmest clothing out of the car," he suggested.

She grabbed her hat, mittens and scarf from the car and waddled over to the four-wheeler to awkwardly climb on behind him. She would never get used to all this clothing.

He gave the four-wheeler gas and they sped off down the rocky shore bouncing along until they hit the ice of the reservoir.

They raced across the frozen expanse, the cold air making her eyes tear. She hung on for dear life expecting to hear the crack of the ice followed by the deadly cold splash of the frigid water.

After what seemed like forever, her driver slowed the four-wheeler, coming to a stop next to what looked like a large outhouse. To her surprise, she could see that it had a stovepipe and smoke was blowing horizontally across the gray sky the moment the wind caught it. Snow had been packed around the bottom of the shack except in front of the door.

"Cade," the man called. "You've got a visitor."

Cade was half-afraid it would be his brother with an arrest warrant.

The first thing Cade had done after talking to Carter back in town was head out to the cabin. He owned half a dozen guns that he kept in a safe in the back room of the cabin. He used to hunt with his father and he kept a .357 Magnum out for protection although he'd never had to use it for that.

Once inside the cabin, he'd gone right to the back bedroom, opened the closet and turned on the light so he could open the safe. It held twelve rifles. He had only three in it and a couple of shotguns along with the .45 his father had given him.

As he turned the dial, his fingers trembling as he tried to remember the combination, he recalled the day Grace had asked him what was in the safe.

"Guns."

She'd raised a brow and he'd laughed.

"You're in Montana. Practically everyone owns at least one, most a whole lot more than that. We still hunt in this state."

"Can I see them?" she'd asked.

"Sure. Have you ever shot a pistol?"

She'd shaken her head. "Could I?"

He recalled her excitement, his mouth going dry, his stomach roiling. Right away, she'd taken to shooting the .45 his father had given him.

"It looks like something one of the Old West outlaws would have used," she'd said.

He hadn't told Andi, but he was more than aware of Grace's interest in outlaws. He'd thought of it more as an interest in the history of the area and he'd encouraged it, wanting her to feel about this place as he did.

He heard a click and reached for the safe's handle, half praying the .45 would be there and half hoping it wouldn't. Without the gun, Carter couldn't prove that the bullet that killed Houston Calhoun had come from Cade's pistol.

But the gun might also clear him—and Grace, as well. He'd been praying that would be the case as he'd opened the safe door.

He'd had a bad feeling even before he opened the safe door that the .45 wouldn't be there.

If Grace shot her brother with it, then she would have gotten rid of the gun, right?

Or put the gun back where it would be found long after she was gone to incriminate Cade.

The gun wasn't where he usually kept it.

Panicked, he'd begun to search the other drawers, knowing he wasn't going to find it. He had sat down on the hardwood floor, sick at heart with what this meant. The only person who could have taken the gun was Grace. Starr, he reminded himself. There had been no Grace.

His heart had sunk with the realization that he hadn't known his wife at all. He'd trusted her. When he'd opened the safe that day to teach her how to use a gun, he'd let her see the combination—no doubt exactly why she'd asked him to teach her to shoot. He would bet Starr Calhoun and guns were no strangers to each other.

He'd gotten up from the floor, closed the safe door and called his brother with the bad news.

All Carter had done was swear. The loss of the .45 was a double-edged sword. Without the gun, Cade couldn't prove he was innocent of Houston Calhoun's murder. But with it, the gun might have seen him straight to prison.

As he'd left the cabin to go down to his fishing shack he was thankful at least that Starr hadn't put the gun back into the safe to frame him for murder.

Maybe there was a little Grace in her after all.

He'd gone fishing, just wanting to be left alone. And he had been until now.

ANDI WATCHED AS a plywood door scraped open and Cade Jackson looked out. He appeared anything but pleased to see her as she swung off the four-wheeler, thanked the fisherman for the lift and waited for him to speed off again before she looked at Cade.

"Aren't you going to invite me in?" she asked when he said nothing.

Without answering he disappeared back inside, but left the door ajar. She moved across the glare of wind-scoured ice and stepped inside.

Being from Texas she'd never seen an ice-fishing house except in the movie *Grumpy Old Men.* This one was a lot like Cade's apartment—small and light on amenities.

"Watch your step," he said, moving around a large square hole in the ice to close the door behind her.

They were instantly pitched into darkness. The only light came from below her feet. The ice seemed to glow, the large hole cut into it like a wide-screen television.

She let out a cry of surprise as several fish crossed the open water in the hole and heard Cade's amused chuckle.

He pointed to a small folding stool. "Since you're here you might as well sit down."

He picked up what looked like a metal pitchfork and stood over the hole in the ice as fish passed beneath them.

"You don't use a fishing pole?" she asked.

He shook his head and motioned for her to be quiet.

Suddenly a large fish appeared. Cade moved so fast she almost missed it.

An instant later he drew the speared fish out of the water and grinned at her. "Hungry?"

"I need to tell you something," she said. "It's about the man who attacked me yesterday."

"Not on an empty stomach, okay?" He gave her a pleading grin.

She nodded, but as they left the fishing house she couldn't help but feel they were being watched.

CHAPTER ELEVEN

ARLENE EVANS WAS at the end of her rope by the time she reached the mental hospital. For days she'd done everything possible to discover the identity of the man who'd fathered Charlotte's baby.

Her daughter had observed her efforts with sly amusement. "You'll never find out because you wouldn't be able to guess in a million years."

And now Arlene had just spent hours in the car with her pregnant, obstinate daughter and her reticent son.

"Why do we have to go in?" Charlotte whined as Arlene Evans came around to the passenger side of the car, opened the door and ordered her adult children to get out.

"Your sister has asked for the three of us to come to Family Day and we didn't drive all this way for you not to go in," Arlene snapped. "Now, get out and shut up."

Charlotte shot her a deadly look but climbed out of the car, making Arlene wonder how she could have missed the fact that her daughter was pregnant.

She flushed with shame as she watched her son slowly climb out of the back seat. He wore black combat boots, a tattered pair of jeans with huge holes in them, a T-shirt with obscenities scrawled across the front and a gray knitted-wool stocking cap, his dirty hair sticking out.

"Do you have to wear that hat?" she demanded.

He grunted and walked toward the gate into the mental hospital.

Arlene followed Bo and Charlotte, afraid there was even worse waiting inside for her.

THE ELDEST DAUGHTER of Arlene Evans watched from the third floor window, smiling to herself. The family had arrived. Bile rose in her throat. Violet Evans had looked forward to this day almost from the first.

Soon it would be all worth it. Soon she would walk out those doors and be a free woman. Excitement rippled through her, but she quickly squelched it.

She had to be very careful now and not overplay her hand. It would be difficult to be in the same room as her mother and not go for her throat. Not to mention let on her feelings toward her siblings.

But she had come this far using her brains and the drugs her brother had been able to sneak in for her.

She knew the picture she had to portray during Family Day. As long as she kept her true feelings hidden…

She laughed to herself. She'd been hiding her feelings since she was old enough to realize what a disappointment she was to her mother.

Violet hadn't known why her mother found her lacking until she got older and heard some of the girls at school saying she was ugly.

She had looked into the mirror and seen a version of her own mother's face.

That's when she'd known the reason her mother hated her: her mother saw herself in her oldest daughter.

"Violet?"

She turned to see the nurse coming down the hall.

"It's time. Your family has arrived and they're anxiously waiting downstairs to see you."

Sure they were. Violet put on her timid, withdrawn look as she nodded and let the nurse lead her down to Family Day.

AFTER A SHORT WALK to his cabin, Cade filleted the fish, seasoned it and put the northern pike on the grill while Andi made a salad. He watched her out of the corner of his eye, her movements precise. He liked her hands. They were small, the fingers tapered, the nails a pale pink, the skin smooth as porcelain.

"What?" she asked and he realized she'd caught him staring at her.

"You make a nice salad."

She seemed to relax. She'd probably been as surprised as he was when he suggested they take the fish back to his cabin for lunch. He'd never thought he'd bring her back here.

"Mind setting the table?" he asked, getting down two plates, knowing she wouldn't.

He watched her for a moment, warmed by the heat of the kitchen—and the closeness of another human being—before going back outside to the grill.

Lifting the lid on the charcoal grill, he turned the fish. Grace had suggested they get a stove with a grill so he wouldn't have to cook outside in the winter.

But he liked grilling when it was cold. Even when it was snowing as it was now. He liked seeing his breath mingle with the scent of the northern pike fillets grilling just under the metal hood.

He felt his stomach rumble and tried to remember the last time he'd been this hungry. Most of the time he forgot to eat and then just cooked up something to keep himself going.

When the fish was ready, he went inside for a serving platter. Andi had set the table in front of the fire. The flames played off her face as she looked up at him. Her features softened and she smiled.

"How is it out there?" she asked. She'd been shocked that he planned to grill the fish outside in this kind of weather.

"It's ready. I hope you're hungry."

She nodded. "Starved."

He went back outside in the falling snow and cold and shut down the grill. With the fish fillets on the serving plate he returned to the cabin to find her waiting by the door.

She took the plate from him. "Oh, it smells wonderful," she said as she carried it over to the table.

Cade knocked the snow from his coat and hat and slipped off his boots before joining her.

She had turned on the stereo. One of his country-and-Western CDs was playing softly.

"I hope you don't mind," she said, obviously seeing his surprise. "This CD is one of my favorites."

He shook his head. It was also one of his favorites.

They ate listening to the music, neither saying much other than to compliment the food.

"Your first northern pike?" he asked.

She nodded. "It's good."

"So's the salad." They were being so polite to each other it was making him nervous. "Look," he said, putting down his fork. "There must be something you and I can talk about other than criminals, isn't there?"

She smiled. "Who knows? We've never tried."

He returned her smile and picked up his fork. "So let me guess, your favorite food is Tex-Mex."

She laughed. "How did you know?"

They spent the rest of the meal talking about food, music, television and books that they liked, bands they'd heard, places they wanted to visit.

After they finished eating, they cleared the dishes together. As he washed and she dried, she told him about what the attacker had said to her.

"I have some news, too," he said and told her about the talk he'd had with his brother—and about the missing .45.

ARLENE SQUIRMED IN her chair as she heard footfalls coming down the hall. It had been months since she'd seen her daughter Violet. Not since the night her eldest daughter had tried to smother her with a pillow.

She didn't like to recall the events of last summer. All her near-death "accidents." Sometimes late at night when she couldn't sleep she would know that she had done a horrible disservice to Violet.

She hadn't wanted the child, hadn't wanted to be pregnant, certainly hadn't enjoyed lovemaking with Floyd. But as her mother said, beggars can't be choosers.

And that was how Arlene had gotten pregnant. In the back seat of a beat-up old sedan. Floyd had only agreed to marry her after her father had threatened him. They'd gone before a justice of the peace over in Choteau and come back to Whitehorse married.

While she was tied down with a squalling baby, Floyd escaped to the barn or the tractor out in a field or town for fertilizer.

Arlene had hated marriage, motherhood and the baby.

She'd just been thankful that the day would come that she could marry Violet off.

And then along had come Bo almost ten years later and then Charlotte shortly after that. Both times only because Floyd had forced himself on her.

After that, she saw even less of Floyd, which suited them both fine. Until last summer when he'd left her for good.

Arlene watched the doorway for Violet, telling herself that it wasn't too late to make it up to her.

But then her daughter appeared in the doorway, stooped, lanky, dull brown hair, hollow eyed, resembling a kicked puppy, and Arlene knew that coming here had been a huge mistake.

ANDI COULDN'T BELIEVE Houston was dead. Murdered. "Your brother doesn't think you killed him."

"No. But I have to admit, I look guilty as hell," Cade said. "Not only was it my gun, but everyone knows how I felt about Grace. For the last six years I've mourned the loss of her and our baby. I would have done anything to protect Grace and our baby."

"Even kill?"

Cade looked away for a moment. "I didn't kill Houston in case you're wondering."

"I wasn't. I know you didn't kill anyone."

He turned back to look at her again. "You could be wrong about me."

She shook her head. "I'm a pretty good judge of character since I make a living telling other people's stories." She said nothing for a moment, then, "You don't seem all that surprised that Lubbock's after the money."

"I'm not. I've thought this was about the money since

I found out about it. I just wasn't sure how *you* fit into it." He met her gaze. "Did you call 911 from your apartment?"

"No, just as I told your brother. I can't explain it. Unless Lubbock called right before he grabbed me. Maybe it was a test to see if I would tell your brother what he said."

"Unless there was someone else in your apartment and the whole thing was a setup," Cade said.

"You don't think I—"

He cut her off. "No. I was thinking more of Starr. If you're right and she's alive."

"Then that would mean that Houston hid the money and she and Lubbock don't know where."

He shrugged as he finished the dishes and drained the water in the sink, reaching for the end of her dish towel to dry his hands.

"Have you ever caught a fish through a hole in the ice?" he asked with an obvious change of subject.

"Do I have to spear it?"

He laughed. "No, you can use a hook and a line if you're squeamish."

"I'm not squeamish," she said.

He'd cocked a brow at her. "It's still light out if you'd like to go back down and fish for a while."

NEITHER ARLENE NOR Bo nor Charlotte moved as Violet stepped tentatively into the room.

"What do you have to say to your daughter, Mrs. Evans?" the doctor said, an edge to his voice.

Arlene found her feet and, opening her arms, moved toward Violet. "How are you, dear?"

Violet cringed as her mother touched her.

"It's all right, Violet," the doctor said. "Please come in and join us." He got up to close the door.

Arlene felt his gaze as it swept from her to Charlotte to Bo. He was looking at the three of them as if they were the ones who needed psychiatric counseling.

Violet, her head down, her fingers picking nervously at the sack-like dress she wore, took a chair near the doctor. Arlene sat down again although what she really wanted was to flee. She should never have come here let alone brought Bo and Charlotte. This was all about blaming the family, making them feel bad.

"Violet, what is it like having your family here?" the doctor asked.

"Good."

"Isn't there something you want to say to them?" he asked.

Violet slowly raised her gaze to her mother. "Where's Daddy?"

Arlene winced. Daddy? Violet and her father had never been close. He'd avoided the child just as he had them all.

"Floyd left after what you did, Violet. I have no idea where he is," Arlene said, getting angrier by the moment.

"Oh," Violet said and dropped her gaze again.

"Is there something you'd like to say to your daughter, Mrs. Evans?" the doctor asked pointedly.

Violet raised her head. What could have been a smile played at her lips. Arlene looked into her daughter's eyes and winced at the carefully hidden hatred she saw there.

"No," she said. "There isn't."

The doctor looked shocked. He blinked, then turned to Charlotte. She was playing with her hair and looking bored. "Perhaps you'd like to say something to your sister?"

"Do they make you wear those awful clothes?" Charlotte asked.

Violet let her gaze slide to her sister. She looked sad and embarrassed as she touched the worn fabric. "I didn't have any of my own clothes."

The doctor looked down at the notebook on his lap. Arlene hadn't seen him take any notes. He seemed stunned by the lack of interaction between them.

"What about you?" he asked Bo. "Isn't there something you'd like to say to your sister?"

Bo also had a bored expression. Slouched in his chair, he scratched his neck for a moment and considered Violet.

"When are you getting out of here?" he asked.

Violet gave him a cheerless smile. "I don't know. When I'm well."

"You look…" Arlene couldn't finish. There was a lump in her throat. "Your sister is pregnant." The words just came out. She felt shame that they sounded like an accusation. But then everything had always been Violet's fault in one way or another.

Violet looked at Charlotte. "A baby? Oh, I'd love to see it when it's born." She looked hopefully at the doctor. "Do you think there's any chance…"

"We'll have to see," he said noncommittally. "You keep making improvements like you have…"

Arlene rose. "I'm glad you're getting well, Violet."

"Thank you, Mother," Violet said, lowering her head again.

"We should go," Arlene said.

"Violet, was there anything else you wanted to say?" the doctor prodded.

She nodded. "The doctors told me what I did." She raised her head. Huge tears welled in her eyes and slowly rolled down her cheeks as she looked at her mother. "I can't believe I would do such a thing. I'm so sorry. I just hope you can forgive me someday." Violet began to cry softly.

Arlene nodded and turned to give her two youngest an impatient look. They finally rose to leave.

"It was good seeing you, Violet," Charlotte said. "If my baby is a girl maybe I'll name her after you."

As Bo walked by Violet, he knelt down and took both her hands in his. "Take care, Vi." He rose again and walked out the door.

Arlene saw Violet palm something in her hand, then secretly slip it into her pocket.

Bo had given his sister something. A note? What?

Violet rose as Arlene started to move past her. Standing, she and her mother were about the same height. "Thank you for coming, Mother."

Arlene was still shocked by the hatred she'd seen in Violet's eyes earlier. Now that hatred was watered down with tears, but still shining brightly, leaving little doubt what Violet would do if she was ever released from here.

"My daughter isn't well," Arlene said to the doctor suddenly. "She has no business leaving here. Ever."

Violet seemed to crumble as she dropped into her chair and put her face in her hands.

"Really, Mrs. Evans," the doctor chided. "Violet was sick but now she is trying so hard to get well."

"You don't know her like I do," Arlene argued over the quietly weeping Violet curled up in her chair like a child. "All this is for show. She wants you to believe that *we're* the problem—not her, but it's not true. You can't let her out."

"That decision isn't up to you, Mrs. Evans," the doctor said sharply. "Violet is an adult. When she's well, she has a right to make a life for herself outside these walls."

"She's fooled you, but she hasn't me," Arlene said. "Look in her pocket. I saw her take something from her brother and put it in her pocket."

The doctor started to refuse but Arlene insisted.

"I'll show you how deceptive my daughter is, Doctor."

With apologies to Violet, he checked one pocket of her loose jumper, then the other.

"Her pockets are empty, Mrs. Evans," he said angrily. "Are there any more allegations you'd like to make before you leave?"

Violet raised her head just enough that Arlene could see the triumph in her eyes.

What had Violet done with whatever it was her brother had given her?

"I'm going to have to ask you to leave now, Mrs. Evans," the doctor said. "I won't have you upsetting my patient further. You will not be welcome here again."

"Don't worry," Arlene said. "I won't be back and I'll fight to keep Violet in here where she belongs. You can't let her come back to Whitehorse. Ever."

"Goodbye, Mother," Violet said, teary voice cracking.

Arlene stopped at the door but she didn't look back. "Goodbye, Violet." As she left, she prayed she'd never set eyes on her oldest daughter again.

CHAPTER TWELVE

ANDI COULDN'T REMEMBER a time she'd enjoyed more. For a while she forgot about everything and just enjoyed herself. This Cade Jackson was fun. They'd laughed a lot, spending most of their time in the ice-fishing house talking until it was too dark to see the fish any longer.

They walked back up to the cabin and she was surprised to see that Cade was armed. She hadn't seen him get the pistol before they'd gone down to the fishing shack. He must have had it hidden under his coat.

It reassured her. She'd thought he hadn't been taking any of this seriously. But the gun proved that he had. The man continued to surprise her.

A sliver of moon peeked out of the clouds and for once it wasn't snowing. The air was cold but walking next to Cade she felt more than toasty, the snow crunching under their feet. The night was bright enough that they could see for a great distance in this open country.

Andi realized she wasn't afraid with Cade. There was a strength about him, a determination that might even match her own. He understood the danger they were in, and she felt safe here with him.

Without looking at her, he said, "You've been through a lot with what happened to your father, the stalker in Texas and now this."

"I was in the public eye," she said, thinking about

what Bradley had said. "Sometimes viewers think they know you. They would send presents or cards and letters. One time on the air I mentioned that my favorite flower was the daisy. I got dozens of daisies over the next few weeks. It's amazing also how much there was about me on the Internet."

"But you said the stalker turned out to be someone you worked with?"

She nodded. "A woman who wanted my job, I guess. She got her boyfriend to help her."

"The police didn't suspect her right away?" he asked.

"Apparently not." Andi frowned. "I still have a hard time believing it. I met her boyfriend once when she brought him down to the station to show him around. He seemed nice."

"She must have wanted your job awfully bad," he said. "It doesn't surprise me that she could talk her boyfriend into helping her. He probably loves her."

"Or did. They both deny it, but apparently the police found evidence that ties them both into the stalking." She sighed. "Anyway, it's over. Now I feel as if I panicked unnecessarily, leaping, as it is, from the skillet into the fire."

"And you're angry with yourself, right?"

She looked over. "Yes, how did you—"

"I've been doing a little running myself so I know the feeling." There was a smile in his voice.

"At least you were grieving for the death of the woman you loved," she said.

He chuckled softly, stopping at the top of the rise to turn to look back at the frozen reservoir. "That's what I told myself. But I think you and I know it was a little more complicated than that." He grew silent for a moment. She could hear the sound of the wind in the trees behind the dark outline of the cabin.

"You asked me the other day if I hadn't seen something that made me question my relationship with Grace," he said quietly.

She held her breath.

"They were such little things. Little doubts that nagged at me all these years even after she was gone." He looked over at her. "A part of me knew something was wrong. I could see her struggling sometimes." He chuckled. "I thought it was a man. The day I met her beside the highway changing her flat tire, I knew she had some past she was escaping from. I just assumed it was from a relationship. When I caught her looking anxious or worried, I told myself she was thinking about him."

Her heart went out to Cade. "I'm sorry it was so painful. I guess the truth wouldn't have been any easier, though."

He laughed and they started walking again toward the cabin. "No, the truth I'm afraid is going to get us both killed."

CADE DIDN'T ADD that being with a desirable woman again was also helping. He felt as if they were in the same boat. Both of their lives on the line. Both of them fighting the ghosts of their pasts.

It surprised him that he could feel that way about Andi Blake. Oh, desire, that was a given. Same with compassion for what she'd been through.

But at some point, he'd actually started liking her. A reporter. He never would have expected that in a million years.

"My car's on the other side of the lake," she said when they reached his front porch.

He nodded and looked back toward the reservoir. He could barely make out the shape of the fishing shack in the blackness of the winter night.

Across the lake, he could see multicolored Christmas lights glittering. He'd forgotten about Christmas, but in a few days he was expected at a party where his brother would be asking the woman he loved to marry him.

The clouds parted and a sliver of silver moon appeared, then dozens of tiny sparkling stars. Suddenly Cade felt very small in this huge universe. He looked up. A few more stars popped out of the clouds while tiny ice crystals sifted down from the cold blue of the sky.

The way he was feeling, he knew the smart thing was not to invite her in but to give her a ride to her car and go on back to his apartment tonight.

But he'd seldom, if ever, done the smart thing. He'd proved that by falling in love with Grace Browning.

Earlier he'd been glad to see that Andi had taken his advice and gotten some warm Montana clothing. She was bundled up, a thick knitted cap pulled down over her dark hair. In the faint moonlight, he could see that her cheeks were flushed from the cold, her eyes sparking.

He reached over and grabbed a handful of the front of her coat and pulled her to him.

She stumbled into him, her eyes widening.

"There's something I've wanted to do since the first time I laid eyes on you," he said.

He cupped Andi's face in his gloved hands and pulled her into a kiss.

He felt her resist for an instant, tears welling in her eyes and then his lips touched hers. He felt a hot tear, tasted the salt. He pulled her into his arms, holding her tightly, telling himself he was in over his head.

But this felt right and for the first time in years, he wasn't afraid to feel. Her lips parted, her breath warm and sweet. He deepened the kiss.

Desire shot through him, heating his blood. He encircled her in his arms, pulling her as close as possible through all their winter clothing.

It wasn't close enough. He drew back from the kiss and realized he'd never wanted a woman the way he wanted this one. Not even Grace. He heard the soft intake of her breath as he pulled her toward him again, dropping his mouth to hers.

She answered in kind as he reached behind him and opened the door to the cabin.

In a flurry of clothing and kisses, they stripped off their coats and boots, hats and mittens, peeling off pants and sweaters as they stumbled locked together toward the couch.

The fire he'd made earlier before dinner had burned down to a few glowing embers, but they didn't need the heat. They were making their own.

Her skin felt on fire as he brushed his lips along her throat. He could feel her pulse quicken as he slipped his fingers beneath the thin fabric of her bra. Her nipples were hard and erect. She moaned as his fingers brushed over one then the other. He dropped his mouth to her warm breast, making her moan, and ran his hand over her flat, smooth, warm belly to slip into her panties.

She was hot and wet and pressing into him with a fierceness that matched his own. He looked into her eyes and saw that there would be no turning back for either of them as his fingers found her center.

ANDI ARCHED AGAINST HIM. From the moment Cade had pulled her to him on the porch, she knew she was a goner. She'd wanted him on a primal level that terrified and excited her. There was no thought, only the feel of him and the fire that shot through her straight to her core.

His fingers filled her as his mouth came back to hers. She could feel herself rising higher and higher, the pleasure building in intensity until she thought she couldn't take another instant. His skin was like a flame against hers, stoking the fire inside her. She could feel it building and building and suddenly she was bursting beneath him.

She gasped and cried out, her head thrown back, pleasure coursing through her veins. She barely felt him remove her bra, then slip her panties down her legs. She lay naked on the leather couch, him above her.

In his dark eyes, she saw raw need flash like a hot spark ready to catch fire. It fanned her own longing as he stood and dropped his boxers to the floor.

With an abandon she never knew she possessed, she surrendered to him completely as inside the cabin, they made love through the night completely unaware that outside it had begun to snow again.

THE NEXT MORNING, Cade left Andi sleeping in the cabin and went outside.

From the cabin he had a good view of the area. He checked the trees behind the cabin and the arena first, looking for fresh tracks in the snow. There were none.

As far as he could tell no one had been around during the night. The news flooded him with relief.

Yesterday he'd thrown caution to the wind, feeling as if he'd been playing Russian roulette. He'd gone fishing when he should have been worrying about the Calhouns and his future. And even crazier, he'd curled up with Andi, making love all night, when they both were in danger.

Not that he regretted either. The memory of their lovemaking warmed him on the cold, snowy morning.

This morning, though, he couldn't keep pretending this mess was going to just go away. He knew what he had to do to save himself and Andi. They were in it together now and no matter what she said, he'd gotten her into it. He was the one who'd married Starr Calhoun.

As he walked down to the ice-fishing shack watching for tracks coming up from the reservoir, he thought of the outlaw books Grace had loved. She'd reveled in this part of Montana's past. The Curry brothers, Butch Cassidy and the Sundance Kid and many more had made this area home for a while.

Some of them were so much a part of the community that area ranchers would hide them from posses and even lie on the stand for them. Not that some didn't fear them and the repercussions if they hadn't.

As he walked, the fresh snow crunched under his boots and his breath in the cold morning air came out in frosty white puffs. It was early enough that he didn't see any other fishermen down by the lake. He liked the utter silence of winter mornings. It was his favorite time.

And this morning he really needed the time to get himself together before he saw Andi. They needed a plan. There were decisions to me made. Lubbock, or whoever had attacked her, would be back. Cade didn't doubt that for a moment.

How the hell they were going to find the missing money, he had no idea. But they had to at least make the attempt because if he was right, someone had been watching them for several days now.

He could hear the ice cracking closer to shore, but he wasn't worried. The ice was thick and would be for months.

He couldn't help but think about yesterday with Andi. He'd had fun. That surprised him. She'd let down her defenses and he had, too. Maybe that's why their love-making had been like none he'd ever experienced. He got the impression that she'd been so busy building her career that she hadn't dated much—let alone gotten close to a man.

As he neared his ice-fishing shack, he slowed. The wind had blown long into the night, but he could still make out the slight indentations in the snow on the lee side of the shack that had once been footprints.

The house was covered with frost. The wind had drifted the new snow up one side of the wall and left the surface of the reservoir perfectly smooth and un-tracked except where someone had stood.

He pulled the .357 Magnum from under his coat and stepped as quietly as possible to the door. As he cautiously pulled it open, the breeze caught the door and threw it back. He jumped back and the door banged against the side of the shack and stayed there. Then everything was deathly silent again.

No sound came from inside. Cade waited a few more seconds before he carefully peered around the edge of the door.

The first thing that hit him was the scent. The ice was an aquamarine green—except where he'd cut the large rectangular hole. Yesterday there had been open water in the hole but during the night it had iced over.

There was something dark smeared along the edge of the thicker ice next to the iced-over hole that made his mouth go dry. He'd smelled enough dead animals as a ranch boy to recognize it as blood.

His pulse drummed in his ears so loudly he almost didn't hear the approaching crunch of boot soles on the new snow. The steps were slow, tentative.

He flattened himself to the side of the shack, the gun ready, but not knowing which side of the shack the person would come around.

"Cade?" Andi said as she appeared to his right by the open door of the fishing shack. She looked from his face to the gun in his hand.

"Stay back," he snapped as he stepped to the doorway to shield her.

But she'd already looked in and no doubt seen the smear of blood on the ice. Her eyes widened and a gasp escaped her lips. As she stumbled back, one gloved hand over her mouth, he turned to see movement beneath the ice.

Only this time it wasn't fish.

A face appeared beneath the ice. The skin was drawn and blue, the mouth open as if gulping for breath, the pale blue eyes staring blankly up from the freezing water.

ANDI COULDN'T GET WARM. She stood in front of the fire Cade had built before his brother had asked him to wait outside in the patrol car.

She rubbed her hands together and looked down into the flames. The sheriff had taken her statement and now stood next to her, making notations in his notebook.

"Where were you last night?" he asked.

"Here. All night."

He looked up from his notebook. "Can anyone verify that?"

"Cade."

He studied her for a long moment, then wrote something down in the notebook. He'd already made it perfectly clear that he didn't approve of her—especially her and Cade. She wanted to assure him that she would never hurt his brother, but the truth was, she already had and she had no way of knowing what the future held any more than Cade or the sheriff did.

"Have you ever seen the deceased before?"

"No." Although she suspected she knew who he was.

"You have any idea why he was killed?"

"No."

"You don't think it might have something to do with why you're in Whitehorse?"

"I came here for a job."

"Right. You just happened to stumble across the fact that Grace Jackson was really Starr Calhoun."

"I didn't bring the Calhouns to Montana."

He nodded solemnly. "But you're up to your neck in this."

"I'm a reporter. I go after stories. I don't expect you to believe this, but someone got me involved in this—not the other way around."

He looked skeptical, just as she'd known he would. "I don't want to see my brother hurt."

"It's a little too late for that."

"I wasn't talking about Starr Calhoun," he said, glancing toward the front window. "He's vulnerable. You're the first woman since Starr. Add to that he feels responsible for what's happening."

She wanted to argue that none of this was her fault, but she knew that wasn't necessarily true.

"When this is over, you'll make headlines again," the sheriff said. "You'll go back to your old job or get offered an even better television job in some big city. Cade won't ever leave Montana. If you think he will, then you don't know him. And even if you were able to get him to leave, well, a big city would kill him. He's a cowboy. He has to have room. This is his home."

She said nothing as he rose from his chair.

He looked as if there was more he wanted to say, but after a moment he turned and left.

When she heard the door close, she walked to the window and peeked out from behind the curtains. Cade was standing by the patrol car. He got in as Carter went around to the driver's side.

Andi turned from the window and stepped over to the fire again, chilled. She knew that Cade had recognized the resemblance between his deceased wife and the man under the ice. It was a Calhoun. It had to be Lubbock since Cade had told her that some remains found down in Old Town had turned out to be those of Houston Calhoun—and according to the crime lab, he'd been there about six years.

If the body was Lubbock Calhoun's, which she suspected, then she had to ask herself: Who killed him?

She felt another chill.

What if Starr really had faked her death and was not only alive, but back in Whitehorse?

CADE WATCHED A herd of antelope race across a wind-scoured snowy hillside just beyond the cabin as his brother started the patrol car and turned on the heater. The heater blew cold air, but not nearly as cold as Cade felt.

His brother was too calm, too much a cop on a case, and Cade knew he was in bad trouble.

"Any idea what a dead man was doing in your fishing shack?" Carter asked after a moment, pulling out his notebook and pen.

"I wish I knew."

"Where were you last night?"

Cade looked over at his brother. "In the cabin with Andi."

Carter swore. "We have an ID on the dead man from some jailhouse tattoos that we knew of from the APB out on him. His name is Lubbock Calhoun."

Cade nodded. No surprise there. He'd known the man was a Calhoun from his resemblance to his sister. Lubbock would have been his first guess since they'd known he had broken parole after getting out of prison.

"Had you ever seen him before?" Carter asked, writing down his responses.

"No."

"You have any idea who might have killed him?"

"None."

"When was the last time you used your fishing spear?"

"Yesterday."

"It appears he was killed with your spear," Carter said. "What are the chances the only prints on it will be yours?"

"I'd say pretty darned good."

His brother shook his head. "This all started with that damned reporter."

"Don't blame her. It actually started with Starr."

Carter put his notebook and pen away. "You're sure Ms. Blake didn't slip out last night while you were sleeping?"

He met his brother's gaze. "I didn't get much sleep last night so yes, I'm sure."

Carter swore. "Glad to see you took my advice and haven't gotten involved with her."

"I know you think I have lousy luck with women," Cade said. "But I loved Grace. Starr *was* Grace, a woman who wanted our baby, wanted this life with me and wanted to put all the rest behind her. I believe that with all my heart. Who knows how this would have ended if she hadn't died?"

Carter shook his head. "You're kiddin' yourself, bro. As long as that robbery money was missing, you and Starr, Grace, whatever, wouldn't have had a chance in hell. The only reason you haven't heard anything from this family is that Lubbock was locked up and Houston was dead. Now you've got a dead man in your fishing shack and I'm willing to bet he didn't break parole to come up here to ice fish."

"No, I think he was looking for the money. But apparently he's not the only one." Cade thought of Andi's theory about Starr. "What if Starr killed him?"

Carter shot him a look. "Starr's dead."

Cade realized it had always been coming to this. He had to know if that was her he'd buried. Or if everything he'd believed about his wife had been a lie. Otherwise, he knew he would never be able to put her to rest. "What would it take to have her body exhumed?"

"What?" Carter demanded. "You think she's *alive*?"

"I need proof that the woman who died in that car wreck was my wife. Andi thinks Starr might have faked her death and taken off with the money. Under the circumstances, I think we should know who all the players are, don't you?"

His brother looked at him. "You knew her. You can't really believe that your wife could kill someone in cold blood with a fishing spear?"

"Not the woman I married, no," Cade said. "But I think Starr Calhoun might have been more than capable of murder. My .45 is missing and Houston Calhoun is dead. Not to mention the body found in her car—if she faked her death."

Carter shook his head. "Well, at least now we have two of her brothers' DNA to compare hers to. If it's not Starr, we'll know soon enough."

CHAPTER THIRTEEN

"IT WAS LUBBOCK, wasn't it?" Andi said as Cade entered the cabin.

He nodded. "Carter ID'd him from some prison tattoos." He stepped to her, taking her in his arms. "Are you all right?"

She nodded against his shoulder, burrowing into him. The fabric of his coat smelled of the outdoors and the cold but the feel of his arms around her warmed her to her toes.

"My brother upset you." He swore as he stepped back to look into her face, holding her at arm's length. "I should never have let him talk to you alone."

She smiled at that. "Like you could have stopped him. This is a murder investigation. He's worried about you."

Cade let out a laugh. "I'm worried about me."

"If it wasn't Lubbock who got me here, then who?" she asked.

He shook his head. "We've known all along that whoever was behind this wanted the money. Someone must think I know where it's hidden."

"But who? If Lubbock was the one who was sending me the information and attacked me, then who killed him?"

Cade looked into her eyes. "I've asked my brother to see about getting Starr's body exhumed."

She stared at him. "Are you sure?"

"We have to know. If she's alive, then…" He couldn't finish at just the thought that the woman he'd loved and married was a killer.

ANDI SHUDDERED AT the thought that Starr Calhoun was alive—and killing off the competition. "If she hid the money, then why wouldn't she just take it and leave?"

He shrugged. "Maybe there's more to it than money. Or maybe she can't find the spot where she hid it. Everything looks different in the winter. There's also the possibility that Houston hid it."

Andi thought about what Bradley had said. "Wouldn't whoever hid it have made some sort of map? Or at least written down the directions?"

Cade moved to the bookshelves with the outlaw books. "Grace did some drawings… I think they were in the back of one of these books. She was always sketching. She had talent as an artist."

"I can see that in her photographs," Andi said.

He glanced back at her with a grateful look that did more than warm her toes. "I still believe she wanted to be Grace."

"I think you're right." She stepped to him and put a hand on his arm. "That photograph of you in your bedroom… She loved you."

He looked away. "Here," he said, handing her a few books. "Let's see if there is some sort of map in here."

They spent the next few hours going through Grace's books. Many of them were inscribed to her from Cade with love. While there were small drawings often in the margins or notes, none of them appeared to be a map or diagram or clue to the missing money.

When they'd gone through her last book, Cade got up from the floor. "Well, that was a dead end."

Andi was just as discouraged. Why had she been given the article about Kid Curry? There had to be some connection. "I need to go to the newspaper. There might be another manila envelope waiting for me."

"I'm worried about you," Cade said. "It's not safe."

She smiled and leaned in to brush a kiss over his lips. "I'll be all right. It's Whitehorse. No one will grab me in the middle of Central Avenue. And anyway, whoever is behind this wants us to find the money. Until we do, I'm pretty sure we'll be safe."

"I hope you're right about that. I'll drive you to your car. I want to do some looking around the apartment. I'll call you if I find anything." He stepped to her, cupping her face in his hands. "Be careful. And please don't go back to your place. Stay with me at the apartment in town."

She nodded. There was no place she wanted to be other than with him right now.

He followed her into town, driving on past as she pulled into the diagonal parking in front of the newspaper building.

Getting out she fought that feeling again that she was being watched as she entered the building.

Her desk had numerous envelopes on it. She dug through, hoping for another manila envelope. At this point, she had no idea what to do next and could use all the help she could get.

But there was no manila envelope.

She did what she had to do at the paper, all the time thinking that she'd missed something at the museum.

Glancing at her watch she saw that it was still open if she hurried.

She went straight to the outlaw exhibit and, starting at the top left, studied each photo, each story. She had to have missed something.

She hadn't heard the elderly volunteer until the woman spoke, "We're closing in fifteen minutes, but you're welcome to stay until then."

"Thank you," Andi said, then noticed something she hadn't seen before. "What is that?" she pointed to a series of numbers and letters at the bottom of one of the exhibit cards, wondering if it referred to another exhibit.

"That's a geocaching site," the woman said.

"Oh, the game you play with a GPS."

"Don't let a hard-core geocacher hear you say that. They take it very seriously. There are two sites in our area. When you find the spot, you look for a container of some kind. Inside can be anything from a coin to a toy or a book to a map."

A map? Her heart began to pound. Bradley had said Starr would have had to have some way to find the money again. Like a global positioning system coordinate?

All she needed to find out was whether or not Cade had a GPS. It was too much to hope for.

But even if Cade had a GPS device, Starr wouldn't have been foolish enough to leave the site on it. She would have hidden the coordinates.

As the volunteers locked up the museum behind her, Andi glanced at her watch. It wasn't even four thirty and it was already almost dark. She could feel the chill in the air as she called Cade's cell, too excited to wait until she got back to his apartment at the bait shop.

Starr Calhoun probably wouldn't have known about geocaching since it wasn't even started until 2000—just a year before she died.

But she could definitely have known how to use a GPS, especially if Cade had one. A lot of hunters and fishermen used them.

The phone rang four times before voice mail picked up. Disappointed, she started to hang up, then changed her mind and left a message telling him what she'd learned at the museum.

"If Starr had access to a GPS, then she might have left behind the coordinates to find the money, but for some reason hasn't been able to get to them. Call me." She snapped shut her phone, wondering where he was.

It was full dark now, the temperature dropping rapidly. Christmas lights tinkled on the houses around the museum and carols played on her car radio. She turned up the radio as she drove, surprised that the songs made her teary eyed. She'd missed Christmas.

Up here in this part of Montana Christmas seemed so much more real than it had in Fort Worth. The snow helped considerably. But it was more than that.

It was Cade, she thought. She was falling for him. The thought sent a jolt of panic through her. She'd worked too hard at her career to fall for any man, especially one who lived in Whitehorse, Montana.

His brother was right. How could she stay here and continue her career? And she couldn't imagine Cade Jackson anywhere but here.

A part of her wanted to just keep going. Get on Highway 191 and head south until she hit Texas. But the rest of her couldn't wait to see Cade, couldn't wait to be wrapped in his arms, as she turned into the bait shop.

Her headlights flashed across the empty spot where he parked his pickup and she was filled with disappointment. She climbed out of her car and walked to the back of the building, her spirits buoying a little when she saw that there was a note on the back door.

The back door was unlocked. She reached inside to snap on the light, stepping in to read the note. A key fell out of the envelope. She picked it up and saw that it appeared to be a key to the apartment.

Andi,
I thought of a place Starr might have hidden the money. I'm driving up there. Stay here. There's a frozen pizza in the freezer. I'll be back as soon as possible.
Cade

She smiled at this thoughtfulness as she closed and locked the back door. The apartment felt cold. She kicked up the heat as she moved through it, taking off her coat. It felt strange being here without Cade.

As she neared the door to the bait and tackle shop, she noticed the thin line of light under the door.

Had a light been left on?

Even stranger, she thought, was that she felt a breeze. Almost as if the front door had been left open.

She hung up her coat and opened the door into the shop. She was hit with a wall of cold air. As she listened, she could hear the front door of the shop banging in the wind.

A faint light glowed near the front. She hurried down the narrow aisle, fishing items stacked almost to the ceiling, anxious to get the door closed.

The temperature was supposed to drop to more than twenty below zero tonight. She hoped nothing in the shop had been ruined because of the door being left open.

At the front door, she reached out and grabbed the achingly cold handle. She had to pull with all her strength to get it closed, the wind was so strong, and snow had drifted in, making it even more difficult.

The door finally slammed with a thunderous bang. She locked it and used the dead bolt as well, wondering how it could have gotten left open. Cade, no doubt, had other things on his mind.

She was halfway back down the aisle, when she noticed that the door to the apartment was closed. Strange, since she was sure she'd left it open. She'd almost convinced herself it had been the wind, when the small light at the front of the shop went out, pitching her into blackness.

CADE JACKSON HAD driven up into the Bear Paw Mountains to the west of Whitehorse. He and Grace had picnicked there early in the fall among the ponderosa pines along a small creek.

She had been so happy that day. They'd eaten fried chicken, potato salad and fried apple pies that she'd made early that morning.

He'd been surprised how good a cook she was. They'd made love in the shade and fallen asleep.

He'd awoken to find the sun behind the trees and Grace gone.

She'd come hiking up thirty minutes later, after he called for her and hadn't gotten an answer. He had been getting worried something had happened to her.

She'd been apologetic, saying she'd just wanted to

take a little walk and had been so taken with the country she'd lost track of how far she'd gone.

He'd thought it a wonder she hadn't gotten lost and said as much.

She'd told him she had a great sense of direction.

The Bear Paws were iced with snow this time of year. The picnic spot looked nothing as it had with ice covering the creek and the boughs of the pines heavy and white with the new snowfall.

He hiked in the way Grace had come out but he'd found no spot that looked like a great hiding place for three million dollars.

It was dark by the time he headed back to Whitehorse. As soon as he could get cell service, he called Andi. The call went straight to voice mail. She must have her phone turned off.

That was odd. He glanced at his watch. She should have been to the apartment by now.

That's when he noticed that he had a message. With relief he saw that it was from Andi.

He listened to it as he drove toward home, anxious to see her. Returning to the picnic spot had brought back a lot of memories—as well as doubts about Grace. How could he not have seen how secretive she was back then?

He knew he hadn't seen it for the very reason he hadn't wanted to. He'd wanted to believe she was exactly who she pretended to be.

"Geocaching?" he said and played the message a second time, realizing he'd missed something.

He listened again, then snapped the phone shut. "Sorry, Andi, it was a great idea, but I don't have a GPS," he said to the empty pickup.

But maybe Grace had one. No, not Grace, Starr. There

was no Grace. The only way she could be more dead to him was if Starr was alive and he found himself coming face-to-face with her.

He turned on the radio, trying to exorcise the memories and not worry about Andi. Christmas carols. It was only a few days until Christmas and he hadn't even shopped.

Not that he'd shopped the last six years, but this year he'd been starting to look forward to it.

As he saw the lights of Whitehorse appear on the dark horizon, he felt his excitement growing. He couldn't wait to see Andi. He just hoped her car would be parked behind the shop and the lights on in the apartment. Hopefully, too, she'd cooked the pizza because he was starved.

But as he pulled in, he saw that the parking space at the back was empty. No light on in the shop. No Andi.

He felt a sliver of worry burrow under his skin as he parked and got out. The note was gone off the back door. That made him feel better.

She'd at least been here. He turned on the light. There was no smell of store-bought pizza. He closed the door behind him, sensing something wrong.

The door to the shop was standing open. The light he always left on was out and there seemed to be a cold draft coming from the darkness.

Without taking off his coat, he moved toward the shop. The moment he was out of the light of his apartment, he drew the .357 and slipped into the darkness just inside the door to let his eyes adjust before he reached for the overhead light switch.

The florescent lights came on in a blink, illuminating

the whole place. He moved swiftly to the farthest aisle where he could see the front door.

It was open. He remembered locking that door. It wasn't something he would forget.

Quickly he moved to the next aisle. Empty. Then the next. His heart dropped at the sight of the pile of spilled lures, the packages spread across the floor as if there'd been a struggle.

He rushed up the aisle and around the end to the counter. Nothing looked out of place—just as he'd feared. He hadn't been robbed. He'd known that the moment he'd seen that the big ticket items hadn't been taken—nor the cash register broken into.

At the front door, he peered out into the darkness. There were tracks in the snow, but the wind had filled them in except for slight hollows. He had no way of gauging how long ago the tracks had been made or by whom.

He slammed the door and bolted it, his heart in his throat. Where was Andi?

The phone rang, making him jump. He stared at the landline on the counter for a moment as he tried to calm down. It could just be a call asking if he had any minnows or if the fish were biting on Nelson.

But as he picked it up, he knew better.

Never in this world, though, did he expect to hear the voice he heard on the line.

His dead wife said, "Okay, now, listen. You do as I say and we're all going to come out of this just fine."

"Grace?"

She didn't seem to hear, her voice clipped. "Do not go to the police. I've left my demands."

"Grace!" But she'd already hung up.

His hands were shaking so hard he had trouble putting

the phone back into the cradle. He dropped to the stool behind the counter and tried to pull himself together.

Grace was alive. What about their baby? The child would be five years old.

He let out a sound, half sob, half choked-off howl.

This wasn't happening. It wasn't possible and yet he'd heard her voice. At first she'd sounded like her old self, then her words had become so unemotional. But it had been her.

Not Grace, he reminded himself. *Starr Calhoun* was alive.

And she had Andi.

He reached for the phone and checked caller ID. Blocked. He dialed *69. The phone rang and rang. No voice mail. Probably a cell phone that couldn't be traced.

He started to dial the sheriff's department, but stopped himself. Hanging up the phone, he remembered what she'd said. *I've left my demands.* He hurried through the shop back to the apartment and looked around, not seeing the manila envelope at first.

The envelope was propped against something in the corner of the counter. As he reached for it, he saw what had been behind the paper. Andi's shoulder bag with her new can of pepper spray. He'd seen it last night at the cabin and been thankful she had replaced the other can.

He'd known Andi had been taken when he'd seen the lures and realized there'd been a struggle. But seeing her shoulder bag brought it all home. Her car, though, hadn't been parked outside. He glanced in the purse, knowing her car keys would be gone. They were.

All his instincts told him to call Carter. As sheriff, Carter could put an APB out on Andi's car. Starr could be apprehended quickly—before she could do anything to Andi. But what if he jeopardized Andi's life? And what if Starr had kept the child, had the child with her?

He looked down at the large manila envelope still clutched in his left hand. *Do not go to the police.* Starr hadn't said anything about the sheriff. She knew his brother was the sheriff. Did it mean anything that she'd said police?

Semantics. He understood what she'd meant. He couldn't risk Andi's life. Houston was dead. Murdered. Lubbock was dead. Also murdered. Starr wasn't bluffing. She had nothing to lose. What was another murder?

Carefully he opened the envelope.

The words had been cut from a magazine so it resembled a kidnapping demand. Which was exactly what it was, he realized.

You have twenty-four hours.
Or your precious reporter dies.
Find the money.
I will contact you this time tomorrow.
Don't let me down.

His mind raced. Starr. But if she'd hidden the money, then she would know where it was. And if Houston had hidden it...

This didn't make any sense. Why would Starr think he knew where the money was? He remembered Andi asking the same question. Only then they'd believed it had been Lubbock who thought Andi could find it.

He began to pace the floor, trying to put it together. Lubbock hadn't known where the money was. Houston was dead. And now Starr didn't seem to know where the money was, either? Who the hell had hidden it, then?

Geocaching. He thought back to Andi's message. But he hadn't had a GPS. He'd since purchased one, but he wasn't very good at using it. Had Starr had a GPS he didn't know about and used it to hide the money and now lost the coordinates?

Twenty-four hours. He swore. How was he going to find the money in that length of time when apparently the Calhouns couldn't find it?

Calm down. Starr thinks you know something, remember something. He jumped as his cell phone rang.

With trembling fingers he dug it out. "Hello?"

"Cade?" It was his brother.

"Carter, hey."

"Did I catch you in the middle of something? You sound...odd."

"As a matter of fact..." Cade said.

"Then I'll make this short and sweet. I got the judge to approve an emergency exhumation. I had to go out on a limb to get this. I've also got the crime lab standing by to run the DNA. Everyone is grousing about the added expense since the ground had to be heated. You do realize it's almost Christmas and colder than hell. But by tomorrow, we'll have our answer."

Cade wanted to tell him not to bother. He already had *his* answer. But he couldn't do that without risking everything. He cleared his throat. "Thanks."

"This is going to be over soon," Carter said.

That's what Cade feared.

CHAPTER FOURTEEN

IN THE WEE hours of the morning, Cade sat bolt upright in his chair in the small apartment living room where he'd spent the night.

Daylight bled through the blinds. He hadn't slept more than a few minutes at a time, waking up with a start, everything coming back in a nauseating rush.

His head hurt, mind still reeling. But as he got up, he hung on to his waking thought.

Houston's body had been found down in Old Town, the original Whitehorse. The town had moved five miles north when the railroad came through to be closer to the line.

Assuming Starr had killed Houston, what was she doing in Old Town? There was little left in the old homestead town. A community center that served as the church and the home of the Whitehorse Sewing Circle famous for its quilts.

There were a half dozen houses, even more old foundations filled with weeds. Most of the population lived on ranches in the miles around Old Town.

The house where Houston's body had been found was known as the old Cherry House. Every kid in the county knew the place was haunted. Hell, Old Town had every reason to be haunted given everything that had happened out there over the years.

Most residents had seen lights not only in the abandoned, boarded-up Cherry House, but also in the old Whitehorse Cemetery. Along with lights, there'd been rumors handed down over the years of the eerie sound of babies crying late into the night.

Cade and his brother had played in the old Cherry House when they were kids even though every kid was told the house was dangerous and to stay out of it. Which only made him and Carter more anxious to go into the house.

He'd taken Starr to Old Town, past it to the ranch his family used to own, and he'd probably mentioned the place.

But still, how would she have gotten Houston into that house to kill him? There wasn't any way she could have carried his body down to the root cellar where his remains were found.

Unless he'd been alive when he'd gone down there. Unless she'd told him that's where she'd hidden the money.

Cade put call forwarding from the landline in the shop to his cell phone just in case Starr called again, then grabbed his coat and headed for the door. The sun on the new snow was blinding as he drove south. This time of the morning there was not another pickup on the road. He passed a couple of ranch houses, then there was nothing but the land, rolling hills that flattened as they fell toward the Missouri River Breaks.

He knew he was on a fool's errand. His brother and the rest of the sheriff's department had searched the entire house after getting an anonymous tip that there was a body buried in the house. The tip said the body was that of a woman who'd been missing for over thirty years.

As it turned out, the human remains were male and had only been in the ground not nearly as long.

Old Town looked like a ghost town as Cade drove past the community center, the cemetery up on the hill above town and turned down by the few houses still occupied to pull behind the Cherry House. He parked his pickup, hoping it wouldn't be noticed. The last thing he needed was to have some well-meaning resident call the sheriff.

Carter's men had boarded up the house again and put up no-trespassing signs. There'd been talk of burning the old place down since the county had taken it over for taxes and had had no luck selling it.

With a crowbar from his toolbox in the back of the truck, he pried up the plywood covering the back entrance enough that he could squeeze through. The job had gone much easier than he'd expected. Apparently he wasn't the first to enter the house since it had been reboarded up.

He was glad he'd brought the .357 under his coat since he wasn't sure who'd been here before him. Starr? Had she come back to the scene of the crime? It still bothered him. If she'd hidden the money, then why would she want him to find it? He had a hard time believing she couldn't find it again. She'd been nothing if not meticulous.

The house was cold, dark and dank inside. It smelled like rotting dead animals. He breathed through his mouth, waiting for his eyes to adjust to the darkness. The floor was littered with old clothing and newspapers.

Houston Calhoun wasn't the first person to die in this house. As the story went, one night more than thirty years ago, old man Cherry took his wife down to the root cellar, a dirt part of the basement where they kept canned goods, and shot her to death before blowing out his own brains.

To this day, no one knew why. The Cherrys left a son who died only weeks later in a car accident between Old Town and Whitehorse. The son left behind a wife, Geneva Cavanaugh Cherry, and two small children, Laney and Laci.

It was said that Geneva couldn't live with the death of her husband and took off never to be seen again.

Laney and Laci had been adopted by their grandparents, Titus and Pearl Cavanaugh, and both had recently returned to Old Town after years away.

So it was no wonder that people believed the house was haunted, Cade thought as he snapped on his flashlight. He had no idea what he was looking for. Something. Anything that would give him a way to save Andi.

For years he'd believed he would never get over Grace—let alone ever fall in love again.

But the first time he'd laid eyes on Andi Blake he'd felt more than desire. He'd felt a strange pull.

It had been push-pull ever since. He'd fought it with all the strength he could muster. But he'd finally given up.

He knew he would be a fool to fall in love with her for a half dozen good reasons.

But he also knew reason flew out the window when it came to love. Grace had certainly proved that. He'd known she was running from something—just as he'd known Andi Blake was. But we were all running from something, haunted by our own personal demons, he thought as he searched the ground floor before climbing the rickety stairs to the floor above.

There was less debris up here. A couple of old bed

frames and mattresses that the mice had made nests in. A few old clothes that had faded into rotten rags.

He shone his flashlight on the walls. Someone had used spray paint to write obscenities on several of the walls. He moved through, stopping at a small bedroom off the back. It was painted a pale yellow. Grace's favorite color.

With the flashlight, he swept the beam across the room. His hand stopped as something registered. He sent the beam back until he saw where someone had written some words in a neat black script.

Like a sleepwalker, he stepped into the room, the beam illuminating a couple of the words. His heart began to beat harder, his breath coming in painful puffs, the room suddenly chilling.

Only you know my heart.
Only you know my soul.
Find me for I am lost.

He shuddered as if an icy hand had dropped to his shoulder. The cold seemed to permeate the room.

Grace's meticulous handwriting. He would know it anywhere.

He closed his eyes. How long had this been there? This cry for help? He backed into a wall and leaned there, wanting to howl, his pain was so great.

He *had* known her.

But the fact that she'd been here, written this, told him how her struggle against her past had ended in this house six years ago. She had killed her brother. And more than likely with Cade's .45.

Had it been self-defense? Had they struggled?

His cell rang, startling him. He fumbled the phone

out of his coat pocket and snapped it open. "Yeah?" He braced himself, ready to hear Starr's voice on the other end of the line.

Years before, he'd reached the woman who called herself Grace. He prayed now that he could reach her again in Starr. That woman had loved him enough to want to have his child. That woman hadn't been a cold-blooded killer. That woman, if he could reach her, would spare Andi.

"Cade? It's Carter. I have news."

ANDI DIDN'T KNOW how long she'd been out. She woke sick, her mouth cottony and her stomach queasy. As she opened her eyes and sat up, she took in her surroundings in a kind of dazed, confused state.

The room was small, windowless, the floor bare except for the rug and sleeping bag beneath her. Off the room was a small doorless alcove that held nothing but a stained toilet and sink. Clearly no one lived here and hadn't for some time.

As she slipped from the sleeping bag and tried to stand, she noted that she was still fully dressed in the same clothing she'd had on yesterday. That alone she took as good news.

She could recall little except entering the bait and tackle shop to close the front door and the light going out. After that, nothing until a few moments ago when she'd come to, but she was sure she'd been drugged. Her limbs felt rubbery and useless. Her legs barely wanted to hold her up.

She heard a sound behind her and turned too quickly. Everything dimmed to black and she sat down hard on the floor. She could hear the steady, heavy tread of someone coming up what sounded like stairs. The footfalls grew louder.

As her vision cleared, she stared at the only door out of this room and saw where someone had cut a narrow slot under the door. The footfalls stopped. In the silence, she heard something metallic connect with the floor just an instant before a metal tray came sliding under the door and into her room.

"Wait!" she cried as she heard the footfalls begin to retreat. "Wait!" But whoever it was didn't wait and soon she heard nothing at all.

Her stomach rumbled as she crawled over to the tray, half afraid the food had been poisoned. But if the person had wanted to kill her, he or she certainly could have at the tackle shop.

The tray held a carton of milk, a small tub of butterscotch pudding and a heated frozen dinner of turkey, dressing, mashed potatoes, gravy and green beans. Beside it was a plastic spoon.

The food smelled wonderful, which told her she must not have eaten for a while. She had no idea how much time had passed or even if it was day or night.

She picked up the spoon, telling herself that she needed to regain her strength. As she ate, she watched the door, wondering who her captor was and why that person didn't want her to see them.

CADE BRACED HIMSELF, afraid just how bad the news would be. *Just don't let it be about Andi.*

"I'm at your apartment," Carter said. "Where are you?"

"At the cabin," he lied. "Why? What's up?"

"Maybe I should drive out. I'd prefer to tell you this in person."

"Just tell me, please," Cade said. He knew he sounded dog-tired, emotionally drained and scared. He was.

"Okay," Carter said hesitantly. "The exhumation took place this morning at daybreak. We wanted to get it done at a time that caused the least amount of interest."

Cade walked over to a straight-backed chair that was missing most of the back. He righted the chair and sat down, leaning it against the wall for stability since he wasn't sure his legs would hold him.

"According to preliminary DNA tests done locally, the body in the grave, Cade, is Starr Calhoun."

"What?" How was that possible? He'd heard from Starr just last night at the shop. It had definitely been her voice. "That can't be right."

"It's her, Cade, and there's more. The coroner was examining the body while we were waiting for the DNA results. She was murdered. Like her brother, the slug was lodged in the skull. The wounds are almost identical. Whoever killed her covered it up with the fire, making it look as if she'd lost control and ended up down in that ravine. They must have cut the gas line to make sure the car burned."

The room began to swim. He could feel the sweat break out even though it had to be below zero in the boarded-up room of the old house.

"The slug was a .45 caliber—just like the one taken from her brother's body," Carter said. "We'll have to send the bullet to the crime lab to be positive that they came from the same gun, but I think it's a pretty good bet they did."

Cade couldn't speak. Starr murdered. Starr and his baby. Not Starr. Grace. He remembered the call from Billings, her news, her excitement. She'd sounded so happy. She'd thought she'd put her past behind her, but it had caught up with her on the highway.

"Are you all right?" Carter asked.

"Yeah." He'd never been less all right. Except maybe the day he'd gotten the news of Grace's car accident. Both Grace and the baby gone.

"Maybe I should come out to the cabin," Carter said. "You shouldn't be alone now. Or I guess, you aren't alone. You have Andi."

You have Andi. "Yeah. I'll be okay. It just comes as such a shock."

"You realize there will be a double murder investigation," Carter was saying. "The state bureau will be involved. I've got to tell you, it doesn't look good. I know you didn't kill them. But—"

"Yeah," he said. "A judge might think I'd found out who Starr really was and did something crazy."

"Anyone who knows you knows that isn't like you," Carter said. "But with the money still missing…"

Yeah, Cade Jackson, the stable one of the family, doing something crazy. Not a chance.

"I gotta go," Cade said. "Thanks for doing this and letting me know." He hung up and sat for a moment, too stunned to stand.

Starr was dead. Murdered. And he was a suspect. It would have been funny if someone didn't have Andi.

Not Starr, anyway. But who?

He got to his feet, but stumbled and sank back down. The chair cracked, one leg barely holding as he held on for dear life. He felt as if he would explode. Turning his face up to the high pale yellow ceiling, he felt the anguish rising in him, choking him as all his pain and anger and fear came out in a howl.

Grace and the baby. He cried for what could have been. The child he never got to know. The life he and a woman named Grace had shared. A life they never could have had even if she'd made it home that night. Grace could never have outrun her past. It would have caught up with her. If not that Christmas six years go, then this one. Blindsiding him, destroying anything they might have built.

Damn her. How could she have done this to him? And now someone had Andi, all because of Starr and her family.

Spent, he stumbled to his feet and tried to clear his head. He couldn't save Starr or the baby, but he had to save Andi. He had to find these people who had killed Grace and the baby before they killed the woman he was falling in love with.

He didn't look at the words Grace had left on the wall. Grace was his past. Her memory was fading like the walls of the old Cherry House.

The voice on the phone last night had been Starr's. That's why Carter's news had floored him. But the more Cade thought about it as he hurried down the stairs to his pickup, the more he realized why the call last night had bothered him.

The first few sentences sounded exactly like Grace, but the rest was stilted, oddly disjointed.

He drove the five miles north, going under the railroad underpass as he went through town to get to his shop.

The tape recorder and tape that Andi had left with him just days ago was right where he'd hidden it. He pulled it out and listened to the tape. He'd been right. The first two sentences were Starr talking to her brother about plans for the bank robberies. The other words had been taken from the tape, spliced together and no doubt put on another tape that was played when he answered the phone.

That meant that the person who had Andi also had a copy of the tape.

He took the message that had been left for him and read it again. All he could think about was Andi. Another storm was coming in bringing both snow and cold. Andi wasn't used to this weather. He prayed she was somewhere warm if not safe.

He told himself that he'd known Grace. He should know where she would hide the money.

Bull, he thought. If he'd really known his wife, then he would have known she wasn't who she said she was, that she was lying through her teeth, that she had three million dollars hidden somewhere.

Why hadn't she just given it to her brothers?

But he knew the answer. She would have kept it. Her ace in the hole in case the day came that someone found out who she was and she had to run.

He read the note again, then balled it up and threw it across the room. The paper rolled under an end table. He started to get up to retrieve it, when his gaze fell on a framed photograph on the wall.

When had Grace put that there? It was in such an odd place that he'd never noticed it before. His heart began to pound. She must have put it there shortly before she died. He'd been in such a fog the last six years, he'd never even noticed since they had lived out at the cabin and never spent any time in the apartment.

He reached to take it down, his fingers trembling. The frame slipped from his fingers, fell, hitting the floor, the glass shattering. He swore as he carefully picked it up and carried the frame into the kitchen to dump the broken glass into the wastebasket.

It was one of Grace's photographs. As he shook off the rest of the shards of glass, he frowned and walked back into the living area. Just as he'd suspected, this was the only photograph that Grace had put up in here.

He felt a strange chill as he stared down at the photo and recognized where it had been shot from—the property where he'd started the house they were to live in as a family.

Heart racing, he pried at the frame. Grace had always dated her photos and written down the locations on the back.

You know my heart, she'd written on the pale yellow wall.

If he'd known her, really known her, then she'd left him this photo because she knew...

He carefully removed the back of the frame to expose the back of Grace's photograph.

There it was. Written in her meticulous hand. The date, the place and under it, taped to the back, was a small white envelope with his name on it.

CHAPTER FIFTEEN

CADE PLUCKED THE envelope from the back of the photograph and dropped into a chair.

Cade,
I hope you will never see this. I plan to come back and destroy it if everything goes well. But if you are reading it, then I never got the chance. Which also means I am no longer with you.

I understand if you can never forgive me for not telling you the truth. Just know that I loved you with all my heart. I was never happier than in the time I spent with you.

I hope you will never have to use this because if you do, then I have failed you, failed us.
I am so sorry,
Grace

Printed in small letters under it were a series of numbers and letters. Latitude and longitude coordinates?

He glanced at the clock. The person who had taken Andi had given him twenty-four hours. It was only a little past noon. He had time if he hurried.

ANDI FELT BETTER after she ate. She hadn't heard another sound from her captor, but she had found a note under the pudding cup telling her to slide her tray back under the door to get more food in the future.

She tested her legs and found herself much stronger. As her mind cleared, she looked for a way out. There was just the one door out. No windows.

The old door was made of thick wood. She realized the lock was also old and required a skeleton key. With growing excitement, she saw that the key was in the lock on the other side.

She looked around for something to use to push the key out. The plastic spoon was too large.

She hurried into the bathroom and removed the top on the tank. The mechanism that made the toilet flush included a long piece of small-diameter metal. Hurriedly she took it apart and armed with the piece of thin metal, went back into the other room to listen.

No sign of her captor.

She dumped everything off the tray but the napkin and carefully slid the tray through the slot under the door. Her fingers were shaking. She knew she would get only one chance.

She poked the metal rod into the keyhole, heard it hit the tip of the key. She pushed slowly and gently and felt the key start to move. *Easy. Not too fast.* Her fear was that the key would fall out of the lock, but then bounce out of the tray and out of her reach.

She felt the key give, and with her heart in her throat, heard it drop. It made a slight thump as it hit. Praying it had worked, she pulled the tray back into the room.

At first she didn't see the key. Her heart fell. But there it was, partly hidden under the napkin where it had landed. She snatched the key up and, holding her breath, listened.

No sound from outside the door.

She started to discard the thin rod from the inside of the tank, but it was the only thing she had for a weapon, although not a great one.

Then carefully, she fit the key into the lock, took a breath and let it out slowly, and turned the key, praying it would open the door.

It did. The door creaked as she opened it a crack and listened. Still no sound. She eased out into the narrow hallway and saw that she was being kept in an old, abandoned house.

At the top of the staircase, she glanced down. The house was empty except for a thick layer of dust. Her room had been cleaned. She knew she should be thankful for that.

It seemed odd that her captor had gone to the trouble as she began the slow, painful descent down the stairs, working to keep each step from groaning under her weight.

Where was her captor? Was it possible the person wasn't even in the house?

She reached the bottom step. The front door was just across the room. With the windows boarded up, she had no idea where she was or if it was even day or night.

It didn't matter. If she could get through that door and out of here…

She inched across the floor, noticing where the dust had been scuffed with footprints. Holding her breath, she grabbed the doorknob and turned, praying it wouldn't be locked.

It wasn't.

She flung the door open, ready to run and stopped short at the sight of the person standing on the other side.

"Hello, Andi."

CADE HAD A FRIEND who was into geocaching and not only owned a GPS, but also knew how to use it.

"You're sure it's easy?" he said after Franklin showed him the basics.

"Nothing to it. If you have any problems, just give me a call."

Franklin had written down basic directions on how to find a certain longitude and latitude.

"Hell, Cade, the next thing you'll do is computerize that shop of yours," Franklin had joked.

As Cade left, the promised winter storm blew in. The wind took his breath away as he ducked his head and made his way to his truck.

Once on the highway north, the wind blew the falling snow horizontally across the highway. He couldn't see his hand in front of his face. The going was slow, but nothing like it would be once he reached the rocky point by the house site. He'd have a hell of a time finding anything in this storm.

It wasn't the cold that chilled him, though, as he drove. It was the thought of Andi and the fear that she was out in this weather. He wouldn't let himself consider that even if he found the money, it might not save Andi.

Snow blew across the highway, the whiteout hypnotic. He kept his eye on the reflectors along the edge of the pavement. Otherwise he wouldn't have known where the road was.

Occasionally he would see lights suddenly come out of the storm as another car crept past. But travelers were few and far between.

Once off the main highway, the going wasn't much better. He plowed through the drifting snow, the GPS on the seat next to him. A gust of wind rocked the pickup and sent a shower of fresh snow over the hood.

He was almost on top of the bare bones of the house before he saw it and got the pickup stopped. Through the blowing and drifting snow, he stared at the weathered wood that his brother and some friends had helped him build. Why had he left it like this?

But he knew the answer. Inertia. He'd been paralyzed by his loss. Until Andi had come into his life. He wouldn't lose another woman he'd fallen in love with. This time he knew what was at stake. This time he would fight.

He picked up the GPS from the seat and turned it on, watching the screen as it searched for a satellite.

"Come on," he said and glanced at his watch.

ANDI FROZE, SO startled that the last thing she could have done was run. She was momentarily so stunned that she forgot about the weapon she had hidden in the back waistband of her jeans. *"Bradley?"*

He smiled and she might have misunderstood and run into his arms, thinking he'd come to Montana to save her. But the gun he pointed at her cleared that up at once. "What...?"

He motioned her back and she stumbled into the house, not even aware that her teeth were chattering from the cold coming through the open doorway.

Bradley's heavy coat was covered in snow. So was his blond hair. She stared at him, realizing that his eyes were no longer brown—but a pale blue.

She felt off balance and wondered if it was the drugs. This couldn't be real. She had to be tripping. Or asleep and all of this, including her almost escape, was just a dream with a nightmare ending.

"I don't understand," she managed to say.

"Don't you, sweetie?" he asked, sounding like his old self. "Why don't we go back upstairs and I'll explain it."

She didn't move.

"Please, Andi, I really don't want to have to hurt you."

She stared at him. "I thought you were my *friend*?"

"That was the idea," he said with a chuckle. "I'm surprised how well you've taken to Montana and Cade Jackson. Ice fishing, Andi? Really?"

He knew she'd gone ice fishing? "You've been in Montana all this time? But when I called you…"

"The joy of a cell phone, sweetie," he said.

"The TV station gossip?"

"Please, you weren't the only person I befriended at the station. I have my sources."

"You did befriend me, didn't you?" she said, remembering the times he'd gone out of his way to talk to her.

He nodded smugly. "It wasn't easy, either."

She couldn't believe she'd been so stupid. "I told you *everything*."

"And I greatly appreciated that."

"You took the research job to get close to me."

He laughed. "Sweetie, that sounds so egotistical."

She was shaking her head, backing up until she stumbled into the wall.

"Andi. You should be flattered. I'd seen you on TV. It was that big story you broke about a woman who killed her husband. Hell, you did all the footwork for the police and solved the damned murder. I was so impressed. I said to myself that woman is really something. And, truthfully, that's when I got the idea. I knew I didn't have a lot of time with Lubbock getting out soon."

She stared at him, realizing something else about him that was different. "You aren't gay."

"No, I'm not."

"Why would you…"

He laughed, a sound that was so familiar and yet alien, that it sent chills racing down her spine.

"As male-female relationship-phobic as you were it was the only way I could get close to you," he said. "You wanted a pal, someone whose shoulder you could cry on, someone you could open up to." His expression soured. "But you certainly didn't have that problem with Cade Jackson, now, did you?"

"I trusted you."

"Yes, you did. Now, start climbing, sweetie, before I have to get angry with you."

She turned toward the stairs. "Why are you doing this?"

"Can't you guess?"

She stumbled on one of the steps.

"Careful," he said behind her.

"Tell me all this isn't just about the money."

"Don't turn up your nose at three million dollars. Like you said, I'm the best researcher you've ever known. I researched you, found out who you were. Imagine my shock when I discovered that nasty news about your father."

"You used that to manipulate me." She felt anger well inside her. It was all she could do not to go for the rod in hopes of catching him off guard.

"And it was so easy. This obsession you have with the Calhouns…" He *tsk-tsked*. "I just did what was necessary to get a job at your station and get close to you. I had faith in you from the beginning that you would come through for me."

She'd reached the top of the stairs and turned in shock

to stare down at him as his words registered. "The researcher position... Alfred's accident—" Alfred Fisher, the station's former researcher, had been killed after a fall down his basement stairs.

"Wasn't really an accident. I just had to open up the job. And Alfred did give me a glowing recommendation before he died, which really cinched it, don't you think?"

She felt sick. Bradley was insane. He'd killed Alfred—after forcing the poor man to write him a recommendation and all so he could get to her? She could feel the metal rod digging into her back. But the barrel of the gun was pointed at her heart.

Bradley shook his head as if reading her expression. "Please don't make me shoot you, but I will since your part is really over. Now it's all up to Cade Jackson," he said calmly as he motioned her toward the room she'd just escaped from. "And you did an excellent job of motivating him, though I was a little surprised when you slept with him."

She clamped down on her anger. He was looking for an excuse to kill her. As he'd said, her part was over. She turned and walked slowly toward the room, mind racing, the pieces starting to finally fall into place.

"My stalker in Texas?" she asked.

"Me," he said with a chuckle. "I was afraid you were starting to get suspicious, though. After all, what is the chance of you stumbling across a story like the Starr Calhoun disappearance? So I framed Rachel and her boyfriend. You never liked her, anyway."

"And the job in Whitehorse?"

"That was just a lucky coincidence," he said. "I happened to see it. I've been following the Whitehorse paper for years. I kept thinking someone would find the money."

She had reached the doorway to the room and turned abruptly to face him. "You've known about the money for *years*?"

"You disappoint me, Andi. I really thought, as super an investigative reporter as you are, that you would have figured it out by now." He made a sad face. "I think it was getting involved with Cade Jackson. It took the edge off your instincts."

Her head still felt filled with fog from whatever drug he'd given her not to mention the shock. She shook her head, trying to take this all in and make sense of it. "You're the one who's been giving me the information. Not Lubbock."

He smiled. "Truthfully, Andi, I had my doubts that you could find the money. But I thought it was worth a shot. I knew I didn't have a lot of time with Lubbock getting out soon. After neither Houston nor Lubbock had managed to find out where Starr hid the money, I knew I wouldn't stand a chance, a stranger in town. And Lubbock was bound to head for Montana and screw everything up like he did the last time."

"The last time?" she echoed, although she knew what was coming.

"He killed Houston, then lost his temper and killed Starr when she wouldn't tell him where the money was. If he hadn't gotten arrested when he did, who knows what fool thing he would have done?"

Her breath caught in her throat. She remembered what Bradley had said about suspecting someone had dropped a dime on Lubbock and that's why he'd been picked up in Glasgow just northeast of Whitehorse.

"Lubbock, as you know, leaned toward brute force," Bradley said, eyeing her neck. "You should thank me for saving your life. If I hadn't made that call from your apartment and taken care of Lubbock…"

She stared at him, wondering why it had taken her so long to put the pieces together and suspected Bradley was right. Cade Jackson had clouded more than her judgment.

"You know what's always bothered me?" she said. "Is who taped Starr and Houston planning the robberies without them knowing it. It would have had to be someone close to them, someone really close."

He grinned at her. "Like one of them?"

WITH A WAVE of relief, the GPS picked up a satellite and Cade pressed the page button to get a list that included waypoints, as Franklin had instructed him.

He scrolled down to waypoints, pressed Enter and scrolled down to New, pressed Enter, and eventually scrolled down to the coordinates.

After pressing Enter, he put in the letters and numbers Grace had left for him.

He followed the rest of the steps, climbing out of the pickup, shielding the screen on the GPS unit as he grabbed his shovel out of the back of the truck, and moved toward the outcropping of rocks that had been in Grace's photo.

On the screen was a compass ring and arrow, just as Franklin had said he would eventually get.

He walked in the direction the arrow pointed. At first he moved too fast, not giving the compass time to move. Numbers came up on the screen telling him what direction the spot was from him and how far so he'd know which direction to walk in.

He hadn't gone far when he spotted the cave-like hole back in the rocks. Pocketing the GPS, he stepped in out of the falling snow, imagining Grace doing the same. She would have hidden the money in the fall.

With the shovel, he pried up several rocks that obviously had been moved to the side of the opening, knowing on a warm fall day he would be able to see the cabin from here, as well as the reservoir.

The money had been stored in large plastic garbage bags and covered with rocks, too many packages for him to take them all. Taking the GPS out of his pocket, he deleted the coordinates he'd put in and put it back in his pocket.

He covered all but two bags, which he lugged back down to his pickup. There was no way anyone could have followed him. Or now be watching. Not in this storm.

Now that he had some of the money, all he had to do was wait for the call. He'd never been good at waiting. All he could think about was Andi. His fear for her had grown during the past twenty-four hours.

From the beginning, he'd known she was up to her neck in this mess. A more suspicious person might think she was involved the way she'd found out about Grace being Starr.

He drove down to the cabin, deciding to wait there rather than drive back to town in this storm. He checked his cell phone to make sure his battery hadn't gone dead before he went inside to wait.

ANDI LOOKED INTO Bradley's pale blue eyes. She'd known he wore contacts. She just hadn't known he'd worn brown ones to cover up his blue eyes. Just as she hadn't known that he had put a dark rinse in his hair. Or that he wasn't gay. Or that he was a liar, a master manipulator, a Calhoun.

"You're the missing brother, Worth Calhoun."

"Or Worthless, as my siblings used to call me," Bradley said with a laugh. "Being the youngest boy, I was adopted by a nice, normal family. But after college, Starr found me. She and the rest of them were always trying to involve me in their crimes. They really lacked imagination."

He had backed her to the doorway of the room. She put her hands behind her, leaning into the doorjamb, waiting for the right moment.

One thing she knew. She wasn't going back in that room. Not if she could help it.

"Why didn't Starr just give Lubbock the money?" she asked, hoping to keep him talking. Clearly he was proud of what he'd managed to pull off and wanted her to know all of the details.

"Don't get me wrong," he said, "Starr was crazy about Cade, but I guess she thought she could have it all, the money and the man."

"Or maybe she knew that if her brother got caught with even one of those baited bills, he would rat her out," Andi said. "Three million wouldn't have done it, anyway. She had to know that the minute the bunch of you went through the money, you'd show up on her doorstep to blackmail whatever else you could out of her."

"I've got to hand it to you, sweetie, you do have a feel for the Calhoun clan," he said with an edge to his voice. "But in the end, I will be leaving here with enough money to take care of me for some time to come."

"You're that sure Cade will find the robbery money?" It was the only flawed part of his plan and he had to know that.

"Actually," Bradley said with a smile, "I doubt he will ever find the money. But after the way you charmed him, he'll do whatever he has to do to save you—including digging into his own pockets."

"Cade doesn't have any—"

"You don't really think he makes a living off that bait and tackle shop?" Bradley laughed. "Cade Jackson invested his share of the money his father gave him from the sale of the family ranch south of Old Town. He's loaded. So see, either way, I knew you would come through for me."

"You really do resent me, don't you? All those jabs about you being a lowly researcher while I got to be center stage in the spotlight."

"No," he cried, mimicking the voice he'd used in Texas. "Although it did help when it came to the stalking part of the plan. Me? I shun the limelight for obvious reasons. If you were willing, I'd take you with me." He reached out to touch her face with the tips of his fingers.

She swung her head to the side, away from his touch, and reached under her shirt to pull the thin rod from the back waistband of her jeans, but made no move to use it yet.

"Come on," he was saying, "We'd be great together. I've often thought about what it would be like to make love to you."

She braced herself, ready to strike. "Over my dead body."

He laughed. "That would be all right, too."

"After you get the money, what then?" she asked,

already knowing. He couldn't let them go. So far, he was the one Calhoun without a record. Like he said, he shunned the limelight.

He didn't answer as he glanced at his watch. "Time to call your boyfriend."

He held the phone to his ear, listened, then shoved the cell at her. "Find out if he has the money. Otherwise, make it perfectly clear that he'd better get it or you are going to die."

She took the phone with her free hand, but the moment she touched it, Bradley jammed the gun into her side, making her cry out as Cade answered.

He snatched the phone from her, catching her off guard as he shoved her into the room so hard that she fell. She scrambled to her feet, the rod in her hand, but he'd already grabbed the key and slammed the door and locked it.

CADE DIDN'T ANSWER on the first ring. He let it ring twice more, picking up only before it went to voice mail. He checked the calling number. Blocked. "Yeah?"

He'd expected to hear Starr's taped voice again. What he wasn't ready for was Andi's cry of pain. *"Andi?"* Another cry of pain, then a male voice he'd never heard before.

"Mr. Jackson, do you have my money?"

Cade had to bite down on his fury. "As a matter of fact, I do, but I will burn every last bill if you touch her again."

The man laughed. "I don't think you're in a position to make the rules." The man had a Southern accent. He wasn't sure why that surprised him.

"I have three million that says I am."

Silence, then, "I see why Ms. Blake has taken a liking to you. So you found the money. Congratulations. You and Ms. Blake have more than met my expectations."

"I want to speak to Andi."

"She's fine."

"Not good enough. I talk to her or we're done here," Cade said, half scared the caller would hang up.

"Maybe we're done here."

Cade held his breath, terrified that the next sound he heard would be the click as the connection was broken. But then again, there were those three million reasons for the man to work with him.

He heard a key turn in a lock, the creak of a door and then Andi's voice.

"Cade?"

He closed his eyes, squeezing the phone in his hand as he dropped onto the arm of the couch and put his head down. He cleared his voice, not wanting her to hear his fear.

"Andi. Are you all right?"

"I'm—"

A door slammed. Andi let out a cry, this one sounding more like frustration than pain.

"Okay, you heard her," the man said. "She's alive, but if you want her to stay that way, then you'd better get me the money."

Cade had had plenty of time to think while he was waiting for the call. "Here's the deal. You come to me. You bring Andi. Once I see that she's all right, I give you the money. I'll be waiting for you at my ice-fishing shack. I have a feeling you know where it is. You've got thirty minutes before I start burning the money."

"I'll kill her," the man snapped.

"I lost my wife and baby because of this damned money," Cade shot back. "Thirty minutes or it all goes up in smoke, every last damn dollar." He snapped off his phone, his hands shaking so hard he dropped it.

When the cell phone rang a few seconds later, he kicked it away, afraid he'd break down and answer it.

Andi. Oh God, Andi.

He prayed his bluff would work and that it wouldn't cost him not only his life, but also Andi's.

As he stepped to the front door of his cabin, he picked up the two bags full of money and headed for his fishing shack.

CHAPTER SIXTEEN

ANDI HEARD BRADLEY go berserk on the other side of the door, yelling and cursing and hitting the walls.

She'd heard at least Bradley's side of the conversation through the door including the last part. *I'll kill her.*

Fear rose in her as she heard the scratch of the key in the lock. She backed up to the far wall as the door swung open.

She knew that Bradley's fury could mean only one thing. Cade *had* found the robbery money. But apparently, he must have refused to pay Bradley to get her back.

Bradley's plan hadn't worked. She didn't need to ask what would happen now. A part of her was glad Bradley wouldn't get a dime. But she was now more than dispensable.

Bradley would have to get rid of her. She was the only person who knew of his involvement.

He stepped into the room, the gun dangling from the fingers of his right hand, his head bowed. He let out an exasperated sigh.

"I can't imagine what my sister ever saw in that man," he said and raised his gaze to her, "let alone what you see in him."

She heard the jealousy in his voice. She said nothing as she swallowed the lump in her throat and waited.

Bradley seemed to brighten. "But the son of a bitch did find the robbery money—at least he says he did." He shook his head. "God help him if he didn't."

Andi wondered what Bradley had been so furious about if Cade had the money and was willing to give it to him.

"Get your coat," he said. "Your boyfriend is meeting us at his *fishing* shack."

He picked up his cell phone from the hall floor where he'd thrown it but she knew he was watching her, probably expecting her to try to get away. She got the impression he wanted her to try. Not that he would kill her. Just hurt her.

If he was going to kill her, he would have already done it. No, he needed her. Cade must have demanded her in exchange for the money. She felt her heart soar.

Also she could tell, by the way Bradley said it, that the fishing shack hadn't been his idea.

"I need to go to the bathroom," she said, sounding as defeated as she could.

"Well, hurry it up then," he snapped and checked something on his phone.

She stepped into the bathroom, making a show of turning her back to him. As she slipped behind the short wall, she hurriedly slid the thin metal rod into the top of her boot and pulled her jeans pant leg down over it. While it would be harder to get quickly, she knew there was less chance of it being discovered before she needed it.

She flushed, washed and came out to find him waiting for her. The look in his eyes told her as she pulled on her coat, hat and mittens that Bradley's original plan had been that she would never leave this house alive.

As Cade prepared for the worst possible outcome, he told himself he'd done the right thing.

He turned on the lantern, illuminating the inside of the fishing shack. With the door closed, though, whoever had Andi wouldn't know for sure if he was inside or not.

He was counting on that. Otherwise it would be like shooting fish in a barrel.

As he looked around the inside of the fishing shack, he couldn't help but think about the day Andi sat in the folding chair laughing as she caught fish and he unhooked them and threw them back until long after dark.

All he wanted was to save her. He told himself that made everything he'd done right. As long as Andi was spared.

Unfortunately he had too much time to think, to speculate on who had Andi. He remembered what she'd told him about the Calhouns. All were now accounted for. Except one. A male who would be just a little older than Starr.

The voice on the phone just now had been a male's. Cade had detected the Southern accent. He was betting the man was the missing Worth Calhoun.

Cade heard the sound of a vehicle's engine. He checked his gun, then set it just inside the door. When he heard the vehicle stop, the engine die, he opened the door of the fishing shack.

Bradley seemed nervous as he cut the engine on the SUV and looked over at her. He'd duct-taped her mouth and used plastic cuffs on both her ankles and wrists, pushing her into the floorboard of the passenger side of the SUV and ordering her to stay down.

She'd sneaked a peek as they'd left where he'd been

keeping her, but she hadn't recognized the old house. It was an abandoned farmhouse and there were hundreds of them across Montana.

With her wrists bound, her door locked and the gun within Bradley's reach, there was little she could do to escape. She had to hope she'd get an opportunity once they reached their destination. Once they reached Cade.

She'd hold her fear at bay. She knew Bradley would have found another way if he hadn't used her, but still she felt responsible for jeopardizing Cade's life.

Now she looked out to see that he'd brought her to the cabin. Cade's pickup was parked out front.

It was twilight. The fallen snow seemed to glow. Earlier the snow and wind had stopped just as quickly as it had begun. Now a couple of stars popped out in the cold, dark blue canvas of the sky overhead.

Bradley reached over and with a knife from his pocket, cut the cuffs on her ankles before quickly picking up the gun. "Take it slow. Do anything stupid like run and I shoot you, understand?"

She nodded, more worried about where Cade was and what would happen next.

Bradley released the lock on the passenger-side door, slid across the bench seat and opened the door. With the gun in one hand pointed at her head, he grabbed a handful of her hair with the other and pushed her out.

She stumbled in the deep snow and almost fell. He jerked her close to him, making a show of the gun pressed into her temple, as he pushed her toward the slight incline to the reservoir.

The door was open on Cade's fishing shack. A wedge of lantern light spilled across the snow and ice.

She could feel Bradley nervously looking around as

if he thought he was walking into a trap. Other than the cabin, there were no other structures nearby—not even other fishing shacks. And what fishing shacks there were on the lake were apparently empty, no rigs parked outside them.

Where was Cade? Inside the fishing shack?

The land around the reservoir was rolling hills. Other than a few outcroppings of rocks and several single trees, there was little place for anyone to hide.

Fifteen yards from the shack, Bradley brought her up short. "Show yourself!" he called out to Cade.

Andi's heart raced at the sight of Cade as he stepped into the light. He wore no coat, just jeans and a flannel shirt. He held up his hands and turned slowly around to show that he had no weapon.

"Let's see the money," Bradley called.

Cade stepped back into the shack and returned with a large garbage bag. He dumped the money into the snow.

Bradley let out a curse. "Where's the rest of it?"

"Inside. Let her go and it's all yours."

Bradley voiced his reservations. "I want to see it all first," he said.

Cade didn't move. "Let her go."

Bradley tightened his hold on Andi's hair, the barrel of the gun pressed hard against her temple. She knew he had no intention of letting either her or Cade walk away. Cade had to know that.

"Either I see the money or I shoot her right now," Bradley called.

Cade didn't move for a long moment. She could feel Bradley shaking with anger.

Cade stepped back into the fishing shack. A few

seconds later he came out with another bag of money, which he also dumped in the snow.

Bradley swore under his breath. "I'm going to kill that son of a bitch."

"That's all you're going to see, now let her go," Cade said, his voice dangerously calm.

Bradley pushed her on ahead of him, his hand still tangled in her hair, the gun still to her head. "Move away from the shack," Bradley ordered as he got near enough that he would be able to see inside.

Andi feared the moment Cade was out of the way, Bradley would shoot him. She tried to warn Cade, but the tape muffled her words.

"Shut up," Bradley whispered. "Move away from the shack!" he yelled at Cade.

She had to get to the metal rod in her boot, but with Bradley holding her hair… She saw Cade start to move aside. She kicked as hard as she could at Bradley's ankle then let her body go slack.

He let out a cry of pain, his fingers digging into her hair as he tried to hold her upright. But the weight of her body had pulled him forward. He stumbled into her and almost went down with her, forcing him to let go of her hair.

As she fell toward the snow, she reached down, pulling up her pant leg to retrieve the rod from her boot. Her wrists were still cuffed but she was able to grasp the rod in one palm, her hand closing over it.

Instinctively Bradley reached for her. She swung to one side and rammed the rod into his outstretched arm.

She heard a howl of pain an instant before the air exploded in gunfire. As she looked up in confusion, she saw the front of Bradley's coat bloom bright red, once, twice.

He staggered, the gun still in his hand, as he pointed the barrel at her head. Their eyes met in the dim, cold light and she saw an even colder light in his pale blue eyes.

Andi rolled to the side. Gunshots exploded. When she looked up, she saw Bradley. He had dropped the gun at his feet. The snow was painted red in front of him. He was looking toward the fishing shack.

Andi rolled up to a sitting position and saw Cade standing in the doorway, the .357 in his hands. Bradley said something she didn't understand and collapsed into the snow next to her.

It had all happened in a matter of seconds.

Over the pounding of her heart, she heard voices, one in particular, ordering Cade to stay back.

Men appeared out of the snow, cloaked all in white. In the lead was Sheriff Carter Jackson.

But before he could reach her, suddenly Cade was there, falling into the snow beside her, drawing her to him.

"Are you hit?" he was shouting as he ripped the tape from her mouth. "Are you hit?"

All she could do was shake her head.

And then he was cutting the plastic cuffs from her wrists and carrying her toward the cabin.

Behind them, more men appeared out of the snow to surround the man she'd known as Bradley Harris. She heard the sheriff say he was dead and then she was inside the cabin and in Cade's arms.

EPILOGUE

ANDI BLAKE LOOKED up from her computer as a sleigh pulled by two huge horses trotted down the main street of Whitehorse. Snowflakes danced in the air to the sound of laughter and Christmas carols.

Her eyes burned with tears as she finished typing and hit Print. The printer whirred. She hurriedly addressed an envelope with the publisher's name on it, signed and folded the one page resignation letter, put it in the envelope and sealed it.

She'd already called Mark Sanders to let him know she was quitting and would leave the letter on his desk. It had been the hardest thing she'd ever done. But her job was waiting for her in Texas. Her old boss had promised her a huge raise and a prime-time spot.

Her story about the last of the Calhouns had made all the networks. Her boss had even sent a special film crew to Montana to shoot her account.

The Calhouns were all gone now. All of the missing robbery money had been returned. Cade had been completely cleared and Andi had done what she could to give her father justice—and peace. There was nothing keeping her in Whitehorse.

Except for the way she felt about Cade Jackson.

She hadn't seen him since the shoot-out at the fishing shack. They'd both been taken to the sheriff's department for questioning. She'd been sent to the emergency room to be checked out. When it was all over, it was morning and the sheriff had given her a ride to her apartment.

She hadn't asked where Cade was because she knew the sheriff was right. She couldn't ask Cade to leave here. And how could she stay? She would have to give up her television career that she'd worked so hard for.

But Cade had definitely changed the way she felt about him, about her career, about herself. He'd shown her a life completely alien to the one she'd lived in Texas. She knew she would never see her old life the same after Whitehorse and Cade, let alone after what had happened here.

Not that Cade had offered her an alternative. He'd called shortly after she'd gotten back to her apartment and asked how she was doing.

"Fine," she'd said.

"You must be packing."

"I guess so." And that's where they'd left it.

No reason to stay around, she told herself. Especially since it was Christmas Eve and she'd heard there was a big party down at the new restaurant that Cade's friends had started.

But the main reason she couldn't stay was that Cade still loved his wife. Andi couldn't compete with Grace. And it was just too cramped in that cabin to live with a ghost, let alone the shadow of the house Cade and Grace were to live in together just up on the hill behind it.

While Cade knew his wife had been Starr Calhoun, he still believed Grace had been the part of Starr that was good, the part he'd loved and was going to have a family with. Andi knew he was hurting all over again at the loss of that woman—and his child.

If Andi left now, she could be back in Texas and settled in by the New Year. And it would make Christmas easier since she had no family to celebrate it with, anyway. Better to be busy finding a new place and getting moved in.

The bell over the front door of the newspaper jangled, bringing her head up.

Cade came in out of the storm, brushing snow from his hat and coat. She felt her heart take off like a shot.

He looked shy and uncertain standing there, so different from the man who had saved her life. The sheriff had told her that it wasn't like Cade to ever ask for help. It had taken a lot of faith, but Cade had called his brother and told him everything long before the meeting at the fishing shack.

"You can't understand what a big step that was for Cade to do that," the sheriff had told her. "That says a lot about how he feels toward you."

Andi had nodded, touched that Carter had told her, and thanked him.

"I know I told you that I don't do holidays," Cade said now as he stepped up to her desk. "But tonight my brother's going to ask the woman he's been in love with for years to marry him and I promised I would be there."

She couldn't have said anything even if he'd asked.

"Everyone is going to be at the restaurant—Laci and Bridger—they own the place, my father, Loren, and his wife, Lila Bailey Jackson, my brother, Carter, and Eve Bailey, she's the one he's in love with, her sisters Faith and McKenna." Cade stopped to take a breath.

Andi waited, not sure what he was doing here or why he was telling her this.

"I went to the house site this morning," he said, the

change of subject practically giving her whiplash. "I burned it down. In the spring, I'll get a backhoe in there to take up the foundation. It will take a while for the grass to come back in. That spot will never be exactly as it was before Grace came into my life, but in time…"

He held up his hand as if he was afraid she might speak. No chance of that.

"What I'm trying to say is that I can't pretend Grace wasn't a part of my life. I can't say I'm sorry that I ever met her. But in time, like that hillside, I'll come back, too. Not the same, but maybe richer for the fact that I loved her."

Tears welled in Andi's eyes. All she could do was nod.

Cade took a long breath and let it out. "What I'm trying to say is that—"

The front door of the newspaper office opened, the bell jangling as Andi's boss came in. He looked surprised to see her.

"I was hoping I would catch you before you left," Mark said. "I just wanted to congratulate you on that story you did. Saw you on television and said to my wife, 'That young woman was a reporter at the *Milk River Examiner*,' at least for a few days," he said with a laugh. "Best of luck in Texas." He shook her hand and left again.

"So you're leaving tonight," Cade said, nodding as he backed toward the door.

"I thought there was something you wanted to tell me." Andi knew if she let him leave, she would never see him again. She could see how hard it had been for him to come in here tonight, how hard it was for him to burn down the skeleton of the house, destroying the last remnants of the life he'd planned with Grace.

"You probably have to get going."

"No. Please. What were you going to say?"

Cade met her gaze and held it. "I can't let you stay in Whitehorse, not knowing how you feel about your career. I saw you on television. You are damned good at what you do. You deserve the best. I just wanted to tell you that."

He turned to leave.

She wanted to call him back, but she knew the moment was lost. Whatever else he'd come to tell her tonight was lost.

At the door, though, he stopped and turned back to her. "It *is* Christmas Eve. If you're not leaving tonight, maybe you'd like to go to the party with me."

She smiled through her tears. "I'd like that a lot. But I will have to change. Can I meet you at the restaurant?"

She'd seen the dark blue velvet dress in the window of the shop next door. Unless she was mistaken, it was her size. She knew the dress would fit perfectly.

He smiled. "I'll be waiting for you," he said as he pushed his Stetson down over his dark hair, reminding her of the first time she ever saw him.

"I'll see you soon," she said to his retreating backside as she picked up the envelope containing her resignation and dropped it into the trash.

* * * * *

We hope you enjoyed reading

DEAD RINGER & CLASSIFIED CHRISTMAS

by *New York Times* bestselling author
B.J. DANIELS

⊕ HARLEQUIN®

INTRIGUE

EDGE-OF-YOUR-SEAT INTRIGUE,
FEARLESS ROMANCE.

www.Harlequin.com

HIBJD0917

Get 2 Free Books,
Plus 2 Free Gifts—
just for trying the Reader Service!

HARLEQUIN

I N T R I G U E

C.J. hated to admit that the cowboy might be right. Before Boone McGraw had walked into this office, she'd been sure Hank's death had something to do with one of his older cases. All of his newer cases that he'd told her about were nothing that could get a man killed.

Now she had to adjust her thinking. Could this be about the kidnapping? Her mind balked because Hank loved nothing better than to talk about his cases. He wouldn't have been able not to talk about his one unless... Unless he did know something, something that he thought could put her in danger...

"Why do you think the hit-and-run wasn't an accident?" the cowboy asked.

It took her a moment to get her thoughts together. "This ransacked office for one. Clearly someone was looking for something in the old files."

"You're that sure it involved a case?"

She waved a hand through the air. "Why tear up the office unless the killer is looking for the case file—and whatever incriminating evidence might be in it?"

He nodded as if that made sense to him. "But if it was here, don't you think that whoever did this took the file with him?"

"Actually, I don't. Look at this place. I'd say the person got frustrated when he didn't find it. Otherwise, why trash the place?"

"You have a point. But let's say the file you're looking for is about the McGraw kidnapping. It wouldn't be an old file since he called only a few weeks ago. When did he turn off his phone and electricity here at the office?"

C.J. hated to admit that she didn't know. "We've both been busy on separate cases. But he would have told me if he knew anything about the case." He wouldn't have kept something like that from her. And yet he hadn't mentioned talking to the McGraw lawyer and her instincts told her that Boone McGraw wasn't lying about that.

That Hank now wouldn't have the opportunity to tell her hit her hard. Hank had been like family, her only family, and now he was gone. And she was only starting to realize how much Hank had been keeping from her.

She had to look away, not wanting Boone to see the shine of tears that burned her eyes. She wouldn't break down. Especially not in front of this cowboy.

Don't miss
ROUGH RIDER by B.J. Daniels,
available October 2017 wherever
Harlequin® Intrigue books and ebooks are sold.

www.Harlequin.com

HIEXPBJD0917

HARLEQUIN®

INTRIGUE
EDGE-OF-YOUR-SEAT INTRIGUE, FEARLESS ROMANCE.

Save $1.00
on the purchase of ANY Harlequin® Intrigue book.

Available wherever books are sold, including most bookstores, supermarkets, drugstores and discount stores.

Save $1.00
on the purchase of any Harlequin® Intrigue book.

Coupon valid until November 30, 2017.
Redeemable at participating outlets in the U.S. and Canada only.
Not redeemable at Barnes & Noble stores. Limit one coupon per customer.

52614965

5 65373 00076 2   (8100)0 12292

® and ™ are trademarks owned and used by the trademark owner and/or its licensee.

© 2017 Harlequin Enterprises Limited

HIBJDCOUP0917